THE MANIKIN

THE MANIKIN

A NOVEL

JOANNA
SCOTT

HENRY HOLT AND COMPANY
NEW YORK

Henry Holt and Company, Inc.
Publishers since 1866
115 West 18th Street
New York, New York 10011

Henry Holt® is a registered
trademark of Henry Holt and Company, Inc.

Published in Canada by Fitzhenry & Whiteside Ltd.,
195 Allstate Parkway, Markham, Ontario L3R 4T8.

Library of Congress Cataloging-in-Publication Data
Scott, Joanna.
The manikin: a novel/by Joanna Scott.—1st ed.
    p.   cm.
I. Title.
PS3569.C636M35   1996   95-21734
813'.54—dc20   CIP

ISBN 0-8050-3974-0

Henry Holt books are available for special
promotions and premiums. For details contact:
Director, Special Markets.

First Edition—1996

Designed by Paula R. Szafranski

Printed in the United States of America
All first editions are printed on acid-free paper. ∞

1   3   5   7   9   10   8   6   4   2

*For Jim, who helped me to
imagine my way through.*

*The author wishes to thank the
John D. and Catherine T. MacArthur Foundation
for its generous support.*

I

THE
LONG
MIGRATION

1

The winter of 1846, when half of everything alive succumbed to the cold, has been stored for over eighty years in the mysterious mind common to the species, and though the owl didn't experience that winter, she remembers it—the poisonous smell of the air, the frost that pinned feathers to skin, the famine. She remembers that time the way a woman remembers her great-grandmother's death in childbirth. So this year, when summer never properly thaws the land and the tidal pools remain fringed with ice, she knows what to expect. Soon the bay will be frozen shore to shore, the ptarmigan scarce, the predators hungry. The owl understands that to survive she must leave early and abandon the north entirely.

She sounds the alarm at dawn on the eve of the equinox, waits for the flock to gather, and sets off. From Baffin Bay to Island Lake and on toward the great expanse of Lake Ontario, she leads the way. Such a strong, sturdy queen of a bird, and so richly attired: gold-ribbed breast feathers, white coat, brazen, diurnal eyes. Lying eyes. The other owls believe her to be fearless. In truth, danger makes this brave, majestic owl as skittish as a gnat. Crossing the vast expanse of Lake Ontario— this frightens her, though she'd never admit it. They are met midway by a mild squall that gains an unexpected intensity as they fly through it. Bursts of hail scatter the owls, and the last sight the bird has of her mate is his wingtip before the mist sucks him into its center. You should let a storm take you where it will, the bird knows—warp and spin across the sky with the wind instead of trying to resist it. But the squall threatens to pull her downward into the turbulent lake, so she beats her powerful wings against the gusts, hovering while the rain swirls around her. All reason is swept away by the storm, leaving only the frenzied effort of life protecting itself and an insidious, creeping exhaustion.

And then, abruptly, the squall passes and the bird flies on through the drizzle to the southern shore. She alights on a narrow strip of sand, tucks her head between hunched wings, peers out at the water. She wonders whether the others would agree to call this beach their destination. Her tired body tells her to stay here through the winter months, and her instinct to go on fades to a whisper. The waves of the lake teeter and collapse near her feet. Yes, she persuades herself, it seems as safe a place as any.

Then she sees the hen. Just a scrawny red hen that must have wandered away from a nearby farm and comes trotting out of the underbrush to say hello. But to the owl, born and bred in the open tundra where there are few surprises, it seems a phantom bird. A demon. Her own goblin double. She lifts up into the air with a panicked flapping, sideslips until she finds a southward current, and pushes herself through the air as fast as she can go.

She bends east, then southwest, then east again, races along haphazardly, escaping not the killing cold but something else, something unnameable. She doubles the distance southward with her zigzags, unable to stop or orient herself. Hours later, her crazed flight brings her to a mossy hillock rising out of an egg-shaped pond, a safe refuge at first glimpse, with the surrounding woods sparse enough for her to see an enemy. She decides to spend the night here. Come morning, she will set out in search of her flock.

She scratches at the wet ground, her talons hidden by thick trouser feathers. She flaps and wriggles and stomps on the spongy earth until she finds a comfortable position. She folds her wings. She bobs and pivots her head to take in the new landscape—the sphagnum moss beneath her, the sumac and myrtle, the saplings with their burning *leaves. Then she blinks her huge eyes slowly and surveys the water, keeping as still as a stone sphinx. This is nothing like her home. But for now she can pretend that she is queen again, that the trees are full of owls and the body of water is her own Baffin Bay. She takes a deep breath and shrieks:* Worship me!

And so Ellen Griswood puts another day behind her, an ordinary day: the kitchen floor was scrubbed thoroughly, the bed linen washed, the clocks wound and antlers dusted and moose-hoof nut dishes wiped clean. Nothing to remark upon. Now that Mrs. Craxton is asleep at last, Ellen may relax. She blows out the candle and moves with her usual confidence across the darkened room—she knows the geography of this bedroom as intimately as she knows the body of the woman she serves, from the horny toenails to the rhythms of the bowels, from the ragdoll legs to the waxy scalp beneath the thin white hair. Over the years, Ellen has learned to divide her attention equally between the house and its mistress and has rarely, if ever, been found at fault. She reminds herself of this as she steps out into the hallway, where she's left a lamp hanging: she's an expert in her way—indispensable. She needn't worry about her position as long as Mrs. Craxton is alive.

And here's the delicious fatigue that proves the hours have been well spent. She turns toward her weariness as she might turn toward the sun on the first warm day of spring, basks in it, retaining just enough strength to drag herself up the two flights of stairs to her bedroom.

The attic room, which Ellen shares with her daughter, is long and narrow, with a sloping ceiling, flowered wallpaper, and a half window at the far end. The twin beds are separated by a table, and in the stingy light cast by Ellen's lamp, the room seems to have the depths of a tunnel that continues beyond the window into the night sky. A desolate space, perhaps, but a haven nonetheless, and if you asked, Ellen would tell you that she'd be content to sleep here every night for the rest of her life.

How different she is from her daughter, who looks forward to the day when she'll sleep between silk sheets on a canopy bed the size of Delaware. That's what eight years at a provincial academy will do to a girl: give her high notions and no useful skills. The insult of Peg's covers still tossed in a frothy mess makes the room seem strange to

Ellen, as though she were visiting it for the first time after many years. A regular princess, her daughter, too spoiled even to make her own bed. The never-ending game Peg plays these days is a fatal one: too much time on her hands and no responsibilities. Even now she's probably up to mischief, wandering through forbidden rooms with young Junket, the groundskeeper's son, treating the Manikin as her private property. Nonsense. From start to finish the game of leisure is nonsense, and if Peg doesn't find a proper job soon, Ellen will . . . what will she do? She has let Peg have her own way until now, so there's not much possibility for correction. Peg Griswood does exactly as she pleases, with or without her mother's blessing.

After Ellen has slipped into her flannel nightgown and cap and eased herself beneath the icy spread, she hovers in this wakeful temper for a few minutes, thinking about how her influence over her daughter, always precarious, has grown negligible. She's at her wit's end—and at the end of a busy day, as well. She has never been one to trade precious sleep for worry. *And remember, Mrs. Griswood,* she reassures herself, *the sure reward for an honest, hardworking life will be a secure future for both yourself and your child.*

Ultimate security is Ellen Griswood's goal—it meant complete devotion to her husband for six short years. Since his death in 1917 it has meant complete loyalty to her employer. Ten years of loyalty, never a lapse. So when she hears, or imagines, Mrs. Craxton's voice whispering her name, a low snap of sound against her ear just as she is drifting to sleep, she responds like a recruit called to attention.

Ellen.

"Ma'am?" she says aloud, sitting bolt upright. The lamp, left burning for her daughter, casts a smoky yellow light, and the room feels more snug now. The house is silent again. It must have been nothing, or, if something, merely the crackle of wind through the hickories. But the possibilities suggested by the whisper have drawn Ellen back to full awareness. Does Mrs. Craxton need her?

As the Manikin's head housekeeper and Mary Craxton's companion, Ellen is responsible for her employer's well-being. What if something has happened to the old woman? Doubtful, Ellen doesn't believe in portents, and the nightly routine guarantees consistency. But the what-if lingers. If Mrs. Craxton needs her and Ellen isn't quick to respond, she'll have to bear the brunt of the old woman's rage. It isn't likely, but it's possible that the imagined whisper had its source in actual distress. Anything's possible in the Manikin, and Ellen won't be able to sleep until she looks in on Mrs. Craxton one more time.

"Lord," she moans in exaggerated misery, weak solace as she descends the back stairwell to the first floor. Inside Mrs. Craxton's bedroom, everything appears undisturbed, but since Ellen has come all this way she will make sure. She leaves her lamp in the hall and drops to her hands and knees, keeping below the line of vision in case the old woman has her night-eyes open. By the time she reaches the bed, her own eyes have adjusted enough to the darkness to make out form, if not precise detail. She sees the stiff billows where the comforter is bunched against the footboard. She sees the crumpled surface on top of the bed. She sees the pillow where Mrs. Craxton's head should be. She sees the carved mahogany bedposts, eagles with folded wings rising up on either side.

Where Mrs. Craxton's head should be. Mrs. Craxton's place is empty. Empty! Neither Mary Craxton alive nor Mary Craxton dead. Ellen's history of competence won't be worth a dime if Mrs. Craxton is missing. It's her job to sustain Mrs. Craxton so the old woman can write her son long, accusing letters while he's abroad and scold him when he's at home. She's been known to work herself into such a temper that she faints; every year their battles are a little fiercer, and with every battle Ellen holds her breath, expecting disaster.

Now here's a disaster, Ellen thinks. Her misperception will pass in a flash. But how brilliantly that flash illuminates her confused fears.

I don't know how it happened, sir. In her mind Hal Craxton sits in his velvet wingback chair, glowering, terrifying. *Your mother simply disappeared.*

Simply? Simply? Mrs. Craxton simply disappeared? An invalid woman can't just sneak from her bed of her own accord, no more than a newborn infant can walk away from its cradle! Someone must have stolen her, there's no other explanation possible. Someone must have gagged her, bound her, and carried off the bundle of aged flesh into the woods. Mrs. Craxton has been kidnapped, and her son will have to pay a pretty sum of money to get her back! The sheriff will want to talk to you, Ellen Griswood, he'll want to ask you a few questions, so you'd better have an alibi ready. Mrs. Craxton has disappeared, and you're going to have to answer for it!

Exhaustion, Ellen will be the first to point out, can turn the mind into a vessel for delusions. In fact, yes, in irrefutable fact, Mary Craxton is still in bed, asleep, her head sunk so deeply into the pillow that the folds almost entirely enclose her face. Which proves not that Mary Craxton has the magical ability to disappear and reappear at will, but that Ellen was mistaken.

Only now does she consider her compromised dignity. She climbs to her feet, shakes her robe so it falls evenly, and walks from the room. She even lets the latch click as she pulls the door shut. *Wake up, you old bat!* Briefly, Ellen is possessed by an overpowering anger. The terrible tricks the mind can play. She wants to indulge in hatred, too. But hatred is just another deception, she tells herself. The lie of senseless blame. She has too much sensible sympathy to hate Mary Craxton. Anyway, by the time she reaches her own bedroom again she feels so tired. This fatigue: her own delicious oblivion. Give her a minute to slip back beneath the blankets, and soon she won't care much about anything.

In 1912, three years before his death, Henry Craxton Senior—founder of Craxton's Scientific Establishment—purchased two thousand acres in western New York State, on the outskirts of the village of Millworth and adjoining state land. The property included a barn and chicken coop, a smokehouse, a gatehouse, and the ramshackle Big House, built in the mid–nineteenth century as a water-cure sanitorium but never fully operational, owing to a continual lack of boarders. When Craxton acquired the deed, the Big House, which he renamed the Manikin after the durable forms used to replace the animal's skeleton in taxidermy, had been sitting empty for nearly two decades. He commissioned the renowned firm of Howe, Partridge, and Stilman to renovate the house—they widened an alcove into a spacious conservatory and knocked down altogether sixteen walls, reducing the number of rooms but enlarging the spaces. Outside, a landscaper planted shagbark hickories in a horseshoe around the front yard, designed a terraced rock garden along the sloping eastern lawn, and crisscrossed the orchards and outlying pastures with paths bordered with currant bushes. The spring was dredged to make a small pool and encircled with a neat brick patio, which was enclosed, in turn, by the full circle of a grape arbor.

Henry Craxton—known as the Founder to his friends and employees—had run Craxton's Scientific Establishment for more than forty years and transformed it from a small taxidermy shop to the largest supply company of its kind. At its height, the company employed three hundred workers, including big-game hunters, botanists, paleontologists, taxidermists, chemists, copy writers, secretaries, and accountants. Major museums around the world depended on Craxton's Scientific for everything from tiny ammonite fossils to dinosaur bones to the full-scale dioramas that were so popular at the time, and Henry Craxton became the Henry Ford of natural history.

After spending most of his life growing rich, the Founder intended to indulge himself. But the Manikin was a greater luxury than he could safely afford. Between the elaborate interior of the house and the grounds, maintenance costs alone exceeded the annual return on Henry Craxton's remaining investments by over five percent. Yet he dipped into his capital without compunction. The Manikin was his reward for success, the refuge that he'd dreamed of for years, splendidly remote, without a telephone or electricity. There were other estates in the area and other society women to quell his wife's boredom, and at her request they kept their home in Rochester so they wouldn't have to brave winter in the country. For Henry Craxton, though, the Manikin represented a last stronghold against the cutthroat modern world, and if he could have sealed himself inside the walls, he would have done so.

Of course he couldn't have foreseen how soon he would be spared the world entirely—he had spent only one full season at the Manikin before he was run down by a mail truck on a day trip he took to Buffalo. Nor had his wife been prepared for the consequences of his death. She was too proud to take a huge loss on the Manikin, so in 1917 she sold the more marketable Rochester home and retired to the country estate to live year-round. As it turned out, she was stuck with the Manikin—an embarrassment, if she'd been willing to admit it, much too large and too isolated. Her bachelor son, Henry Junior—Hal, as he was called—hated it so that he took to traveling, staying away for months, even years, at a time, selling shares in the family business to pay for his tours and leaving his mother to manage the upkeep on her own. Which enraged Mary Craxton, of course, and after she slipped down the front steps and injured her hip, she came to believe that her husband and son had conspired to build this house not as a retreat but as her prison. Like that other Mary in the tower, she mourned her lost life and plotted impossible escapes.

By 1927 Ellen Griswood had been the Manikin's head housekeeper and Mrs. Craxton's companion for seven years, on the staff for ten. She had never lost a day to sickness, nor did she bother to take vacations. She had subdued dust and mold and her employer's fury. Despite the burden of work, she had grown comfortable and couldn't be tempted by a change. She was a domestic servant, no more and no less, and was proud of it. Ellen worked hard, and this became the simple justification for her life.

With Mary Craxton as its captive and Hal away more often than not, the Manikin came to belong, at least in spirit, to the servants. Thanks to Ellen's supervision, the rooms always looked newly furnished, the oak-paneled walls shone a lustrous blond, the mirrors were spotless. Even the animals left in Henry Senior's Cabinet of Curiosities were dusted and their glass eyeballs polished weekly. The gibbons and bats, the giant sea turtle, the macaw, the cougar, the tiny dik-dik, the peacock and quetzal, the crocodile, along with local specimens—a raccoon, a family of striped skunks, two beavers: all continued to look freshly skinned and stuffed, the fur and feathers sleek, as though their memory of life was just hours old.

Only outside did time leave its mark, scratching and clawing at the roof, beating relentlessly against the doors, bubbling the whitewash. Henry Craxton had chosen a harsh climate for his country estate; here in this pocket of northern wilderness, the weather, unlike the housekeeper, was inexhaustible.

But there are those who prefer the open sky to a ceiling, the busy silence of nature to the deadening quiet inside the Manikin. They love to feel a birch-bark canoe gliding over water and to bloody the wrinkled, melancholy faces of deer. Most of all, they love this irascible climate, especially the long winter, with its blizzards and shocking cold. You might even say that the weather forces them into an intimacy that wouldn't have been proper or possible otherwise; so Peg Griswood has a father in Lore Bennett, the groundskeeper. And she has a brother in Lore's son, Junket. And maybe Junket's dog, Machine, cocks her tufted ears forward not because she's trying to hear something but because she, too, loves the challenge of the weather and is captivated by the first scent of winter.

Last week Lore gave Junket a Maynard for his fourteenth birthday. Peg doesn't own a rifle, but whenever they hunt together Lore lends her his old breech-loading shotgun, the weapon hardly more than ornamental, since the few times she has fired out in the field she's never come close to her target. They're out jacking to reduce the crowded whitetail population—the deer come down to the pond to drink, and when one raises its head from the water Junket will attempt to put a bullet in its heart. Lore might try for a muskrat. Of the two, Junket is already the sharper marksman, and the Maynard—.40 calibre, with an extralong cartridge—is designed for high accuracy. It will take weeks, though, before he's comfortable with the rifle, and during that time there will be plenty of bungled shots.

The glow from the jacklight washes across the water at an angle, collecting in puddles of melted silver. The full moon hangs low, and they can see the shore with unusual clarity, poplar and beech yellowing above the mossy shore and behind them peaks of fir. Lore cuts his paddle into the water soundlessly to ease the canoe full around so they can survey the opposite shore. Junket will probably be the first to give the soft chuck in alarm. Whatever might escape his new gun won't escape his eyes. Or maybe he'll prove that his skill as a marksman is unconditional. The gun has confused the odds of the hunt—now it's anyone's guess.

Peg loves the wonder of a hunt, when the momentous act hangs just in front, in the invisible future. Imagine life without wonder: the life of an ox, for instance. Wonder has been broken out of the species. Out of the cow, the horse, the pig. Wild animals are different. Just look at the stuffed cougar in the Manikin's living room—the eyes are glass, but still you can sense the intensity in its expression. An amazement, as though at the moment just before its death it had suddenly been overwhelmed by wonder. *How can you do this to me?* it seems to ask. Boggio, Craxton Senior's leading artisan in the taxidermy department for forty years, now retired and living on the grounds of the estate, supervised the mounting of all the trophies in the Manikin. And they all have the same taut look of amazement. *How can you do this to me?* The working animal never asks this question, not even when it fights for its life in the slaughtering pen.

Peg's mother is a working animal—does what is expected, no surprises. Up before dawn, asleep by ten o'clock. As steady and predictable as the hands of a clock. As an ox. She is a dumb, domesticated brute, no self separate from her role as housekeeper, while Peg is as untamed as the Craxton cougar. But unlike that animal, she has the advantage of a future.

However much she enjoys the thrill of the hunt, her future is elsewhere. Where, she's not sure. She simply knows that she wants to see more of the world, to experience it in the way that her sixteen-year-old mind imagines other people do. She's never been farther than Syracuse, while her mother hasn't ventured outside the region for more than twenty-five years. Ellen has the nasal, dropped-ending accent of an upstate native, and in her cheap charcoal-colored uniform, a kerchief tied over her hair, she's easily mistaken for Amish. Not Peg, whose foot-long bundle of hair is more brilliantly red than Craxton's freshly painted barn. And that wild future, her own hidden behind the silence—it is waiting to be snatched, seized, bloodied.

Lore has tried to impress upon her the importance of this belief: a hunter doesn't shoot any white-tailed deer—he shoots *his* deer, the one that belonged to him long before he marks it and fires. At the moment an animal crosses into his line of vision, it gives up its life. But the hunter must kill his game with one shot, mercifully shortening the span of dying. No experienced hunter likes to watch his victim die. Bound up in its fate, he suffers with it. He wants to possess the animal that is rightfully his, to eat its flesh or wear its skin. Killing is the means and should elicit only minor pleasure, a sturdy satisfaction, nothing more.

Somewhere out there is Peg's future. Beyond the silence. A silence that encompasses the meager chirping of the season's last crickets, the *burr-ah* of a lone bullfrog, the splash nearby as a fish leaps, as though startled out of sleep by its own dream. Summer and winter both can be felt in the breeze and in the warm currents mingling with cold in the pond. As Peg lets her hand drag through the water she asks herself whether she'll miss her home after she leaves, forgetting for a moment that she has no home. A housekeeper's daughter cannot call her mother's place of employment *home*. Her mother. God knows what she'd have to say about Peg sitting in a canoe between Lore Bennett and Junket, a shotgun tucked under her arm.

So Peg's thoughts go, swirling on the same side of silence as the canoe, as Lore and Junket and Machine. And from the other side a twig snaps, and Peg looks toward the bank and sees something move—the object is too vague for her to make out its shape, but the motion attracts like an artificial light, absorbing her concentration even as the image disperses into a blur. Junket raises his gun; Machine lets out a low, barely audible growl and lifts her front paws onto the rim of the canoe. And just as the vision folds into the darkness again, just as Peg thinks, *Oh no,* Junket's Maynard goes off. The report of the gun tears the silence in half, the air fills with the echo of the explosion, and another sound follows—the crash of a heavy body rolling down the bank toward the water. And then a splash.

Peg doesn't finish the thought that was interrupted by the shot, so she'll never know exactly what she feared. But she hears herself screaming out Lore's name, appealing to him, as though he could reverse what has just happened, forcing, with a great heave of his strong arms, time to go backward. Instead, he bursts into laughter. Demonic laughter. And he sends Machine, who claws the wood and whines frantically, into the water with a "Fetch!" the command sandwiched between guffaws.

Junket shouldn't have fired—that's all Peg can say for sure, even before she knows what he has killed. He is panting, grinning uncertainly at his father, until Peg turns her rage on him: "Stupid, stupid boy!"

Junket's smile flattens, and his eyes widen in humiliation, asking, *How can you do this to me?* The boy's face, she senses right away, is one of those images that will remain in full detail in the front of her mind, easily recovered. And if she could have ignored the feeling that provoked her outburst, she would have pitied him.

But now Machine is paddling alongside the canoe, throwing back her head to raise the sopping bundle out of the water. Lore, still laughing, dips both arms and tugs at the prize, coaxes the dog to release it with a gentle "Drop it now, come on, 'atta girl." Not until he pulls the body into the canoe does Peg see that there hadn't been any atrocity at all. It is an owl, a white owl as large as a plump, two-year-old child, half its head smashed in, its broad, feathered chest webbed with blood.

A snowy owl. Peg recognizes it from Audubon's painting. A snowy owl, beautiful yet dreadful, like a mournful ghost owl from some forgotten legend, whose job it is to warn a person of approaching death.

Renamed by his father shortly after his mother died. Born Steven Bennett at the maternity hospital in Utica, where his father worked as a nurseryman. Now Junket. To be Steven Bennett again by his own choice when he is eighteen and living in the true wilderness, not this make-believe version. Junket, called by his father in fondness *Junk*. Whatever he might have been, his father has made him laughable. Named him after the food he loved so well as a baby: a dish of sweet milk set with rennet. Cuts his hair in sloppy haste. Never had the inclination to teach his son much of anything, except to shoot. Keeps Junket by his side, as much his possession as the locket attached to a chain around his neck. The locket, containing a single petal from his dead wife's prize-winning violet collection, will hang from his neck forever. Adores his son, as Junket well knows, but years ago took to keeping him home from school so regularly that Junket finally gave up school altogether. Yet despite the stunting effect of his father's devotion, the temptation to stay by Lore's protective side, to do as he says, to bring him good luck and keep him company, is strong. And if Junket had had his way with Peg Griswood, he would have stayed for much, much longer.

How natural, for the groundskeeper's son to love the housekeeper's daughter. But tonight nothing seems natural here at the Manikin, especially not the Craxtons' two thousand acres. This land is no wilderness, it is a preserve, sugared and boiled down like plums into jam. After only two years in the field, Junket is well on his way to becoming a master hunter. So what? It is a simple game, systematic and regulated. Whether he aims at a Coca-Cola bottle or a white-tailed deer, he will hit his target. He always hits his target. And by now would have already moved on to some other diversion if it hadn't been for Peg herself, who became his prime target, working her way into his mind until he could hardly concentrate.

But the owl has changed everything. The magnificent white owl from the Arctic, a rare visitor this far south, and so early in the season.

Shot, struck, felled—by mistake. By mistake! Never in his life has Junket made such an awful mistake with a gun. He committed the supreme sin, firing before he had identified his target. The bullet pierced the owl's eye and exited messily through the back of the skull. Lore, usually a man so reticent that he can go through an entire day without uttering a conversational word, had exploded in laughter. He still doesn't realize that Junket fired too hastily, and Junket won't bother to explain. Why spoil it? Let Lore believe in Junket's purpose. Then Lore needn't be humiliated, as Junket was humiliated by Peg.

Stupid, stupid boy. At last he comprehended that she would never have him. Never—a crushing verdict for a fourteen-year-old boy. But he's wise enough to accept her rejection without despising her. To do so privately. Peg wasn't oblivious, though—not entirely. As they were crossing the lawn back up to the Manikin, she caught Junket by the arm and whispered, "I thought . . . oh, I don't know what I was thinking back there!" laughing with unconvincing lightheartedness. She meant to soften the impact of her rebuke, Junket believes, to win back his friendship. And then she did what she hadn't for years—she took his hand and they walked together toward the house. Only then, and only briefly, did Junket want to return her malice and hurt her as she had hurt him. But the desire for revenge, connected as it was to the contact of flesh on flesh and to the hair that blew like threads of fire against his face, passed as soon as she released his hand a few steps later, leaving him more acutely alone than before.

Machine, jolly as Lore, bouncing on the trampoline lawn, might have lured him backward by reminding him of the more sentimental attachments of childhood. A boy and his dog. But wasn't there still a spray of blood across Machine's snout? Wasn't the dog's joy bound up in the death of the owl? Machine reminded Junket only of the barbarity of his last kill, and the owl reminded Junket of Peg.

They went separate ways at the Manikin, Peg up the stairs to her bedroom, Machine and Lore to the kitchen with the owl carcass to see what Sylva the cook could do with it, and Junket up the drive to the old gatehouse, where he has lived with his father for ten of his fourteen years.

Junket. Cast-off Junk. Plain Steven Bennett. He'd leave tomorrow if it weren't for his father, whose penny-ante consolation would be

You're young, you will outgrow this, you'll fall in love a dozen times before you're twenty. But Junket knows that there will be no healing, since almost every worthwhile memory he has of his life includes Peg Griswood, and to forget her would mean obliterating his own self. Or maybe that's what he wants—to dissolve into the night. Inside his bedroom he lifts the window, leans on the sill, and inhales the darkness, imagining that he is alone in the middle of nowhere—wherever that is—surrounded by miles and miles of unmapped land. The thought of such wilderness soothes him with its promise of vast silence, a *natural* silence, without the intrusion of voices. Only the sounds of animals and weather, of life in motion.

Soon he hears the scratch of pebbles as his father and Machine come up the driveway. Then a pause, which the dog fills with an impatient bark. Junket sees Lore standing in the middle of the drive, head slightly cocked as though he were trying to regain his bearings. He holds the owl by the legs and has been letting the head drag so there is a groove in the dirt behind him.

Of course Sylva refused to cook this carrion bird. So what can be done with the carcass? The answer is obvious to anyone acquainted with the old taxidermist Boggio, though Lore, who detests the man and his useless profession, would never admit it. "Bring it to me, Papa, I'll take it," Junket calls. With a wave of his free hand Lore acknowledges, and he slings the owl over his shoulder, arches to absorb the thud of the dead bird against his back. He's lost his pleased-as-punch smile, is considering at last, Junket assumes, his son's error. It isn't right to kill such a noble animal, a godlike bird, just for fun. It is, Lore must be thinking, as close as a hunter can come to blasphemy.

At last, by midnight, the spell has been cast, the Manikin stands luminous in moonlight, everyone is asleep. But no one sleeps as soundly as Ellen Griswood. Whatever worries she carries around with her fall away, and Ellen sleeps the carefree sleep of someone who has washed her hands of the day. No remembered dreams to trouble her. No startles or insomnia. She doesn't even hear her daughter enter the room and rustle about as she gets ready for bed. Sleep is Ellen's reward for a good day's work, and she guards it as carefully as a miser guards his gold. You won't catch the Manikin's housekeeper at rest during the day, but at night, when no one is watching, Ellen indulges herself with this great luxury, draws the starched cotton sheet up to her nose, and disappears for seven solid hours.

If she could remember the travels of her sleeping mind, however, she might not be so eager to give up consciousness. A carefree sleep—and all her freed cares mix together in skittish visions. Perhaps tonight she'll dream of music rasping as the gramophone needle scratches to a halt on the record, and it's her fault. Or she'll dream that the lamp beside her bed crashes from the table, the flames spill across the floor with the kerosene, and it's her fault. She'll dream of cobwebs in the corners, of tiny white larvae in the millet, of worms in the eye sockets of the cougar. Where is Mrs. Craxton's fox fur and where is Mr. Craxton's newspaper? Where is Peg when she's needed? In her dreams Peg will be just a wee thing again, crying that little lamb's bleat of a cry. She'll hear her husband groan as he spills into her. Ellen! Foolish of her to have put off sweeping the front steps, and now the rain. Did she wind the clocks on Monday? And who is that child leaning back on her heels, refusing to go on? Why, herself a little girl again, imagine! She'll notice dust on the antlers above the mantel, ashes in the ashtrays. What else has she neglected? *Mrs. Craxton?* she'll call, knocking on the door that has been locked from the inside. *Are you there, Mrs. Craxton?* And there she is again, a young girl standing barefoot on hot sand, refusing to go on. The surf roars like a huge fire on the other side of the dune, no wonder she's afraid. The sun has fallen from the sky, water burns, dust is sand, and men are made of wax. A tall woman, her mother, stands at the top of the dune, a cardboard silhouette. *Come on, poppet*, she urges gently. *Hurry up, poppet. Let's go and find the sea.*

And after all this, Ellen will wake at dawn, thoroughly refreshed, the tumult of the night forgotten. Even before she rises from bed she'll contemplate her sleeping daughter while she plans how to do everything that needs to be done.

2

If you make your way to Millworth, New York, you'll find gaslights still burning twenty-four hours a day on the streets, ornate black bars over the teller's window at the bank, a wrought-iron bench in front of the post office where you may sit for hours. Both bars in the village are equipped with brass spittoons. There are three churches, one school, one small grocery store, and a white clapboard public library, formerly an academy for girls. Only the children complain that there is nothing to do here. The adults fancy themselves keepers of an important history.

Over breakfast at the local inn you can browse through old photo albums while Mrs. Perry, the owner, tells you the story of the village. She'll describe with possessive pride the annual Chautauquas that drew visitors from all over the state. She'll tell you an anecdote about Theodore Roosevelt, who killed a black bear nearby. And of course she'll tell you about the Craxtons, about their wealth and extravagances, about the strain of madness in their family and their feuds.

It is not that Millworth has remained immune to time. The quaint nineteenth-century touches are, in fact, recent attempts by the few hundred residents to put their tiny village on the map by turning it into a living museum. One young couple opened a Christmas shop last year. Some families have turned their barns into antique shops. The gas lanterns were repainted, the spittoons imported. The inn now serves two dinner entrées: prime rib and roast duck.

In the nineteenth century, the region gained renown for its mineral springs, and aristocrats from upstate cities built mansions to serve as summer retreats, mostly Greek Revivals that exist today in varying states of disrepair. But the leading attraction will be the Craxton mansion, a fifteen-minute drive from the center of the village, on the eastern side of Firethorn Mountain. Renovations will begin as soon as sufficient money can be raised. For the time being, the Manikin remains closed, the windows boarded shut, paint flaking like old scabs from the shingles, wood showing through the broken plaster of the pillars, the portico crumbling, the yard overgrown, nettles knee-high by the end of June. The wild loneliness of the place scares away most visitors, but a few are tempted by the proximity of the past, and they slip inside through a cellar window that was broken open by village scamps years ago and never repaired.

The only permanent residents are gray rats who live in the cider barrels. They consider the Manikin rightfully theirs, having inhabited it for generations. On the wall of the old coal bin the penciled numbers marking dates and tonnage are faintly visible. Most of the rooms on the first floor are empty of everything but dust and bat scat. In the dining room, however, you can see the original painted wallpaper (a scene of a bloody battle between primitive hunters and a saber-toothed tiger), and in the conservatory the leaded glass doors are still intact. The carpets have long since been sold, but their impressions remain— rectangles of dark oak parquet framed by lighter borders. The library and dining room share back-to-back fireplaces with marble mantels, and both rooms smell of damp ashes (vagabonds have lived here for months at a time). The oak panels of the library were once covered with celadon silk but are exposed now. The expansive staircase narrows at a landing, then splits in two, both sides curling to meet again on the second floor. The banisters are mahogany, with spindles carved into coiled ropes.

Many of the bedrooms are still cluttered with Craxton's Scientific paraphernalia—common fossils, horns and tusks, skulls, claws, feathers, bird nests, seashells, coral, and the animals themselves. Craxton

Senior's main love had been fossils, though his company was best known for its taxidermy department, and at one time his private collection included a rare Madagascar moth with a twenty-inch tongue, a six-banded armadillo, and a resplendent quetzal. In recent years, unfortunately, the more exotic specimens have disappeared, presumably into the knapsacks of thieves.

The remaining items in the zoological collection are gathered in the master bedroom of the Manikin—all long dead and still wide-eyed, as though frozen by a gorgon's gaze. Only a female gibbon remains from a pair, her arm curled to embrace her absent mate. A snarling cougar lifts a filthy lip, exposing pink, papier-mâché gums, a moose head drips cobwebs, and smaller animals—squirrels, weasels, rats, shrews, lizards, beetles, birds, and fish—are crowded on the shelves. The windows have not been boarded over, so on a bright summer day the sunlight streams in, separated into strands by the grimy windows. With the dust motes hovering in the air, it may seem as though the room has been submerged in water, and the animals are floating around you.

Of all the animals, it is the snowy owl that appears most insistently alive. Mounted above the door, it stands guard over the collection, and though its feathers are pasted to its skin with a cakey violet mold, the mouth has been wired open to evoke a scream, and the bird is hunched forward slightly, its wings spread into a canopy, its eyes staring not with the ubiquitous wisdom of all owls but with a murderous envy, despising anything more animated than itself. With its round-tipped spuds of feathers and glaring eyes, the white face armored with tiny scales of gold, the fluffy white collar surrounding the open beak, the bird seems a monstrous imitation of a white Bengal tiger.

A crack runs along the panel from hook to ceiling, evidence that long ago someone tried to rip the owl from its mount. But the owl hasn't been tampered with for years. The locals warn that the snowy owl can never be moved, not without bringing down the entire Manikin upon the head of any would-be thief. And only the most hardened cynic would take the risk to prove this superstition false.

If this were a medieval court, Boggio would be the aged fool, kept on by order of the king, taunted by the children, fed table scraps by the cook. An ugly, unshaven fool, his skin a sickly shade slightly lighter than his tongue, the stench of dead animals clinging to him. He's too horrible to be pitied by the other servants—to them, he's the vision of what they will become, if they're not careful. To Mary Craxton and her son, he's the image of their opposite: a misfit, a pauper, a pleasant reminder of their advantages.

Fools are supposed to survive by their wits. But Boggio never has had much quick humor in him. He is too passionate to be witty. Passionate about his trophies, and passionately bitter. He's as much an expert at what he does as Ellen is at housekeeping—more so, perhaps, if you equate intensity with genius. But his belief that he's been cheated threatens to corrupt him entirely. Craxton Senior dragged his most talented artisan out to the Manikin and into retirement before Boggio was ready. Damnable man, but he's dead now, and his son's a rogue. Boggio has neither friends nor admirers in this godforsaken place. All he has is a roof over his head and a meager pension that could be revoked at any time.

Those who know him assume that he's long since used up, but Boggio himself looks forward to a change in situation. He's not in retirement, as he sees it—he's merely unappreciated. He's got a rare skill, and local hunters still come round from time to time with a hide for him to mount, in exchange for a pint of bootleg whiskey, which Boggio trades for supplies, since he's come to prefer sobriety to the early death a doctor once predicted for him. He's holding himself together, and someday he'll have another go at a champion, just as he did back at the start of his career. He was only twenty-two years old when the great P. T. Barnum sent an SOS from St. Thomas, Canada, to Craxton Senior. And, as it turned out, Boggio was the first to devise a strategy for this formidable job: the mounting of the circus elephant Jumbo.

On Boggio's recommendation, the team from Craxton's hired a dozen butchers to help them carve up the elephant. Jumbo's skin was shipped straightaway, in a tank of saltwater and alum, to Craxton's headquarters in Rochester. The rest of the carcass—the skeleton, the viscera, the heart, the eyes, the stomach (containing seventy-three pennies, a bunch of keys, and a policeman's whistle)—was saved for research purposes and took three days to crate. A new barn had to be erected on the grounds of Craxton's Scientific Establishment to house the twelve-foot-high wooden manikin. *Make him bigger, make him bigger!* Barnum wrote to Craxton. And the whole project turned out to be a bigger success than anyone could have dreamed. Akeley took all the credit, but it was Boggio who had the insight to secure the skin with hundreds of countersunk nails to the wooden skeleton and so prevented the hide from shrinking. And though the elephant's skull had been smashed to bits by the train that had killed him, Boggio was able to reconstruct it exactly with papier-mâché and wood. Never again would the spotlight shine quite so brightly on Craxton's Scientific as it did during the stuffing of Jumbo. Ears nearly six feet wide, legs as tall as doorways, glass eyes the size of baseballs, and that most important and awesome member . . . piece by piece, the puzzle of Jumbo had been assembled. Although officially Boggio had been Akeley's assistant, off the record Craxton attributed all the talent to Boggio—it was an extraordinary coup for Boggio that early in his career. The greatest triumph of his life.

So far. But Boggio wants to outdo himself. His ambition hasn't been diminished by time. Just the opposite. He is a locomotive with failing brakes plunging toward another Jumbo. *There will be another Jumbo*. His longing for an equal challenge has become so consuming that it has physically weakened him.

And now he has Junket's snowy owl, an unexpected gift, the first recognition that Boggio has had in years. The owl is a tribute, as well as an admission that all the wasteful killing for sport must come to an end. Species after species disappears, and it is up to the expert taxidermists of the world to document rare animals before they become extinct. Just recently police investigating an anonymous tip found in a cold-storage warehouse in New York City no less than twenty thousand dead birds—snow buntings, sandpipers, plover, snipe, yellowlegs, grouse, quail, ducks, bobolinks, and woodcock—all slaughtered to provide pretty plumage for the ladies' hats. Because of incidents like this, Boggio's dedication, along with his sense of self-importance, has intensified over the years. He casts himself as nature's savior, the supreme archaeologist not of man-made trinkets but of God-made art. Unlike Craxton Senior, Boggio was never interested in the commercial aspects of the trade. He stuffs animals that other men have killed in order to keep the memory of nature alive.

But his purpose has always been grander than simple reconstruction. Boggio tries to *improve* the original animal through careful refinement. Live animals can be more grotesque than beautiful. For this reason alone they are taken into captivity and forced to eat their meals with a fork, to jump through rings of fire, to lick their trainer's boot. The comedy of degradation—this is the appeal of the circus and the zoo. But take the great elephant Jumbo, empty the beast of gory life, and sew the pelt to an intricate wooden frame covered in clay—this is a show fit for a museum. A natural history display: more natural, more dramatic, more lifelike than life itself.

At last, thanks to Junket, Boggio has a new task at hand. Sweet Junket—a good boy, Boggio has decided. Boggio himself is a dwarfish man, thick-limbed, with an odd, prominent nose that bends toward his right cheek, but he can admire Junket's beauty without jealousy. The boy is among the finest examples of bipeds, with his sinewy limbs and jackal ears, a spray of freckles, narrow, mischievous green eyes. What a shame that the boy has Lore, such a coarse, ignorant bull of a man, for a father.

He was unprepared for the boy's visit earlier this afternoon, and he had to clear pliers and bits of stuffing wire from a chair before offering Junket a seat. Boggio lives and tinkers in the old smokehouse that has been his ever since Henry Craxton bought the estate. Once a week Ellen sends a maid to straighten up, and until then the mess accumulates as steadily as sand in the bottom of an hourglass.

"Please?" he said, motioning to the chair, allowing a strain of desperation into his voice in hopes that sympathy would make Junket linger. And to Boggio's surprise the boy sat in the designated chair and folded his hands over his lap. Like a woman, it suddenly occurred to Boggio, who came with bad news.

But Junket anticipated him. "Don't worry, nothing's wrong," he insisted, a touch snootily, kicking a ball of string by his foot, watching as it unwound across the floor. "Nothing's *wrong*," he repeated, which of course made Boggio sure that something was terribly wrong, and during the few seconds spent waiting for him to explain he considered various possibilities, most convincingly, since he'd thought of this before, that Mrs. Craxton had decided to evict him and sent Junket to deliver the notice.

Where would he go? He's an old cur of a man, he knows that. Only half his teeth left, lately he can't hold his urine and wakes up in soaked sheets in the middle of the night, can't get back to sleep, doesn't bother changing the bed, just lies close to the wall, eyes burning, the pulse in his neck bumping faintly against the skin, his mind as alert as ever while his body falls apart. He's an old man—what would he do if he were turned out? He's an old man with plenty of stamina, but—

Junket put an end to Boggio's escalating panic. "I've brought you something, is all."

A different panic filled him—an eager, fearful greed. "What?" Boggio swallowed the word and all that came out was a shallow bark. What would the boy bring him? Maybe he'd come to play a trick on poor old Boggio—some humiliating practical joke, the manure cookie kind of joke. It wouldn't have been the first time.

Junket bit his lower lip and scowled, apparently considering whether or not to go through with his plan. Then, without a word, he returned to the door and disappeared outside for a moment.

"This," he announced, standing at the threshold, holding the limp bundle of feathers at arm's length in front of him in distaste, though it was a marvelous bird, Boggio could see at once. Within the blood-stained plumage was an owl, an exquisite white owl.

"To mount?"

"To keep," Junket said, and dropped the owl on the floor. He left in such a hurry that for a moment Boggio hesitated to reach for the bird.

But there it was: one of the magnificent owls from the north. Not Jumbo's rival, of course. Not a black bear. But an impressive specimen, however mangled. He calculated its weight at twenty pounds or more. A bird so wonderful it hardly seemed real. More like a creature plucked from a fairy tale. A female snowy owl. Boggio picked her up, cradled her broken head as though she were an infant. He'd put together a shattered animal before. He'd do it again, he told himself. Perfectly. Brilliantly. Pushing aside the clutter on the table, he laid down the owl and ran his hand over the body, starting at the broken head and over the woody, pocked beak and down the breast. With his thumbnail he absentmindedly scraped off flecks of dried blood.

Then he noticed that his fingers were trembling. He looked at them in surprise. *Shh-shh-shh*—they made this slight noise as they brushed against the feathers. He tried to stiffen his hands, but he could not stop the shaking. His ten little slaves. He closed his fingers into fists but they were still trembling when he opened them again. Ten little mutineers dancing anarchical jigs. First it was his bladder. Now his fingers. *Come on*, they whispered to the rest of his body. *Follow us.*

But Boggio, stern captain, wouldn't stand for it. He rapped both hands against the table hard enough to split three knuckles. Hah! That shut them up, for the time being.

Outside, Indian summer fills the air with a ghostly sort of warmth, soothing and foreboding at the same time. Lore's muscles bunch into hard knots of strength as he lifts a full bushel. He hears Sid whistling from the far side of the orchard. He hears the rattle of a woodpecker, the screech of blue jays, the buzz of horseflies. The sky is pearl white, and the intense, cidery fragrance of neglected windfalls is dispersed from underfoot by the breeze. Lore's belly grumbles with hunger. He sets the bushel on the back of the truck, slips an apple into the deep pocket of his overalls, and reaches for another bushel.

As he works he thinks about the season ahead, his three-month battle against the tidal snow, and then the early spring plantings and the expanse of lawn to seed and then cut back. And then the fall again, apples to harvest, bulbs to plant. If he were a different sort of man his work might bore him with its repetitions. But he has never doubted the usefulness of his labor—he's well aware that every apple he gathers contains a few hours of sustenance and so will help to keep alive a stranger, a friend, a child, himself.

Inside, the scents of wood polish, Baume Bengé, and lemon teacakes fresh from the oven mingle in the air. Ellen pauses for a moment to dig out silt from under her thumbnail. Her joints make a slight clicking sound when she crouches to brush a dust bunny into the pan. She sneezes. Sylva reprimands a child in the kitchen—"You know better!" Above Ellen's head the boards creak as Eva cleans the bedroom. Ellen must remind her to wipe down the windowsills. And where is Billie? Billie should be back from the vestibule by now, carpet sweeper in tow.

Just then the harsh jingle of Mrs. Craxton's bell sounds in her bedroom, and Ellen quickly empties the dustpan into the wastebasket, wipes her hands on her apron, and tucks the loose strands of hair behind her ears. The bell rings again, more insistently, and Ellen hurries off, mildly irritated because there aren't enough hours in the day and nothing she can do about it.

But there is one advantage she's determined to claim, extra help to be had, and after Mrs. Craxton has eaten her lunch and retired for her nap, Ellen goes looking for her daughter. Peg may be an educated girl, but since she finished her schooling she's shown no interest in looking for work. Well, there are plenty of jobs to be done around the Manikin. Peg could grind the coffee or clean the glass in the conservatory or even set up the coffee table, with supervision. But Peg is neither in the library nor in the kitchen. Ellen calls out the door, "Peg? Where are you, Peg? Peg? Sylva, have you seen my daughter? Peg! Peg!"

When Peg was little, Ellen could keep her within the boundary of the lawn by telling her stories about wolves and witches lurking in the forest's depths. The girl would wander to the edge of the woods, but never farther. And if a sudden, sharp noise came from the mysterious center, the coven where witches danced and chanted and boiled children in great vats of broth, Peg would run as fast as she could back to the Manikin, back to Ellen, and bury her face in her mama's skirt.

Things were so simple back then—as simple as the fairy tales that Ellen told. The same that her mother had told her. And the songs: "Come my Dolly, come with me, dance beside the frothy sea." But now Peg goes where she pleases—deep into the Craxtons' forest, deep into the Craxtons' library. If Ellen only had the time to look . . . but she doesn't, and it's too late to do anything about it. Throughout her daughter's childhood, Ellen spared her both from chores and from punishment, as she herself had been spared for the first eight years of her life. But after her parents died within six months of each other, she and her brothers and sisters were dispersed to relatives. Ellen went to live in America with her aunt Lila, who taught her how to tuck a sheet around the corners of a mattress, how to dry china without leaving streaks, how to sweep, how to dust, how to arrange a tea service, how to obey. Not that her aunt was unfairly stern. A mild woman, herself a maid in a boarding house for many years, she wanted only to secure a position for her niece. *A position.* Ellen was brought up to aspire only to this.

No one was more surprised by Ellen's marriage, at the age of seventeen, than Ellen herself. And when her husband died six years later, leaving her with a meager pension and a young daughter to raise, the shock of widowhood passed quickly and Ellen settled into the life she had expected for herself. She found a position easily enough in the Craxton household, thanks to Aunt Lila's training. She moved up from the rank of scullery maid to chambermaid. And to housekeeper seven years ago, when Mrs. Webster left.

But knowing what she does about work, and recalling with nostalgic abandon her youth on the coast of the North Sea, she has been determined to let Peg enjoy a full childhood and a decent education, never foreseeing the impudence spawned by freedom. Ellen can manage the upkeep of twenty-seven cluttered rooms, but she cannot manage her own daughter.

"Peg!"

Now that it's time to put her to work, Peg is nowhere to be found.

Here she is: deep inside the Craxtons' two thousand acres, paging aimlessly through a book about owls. Gathering more information to add to the hodgepodge in her head. Peg wanders at will through the shelves of books and the grounds of the estate. But despite her schooling, or perhaps because of it, her knowledge remains piecemeal—an arbitrary accumulation. From her teacher she knows what a middle-class girl her age is supposed to know in order to make a good housewife. From the books in the Craxton library she knows about the life of the honeybee, variations in domestic breeds of pigeons, hybridism, falconry, heredity, Galvani's experiments on frogs' legs—and, most recently, the migratory habits of snowy owls. And thanks to Lore, she can find fossils in a creek bed where most people would see only rocks, she can load a rifle, bleed a deer, skin a rabbit. Yet it is all as useless to Peg as an index that refers to nothing.

Peg Griswood, daughter of a housekeeper. Daughter of a housekeeper. She reveals her background in the way she sets her lips together or holds her fork or speaks. Daughter of a housekeeper. Modern chattel. Her mother hoped she'd go directly from school into a profession—teaching young children, perhaps, or cataloging books in a library, or any other job that would make good use of her education. *An educated girl can find decent work, and she won't have to marry the first griffin who comes along. Work, Peg, work until you drop.* That's what her mother wants for her—a career that is just a shade more dependable than domestic service. So of course Peg wants just the opposite. She wants to be a modern girl, whatever that means—

she's not sure, but she imagines city streets at night, bathtubs full of champagne, rooms thick with cigarette smoke, couples necking in dark hallways. She wants to have the wildest adventures the era has to offer, and to have enough money to pay for them. A borrowed dream, she'd be the first to admit, unworthy of her tough intelligence, though how can she help it when she has so little experience of the world?

Mr. Hal Craxton, world traveler, might have been more useful in this matter if he'd had decent manners. Hal Craxton, with his greased hair combed forward to cover his bald pate, the smell of smoked fish on his breath, his fingers expensively manicured. Peg likes to shrug him off as the necessary mistake of a young girl who didn't know the first thing about romance. She knows a little something now, thanks to Mr. Craxton.

One day summer before last he'd surprised her by giving her permission to browse through his father's books whenever she pleased. Until then, every room except the kitchen and her attic bedroom had been off limits, but for some reason—easily deduced, had she been shrewder—Hal Craxton offered Peg this special favor. And the very first evening she'd gone to select a book, he'd joined her in the library, sat on the arm of the wingback chair where she was curled up reading, and without a word had started combing his fingers through her hair, gently easing his way through a tangle. The memory is powerful enough to cover her with gooseflesh. Why had she let him touch her? Maybe it was the surprise of the encounter that made it seem so natural—one moment she was just a child, the daughter of the housekeeper, and the next moment she was desirable. The fact that she found him vaguely repulsive only added to the thrill. His touch was too proficient to be resisted, and she felt herself succumbing to an unfamiliar state of docility.

If her mistake was to let him touch her at all, his was the common one of a man accustomed to paying women for their favors. How quickly his tenderness moved toward its own selfish fulfillment. In a matter of minutes he'd snuffed the reading lamp and was leaning over her, kissing her greedily, groping, squeezing, so there seemed to be at least two men bearing down on her, and the encounter suddenly felt like an assault. It wasn't that he frightened her; rather, his casual lust angered her, and though she would have liked the experience that an experienced man thirty years her senior could have offered, she pushed

him away and made a fast, silent exit, leaving him enraged and humiliated—or so she thought.

She had expected trouble from him after that, but he'd given up the
pursuit without a whimper, and during the remaining days of his stay
he hardly glanced at her on the few occasions when their paths crossed.
Peg wanted to believe that she had won his respect by refusing him. Yet
she suspected that Hal Craxton ignored her only because he didn't
want to bother with such a trifle.

He left the Manikin for Europe at the beginning of July, and he
hasn't been back for over a year. She doesn't dread seeing him again,
since it's become clear that he's had hundreds, thousands, of similar
encounters, some successful, some not, and he had swiftly forgotten
every one. Fine with Peg, since she prefers to think of Hal Craxton as
a false start.

She will try again soon, though to tell the truth she doesn't mind
lingering here for a while, passing time in a birch-bark canoe or a
library or an old hunting blind, floating through life. As hungry as she
is for a taste of the modern world, she's grateful for this temporary
calm and solitude. In some ways she'd prefer to stay in this forgotten
hunting blind forever and spare herself all the trouble of change.

Through the roof of dead hemlock branches, Peg can see the flat
white of the sky. The damp bed of needles is home to a large wolf
spider, which occasionally crawls in its emphatic fashion over her boot
to remind her of its claim to the blind. As long as she minds her own
business, the spider leaves her in peace. Her skirt forms a tent over her
legs, trapping hot air between her thighs, making them itch, and she
reaches beneath the hem and scratches first one leg and then the other.
She notices a red ant crawling up her arm, and she blows it off with a
gentle puff, only to find it climbing along a spiral course up her ankle
a moment later. She flicks the ant onto the ground and watches it
disappear beneath a decaying pine cone.

Smashing anthills, stealing Sylva's teacakes, tormenting old Boggio—this used to be daily fare for Peg and Junket. Not anymore, now
that Peg is no longer interested in childish things. She won't admit to
herself that Junket has come to love her—instead, she thinks of him as
a favorite pet that she has nearly outgrown. And since she won't take
her place among the adults who work at the Manikin, she has no place.

Peg wants an absolute freedom and assumes that the crowded world

outside this estate will be her refuge. She is prepared to leave everything behind: her mother, the Manikin, her past. But without any
money of her own, she has no means of escape, and for now she makes
do with imagining the future, relishing its intrigue and mystery, believing that she can make up the story of her life and exclude from it
whomever she chooses.

3

Picture this scene as a museum diorama, all the life-size human fig-ures as motionless as the furniture, modeled to evoke an animated gathering among women of the American leisure class in the late 1920s. Imagine that all the details are so painstakingly exact, the whole scene so convincingly realistic, that it asks for your apology, as though history required an invitation and you had come without one.

On the plush pink satin-buttoned settee is Mrs. Audrey Stone, fifty-seven years old, not at all the rigid woman that her name implies but fat and pliant, her skin shining like the stretched surface of a balloon. She has pinned a yellow silk rose to her cloche, and perfect kiss curls, dyed black, hide her ears. She wears a shin-length pleated voile dress with a sailor collar and a navy belt, white nubuck shoes, and white silk stockings. Her hand is poised above a tray of teacakes, her mouth already open in anticipation.

Nearby sits the hostess, Mrs. Craxton, dressed in a red silk lounging gown. She is seventy-five years old, and during the eight years since she fell and broke her hip, she has lost interest in her canes and instead prefers to pass her day in her wheelchair. Her white hair hangs like bands of gauze down to her shoulders. Her feet, in black kid-leather tie shoes, rest on the leather bar a few inches above the floor. She has draped her pearls, as large as pigeon eggs, in long loops around her neck, and her mouth is puckered, as though she were pronouncing a *pu* sound: "putrid" or "prudent."

The young woman across from her is Lilian, Audrey Stone's daughter, by many years the youngest woman in the group. She is also the most fashionably dressed, in a knee-length straight jumper—sleeveless, despite the season—a slave bangle around her arm, an ostrich-feather fan on her lap. She sits in an armchair by the window, and though she faces the center of the room, her eyes seem to focus past Mrs. Craxton on the window and the garden.

The other elderly women, Dorrie Cooper and Edna Jacobson, sit on the sofa side by side, their hands folded in their laps. Dorrie wears a brown linen skirt and muslin blouse. Edna wears an ankle-length pleated gown of Victorian character, though with a few touches of contemporary fashion, such as the low waist and wide shoulders.

The remaining figure in the group, the housekeeper, leans over the settee's arm to present the tray of cakes to Audrey Stone. She wears a gray rayon dress with a white apron and has pinned her hair up in a tightly wound bun.

Inside the diorama, lights have been positioned to illuminate Mrs. Craxton and her guests independently, so you can see the subtle differences as well as the more obvious ones—the grains of powdered rouge on Audrey Stone's cheeks; a scar cutting down from Edna's ear to the corner of her lip; the liver spots mottling Mrs. Craxton's neck and hands. Only the housekeeper is partially obscured by shadow, more for reasons of composition than to suggest something about her character or class. Murals on the three walls give the illusion that the conservatory extends to broad windows on either side, and in back to a grand piano and an open door crowned by magnificent elk antlers. To ensure continuity, two plastic potted palms in the space are repeated with two painted images. Through one window you can see the yellowing leaves of a trumpet vine; the unobstructed view through the other window is of a hillside, the sky, and dabs of clouds.

Life as it was among genteel ladies in western New York, 1927. The culture expected them to wear their clothes and carry themselves and speak exactly so, and they complied, since even though the culture was severe, it was also devoted, like a child to her dolls, and loved best the fact that they were helpless.

At the last gathering of the Wednesday Friends, Audrey Stone had described the plight of her daughter with such histrionic gestures that at one point she threw her hands back, forgetting that her cup was full of coffee, and the liquid flew like a quick brown bird, a swamp sparrow, and splattered the yellow satin floor-to-ceiling drapes. Ellen and Eva had devoted considerable effort through the week to trying to remove the stain, but still the outline remains, and you can see it in the late afternoon, exposed by the setting sun.

At today's gathering, Audrey brought along her daughter to explain her predicament in her own words. Ellen had to leave the room to fetch the cakes and again to refill the creamer, but from what she did hear she surmised that Lilian Stone's version of the affair was quite different from her mother's. As Audrey had told it, the gentleman pursuing her daughter was a penniless cad. In Lilian's version, he was a decent fellow, not without charm, though she acknowledged that there were more distinguished husbands to be found. From the way the young woman kept eclipsing her sentences with sighs, Ellen wondered whether she might have been lying about her disinterest. Lilian agreed with her mother that she would benefit from a period of seclusion. And since she didn't want to be too far from her own family, who summered in Millworth but returned to Rochester at the first dusting of snow, she hoped to make the Manikin her winter home—if Mrs. Craxton would have her.

It had been Audrey's idea, and she'd tried it out on Mary Craxton last Wednesday. Mrs. Craxton had been overjoyed at the suggestion. She would have company through the long winter ahead: a charming, educated young woman. They could play patience together. They could work on the intricate puzzle of the Swiss Alps that her son had brought to her after his last trip abroad. She had always wanted a daughter, and now, after a few exchanged courtesies, she had one—on loan, so there was no question of inheritance. The girl didn't want Mrs. Craxton's money; she wanted only a temporary refuge.

But Ellen wasn't convinced of Audrey Stone's innocence. And the girl, Lilian: Why would she cloister herself on a remote estate with a seventy-five-year-old invalid woman? There are easier ways to avoid a lover—or to test him, if that's what she really intends. Surely there is more to it, and though Ellen had hidden her suspicions as she passed the cakes, she kept eyeing Audrey and Lilian, especially Lilian, searching the girl's face for another motive, one that put Mrs. Craxton at risk.

"Ellen, tell Sylva that starting Sunday there will be another mouth to feed!" Mrs. Craxton says proudly, after her last guest has left. Just like a woman announcing her pregnancy, Ellen thinks, and wishes she were in the position to warn her mistress. But that position would leave her without any position: the messenger pays with his life. She'll keep quiet. But she'll also keep watch and gather evidence, and if Mrs. Craxton ever asks her what she thinks about Lilian Stone, she'll tell.

Mrs. Craxton won't ask, however—she never asks Ellen anything, except for the time. The grandfather clock in the front hall chimes every fifteen minutes and is joined on the hour by a glass-domed rococo clock with revolving brass antelopes in the living room, a mantel clock with monkeys that clash tiny cymbals, and assorted smaller clocks scattered around the house, but still Mrs. Craxton relies on Ellen to keep track of the time. Perhaps she believes that implied in the question is a sense of urgent purpose, as though she, like the White Rabbit, had an important date to keep.

She does have a date, at last: Sunday afternoon, when Lilian Stone will arrive with her trunk full of winter clothes. The girl will be the antidote for Mrs. Craxton's most dreadful ailment—boredom—though the old woman doesn't stop to consider the high price she'll have to pay.

"Ellen," Mrs. Craxton says as the housekeeper adds another empty cup and saucer to the stack on her tray, "we must make her feel at home."

Bird. Beautiful bird. From the tip of her head to the tip of her tail an amazing twenty-seven inches! Wrapped in her abundant feather coat, the white plumage speckled with gold, her beak almost concealed, one eye still staring with wild intensity, a bloody crater where the other eye had been. This is the way the world will end, Boggio dreamily tells himself, turning the bird from one side to the other. It will be shattered, the center will spill into the sky, the shell will collapse. Foolish bird, to have wandered thousands of miles from your circumpolar haven to Craxton's land. Well, Boggio will repair you. Whoever you are. Emblem of wisdom, companion of witches. If you tie an owl to a tree and walk round and round, the owl will keep revolving its head to follow you until it wrings its own neck. Beautiful bird. Owl the far-seer.

Boggio measures the wingspan, the tarsus, the claws and head, and in his haste he records the measurements right on the table. He pants lightly, as though he were overheated. And there is the problem with his fingers again—their rebellion. They are more docile when engaged in some mundane task, so he sets the owl aside and begins sorting his tools. A penknife, a pair of six-inch cutting pliers, forceps, a nine-inch flat file, a stuffing rod, wire, a piece of wood, bundles of straw. He inhales deeply, draws in the dusty, summery smell of straw. How he loves this work: the art of lifelike representation. Long ago, men preserved skin and horns and skulls as souvenirs. In the sixteenth century an Austrian baron mounted skins of aurochs over a framework of boards. Darwin mastered taxidermy before he composed his theory of evolution. And then Jules Verreaux purchased a booth at the International Exposition in Paris in 1867, and his display of two lions attacking an Arab courier on a camel became a great sensation. Henry Craxton Senior happened to attend the exposition on its opening day; as he stood admiring the Verreaux diorama, he invented the company that would make him rich: Craxton's Scientific Establishment. And with the help of such men as Critchley, Webster, Denslaw, Hornaday, Akeley, and Boggio—yes, Boggio was preeminent—he built an empire.

Mad old Boggio. He knows what people say about him. But Craxton wouldn't have been so successful without Boggio's help. He has a chance, at last, to revive not just the memory of the living owl but of himself as a respected young man.

The first thing he must do: break the bird's wings. *Snap, snap.* The effort makes him light-headed. He sits back on his stool to rest for a moment. He doesn't mind handling the carcass. What unnerves him is the commitment—once the wings are broken he cannot turn back. Some taxidermists make sure to have two animals to work with, in case of error. Boggio has never needed more than one specimen. But he's not as steady as he used to be.

Rain splashes the studio window with each gust of wind. Boggio pushes a wad of cotton up the bird's vent. He cuts open the bag of cornmeal, stolen just this afternoon from the kitchen, and fills a bowl. He moves the lantern closer to the bird. He prepares to make the first cut, but his fingers give such a twitch that he drops the penknife. Old man—ridiculed by his own body. Listen to the storm, heaving and bursting wickedly. If Boggio is mad, then he caught his madness from the natural world. Mad nature, rabid, vicious. It has passed its frenzy to mankind. Boggio wonders how it began: as a dance, perhaps. Women danced, men beat stones, but the madness didn't yield, so the people made arrows and ploughs and inflicted the first injuries upon the earth, and then upon each other. The Age of Stone gave way to the Age of Iron. We live in the Age of Gunpowder—Boggio believes it is only a matter of time before civilization commits the ultimate violence and turns the gun upon itself. Madness. Wildness. Boggio is the sanest of all because he understands what is happening. The sky laughs and spits; his fingers tremble. Wildness will undo the work of mankind in one agonizing fit. Death will follow. Everyone will follow Boggio. They try to deny it, but Boggio knows what's coming. Everyone will die. Boggio's job is to bring life to death, to wrap a skin around a wooden frame and keep memory alive.

Keep the hands moving and the mind can't wander. Now his hands want to move of their own volition. Not surprising to a man who has always known his control to be tenuous. Boggio has devoted himself to representing the sublime as perfectly as possible, and yet he has always left out the vulgarity of nature—the slavering and convulsions. The point has been to improve life, not to reveal its depraved secrets.

But now that he is so close to death himself he wonders whether he has cheated his work of its potential power. In the form of the single animal rests the wildness that will undo mankind. Expose it, represent the living animal exactly, capture all its virulent madness, and perhaps the madness can be resisted.

Boggio loves the natural world; fears it; hates it; believes himself to be, even in his self-acknowledged madness, a prophet. He assumes that age and a solitary life have given him an advantage: Boggio the far-seer. He will use the owl to convey what he knows—how to do this he's not sure. Somehow he must revise his old methods. But the ambition is clear, as well as the importance of speed. Time is running out.

He lays the bird supine, parts the feathers in a straight line, and holding the penknife firmly he plunges in and cuts the skin from the center of the breast down to the end of the breastbone. He's careful not to slice through the abdominal wall—what a mess of intestines he'd have on his hands then. And as though his hands want to avoid that trouble, they remain docile, willingly follow their master's directions. His confidence growing, he skins down each side of the bird to the knee joints, turns the skin of the legs inside out, snips off the tail and both wings. He stops to spread a paste of cornmeal wherever the sluggish blood has begun to ooze, and then he thrusts a metal hook through the pelvis and hangs the bird upside down. He separates the skin from the back, pulls it down over the neck and head, stretching it with his thumbnail to lift over the skull. He cuts through the membrane around the remaining eye and skins to the base of the beak.

With the skin off—and how efficiently it was done, so quickly and delicately, so little blood!—he beheads the bird, removing what's left of the brain and scraping away the flesh from the broken skull. Then he cuts the eye from its socket and severs the tongue. When he is through he sits in a chair at the end of the table, cups one hand inside the other, and contemplates his work.

Money: Lore Bennett has shredded it, rolled it into a ball the size of a cranberry, burned it. Lore despises money the way the teetotalers of his day despise whiskey. Money breaks a man's back, corrupts his children, destroys his self-respect. Lore lost his wife to money. Lost his home to money. Lost his little bit of savings when a stranger from Cincinnati convinced him to invest in—of all things—a toilet factory. Money's shit, and Lore flushed what he had down a fancy, imaginary toilet that was never assembled because the factory was never built. Junket doesn't remember any of it, and Lore has yet to tell his son the details: how they moved into a two-room apartment above the post office in Utica, how that fall the nursery shut down for good, and Lore lost his job, how they had a single kerosene stove for heat, how he and his wife used to climb into bed with young Junket in the afternoon to keep him warm. Unbelievably, they all survived. Spring brought odd jobs and a little income. In May Lore's wife announced that she was pregnant with their second child. And then in the peak of summer, when their misfortune seemed only a bad memory, Lucy caught a virulent strain of pneumonia and was dead within a week.

The baby would have been a girl, Lore has always supposed, sentimentally picturing her for all these years wrapped in bunting, smiling up at him. After losing his wife, Lore couldn't stand his own life and knew he had to change it or end it. Fortunately he chose change—he took his three-year-old son Junket by the hand and joined a group of migrants moving west across the state with the apple harvest. They had reached Millworth when the snow began—the other workers headed south, but Lore stayed behind as a day laborer at the Manikin. And when the former groundskeeper retired the following spring, Mrs. Craxton hired Lore Bennett to replace him. He and Junket have lived in the gatehouse ever since.

Lore doesn't blame the pneumonia for his wife's death. He blames money, a fatal virus. His fear of poverty is matched only by his fear of wealth. He goes out of his way to avoid an encounter with either of the Craxtons, watches over the property as if it were his own in an effort to avoid any need for directions. Hal Craxton, who doesn't even know where the family's land begins and ends, is usually either traveling abroad or busy planning his next trip, and Mary Craxton is too feeble to care, so mostly they leave Lore alone.

But despite the great loss, despite the worn-out longing to hold his wife in his arms again, Lore considers himself lucky. He has a fine job and a beautiful son. The pleasure he takes in his work keeps him vigorous. He thinks of himself as a simple man, congratulates himself for having such simple tastes. How he loves to clutch a fistful of soil in his hand after the last frost of the season or to hear the noise of the crows flocking at dawn and dusk, the rustle of groundcover as a deer lopes through the woods, the crack of a gun. He'd grown up on a small farm in Herkimer County—his father had taught him how to use the natural world, and his mother showed him how to tend it. Now Lore can coax from the orchard the most extraordinary apples—Ida Reds the size of grapefruits, perfect Macintoshes, green apples so abundant that Sylva can hardly boil them down fast enough. Sage, mint, basil, and wormwort spread in luxuriant tangles in the rock garden, the daylilies alongside the creek grow five feet high, and tender puffballs spring up in Lore's footprints in the mud, as though the earth were proving its love for him. Even the wild animals seem to respect a contract that gives Lore the right to kill them. It is widely believed that the beaver, grouse, and deer are more abundant on Craxton's estate than on surrounding land, and such uncommon visitors as moose and lynx have made their summer homes here. Lore tends fairly, if not gently, and over the years has turned this swatch of wilderness into a paradise.

But the one person meant to benefit from Lore's work has lately grown indifferent. His son seems miserable these days, wandering list-lessly through the woods and spending long hours gazing out his bed-room window into the night. What does the boy want? Junk wants something that Lore can't give. It took him over a year to save enough to buy the Maynard, and look what happened: Junk shot a white owl and in the two days since hasn't picked up the gun again, not even in practice.

When Lore saw the white bundle of feathers crash against the steep ground and then roll heavily into the lake, he felt such pride—a famil-iar enough feeling, since though his son has remarkable aim, Lore is surprised every time he hits his mark. *The boy's extraordinary,* Lore has said to himself over and over. *My boy is extraordinary!*

Yet he believes what the Senecas do—that all animals are inhabited by spirits—and fears that Junk will have to pay for his infallible aim. The owl's spirit must have been as pure as the arctic snow, sacred, untouchable. Maybe Junk regrets bloodying those silky feathers and wishes that he had missed his mark.

On Wednesday evening rain keeps most of the help lingering in the kitchen after dinner. Ellen is still with the old woman. Boggio never showed up for his meal. And Sylva's husband, Peter, has gone to close up the barn for the night. But the rest have settled back into their chairs, and Sylva has just set a pot of fresh coffee on the table. Billie, the chambermaid, takes out her sewing. Machine lies across the thresh-old of the pantry and drowsily watches as Sylva's two boys build and destroy card houses on the kitchen floor. Sylva's eight-month-old baby is asleep in a bassinet. Sylva's niece, Nora, a wisp of a thing with splotchy skin and short knots of hair, rinses the dishes. Lore pours his coffee and while he waits for it to cool he contemplates Nora's skinny backside. She's the daughter of Peter's brother and came to the Man-ikin from Chicago for one purpose: to be fattened with good food.

She's been here nearly six months, though, and Lore hasn't noticed any change. Must be she's working too hard, he tells himself. He'll discuss it later with Sylva.

His gaze moves to Ellen's Peg, who has moved her chair against the wall and opened a book. She'll be a handful, Lore thinks. He's always been amused by her willfulness. She bats Junk around like a cat teasing a mouse. But the boy's resilient enough—he can take care of himself. Lore turns to look at his son, who sits at the end of the table paging through his old arithmetic primer. In a few years he'll be every girl's dream. Lore's Junket. He adores the boy. All the richness of the physical world is contained in him. He can do anything if he sets his mind to it: shoot the moon out of the sky, shoot the eye out of a snowy owl. An impressive kill, you have to admit, even if it was unlucky.

Lore rolls a cigarette down the table. "Hey!" he calls. His son catches the cigarette, taps it against his open palm, and lights it with an effort at nonchalance. He resembles less a man than a boy trying to act like a man, which only makes him more impressive to Lore. He is at that age just before his prime, when elegance struggles to subdue awkwardness, and the ungainly body works to collect itself into a powerful unity.

What do you want? Lore should shake him to stir his senses awake. *What do you want?* He'd bring his mother back to life, if he could. *I'd do anything for you,* Lore tells him in a language that Junket can't understand, the abstruse language of thought.

Still, he never stops feeling grateful for his son. And for his people: Ellen and her daughter; the colored folks—Sylva, Peter, and their kin; Sid the gardener; Red Vic; Billie; the second maid—a German girl named Eva. And his employers—he's grateful for them, if not to them. Even Boggio, contemptible old Boggio—he's a necessary part of the whole. When from time to time he tries to beg a carcass, Lore turns away in disgust. The old sot, so useless and so arrogant, offends Lore's sense of decency. But he belongs in their midst, as essential to the balance as the devil himself.

If Lore knew that Junket had that same day given the snowy owl to Boggio, he would have been too stunned by the boy's betrayal to be angry—Junket understands how Lore feels about preserving animals as trophies. But he believes what the boy told him: that he'd carried the carcass back into the woods and buried it, deeply, he hopes, for this storm would wash away a shallow grave.

Tomorrow he will wrap the trunks of the blighted elms along the drive with muslin soaked in a solution of baking soda and witch hazel—an old remedy that his mother taught him. Then he'll take Junk and Peg hunting again, if the rain lets up. There's been too much rain this season, usually presaging a harsh winter. Come winter, it's up to Lore to keep meat on the table. He exaggerates his importance, though; unless there's a full-blown blizzard, Sylva continues to make her weekly trips to the market for supplies that include fresh butter, Florida oranges, and five pounds of grade A aged Angus beef, shipped in from Chicago. But Lore likes to think that all the residents at the Manikin are dependent upon the land, and he casts himself as the leader of the tribe.

Sid and Red Vic share the most recent newspaper—three days old by the time it reaches the Manikin. From time to time Red Vic reads a headline aloud; Sid grunts, turns the page of his section, and sinks back into it as though into sleep.

They all know that the kitchen, where the Craxtons and their guests never set foot, is the only hospitable room in the house. The thick pine table has absorbed the scent of onions and cloves and the bread that Sylva bakes twice weekly. The huge cast-iron stove radiates enough warmth to moisten foreheads with sweat. Copper pots hanging from the ceiling wear skirts of black where the flames have licked against their sides. The wide floorboards have been swept clean. On the windowsill the last tomatoes of the season are ripening—fat orange beefsteaks stained with deepening red. Strings of sausage and dried corn hang in the pantry, and the shelves are crowded with jars of Sylva's jams and relishes.

A *fine life,* Lore tells himself, warm with satisfaction despite the burden of his important responsibilities. *And my son.* Junket is scratching calculations with a pencil on the inside cover of the primer. He doesn't usually go in for books—it's unlike him to be so intent. Lore watches him, trying to decipher Junk's purpose, though he's still comforted by his solid affection for the boy and by the knowledge that he is his father. *My son.*

Junket absentmindedly swipes a hand through the air, but he doesn't look up to see the pair of moths dancing in front of his face. Lore smiles to himself. *My son.* At that moment, he sees in the boy's face the child his wife was carrying at the time of her death—not simply resembling but replacing Junket, a baby girl with a shock of black hair, brown-eyed, smiling sleepily. It is an odd sensation, overpowering in its suddenness. And just as suddenly the image disappears as Junket rises angrily from his chair, flinging his pencil across the room. Everyone looks up, and the moths dart off, each to opposite sides.

"Take this rich man," Junket says, as though intruding into a conversation begun without him, "he gives . . . let me see . . . he gives away one fifth, one third, and one sixth of his money to three different charities. So how much does he have left?" No one speaks. The silence of the room is filled by the trickle of rainwater spilling from a drainpipe beside the kitchen door.

"I couldn't figure it either. I tried. It's a problem from a fifth-grade primer." Junket's voice breaks to a near whisper. He's relieved that he's stumped his audience with the problem, but he's also embarrassed by his outburst.

From the corner of the room comes Peg's voice, gently condescending. "It's so simple."

"What?"

"It's the simplest kind of problem, Junket. I'll show you."

For another moment the boy continues to look baffled, and then humiliation stains his face scarlet. He snaps the textbook shut and rushes from the table, leaps over Machine, who scrambles up and follows him out the door. After he is gone Nora and Billie laugh outright, others exchange smiles, and Peg murmurs, "What did I do this time?"

Sylva cuffs Peg on the ear. "Smart aleck, girl," she says.

Lore doesn't bother to defend his son; in fact, he is quietly pleased, not because Junk has been chaffed by a girl but because such corrections help a boy find his place in the world. He looks forward to the day when his son can laugh at his own expense, making and admitting his mistakes with equal good humor. As he watches the smoke rising from the abandoned cigarette, he considers life's blunt paradox: stuff from nothing. He lazily tries, and fails, to conjure in his mind the faces of the generations that will follow.

4

By the mid-twenties, the village of Millworth had converted from gas to electricity. But the cost of stretching the electrical lines the extra few miles to the Manikin, as well as wiring the interior of the house, would have been, as Mrs. Craxton was told by her accountant, prohibitive. And rather than organize a federation with neighboring farmers to bring the lines over Firethorn, Mrs. Craxton simply did without. So the famous Craxton hauteur was compromised by coal and kerosene and candlelight. During the long winters, the Manikin received few guests and sank into a heavy, hibernating somnolence. The cloud cover hung over the house like a granite ceiling. The wheels of the touring car were deflated, the gas tank drained, and the automobile shut up in the garage until March, or April during years when the thaw came late. A pickup truck was used as long as the roads were navigable, but after heavy snows trips to Millworth were made by horse and sleigh.

Though Mrs. Craxton insisted to her friends that she preferred an old-fashioned country winter and scoffed at their dismay, after they were gone she felt as though she were looking through the wrong end of a telescope at civilized society—she knew it to be there in front of her, as close as the library full of her husband's unreadable books, as close as the piano, which she no longer played because she despised the noise her clumsy, arthritic fingers made, as close as the bell that summoned Ellen. There was Ellen, at least—Ellen, and every evening a cup of hot cocoa. But the cold defied coals and hot baths and cocoa, so Mrs. Craxton's bones ached day and night. Night was worse, with its wind demons and clamoring solitude. What had she done to deserve this? After all the unspeakable suffering of her lifetime—the loss of one son to diphtheria when he was sixteen weeks, the loss of another son in a climbing accident when he was twenty-two, her husband's sudden death twelve years ago, not to mention her own fractured hip—she deserved to be comfortable, to enjoy all the luxuries of the modern world. Instead, she was living like a savage among preserved skins and skeletons, and therefore she felt entirely justified in indulging her savage disposition.

But though she despised her one remaining son for leaving her to rot alone in this godforsaken place, she didn't blame him, not entirely. He could not help his faults. So she scolded Hal even as she privately forgave him for his neglect, and she clung to the hope, what she assumed would be the last hope of her life, that the next time he returned to the Manikin, he would stay put.

Then Lily arrived, and Mrs. Craxton changed her mind: she'd rather have Lily than Hal for a companion, she decided. On that gray day at the beginning of November when Red Vic fetched Lily, Mrs. Craxton set out to convince the girl to make the Manikin her permanent residence. And since she wanted Lily to fall in love with the house, Mrs. Craxton dreaded the coming winter more than ever.

Lily: as colorful as a fresh nosegay, her heels sinking into the mud, leaving egg-carton prints. Red Vic should have driven the car right up to the front door. Mrs. Craxton shoots a glance that says, *Stupid man, an Indian, no wonder! I'll have a word with you later.* Not now, though. Now she welcomes Lily Stone with open arms and a smile to assure her that she will fit right in, she'll be the center of attention, as beloved as a daughter. It's one of the many sad facts of Mary Craxton's life that she never had a daughter. But here's Lily to make it up to her at last.

The novelty of her arrival—not just an afternoon visit, the girl intends to stick it out through the winter—draws a crowd. Billie, Eva, and Ellen stand behind Mrs. Craxton's chair on the porch. Peter walks up from the barn, chewing on a sprig of hay and wearing such a slaphappy grin that Mrs. Craxton would have admonished him for his impudence, if she had noticed. Nora carries the baby and follows Sylva around the side of the house—Sylva holds her sons by their wrists to keep them from bolting across the muddy drive and knocking the delicate young lady flat on her back. Even old Boggio leaves his studio to observe the scene.

"Welcome, Lily." The occasion warrants a special effort, so Mrs. Craxton rises from her wheelchair and extends a hand, which Lily presses between her palms. Then Mrs. Craxton sinks back into her chair, gesturing toward the door. Ellen wheels the chair around, up and over the threshold, and into the living room, where a tray of Sylva's shortbread and a pot of coffee have already been set out, as though to convince Lily that the Manikin's treats are generated by an unspoken wish, that the servants will not only heed her but anticipate her.

And mock her—though they give her no reason to suspect this. They mock her for her high-heeled shoes, for her shin-length leopard-print coat, for her jewels and the hours she wastes masking her face. Their laughter as they huddle together has a shrillness to it because already they sense that her demands will be impossible, that like all spoiled city girls she will expect them to turn off winter entirely with a flick of a switch. And to turn it on, so she can watch the snow dancing merrily behind the windowpane. She is trouble, this modern bird. Whoever fails her first will be the first to go.

No one is more acutely aware of Lily's influence than Ellen. She considers the danger as she watches the girl from her sentry's position a few feet to the right of the wheelchair and listens to Mrs. Craxton's fawning inquiries: "How was the drive, my dear? Do you play patience? Do you miss your family?"—so many questions, with ample time ahead for them to become better acquainted. There is more at stake than a season's friendship. From other people, Mrs. Craxton has always demanded respect. From Lily, she wants the kind of devotion that excludes others, an impossible desire, Ellen knows, as consuming as it is futile, especially for one as inexperienced in affection as Mrs. Craxton. Lily Stone has come to the Manikin not to devote herself to her hostess but to use her—to what end, Ellen still can't say. But no good will come of it, she's sure. The old woman has never seemed so pathetic, or so ancient, even as she flutters her hands about to impress the girl with her gaiety. And when Lily makes a weak stab at wit—"If I keep eating this way you'll have to add me to your collection of stuffed beasts"—Mrs. Craxton erupts in such a howl of laughter that Lily turns to look at Ellen, as though to assure herself that the banshee's keeper were nearby. Ellen returns her glance as coldly as possible, instantly regretting it, for in that brief exchange she has earned the girl's contempt.

A few minutes later, at Mrs. Craxton's direction, Ellen leads Lily up to her room, a grand corner room with an eastern and southern exposure, a massive fieldstone fireplace, a four-poster bed. Ellen draws open the curtains and prepares to leave, but there is one task left, apparently.

"Undress me," Lily says. The direction takes Ellen's breath away, and she turns around to see the girl standing in the middle of the room, arms akimbo, as though waiting to be fitted by a dressmaker.

Ellen swallows her outrage and manages to reply quietly, "Yes, of course."

This is only the beginning, Ellen thinks as she struggles to free the clasp above the buttons. Lilian Stone may be a slender-thighed, small-breasted, fashionable nymph, but the effect of her is that of a boulder rolling down a hill, crushing everything in its way. She has grown into her surname. She wears it well, like her expensive clothes. And will flatten Ellen if she doesn't jump aside at the last minute.

The naked girl rests her hands on the back of her neck in a gesture that suggests an experienced tease, then stalks across the room to stand exposed at the window. Ellen follows and reaches around her shoulder to shake out the curtains, knowing even as she does it that such an act will not go unpunished.

"Leave me," Lily says, staring at the curtains with her penny-colored eyes.

"I was just—"

"Leave me."

If she were a different sort of housekeeper, Ellen would go directly to Mrs. Craxton and report the girl's vulgar display—without a stick of clothing, for the world to admire! But she is the sort whose anger

finds relief in physical exhaustion. She spends the next hour washing
Lily's dirty prints from the floor of the front hall, and by the time the
marble is clean to her satisfaction, she's ready for another job: Mrs.
Craxton's bath. Then dinner. The day will be over before she knows it,
she tells herself. In the blink of an eye.

From the edge of the backyard, Peg watches the stranger at the window for a few long seconds before the curtain hides her again; even
from this distance she can see that the girl is naked. She stands as
though on display, as though daring Peg to stare. It is like a statue's
dare, composed, indifferent to the judgment of her audience. The image so enthralls Peg that she forgets completely about the chance of
being discovered, gun in hand, by her mother, and she forgets as well
about Junket, who stands beside her, breathing lightly, his Maynard
propped upon his shoulder pointing at the figure in the window.
    "Pow."
Now Peg remembers him, turns to witness his childish joke. He
jerks backward with the kick of each imagined shot. "Pow. Pow.
Pow." Easily hitting his target at one hundred yards' distance. Shattering her, until the curtain closes.
    Urged out by Lore, Peg and Junket are on their way to Craxton's
Pond to dismantle a new dam and perhaps bring down a mallard or
two. Junket hasn't spoken a word or even looked Peg in the eye yet.
But she is resolved to repair the damage she's done to their friendship
and convince Junket to forgive her. So even though she'd like to crack
his fancy new gun in half, she lets him be. The beautiful girl won't ever
know how Junket has humiliated her, and Junket can go on thinking
there's nothing funnier. Target practice. *Pow.* No harm done.
    Machine romps out of the woods to fetch them. They can't see Lore
but they hear his whistle, and they hurry down the slope with the dog,
slipping along the path leading into the woods, kicking up pine needles
and wet leaves as they go, woolly mockernut hickory, orange maple,
and the thick, canoe-shaped leaves of the chinquapin oak. Closer to
the pond the ground is yellow with beech and poplar leaves, the trees
almost bare, each like an exclamation point. The beavers love the poplars best—they gnaw at the trunks to get to the gummy inner bark,
toppling the trees and carrying off the branches to pile on their dam.

As they follow the pond to the mouth of the creek Peg falls behind, not because she can't keep up but because she's still thinking about the figure in the window, Mrs. Craxton's guest for the winter. Ellen has been fretting all week that this visitor will disrupt the order so carefully established at the Manikin. Another occupant is like a new tax levied without warning—she thinks it unjust that she has no say in the matter. She can look after this Lilian Stone readily enough—she could look after one hundred guests. But there should be no other guests. Mrs. Craxton is hardly more than a ghost, and Hal Craxton just a fleeting shadow. Ellen has grown comfortable with the arrangement. It is as though she is managing an extravagant hotel and prefers it to remain empty, pristine, undefiled. The overwhelming absurdity of the Manikin is just this: a staff of eight, and little to do. Oh, Ellen makes vigorous work for everyone. But Peg is convinced that the house and grounds could be managed by a staff of two.

A guest on an extended visit might see through the pretense of hard work to the truth. She might tell the truth to Mrs. Craxton. And Mrs. Craxton might decide to trim some of the fat. Ellen surely knows the truth, and that's why she fears the Manikin's new guest, even if she won't admit it. Peg feels free to admit it, though, just as she feels free to blame her mother for her loneliness. And feels free to leave at any time. She means to exercise this last freedom soon enough, but until then she has to be content maintaining a position of quiet superiority: the privilege of insight and honesty.

Who is this Lilian Stone beyond her name and wealth? In order to find out, Peg needs opportunities to observe her more closely. She will volunteer to carry trays and clear dishes and make beds, to do whatever she must to be near her. She even considers gathering a bouquet of the late-blooming orchids, white and yellow lady's slippers still freckling the marshy land at the south end of the pond, to put in the guest room. No, she's not lovesick. What Peg wants, clearly enough to admit it, is to become that modern girl, to change places.

After losing sight of Junket and Lore, Peg wanders back along the path and then steps out to the water's edge. Brown water sloshes against the shore, and the tip of the beached canoe bobs slightly, buoyed by an extra few inches of water after two nights of rain. Junket and Lore will be wondering where she's gone off to—she catches sight of Lore's jacket through the trees on the opposite shore. She steps away from the water, and the clatter of rocks underfoot stirs an otter from its hiding place; it darts from the bank and in good otter fashion splashes out, glides underwater for a few yards, rises and twists onto its back, plucks at its whiskers, swishes its heavy tail and propels itself in a serpentine course, rolls onto its belly and disappears, surfaces on its back, claws the air, and glides effortlessly into a clump of reeds, like a toy sailboat pushed by the gust of a child's breath. Other than a soft splashing it makes no sound.

Even as Peg watches the otter's antics, she feels someone's gaze on her, and when she finally turns around she almost expects to find Lilian Stone standing next to her, clothed again, smiling, her expression artfully frozen, one brow arched, the other flat above a half-winking eye. In a subdued voice she would ask, *Why didn't you shoot?*

"With this?" Peg says aloud, holding up Lore's old shotgun to the woods, and thinks, *Pump an otter full of shot?*

You're delightful, she would say, the girl in the window, the Manikin's winter guest. Then, Peg is sure, she would burst into mocking laughter.

Rosettes of water-chestnut weed floating on the water. Quackgrass. Feathergrass. Cattails. Who lives here? Dabbling ducks. Swamp rabbits. Brown trout. Beavers. Muskrats. Otters. Beech and birch and spruce. No slurring sound of conversation, no smell of kerosene hanging in the damp air. How it is in Lore's paradise: imagine. No change other than the slow, necessary deterioration of the earth. Listen to it groan. The tangy smell of wet leaves and bracken. Bones. The dream of soft flesh tearing. A dog's dream. Fathers. Sons. A gun swallowed by muddy water. Buried bones. A gun's dreamless sleep. The sleep of the drowned. Bulrushes. Ironweed. Pied-billed grebes. Marsh wrens. Tiny bitterns. A gun. A pond. A splash. The only echo a father's soft groaning. A drowned gun. A boy's spite. Everything remains alive, except the gun.

The Maynard, goddammit! Lore saved for a year so he could buy that Maynard, and what does Junk do, Junk his only son and the reason for Lore's life? Why, the little savage tosses it like a spear into the heart of the pond. A boy's spite. There's nothing more vicious. A boy's spite and, even worse, his lack of remorse. If hate were possible, Lore would force Junket to pay, to reimburse his father for that lost year. But where Junket is concerned, anything, absolutely anything, can be forgiven. Lore doesn't have to wait for the wisdom of hindsight to know that the Maynard is a trivial loss compared to other possible losses.

The flight of metal caught Lore's attention, and he turned just in time to see the gun dive, barrel first, into the water. And there was Junket on the bank looking as thoroughly satisfied as he ever did standing over a kill. What went wrong? They had been heading toward the mouth of the creek, Machine trekking ahead then falling back to sniff his spoor, Lore walking about fifty yards in front of Junk. With the suddenness of an accident, the boy turned evil—or mad—and tossed his gun into the pond.

Even now, he meets his father's astonishment with a grin. Junket's expression would shame Lore, if he let it. Instead, he feels incited by the challenge, and under his son's gaze he peels off his jacket, removes his wool hat, unbuttons his flannel shirt, and steps out of his trousers and boots, all with the slow, deliberate movements of a striptease dancer. In his checkered boxers he slurps through the mud and reeds into the water. And just like the gun—or, a few minutes earlier across the pond, like Peg's otter—Lore dives, disappearing beneath the surface.

Instantly the cold seizes him, binds his limbs so he can't pull himself up for a gulp of air, and for those few seconds until Junket pulls him out, Lore hovers somewhere between delirium and consciousness, his mind awake but bewildered, the cold penetrating like electricity, pain so overwhelming that the sentient aspect of himself separates from the body, and he knows he feels, without feeling, the cold. He hears his exhaled breath bubbling through the cloudy water. It doesn't occur to him to distinguish between the surface and the muddy bottom of the pond. What has happened to the sky? The gun must be resting somewhere on the bottom of the pond, as comfortably as a feather on grass. What has happened to direction? Lore doesn't think to ask. He doesn't care. And time? What has happened to time? A fraction of a second lasts long enough for him to wonder how much time has passed. A minute? An hour? And then he gulps, cold water rushes into his throat, and he becomes a tangle of reactive nerves twisting and jerking with almost suicidal effort, like the loon he once caught in a fishing net. The bird had panicked and in its struggle managed to strangle itself before he could set it free. The loon. The long, limp neck of the loon—this is the only image that remains in his murky consciousness.

Afterward, lying on the sloped bank gasping for air, his first thought is oddly pleasant. *It is surprisingly easy to die,* he understands now. If he weren't such a responsible man, he might have given in to the seduction.

But he's Lore Bennett, groundskeeper of the Manikin, so he climbs to his feet as soon as his strength returns and slaps his hands against his arms to hasten the warming blood to the surface. *Well, I'm the fool,* he thinks. Yes, he's the fool, thanks to his son. He doesn't bother to ask the simple question *why.* But Junket tells him anyway, trying to contain the clacking of his own shivering teeth while Machine nuzzles his cupped hands, whispering, as though to keep the trees from hearing: he threw away the gun because he's bored with Craxton's acres; because he needs a change; because there has to be more to life than harvesting another man's orchard and shooting his game. And even though the boy's apology is implicit, he doesn't come right out and admit that what he'd done was selfish. As Lore reads him, Junket is sorry for goading his father to a point beyond sanity, but if the Maynard had been retrieved and returned to him, Junket would have disposed of it in some other fashion. So no adequate reconciliation follows. Lore gives his jacket to his son and dresses in his dry shirt and trousers while Junket tries to explain himself. When the boy drifts off from his shivering whisper into silence, Lore doesn't encourage him to continue. The silence that replaces Junket's voice is not the same as the silence of the forest—between father and son will remain an empty borderland, a desert, impassable, uninhabited. Or this is what Lore fears—that they will not even attempt to cross over this no-man's-land. They will be like foreign nations, dependent upon treaties and pacts to keep their peace, with different languages and currencies and laws.

Lore will never know that while they were heading toward the beaver dam, Junket had seen Peg on the opposite shore, her back turned to him. With the pond between them, she'd made a perfect target, the distance in itself a challenge, the block of her coat a smoky blue. He could have taken her down with one perfect shot between the shoulder blades. For the second time that day, Junket had located a girl's body in his peep sight and centered his shooting eye. Another joke, more wicked than the first—with his finger resting on the trigger's paddle, he'd thought, *Accident.* Implied in the word was his defense against the accusation: Peg's death at Junket's hand. *Accident.* The whole narrative—murder, accusation, and the jury's pardon—was contained in that single word.

And beyond that word, self-disgust. How could he have allowed himself to take the joke this seriously, this far? Suddenly the gun had seemed contaminated. He hadn't been able to hold it, to look at it, especially to own it. So he'd thrown the gun into the pond in an effort to avert the hateful accident, causing another, as it turned out. His father had nearly drowned because of him. This is what he should have used as his explanation, he thinks after he has already fallen silent: *Not because of boredom or impatience, Papa. Because of me.*

Peg is waiting for them midway up the path, and along the walk home Lore spins an unlikely tale to explain their wet clothes and the missing gun. Junket stumbled, Lore says, and dropped the gun in the water, and, crazy boy, he went in after it, so Lore went in after Junket and dragged him to safety. But Peg hardly seems to be listening, and back in the yard she turns away without a word, slowly, mechanically, like a china doll in a music box. Here are Junket and Lore, hair dripping, lips blue in the autumn air, and she doesn't care what happened. Hoity-toity, the servants called Mrs. Craxton's visitor even before she arrived. Miss Hoity-toity. And now it's Junket's impression that Peg is aspiring to the same.

Lore and Junket go to their separate rooms. Junket strips off his wet clothes and climbs into bed, the natty wool blanket prickling his skin. He doesn't need sleep—he just wants to be alone. But sleep comes to him anyway, surreptitiously, so he thinks he is only dozing until he opens his eyes and finds the room dark. He assumes he has slept through most of the night. The memory of the afternoon returns to him: his gun, and the startle of that first splash when the Maynard hit the water. His father's doomed attempt to retrieve it. The rescue. But he can't take credit for dragging the wet lump of a body from the water, no more than a man can take credit for denouncing himself as a murderer. Remember murder, Junket? The idea of it, and the story you would tell to absolve yourself?

Adventure for Junket has been bound up in blood ever since he was old enough to accompany his father on a hunt. As a young child, he tended to give human qualities to animals; now he has imagined Peg as his prey, himself as a murderer. He took the analogy too far and had to sacrifice his gun in penitence. He won't hunt again. He is afraid of himself, knows now that he is capable of murder. He went beyond the conception, stroked the velvety trigger and felt a warm blush of pleasure at the idea. That he could accept it as possible: murder. How *macabre*. Even though Junket doesn't know this word, he imagines its meaning—the dance of death, Peg leading the way to the cemetery in Millworth, himself hard on her heels.

"You awake?" His father stands in the doorway combing back his hair. "Hurry up, if you want supper." So it's only early evening. Oriented in proper time again, Junket feels groggy, as if his father had woken him at 3:00 A.M., and he remains in bed listening to his father's chatter continue from the other room, one of Lore's rare attempts at conversation. He predicts a hoarfrost tonight. He remarks upon a pumpkin in the field: "Must be eighty pounds by now"—has Junket seen it lately? When Junket doesn't reply, Lore gives up. "I'll be up at the house," he says.

Junket hears the clop of his father's boots down the stairs and outside. Soon the ground will be frozen. He imagines the footprints and ruts in the mud hardened like plaster molds. And the skeletons dancing over the surface, shaking tambourines that make no sound.

Yet how tame Junket's imagination is now compared to his early childhood. Peg's as well. They've forgotten so much, all their wild games and childish passions. There was one game in particular that lasted through a summer, though it had promised to go on forever. Every day the floor of Junket's bedroom would collapse, and they'd fall into a different world, where rocks could sing or trees grew five hundred miles high or people were made of glass. The test was to exist inconspicuously in these dangerous, invented places, so most of the game involved hiding—from the glass sheriff, from monstrous birds, or even from Machine, then just a puppy with lollipop paws. Sometimes they would have to leave Junket's room in order to escape, and they would hide in the hayloft or the cellar. Once, they crept into the Manikin's kitchen, past Sylva, who was stirring a pot of soup at the stove, and instead of heading up the backstairs to Peg's room they snuck through the dining room, where they caught a glimpse of Mrs. Craxton sitting before her audience of stuffed animals in the living room.

They padded up the front staircase to the absolutely forbidden second floor and followed the long corridor, counting fifteen doors in all. Peg opened each while Junket kept watch behind. The rooms were furnished lavishly, with sitting chairs and sofas and beds as wide as hay wagons.

When they heard a woman cough lightly on the backstairs—a maid coming to dust, probably—Peg pulled Junket inside a room and quietly closed the door behind them. This was the room, years later, where Lily Stone would come to live for the winter. But on this day they were in a world where adults drank the blood of children and maids carried handy jackknives in their apron pockets for the purpose of slitting little throats. So it wasn't enough to hide behind one closed door. They'd be safer in the closet, Peg decided, and Junket agreed.

They spent the rest of the hour in the dark walk-in closet in the Manikin's grandest guest room. A few of Mrs. Craxton's old dresses and silk bathrobes hung on the rack, but other than these and a stack of hatboxes the closet was empty. Did Junket smell stale blood? Peg wanted to know. Yes he did. And bones—he said he smelled old bones. That's because they buried the slaughtered children in the walls, Peg explained. They were sitting on the floor, their knees drawn up to their chests, and Junket squirmed sideways until he was touching Peg. When he drew in his breath, he hiccoughed loudly; Peg clapped a hand over his mouth. His second hiccough was somewhat muted, but the jerk of his shoulders caused Peg's hand to slip partly over his nose. Junket panicked when he couldn't inhale properly, yanked her hand away, and hiccoughed with such force that he fell backward against the boxes.

The bar of daylight underneath the door made shapes visible, enabling Peg to see enough of Junket's body to grab him by the shoulders and pull him toward her. Then, in desperation, she kissed him. She even pushed in her tongue, slid it along the smooth enamel and the ridges where the teeth overlapped. Junket's tongue shrank back, made timid by the surprise. But Peg continued to kiss him, and he found himself cracking his mouth open a little wider to see what she'd do. She hesitated, which made Junket bolder, and he pushed his tongue forward to meet the tip of hers. The surge of intimacy was irresistible. Junket's fingers, still childishly plump, crawled inside Peg's blouse and up to feel those mysterious bumps, not hard like acorns, which is what he'd expected to feel, but more like the rubbery cartilage of kneecaps. And her skin felt so silky, so expensive, that he wanted to wrap it around his own shivering self.

Later, Peg matter-of-factly explained that her method was the best cure for hiccoughs. It worked, yes? And when they had left the vampire castle behind and were back in Junket's room, he asked her where she'd learned to kiss like that. "Like what?" she said, obviously offended. Junket shrugged and never mentioned it again.

5

The first snow is like volcanic ash, so feathery light that it floats in the air without settling. For a few brief days the colorful patchwork of fallen leaves shines through the branches, until, overnight, the brilliance dulls to browns and grays. Audrey Stone has already returned to Rochester, but with her husband and two sons she plans to make a special trip to the Manikin for a Thanksgiving feast, if the weather holds out. Hal Craxton should be home from Egypt by then. Lilian will have had two weeks to get used to her situation—if she chooses, she may accompany her family back to the city. But this will be her last chance to change her mind.

It is up to Ellen to keep the interior of the Manikin presentable for its inhabitants and guests. Twice a year, in autumn and spring, Ellen turns the mansion inside out and attempts to renew it. The process lasts five days. "Stay out of Mrs. Griswood's way," Sylva will warn her boys, giving them each a sharp slap ahead of time, since they're sure to be a nuisance. But to stay out of the way you'd have to go to the next county—so the men reason, and they won't even set foot in the kitchen during Ellen's house-wrecking campaign. "Do you prefer pestilence?" Ellen will call out to Sid the gardener from an open window as she wipes the glass. "I prefer peace!" Sid will shout, waving his rake at her.

Housecleaning, of course, is women's work. First thing Monday morning, Sylva attacks the stove—blacking it to keep it from rusting, sifting out ashes, scouring its greasy burners. She puts Nora in charge of the pantry—every jar and can must come off and the shelves be wiped down, and then everything must be returned to its proper place. Eva will wash the drapes and carpets and blankets, rejuvenate the pillow feathers, and clean the mattresses. Billie will polish the furniture and floors, banish the cobwebs from the ceilings, and clean the windows. And Ellen will start with the basement, then close up the conservatory for the winter, and finish off with the Cabinet of Curiosities, grooming and polishing the trophies with special attention.

During this week it is always the repetition of her responsibilities that threatens to overwhelm Ellen: still the wicks need trimming, stairs need to be swept, the clocks need to be wound, Sylva needs time to bake, and Mrs. Craxton needs attention, though not as much as she used to, thanks to Lilian. Who'd have thought Ellen would be grateful to have Lilian Stone around? It's just for this one week—afterward, Ellen can resume her place as Mrs. Craxton's main companion. The trick during these seasonal cleanings has always been to fool Mrs. Craxton into a state of complacency. Ellen would lay out a game of patience and crank up the gramophone and leave Mrs. Craxton alone, sometimes for as long as an hour. Now Lilian can help stretch that hour into two and Ellen can go on about her work.

Ellen's the fool, as it turns out. Lilian Stone has better things to do than to sit around playing cards and breathing in an old woman's sour exhalations. Early in the morning she wanders off no one knows where, leaving Mrs. Craxton so affronted that she ignores her breakfast and stares blankly at the dining-room mural, refusing to be consoled by Ellen or even to be moved from her place at the head of the immense cherry-wood table. So Ellen has to let the basement wait and instead busies herself with the minutiae of the dining room, dusting the porcelain tea set, removing the lambrequins from the windows, and finally settling to the tedious work at the étagère, taking out all the fossils and teeth and seashells on display so she can clean the glass shelves, all the while keeping her mistress within sight, in case the strain of disappointment becomes too much for her.

Noon comes and goes, and Mrs. Craxton speaks only to decline lunch. Ellen suggests sending Sylva's boys to Millworth to fetch Dr. Spalding, but Mrs. Craxton scoffs at the idea—the trouble, she says, is not inside her body but outside the house, wandering through the forest. Girls these days think themselves invulnerable, and though Mrs. Craxton doesn't really fear for Lily, she obviously fears this precedent of inconsiderate behavior. There will be trouble when Lilian returns, harsh words, a falling-out. Ellen must bolster the old woman. Perhaps she could tell her about Lilian's bawdy performance at the window yesterday, and Mrs. Craxton could indulge herself with self-righteous disgust at young people these days, their lack of manners; every girl's a tramp. But Ellen decides that telling tales wouldn't do anyone any good, so she resigns herself to a wasted day. Tomorrow she will wake an hour earlier and set to work on the furnace. For now, she will see to it that Mrs. Craxton, pitiful old thing, gets whatever she wants.

She wants a girl—one girl in particular, though as it turns out, Ellen's Peg will have to do. There's Peg in the kitchen gobbling a sandwich, nose pink and wet after a romp outside. She's a lovely sight to her mother, bursting with life. Still a child in many ways. So what if she's strong-willed? Today, Peg's health seems the reward for Ellen's leniency, the girl's insolence only an annoying habit. See how the color in her cheeks matches her hair. Someday Peg will look back upon her childhood and realize that her freedom was her mother's greatest gift, and she'll be thankful. She knows how to be alone with herself, she isn't weak or timid, and she won't have to borrow a personality from her husband. Give her a few more years, and she'll have a rare kind of composure that can't be bought.

Peg leans against the kitchen table as she eats, lost in thought. Ellen stands on the threshold between the two rooms and scrubs fingerprints off the swinging door. She watches Peg take a long drink of milk, winces but manages to keep quiet when her daughter wipes her lip with the back of her hand. Now's not the time to remind her about the use of napkins. Ellen has work to finish. Her daughter, educated but still half wild, must be civilized gradually, gently.

"What may I do to help you, Sylva?" Peg asks, as if she has overheard her mother's thoughts.

"I expect your mama has an idea. 'Bout time you pitched in, kitten." Of all the people at the Manikin, Sylva is the most honest, and Peg flinches visibly at this simple truth.

"Mother?"

"You may keep Mrs. Craxton company." Ellen blurts it out before considering the consequences, and it's too late to retract. She's never put the old woman in anyone else's charge before—why should she begin with Peg? But she knows that Mrs. Craxton has overheard the exchange. And even while she searches for a way out of the predicament, her daughter is already obliging, smiling courteously, approaching Mrs. Craxton with the sprightly step of someone who doesn't much care how she's received.

"I challenge you to blackjack," Peg announces, opening the drawer in the sideboard where the cards are kept. Ellen feels weak about the knees, horrified by Peg's impertinence. Blackjack, indeed! Why not strip poker while you're at it, Peg? Hey, young lady, where's your Havana?

"Don't like that game," Mrs. Craxton mumbles. But any response is better than none, so Ellen refrains from interfering, pretends to busy herself with cleaning and waits to see how Peg will manage.

"Old maid, then."

Oh, Peg.

"I always win," says Mrs. Craxton, cracking a smile as Peg settles into a chair.

"I won't let you win."

"We'll see."

Ellen has been tending the fire in the dining room all day, and she throws in another log, watches as the flames slip under the warped bark. While Peg deals out the hands, Mrs. Craxton asks her twice for the time—evidence that she's reviving. Ellen waits until the flames have wrapped snugly around the log, then leaves the room without a word, comforted, as though she'd just listened to a lovely piece of music. So Peg's at work, finally—occupying Mrs. Craxton, not an easy task by any means, especially with the difference of almost sixty years between them. And Ellen is lost somewhere in the middle.

Down in the basement she sweeps the floor, then sets to work on the furnace, stirring the white coals in the belly to force down the loose ashes to the lower shelf. A salty tear of perspiration drops into her eye, and she shuts the dry eye and looks out through the blur into the throbbing heat. She wonders about herself at seventy-five. Maybe she'll be long dead, her body resting in her grave while her spirit dashes about with the north winds. That's what she wants for herself, eventually: to be weightless. Not to fly—she wants the motion to be effortless, as in the delicious moment just after all her strength had gone into the squeeze of pleasure, and she lay limp in her husband's arms. Remember? His body encasing hers. The heat spreading inside her. But that old memory, however tempting, is incompatible with the task at hand, and she sends it back to the depths of her mind. Shoveling yesterday's ashes, hauling them in the wheelbarrow up through the bulkhead, dumping them in the bin until the furnace shelf is empty and she can brush and scrape away the sooty crust that remains—always the perfectionist, Ellen is, not satisfied until she can see the gleam of metal again.

She stops to rest for a moment and sifts through the ashes in the wheelbarrow. Even water would feel coarse in comparison. So soft are the ashes that when she closes her eyes and holds them in her cupped hand she can imagine she's holding goosedown. Or cobwebs. She had better check on Billie later to make sure she's reaching the cobwebs in the highest corners with her feather duster. And Eva—she joined the staff in August, and though she says she's washed mattresses before, Ellen doesn't entirely believe her. These girls don't care about the quality of their work, since they consider themselves temporary help and are always chattering about better jobs to be had. The maids usually last no more than six months, a year at best, convinced that they'll move on to a better position, and beyond that, to marriage, a Sears mail-order house, a picket fence, four children. Ellen understands the impulse—when you're young, you want to believe that life's a steady climb to a flat-topped summit. But too often disappointment cancels out the bliss of hope, so a woman's ambitions should be modest. Ellen wants to spare her own daughter, to prepare her for the inevitable hardships. Peg had better know about the business of living before she sets out on her own, for there's nothing respectable about a young woman on the move, and the usual direction is down. *Work. Work so hard that you make yourself invaluable.* Work saves a woman from vice, Ellen believes, from the abuse of men, from poverty. *Work, Peg, work for the sake of security.*

The older servants are appropriately grateful for their jobs. Lore Bennett has been at the Manikin for ten years and has made no noises about leaving. Sid is a restless sort, but he's nearing fifty and has confessed to Ellen that he's tired of the unexpected. He'll never marry, though he has a tendency to cast an invitational wink in Ellen's direction, and she doesn't like to be alone with him. Peter and Sylva have their three children—and Nora, too—so they're not going anywhere. Red Vic, at sixty-three the oldest member of the staff, knows he's lucky to have a job at all.

The girls, including Peg—*especially Peg!*—could learn a lesson about appreciation. Ellen forgives them when they complain about the Manikin and its backward aspects, but she loses patience when they balk at hard work. They act as though some innate superiority puts them above Ellen, as though they each had a Lilian Stone inside waiting to come out. Soot under her fingernails, soot in her hair, soot covering her face and neck—this is what the world will give a woman who doesn't have the wealth to support her ambition. Ellen has to admit it to herself, if to no one else, that she hates this necessary stage of cleaning, when she's imprinted with the dirt she's worked so hard to remove, when she's unspeakably filthy from the contact. But she stops just short of feeling sorry for herself. It could be worse: she could be working twelve hours a day in a factory or in the fields or in a poorly ventilated office picking out letters on a typewriter. She's grateful for her position, and though in good American fashion she's tried to give her daughter opportunities she herself never had, she's not ashamed of her work. Far from it. It suits her perfectly. She perceives herself to be a plain woman with skin stretched too tightly over her bones so the skeleton shows through with disturbing insistence. Ascetic and obedient, Ellen fits the role of housekeeper exactly, carries herself with the tired poise of an actress who has performed the same play every night for eight years. So rare are her lapses and hesitations that even those who know her best know only the housekeeper and not the self independent from her work, and she sees no need to remind them of the difference. She enjoys her power, or, as she prefers to think of it, her *influence*, and always exercises it judiciously.

But she's never more proud than when she's in Mrs. Craxton's company and receives directions instead of giving them. No one is as completely dependent upon her as the old woman, and perhaps this alone explains Ellen's pride—she believes herself to be superior to her employer. Or is it that Mrs. Craxton needs Ellen only as a witness, and almost anyone could replace her? Peg is an adequate substitute. More than adequate, apparently. Ellen pulls herself up from the basement ladder into the kitchen and finds Sylva and Nora peering around the door into the dining room, where the old woman laughs with the lusty heaves of a woman half her age and Peg giggles in return.

Sylva motions to Ellen, puts her finger to her lips, and whispers, "The Steffan boy brought a telegram. Mr. Craxton's heading off to Italy instead of coming home for the holiday, turns out."

Ellen looks over Nora's shoulder. Mrs. Craxton is in her chair facing the fire and Peg stands beside her. What are they laughing at? Punch and Judy dancing in the fireplace? Mrs. Craxton points a finger at the flames and says, "There he is, there!"

"Burnin' that telegram," Sylva explains. "Had Peg read it out loud, then she tossed it in the fire." She wipes her hands on her apron and turns back to the stove. "Shame on that man," she mutters.

"Don't look like she cares a stick, Aunty," Nora says.

"She don't ever look like what she feels," Sylva replies, casting such an implicating glance Ellen's way that Ellen says defensively, "She's given up on him. Any mother would, by now," convincing no one. They all hear the agony in that laugh, and if Mrs. Craxton had dived headfirst from her chair into the fire, they wouldn't have been surprised.

For weeks the skin of the snowy owl has remained inside a square, airtight metal box in Boggio's studio, sprinkled with naphthalene crystals and a few teaspoons of old carbon bisulfide. No lice, fleas, or maggots are going to infest Boggio's rare specimen before he has properly mounted it. But here's the riddle: What is proper? He might as well be trying to mount the skin of a fallen angel. He has never seen an angel, though he hopes to one day. And he has never seen a snowy owl in the field. He must model his snowy angel after its former self and capture some motion of life in the pose. His little Kodak can't help him here. Every morning upon waking he stares at the ball of fine excelsior on his table and wonders how to go about it. How to continue with the work he's begun. How to do justice. How to represent life in precise detail.

A job has never stumped him so thoroughly. For lack of anything better, he spends the afternoons in an old hut that he has claimed as his bird blind, overlooking Craxton's marsh. He doesn't hope to find another snowy owl, but he might snap a picture of a different species—a red-tailed hawk or, if he's lucky, a great horned owl, a common enough marauder, every farmer's most detested pest. But even this is an unsatisfying prospect—making do with such a peasant bird. There must be other possibilities.

He reminds himself as he walks quietly along the path of the simple rules that apply to the mounting of any large bird: Be sure that the artificial manikin is smaller than the natural one; bind the roll of excelsior with linen thread to give it strength; fill the space between the artificial body and skin with straw; and use a heavy, galvanized wire to support the head. Guidelines make any operation sound easy. But the combination of surgery and art demands a unique sort of talent, as rare as it is useless in any other line of work. Forty years ago Boggio tried his hand at accounting and failed miserably. He is sure he would have failed at everything else, including women. Especially women. All the palaver and deceit involved. He has been alone for his entire life—this in itself is an accomplishment. By his age most other men are struggling to resign themselves to their cowardly marriages. Solitude is a challenge that Boggio has met as fearlessly as the snowy owl herself, who left behind her arctic home in search of a more temperate solitude. Lovely bird. She'll never see the blossoms of the dogwood or the speckled carpet of lily of the valley underfoot. She'll never crush a wild strawberry upon her tongue. Think of all she'll miss because of Junket's expert aim. Boggio would like to represent this as well: the unlived future. To show what has been lost. It is a melancholy tale, the tale of the hunted.

The snow has begun to fall again, and with every step Boggio pushes through an ice curtain that melts upon his face. A quarter mile away lies his hut, built a century earlier, according to local history, by a farmer to house his mad wife. Boggio replaced the door years ago, and he alone carries the key, so when he finally reaches the hut he is surprised to find the door ajar. *You old idiot,* he chides himself, *can't even remember to latch a padlock.* Then he sees that the bolted lock has been busted right out of the wall. He steps into the dank room and while his eyes adjust he inhales the familiar smells of the moldy wooden floorboards, of damp brick, of cold. But there is something else, too. Boggio smells the wool blanket before he sees it crumpled like a child curled upon itself to keep warm. Or a small man. Some mudlark taking advantage of Boggio's forgetfulness? Some weary Willie with nothing to do but to set up home in Boggio's private blind? He grabs the blanket and rips it off the infernal good-for-nothing . . . nobody. There is nobody, only the same dirt and cobwebs that give the room its character. *Filth,* Mrs. Griswood would say. But it's one hundred years of filth. Familiar filth. Everything's familiar here, except the blanket—and the white silk undergarment that flutters out from the folds of the blanket and wafts as gently as a feather, as a butterfly, as a tiny angel, to the floor.

Listen. Boggio hears it before he conjures an image—an echo, like a mermaid's song that can be heard under water from hundreds of miles away. The song of lovers. And now he imagines what he hears: a man's pale, spongy buttocks rose and heaved, a woman's thighs jerked with each thrust. The room filled with their howling and groaning. A rutting song, that's all—he has no illusions. Just a cheap burlesque in the woods. And here's Boggio's souvenir.

Wretches, whoever they were. Boggio doesn't want to know. The progeny will be given to a foundling hospital, he wagers. They will abandon it, just as Boggio was abandoned when he was two weeks old. No pity wasted, though. The world is a haven for bastards and orphans. Boggio, by virtue of his long-suffering independence, has little to lose.

He holds the frilly panties to his nose. There's a smell of buttered bread in the middle, and the panties are damp at the puckered edges where they've been resting against the wall. Boggio's wall, violated. The insult of it hits him—a rogue and a slut had their fun, at Boggio's expense.

But insult can inspire the open-minded man. Boggio clutches the panties in his hand, squeezing from them a wonderful new idea. He did hear the song, didn't he? He heard it with remarkable clarity. *Now listen carefully:* an owl is singing. He will make the bird sing. He's been wrong to try to start with an image of action. To simulate life, he must construct his animal in such a way that anyone can hear the voice. He imagines the effect: a man enters the gallery, strides across the room to examine Boggio's famous owl, and as soon as he's within arm's reach he hears the voice, a violent whoosh of sound and then the scream of a predator, the cry too lifelike to have come from a recording device.

The man knows the owl is dead, stuffed, inanimate, but just as certainly he knows what he heard—the voice of the dead owl. *Impossible*, he tells himself. But this is the beauty of Boggio's idea: miracles are never forgotten.

He's indifferent to the snow on his walk home. He's thinking about the challenge in front of him. He will spread the owl's wings and stabilize them with wire mesh. He will fill the head and neck with cork dust mixed with shellac—he'll need about two cupfuls, he figures—and then he'll shake and tamp the head until it is completely filled. He'll have to stuff the beak with a wad of chopped tow, since he plans to leave it open and pull the mounting wire through the mouth rather than through the skull as he usually does. He will wire the mouth open and bend the papier-mâché tongue to evoke, exactly and irresistibly, the sound of a scream. And he will paint the beak with a coat of umber, then seal it with beeswax. The finished bird will be his fiercest animal. She will recall her wild self more convincingly than any other of his creations.

Now that he has his idea, the execution will follow easily, naturally. He picks up his pace as he nears the Manikin, but instead of returning directly to his own quarters he circles the house, searching the windows for some sign of activity. On his third trip around he finally sees the housekeeper washing the glass door in the conservatory.

"Mrs. Griswood," he calls, tapping on a pane of glass and grinning. He holds up the panties. "You want filth, here's filth for you!"

Snow, at last. True snow. Not the furtive or dishonest snow that has started and stopped and started again for weeks. Not the mean-spirited, sleety snow or the snow that coats the trees with ice. This is snow that gains in bulk and weight with astonishing speed, snow that transforms the forest within minutes into a whitewashed maze of compartments and aisles, snow that lands in tempting dollops on the tiny red berries of the bitter nightshade, snow that sticks to the hairpin edges of rhododendron leaves, snow that skews perspective, making even the trees close by wave like seagrass. It is not yet the harsh snow with blizzard winds that sweeps south from Canada. This is snow that seems indigenous, falling vertically with a soft hiss, gathering in mounds shaped by the contours of the earth. It is a snow that marks the beginning of winter. A snow that buries.

No other season in the region is as immutable. Once winter sets in, people forget the context of the year. It is winter. It will always be winter. Memories of summer days are blurred by the insistent snow. The forest without snow would look denuded; with snow, it is utterly confident. The weather takes on the logic of natural selection, casts itself as the culmination of seasonal change, having evolved from the weaker seasons into a white-bearded, indomitable Thor, whose main fraud is constancy. Winter will never end—this lie drives unsuspecting homesteaders to despair. Settlers who choose to live outside the towns and cities give up their farms to winter, and only the most trusting believe that someday their land will be returned.

The Manikin had been renovated not with comfort in mind, at least not the comfort of its inhabitants. It was designed to be dressed up and admired—Henry Craxton Senior named it with perceptive irony. But how cruel the irony seems once winter sets in and the admiring spectators have fled back to their electric lights and oil furnaces. The immediate meaning of the season's first heavy snowfall is so obvious that no one bothers to say it: There will be no Thanksgiving party. The Stone family wouldn't dare leave civilization to gather in no-man's-land for the holiday. Whether or not the highway has been cleared, a person risks his life to travel in a sleigh from Millworth over Firethorn Mountain to the Craxton estate.

For Thanksgiving dinner, Sylva boils a corned beef, on Mrs. Craxton's order. Usually the old woman has a more refined, if limited, palate, alternating between poached fish and pink roast beef, with turkey and all the trimmings on the holidays. She's always liked to put on a show for guests and expects the staff to share the feast in the kitchen. But plain boiled beef is hardly something to relish. They grumble their way through this Thanksgiving meal while in the dining room Mrs. Craxton punishes Lilian with silence.

At formal dinners Ellen pours the cider and Billie serves the food. Today, Billie has been replaced by Peg, who lately has been working with such tireless effort that she doesn't leave the two maids enough to do. But Peg is more eager than skilled. She hasn't been trained to ease out of the kitchen by slowly pushing the door open with her hip, and the creak and whistle of the swinging door breaks into the quiet. Yet here she is in a black rayon uniform and white apron trying her best to help her mother. What's come over the girl? Ellen wants to believe, but doesn't quite, that Peg has taken stock of her situation and understands what she must do to survive. By nature, Ellen is cautious—she needs to know the reason for Peg's conversion. Even the word "conversion" makes her suspicious. Peg is too used to her freedom to give it up lightly. They should have a talk later, in private. But Ellen has lost the ability to talk intimately with her daughter and prefers to take refuge in the briefest, most insignificant exchanges.

Careful, she thinks, watching Peg set a pewter gravy boat on the sideboard. But it's a warning to herself, as well. Careful, because banality leads here, to this funereal silence. And when the silence signifies a contest of wills, as it does today, there will be bloodshed. There will be a victim.

In this contest between Mrs. Craxton and Lilian, Ellen can see that the mistress of the house will win. She has gained the upper hand with her unexpected powers of restraint. Never before has she seemed so stolid, so coldly dignified. Ellen has lost count of the number of times her rakish son has laughed at his mother because she can't control her rages. Hal Craxton always wins their battles with laughter and has maintained for himself the right to come and go from the Manikin as he pleases.

Surely the antagonism between generations is not a problem peculiar to the century, though modern trends of education have only made the rift more pronounced, Ellen believes. Perhaps it is an American problem. America breeds insolence. To come to this country you have to leave behind all comforts and pretend to be naturally brazen. In no time the mask grows onto the face. Americans fancy themselves a tough lot, when in fact they are the first to take refuge in fashion and quack religions. The wealthy are even more vulnerable. Ellen believes that families like the Craxtons suffer greatly for their privileges, and she's quick to insist that she wouldn't want to change places.

Who would want to sit where Mrs. Craxton is sitting, in a hand-carved, leather-upholstered wheelchair, with her imperious face looming over the table? Though there's nothing but a weak hip wrong with her, she won't last forever, Ellen reminds herself, wondering in a distracted way how she'll manage after Mrs. Craxton's death. Her employer would drag her into oblivion, if she could. And Lilian—even now Mrs. Craxton wants to break the girl's spirit. Nothing would delight the vengeful old woman more than to watch Lilian Stone languish.

"I have eyes in my head, Ellen," Mrs. Craxton had said the previous night, meaning, *I know what that girl is up to.* They all know—the staff, the children, Mrs. Craxton herself. Unexplained absences are easily interpreted. Last week, the postal clerk mentioned to Red Vic that a young man, a painter by profession, was lodging at the Millworth hotel for the winter, which made it simple for the servants to match Lilian's daily absences with her purpose. They all have eyes in their heads. Ellen threw away the undergarment that Boggio had found, but who needs evidence when the motive is so obvious? Lilian Stone came to the Manikin to escape her parents' supervision. Out here, she can meet her lover daily, clandestinely. But for visitors there is no dependable privacy on the Craxton estate, and the servants watch the girl's secret maneuvers with scornful interest, while Lilian remains oblivious of her audience.

But Lilian isn't the only one excluded from the circuit of gossip. It dawns on Ellen that her own Peg reveres the Manikin's guest, that Peg's attention even now is focused entirely on Lilian Stone. So assiduous is she that after removing Lilian's dinner plate, she leans over and brushes away the bread crumbs still clinging to the linen tablecloth.

Ellen sees it's time to move her daughter on, so she sends her into the kitchen for the next course. Dessert is an applesauce cake with a molasses sauce, which Sylva always bakes at holidays. To refuse it would be too obviously rude a gesture, so Mrs. Craxton allows the cake to be served. Lilian eats her piece with steady appreciation, and when she asks for a second helping, Ellen almost softens to the girl. But the affection disappears when Lilian seizes Peg's wrist, pulls her close, and whispers something in her ear. Peg holds her laughter inside with a cupped hand.

"Peg Griswood!" Mrs. Craxton barks, and they all freeze.

"Yes?"

"Clear my place."

Just what the girl needs, Ellen thinks—a firm order to remind her that, above all, Mrs. Craxton expects absolute submission from her domestic help. Humiliation brings a flush to Peg's cheek. This is her first hard lesson—painful but as necessary as the many tumbles a child takes when it is learning to walk.

Peg doesn't move. *Didn't you hear!* Ellen wants to scream. Mrs. Craxton glares. Lilian grins. For a horrifying moment Ellen thinks her daughter means to turn her back on Mrs. Craxton and leave the room. But finally, with averted eyes, she does what she's been told, thank God, and stacks the dishes on her tray. Ellen moves aside as Peg brushes past. She wants to slap Peg for almost costing her mother her job; but she also wants to kiss her and apologize, because right then she remembers her own humiliation when she was forced to undress Mrs. Craxton's guest.

What will she say to Peg later, when they are alone in their bedroom? Nothing. Nothing at all. She doesn't even want to know what Lilian whispered. They will not speak of it, she tells herself, accepting her decision with guilty relief.

"Will you come to my room tonight? Come late, after they're all asleep." A whispered invitation, full of intrigue and promise. Peg can't believe it—this is more than she had hoped for. Yet she does believe it. *Will you come to my room tonight?* The intrigue is what separates Lilian and Peg from "them"—the rest of society. The promise is that Lilian Stone will make Peg modern.

Maybe they'll paint their lips. Maybe they'll smoke opium and tell dirty stories. They will have to bury their faces in the feather pillows to muffle their hilarity. They'll drink absinthe and prick their fingers and smear their blood together. They'll sneak downstairs in the middle of the night and raid the pantry. They'll eat up Mrs. Craxton's marshmallows, every last one. Lilian will teach Peg French obscenities, and Peg will teach Lilian to whistle. They'll go hunting with umbrellas. Peg will take down the stuffed cougar with a single bullet between its bright eyes. Lilian will ride on the back of the giant green turtle. They will smash the glass of the étagère. They will burn holes in the satin drapes with their cigarettes. They will lock Mrs. Craxton's bedroom door and hide the key. They will run away together to New York City, where they will open a nightclub. They will dance for men and grow rich from the tips, and in a year or two they'll have saved enough to buy a mansion. They'll have twenty-seven rooms and as many servants. But they will be kind to their help—their servants will join them at the table, and every dinner will turn into a wild party.

In the hours before Peg creeps down the dark hallway to Lilian's bedroom, she imagines a thousand different scenes. But the promise is always the same: Lilian will make her modern. And later—after she has sat up with Lilian until dawn, after Peg has returned to the room again the next night and the next, week after week, after she has lost so much sleep that during the day she can hardly speak a full sentence without reversing words, after they've learned everything there is to know about each other, Peg will feel very modern indeed.

II

BEAST
AT
BAY

6

In the countryside surrounding the Manikin, wind rules a winter's day. Whether or not it is frigid or snowing, bleak or brilliantly clear, wind gives the day its personality. When a gusting wind whips the chill into a froth, wild animals and sensible people will go hungry rather than go outside. Blustering cold is the worst kind, and though a strong wind animates a forest, cracking frozen branches from trunks and filling the air with swirling snow, it is an illusory life. If such a wind suddenly ceased, the forest would become as eerily still as a photograph of itself.

Compare that stillness to a day with only the softest of breezes—at first the snowy scene is quiet, but it takes only a few seconds before a blue jay screams and a cardinal pipes sweetly in reply. A sandbag's worth of snow falls from the top of a pinetree. The delicately placed pawprints of a fox lead across the path and over the raised bank. Here and there little pockets in the snow are filled with deer droppings, and the crisscrossed marks of bounding rabbits show how busy life has been.

Life spreads out across the Craxton estate when the wind is down. Steady cold can be held at bay with a well-made woolen coat. There's

Lore trekking across Firethorn's lower slope in search of a fat old buck. Behind the garage Junket splits logs, not because they need more wood—the shed is stocked to the roof—but because driving a blade through a resisting log temporarily knocks out his confusing emotions. Boggio watches him in the distance from his small window. He's got nothing better to do now that he's finished his owl, except to rearrange the feathers to make sure they are evenly fluffed.

Inside the Manikin's kitchen, Ellen fills a bucket from the stove's hot-water reservoir, Eva puts a wet sheet through the wringer, and Sylva leaves her dough half kneaded and rushes off to the toilet.

In the living room, Peg lifts Mrs. Craxton by the shoulders, transferring her awkwardly from her wheelchair onto the sofa. The Craxtons' lawyer is coming all the way from Rochester to attend to legal matters that "cannot wait until spring," Mrs. Craxton had insisted. In front of her, the animals stand in various poses on crowded platforms—but she's unimpressed by them, unmoved by their discomforting gaze.

Upstairs, Billie dozes in the armchair in Lilian's room, where she's been dusting.

In the barn, Peter sweeps the aisle. A black cat, missing one ear, hops from a stall door onto the back of an indifferent cow and twists around in three full circles before settling.

Sid rests against his snow shovel on the path leading from the Manikin to the barn and other outbuildings. He talks to Nora, who is distributing a bag of oatmeal cookies among the men.

In the woods, within calling distance though not within sight, Sylva's two boys eat pancakes of snow sweetened with maple syrup.

A quarter mile away, in Boggio's hut, Lilian Stone lies beneath the man who calls himself her lover. Because of the cold, they have taken off no more than necessary. Lilian can't keep her thoughts from wandering. For no apparent reason, she recalls her performance at a recital when she was ten. It had been a struggle—the black-and-white pattern of the keyboard filled her mind so completely that for a terrifying minute she couldn't remember where to begin, and then she'd let her hands go where they would and watched in wonder as they danced from beginning to end of the little Chopin piece.

Back in the kitchen, Ellen shakes a rattle above Sylva's baby.

Outside, Machine barks when a chip of wood flies from Junket's ax.

In the barn, the black cat twitches her one ear but does not raise her head. Peter mucks out the empty stall of the Craxtons' horse, a tranquil, fifteen-year-old stock horse named Emily.

On the path, Sid tries to kiss "that mousy mulatta," as he calls Nora behind her back, but she slips past him.

Mrs. Craxton says to Peg, "I won't survive the winter. I can feel it in my bones."

In the old smokehouse, Boggio admires the exquisite workmanship of his bird, far superior to the scrawny snowy owl on display at the American Museum. So what if that one was shot and mounted by Theodore Roosevelt himself?

In Boggio's hut on the edge of the marsh, Lilian thinks, *Stupid pig,* and giggles to herself. The man lies on top of her, too exhausted now even to raise his head.

In the Manikin's bathroom off the kitchen, Sylva dries her lips with a handkerchief. It's been the same each time—queasy all day, sick to her stomach once or twice in the afternoon, and then she's ravenous. When she steps into the kitchen, Ellen asks her if she's feeling all right.

"Fine as ever," Sylva says. "Better than fine," with a smile so peculiarly modest that Ellen understands Sylva's meaning immediately. As she kisses Sylva on the cheek, the baby shakes the rattle with furious hilarity.

The afternoon sun is not as blindingly brilliant as it could be—wispy mare's tails dull the light, and the shrubbery around the Manikin, thick-ribbed with snow, glistens only in patches. The old gatehouse at the end of the drive, where Lore and Junket live, looks as though it is made of slabs of gingerbread with a vanilla cream roof. The gate has been left open, and snow has collected on the flat, horizontal bars of the lattice. Deep hoof marks and ruts show that Emily and the sleigh passed along the drive after the last snowfall, which ended early this morning.

Red Vic left right after breakfast to meet Mr. Edward Watts, Esquire, who offered to drive with his assistant in his own motor as far as Millworth. How picturesque the scene will look to Mr. Watts's myopic urban eyes as he passes through the gate in the Craxtons' sleigh. For the first five hundred yards the drive is bordered on either side by elms, and beyond, the front yard slopes up to the house in gentle mounds. The crisp air smells of wood fires. The Manikin waits sleepily for visitors. Despite the renovations, the manor has an aura of quaint shabbiness. Like the nobly born Seneca who holds the reins, the Craxton estate deserves a more deferential century.

White spruce kindling for their fire. Red pine needles for their bed. Even in midsummer the nights were chilly and they had no blankets, only the clothes on their backs. They would embrace for warmth as much as for love, and they'd sleep with their legs braided together, but still they'd wake up shivering. "Hop to, hop to," she'd say to him, pulling him to his feet, and as quickly as possible they'd stir the fire to uncover the warm embers, add tinder, and puff and puff until the flames rose.

Every morning they'd follow the creek upstream for a half mile to the waterfall. By July the cascade over the far edge of the grotto had dried to a trickle, a faucet's worth of water that made the moss shimmer, but the pool was still deep enough to cover their heads when they stood on the bottom. In one of the curved granite walls, about ten feet above the pool, a rectangular opening had been carved, probably by Indians, though for what original purpose they could never figure out, since the hole was too high up the sheer wall to explore. Birds used it now—bitterns that darted in and out like flies.

They ate wild plums and blackberries and whatever fish they could catch with their hands. Once when she was hungry she said, "I'll eat you!" and sank her teeth into his arm. She'd only meant to play, but she managed to break the skin and draw a bit of blood. He had great fun teasing her for it.

They both knew they'd have to move on when the weather turned. For weeks on end they'd take off their clothes in the morning and put them on at night—in the warm, mottled sunlight, they went naked. They vowed to stone to death anyone unlucky enough to wander into their paradise.

Tucked between two boulders at one edge of the pool was a sandy strip about three feet wide and six feet long. After they bathed they'd fall onto the sand and they'd kiss and dandle. When he grew hard he'd find his way into her body. Years later, he can recall the sensation of water dripping from her hair onto his chest. And the smell of tannin everywhere. He remembers the sharpness of her ribs and the salty taste of her nipples. He remembers the tiny cracks in her lips. He remembers thinking, This isn't happening. *He remembers her vividly. The dream of her. Sap beneath their fingernails. The shock of cold as they plunged together into the pool. The shadowy water.*

Such places exist, even though they seem to belong more to the imagination than to the world. The grotto and waterfall are hidden at the bottom of Firethorn Mountain's western slope, just beyond the boundary of the Craxton estate. The place is real, and everything else is possible. Junket probably will grow old; he will always remember loving Peg Griswood, though never making love. They'd swum in the grotto—the Devil's Cauldron, as Lore had named it. As children, they'd swum naked on dusty summer afternoons and stained their lips with the juice of wild berries. The little beach would have made a perfect bed, though it serves this purpose only in Junket's fantasy, which he tries to disguise as memory.

Junket thinks he loves Peg a little less each day. But then at night, his mind turns toward the future that has always included Peg. Sometimes he wonders whether it is even love he feels or the passion born from intense friendship. For three quarters of his life they have been like brother and sister, at ease with each other and fiercely loyal. But neither can pretend to continue this affection anymore—Junket hardly blames Peg for wanting better. He's just a scrubby, raffish yokel who can't add fractions. He understands that time usually dulls even the most mystical pain, and he can comfort himself during the day by ignoring Peg, but when he lies in the darkness, his love threatens to drive him mad if it is not satisfied. A mad old hermit with his beard tangled in his toes—this will be Junket. No, he will be nothing without Peg. It's as though he's been following her farther and farther into a forest, and now she has disappeared, leaving him to fend for himself. She has judged him capable, self-sufficient. Not at all. He's inept on his own. The idea of solitude fills him more with terror than with pride these days. So he indulges the desire that he should be forbidding himself, tries to twist it into hindsight. He will love Peg in a future memory. He will remember loving her.

So far the winter has been like any other, perhaps harsher than most, which suits Junket just fine. He dreads spring and its erratic thaws and rain and waxy green shoots that smell like rotting meat. And summer. How can he bear to live through a whole summer?

During the day he splits logs and transports wood from the shed to the house, he carries buckets full of kitchen slops, he helps his father skin and gut his game, all the while remaining within view of the Manikin, just in case Peg is watching from her third-floor window. He wants her to see that he isn't thinking about her. But night after night he thinks about her plenty, succeeds in calming himself only after he has indulged the fantasy of loving Peg. He should be loving her less. He'd wanted to leave the Manikin in order to forget her. Now he doesn't want to leave at all, since as long as he is near Peg Griswood he can pretend to ignore her.

Rarely do children of Junket's age commit themselves to failed love with such relentlessness—ordinarily, adolescence diverts emotions, mending through sheer distraction. But Junket loves with the fervor of a much younger child, convinced that this love is necessary, that Peg had incited him to depend upon her and then abandoned him. He falls more deeply into love, into an unreal future, and denies himself the chance of any future at all.

If he can't have Peg he wants to remain at the edge of childhood, no older, no more separate from Peg than he already is, and then to swoop forward to some distant point beyond life. He wants to linger and then leave the world. In this sense he is vastly different from his father, who refuses to let even the most monstrous changes overwhelm him. Lore is a great believer in stasis and accepts change by convincing himself that he must conform to the patterns of nature. He is the kind of man who, in the face of devastating loss, will quietly and efficiently rebuild his life.

Junket doesn't have enough of a life to rebuild. When he lies awake at night thinking of Peg, of his expectations, of the empty future, it feels like slow suicide.

"I know the reason . . ."

It is late, and Lore and Ellen have found themselves alone in the kitchen. Mrs. Craxton sat up for almost two hours playing a game of grandfather's clock patience, making her clock-packets and packing upward with unbearable slowness, as though her own internal clock were ticking at half time. And of course Ellen couldn't leave until the old woman had fallen asleep. The long meeting with her lawyer must have overtired her, and she'd passed beyond the reasonable fatigue that precedes sleep into irritable wakefulness. After lunch, she'd closed herself in the library with Mr. Watts, and at three o'clock they'd sent for Sid. The gardener Sid, inexplicably! He came out of the library a quarter of an hour later—he said he'd been sworn to secrecy, and if ordinarily secrets weren't safe with him, on this occasion pride kept him tight-lipped. Mrs. Craxton could have enlisted the help of any employee, but she'd chosen Sid. He had no intention of betraying her. Yet he couldn't help mumbling as he collapsed into a chair in the kitchen, "Mean old goose!" Then he'd rested his forehead on the table and laughed until he started to choke and Sylva had to slap him between his shoulder blades to help him catch his breath.

They've gone off to bed, all but Lore, who arrived late for supper and dallies afterward, smoking, pondering the ceiling. That's how Ellen finds him when she returns to the kitchen. So his voice startles her when he finally speaks.

"I know the reason now," he repeats with a wink.

Lore and Ellen share a well-worn familiarity born of similar experience. They've lived at the Manikin longer than the rest of the staff, except Sylva and Peter, who were the only employees willing to move with the Craxtons from Rochester. They've both been widowed and are raising their children alone. And they do not complain about hard work. But for all the pleasant sympathy they feel toward each other, they have rarely had a private conversation. Ellen manages the interior of the Manikin. Lore tends to the outside. Their different jobs depend upon quite different personalities—Ellen insists upon order, cleanliness, polished surfaces, and rigid routines; Lore can only hope that nature offers him profitable opportunities. So while Ellen always seems to have rehearsed her part, Lore is more of an improviser. If he weren't such a subdued man, he'd be foolishly impetuous, or so he fears. He has trained himself to observe, to wait for an advantage while keeping his first impressions to himself.

Between Lore's reticence and Ellen's poise their encounters have never been more than superficial. There was a time early on when a vague awkwardness between them might have betrayed a depth of feeling, but they were too involved in the many demands and adjustments of their new positions to notice. Since then they have grown used to each other without becoming more intimate.

So Lore's declaration throws Ellen off guard. *I know the reason*. He lets the words fly almost aimlessly out of his mouth, and now Ellen must catch them and bring them back.

"The reason?"

"My boy's in the doldrums, and I've finally figured out the reason why." As though to ensure that Ellen pays attention, he waits for her to push him on. But instead of repeating her question, she tries to diminish the problem. "I hadn't noticed anything wrong. Junket's a good boy."

"He's not himself."

"What do you mean?"

"I know the reason why." He winks again, but Ellen has grown impatient and doesn't answer. After a long silence Lore explains. "It's your Peg. She's the reason. Foolish of me not to have figured it out right away."

"What has my daughter done?"

"She's who she is—that's what. Junk's been moping over her. Brokenhearted. I didn't even notice. Lovesick. But she's much too good for him—I've always thought so. She's beautiful." Lore squints at Ellen, subjecting her to his amused scrutiny, as though, Ellen thinks, he'd really said, *You're beautiful,* and was gauging her reaction. But Ellen believes beauty to be a cosmetic quality—Lilian Stone is beautiful, her face a living portrait, perfectly painted and framed by her silky pageboy hair. Peg is merely pretty. And Ellen herself—she's about as lovely as . . . the giant green turtle in the Craxton collection! Her lips twitch toward a smile at the comparison. But why does Lore stare at her that way?

"She's become quite the sophisticated young lady," he continues in a tone of voice so soft it is almost sinister. "She won't give Junk the time of day anymore. Hasn't been out on a hunt for weeks, though I've invited her often enough."

"Oh, Peg won't have anything to do with guns."

"You don't know your daughter, do you?"

Ellen is adept at containing a swell of rage, but Lore has stumbled upon a charged subject. "That's none of your business!" she says, pushing out of her chair. She might as well have hurled a brick through the kitchen window. Her defensiveness is so foreign that disbelief almost entirely consumes her anger, and she has to sit back down. Did she tell Lore to mind his own business? It's the kind of thing she can easily think a hundred times a day. But to speak it aloud?

Lore looks surprised, though not crestfallen. He sputters an apology, and though Ellen interrupts to say, "I'm sorry . . . please, it doesn't matter," she's lying. Lore probably doesn't realize how much his question does matter. No, she doesn't know her daughter anymore. And because of Lilian Stone, Peg has become ashamed of her mother. She doesn't say so, but she won't even look at Ellen these days, if she can avoid it, won't admit that they share blood and history.

Ellen sinks back into the silence that usually would seem ordinary but now is charged with tension. So Lore's son has a crush on her daughter. Puppy love, she tells herself. He'll outgrow it. And Peg has a crush on Lilian Stone, who acts like she's just stepped from a movie screen to have a look around at real life. Peg is dazzled. Peg, the daughter of a housekeeper.

Now Ellen and Lore could try to pretend that they never had this conversation—Lore's preference, apparently, since he's counting the ceiling cracks again. Or they could follow through and say what remains to be said. Uncharacteristically, Ellen decides to try the latter, partly because she's sorry for lashing out at Lore and partly because she needs to unburden herself.

"You're right—" She stops to wait out the nine chimes of the clock in the hallway, then she starts over. "You're right to blame Peg."

"It's not her fault. She was born lucky. If being beautiful is lucky. I'm not sure. Is it?"

"How should I know!" she says laughing, unable to suppress the coquettish lilt in her own voice. She touches her cheek, as though to feel the inevitable blush. "It is Peg's fault," she insists, impassioned by embarrassment. "Peg is silly enough to think that Mrs. Craxton's guest has taken an interest in her. An interest! Lilian Stone will forget Peg as soon as she is among her own people again. My daughter has expectations. She thinks she's slated for the high and mighty. Lawn tennis and caviar. I don't know what to do with her, Lore."

As soon as she utters Lore's name, Ellen regrets telling him so much. Implied in the name is excessive trust. And more than that. It's as though her worry over her daughter had become a pretext as she'd spoken, until, by the final sentence, she hears herself appeal to Lore for something else, a personal kind of reassurance. Not that she's attracted to him, no more than she longs to possess any object in the house. But for a brief spell she let loneliness get the best of her. There is no mistaking her meaning. So she understands why Lore chooses to end the conversation here, politely but resolutely.

"Don't blame Peg," he says, resting one hand on top of Ellen's. "Blame the influence." His palm is wide, thickened with calluses, slightly damp in the center yet with a smooth surface like sanded plaster. Ellen waits for him to go on, to fill the room with the noise of his voice and drown out the pounding in her ears. But he's given Ellen a worthy piece of advice, and that's enough. She slips her hand away, manages a nod, and leaves him to the less shrill cogitations of his own mind.

Whatever her suspicions, Ellen forgets them in sleep, so she's unaware that during the dead hours of most every night, Peg sneaks down to Lily's bedroom. Now here's Lily lying on her immense bed blowing doughnuts of cigarette smoke into the air while beside her Peg searches the pillow for feathers, pinching each tiny shaft between her thumb and forefinger and pulling the fluffy down out through the cotton. They are such fast friends, though they've known each other only six weeks. Who would have thought? Peg hadn't realized how desperate she'd been for proper company, nothing to do for fun in this howling wilderness but blow apart owls. Now this is fun! Lying on a king-size bed and whispering. Peg can imagine the sun beating down—they are castaways floating on a raft, they've been given up for lost, they will never go home. But this brings to mind the one difference between them. Not money—since Lily doesn't care that she has it. Not education—Lily may be more refined, but Peg has more information in her head and can entertain Lily for hours describing such bizarre things as the breeding habits of garden slugs. And not adventure, as it turns out. For every chapter Lily adds to the story of her upbringing, Peg can tell her about falling through the ice into Craxton's Pond when she was seven, skinning a deer, or shooting snowy owls. Lily has helped Peg to appreciate her memories, has even taken to wandering through the woods alone for hours at a time because, as she says, she wants to memorize the beautiful countryside and take it home with her.

But this is their point of difference: *home*. Lily has a home. She can leave it and return. That Peg and her mother have a garret room to themselves at all is a favor bestowed upon them by a petulant old woman who prefers not to live in an isolated mansion by herself. Peg has come to despise Mrs. Craxton for her power, though lately she pretends, in her mother's place, to dote on her. *Home.* She privately wishes that Lily would invite her home. There she would live as a guest, not as a servant, and over time she would be treated as a member of the family. This used to be an idle daydream, but as their friendship has intensified, Peg has let herself think of it as a real possibility. Why not? Lily makes no effort to hide her affection for Peg. In some ways, she seems the more rapacious companion—she hates to pass a night apart and is generous with hugs and vows of commitment. They've already anticipated the dismal separation ahead and have promised to write each other every day after Lily has left. But perhaps she won't be satisfied with letters. Perhaps she's weighing the options while she smokes her cigarette.

There's something on her mind, something important, Peg senses, and she's decided to wait for Lily to reveal it on her own. The circlets of smoke make up a coded message. What could she be thinking? She's been quieter than usual tonight, almost timid, or perhaps she's just collecting reasons for inviting Peg to live with her next spring. Is this what she's contemplating? Are they close enough to share thoughts? Peg still can't believe that she has such a grand friend, and she's sorry that they have to keep their friendship a secret. But Lily fears Mrs. Craxton would disapprove. Maybe so. Peg's no excitable young man with bursting glands, though—there's not that kind of danger! But Lily may be right, and Peg doesn't want to risk an early separation by testing the old woman's jealousy.

When Lily finally speaks, the subject, so distant from the one in her own mind, disappoints Peg. "Last night I had the strangest dream." She pauses to stamp out her cigarette. "I dreamed that I was in a desert outside Jerusalem with my family, on one of my father's expeditions." Peg listens with a dazed curiosity just short of rapture. She rolls onto her back and stares at the ceiling as though reading the text of Lily's dream in the cracks. "My brothers were finding all the pretty trinkets, while I found nothing," Lily continues. "But I kept on digging, and finally, my fingers scraped against a hard object—a piece of tile loose enough so I was able to wrench it free. I remember cool air blowing against my face as I put my hand through the hole left by the tile. I pulled away more tile, and when the hole was wide enough I lowered myself into the room below.

"I knew—the way you just know things in a dream without having to ask—I knew that I'd discovered the true Jerusalem, more ancient than the existing city. It was the oldest city in the world, and I had found it. I saw stone steps leading from one side of the room to a dirt corridor, and from there . . . from there, I assumed, into the maze of the streets. But suddenly I felt scared—I'm not sure why. I guess I didn't want to be alone anymore.

"I climbed out of the hole. My family had disappeared. The desert stretched as far as I could see. I started to walk, hoping that I was heading in the direction of Jerusalem—the fake Jerusalem—and our hotel. In the distance I noticed a speck of gray bouncing along the sand. When it came nearer I saw it was a bull, its horns glittering, as though tipped with diamonds. I started to run away, but I knew I couldn't escape, that sooner or later it would catch up and kill me. This was the feeling that woke me—the terrible certainty that I was going to die."

Peg believes, in the same strange way that Lily had described knowing in a dream without having to ask, that this dream concerns her. Though she wasn't present, somehow, implicitly, she figured in the dream, and as much for her own sake as for Lily's, she wants to make sense of it. A desert. An underground city. A bull with diamond horns. Diamond horns? She decides that a bawdy gloss on the illusive dream is called for, and she starts to laugh before she has come up with an appropriate joke. She glances at Lily, expecting her to answer with a giggle since they're so in tune, so perfectly matched that they don't even need a punch line. Their laughter is infectious—usually. But Lily's expression remains unchanged, indecipherable, except for a slight crease between her eyebrows, which suggests that she has taken her dream much too seriously. And before Peg can figure out how to reassure her, Lily's eyes glaze over, and a tear spills out and slides halfway down her cheek with the rubbery bounce of a spider dropping on a thread.

"Oh Lily!" Of course Peg throws her arms around her friend. Of course she smooths her hair and hushes her, though Lily hasn't made a sound. And of course Lily buries her face in Peg's neck. They love each other. What follows, then, seems natural, and if in the back of their minds these two girls know that this is no experiment of youth, the import of their actions only makes the loving more solemn.

One moment Lily's hand rests innocently on Peg's shoulder, and the next moment it has crawled down and is caressing her left breast—tentatively, while Peg lies still, barely breathing, and then, because Peg doesn't resist, more confidently. With a few quick tugs Lily undoes the buttons of Peg's nightgown and slides her hand inside, against the skin. Peg notices the other hand cupped against the back of her head only when the pressure increases slightly, and she relaxes her neck and tilts her head forward. This is what Lily wants, isn't it? Yes, she has raised her lips to meet Peg's, and they kiss, sinking into each other's mouths. Peg's excitement feeds upon itself—the thrill of this love makes her insatiable for more, and instead of simply receiving Lily she slides on top of her, separating her thighs with her knee and then pressing up against her groin, an act in itself so full of consequence that for a split second paranoia subsumes pleasure, and Peg pulls away and looks toward the door, certain that someone is watching. The door remains closed; they are alone. But she has broken the spell, and when she looks down again she sees fear—Lily's, or the reflection of her own fear in Lily's eyes. She rests her head on Lily's chest, knowing that now they can't continue, not tonight, at least. The effort of transgression has exhausted them, and they lie in each other's arms without speaking.

Take away the hum of a refrigerator, the click and rush of forced-air heat controlled by a thermostat, the buzz of telephone wires, the distant whine of a highway, and the dense silence of a country house in winter crushes against the ears with the deafening pressure of many fathoms of water. Even the mechanical ticking of the clocks scattered throughout the Manikin doesn't relieve the haunting silence. And this is the paradox: that an enclosed space could be so deafening and silent at the same time, so full and so empty, as if inhabited by ghosts. Perhaps our minds conjure spirits because we cannot stand such complete silence. And maybe all the stuffed animals in the world—not just the ones with real hides and feathers but the nursery animals as well, and dolls with glass eyes, statues too, and portraits, photographs, postage stamps, coins embossed with images of monarchs and presidents, bas-relief heads, gargoyles, masks, puppets, wooden angels, and anything else that never closes its eyes in sleep—maybe all of them are made not to be seen in daylight but to exist unseen at night, to fill the emptiness as nocturnal animals fill the woods, invisibly, so that there is no interior without life.

The Manikin's collection of animals has this effect. To someone wandering through the living room in the middle of the night, with only a paltry bit of moonlight to see by, the animals crowded on the platform seem alive and dead at the same time, frozen forever in their last act. The apprehension they inspire at that late hour can be oddly comforting, more so to the residents familiar with the animals in daylight than to the stranger who has crept in through the unlocked kitchen door, walked slowly down the dark hallway into the living room, and after a few minutes made his way out again. Such a man requires a strong nerve, or else he'll move too hastily in an effort to escape the animals, and he'll knock over a coffee table or a chair and will raise the household with his clatter.

But phantoms retreat at the first hint of morning, their purpose made obsolete by roosters and dogs and crows. *Wake up, everyone, wake up!* the world cries. *Christmas is only a week away!*

7

Biscuits, ham, scrambled eggs, coffee. Cocoa and a boiled egg for Mrs. Craxton. Then Sylva punches down the dough that she left to rise overnight, smears it with the heel of her left hand, and sets to work pressing, folding, and turning until the sponge loses its bubbles and creases. Caked with flour paste, her large fingers look as though they belong to a potter, or to an exhumed corpse. But it's bad luck to think of death when you have life growing inside you, she reminds herself. No visible change yet other than the sickness, which seems to be on the wane. The child will be a June baby, a little girl, she hopes, to even out the balance.

By this time next year little Gracie will be toddling about on her strong legs, poking and pinching the new baby at every opportunity. Imagine—another winter, another child to feed. Sylva and Peter have added two dollars to their savings every month for as long as they've been married, and starting in the fall they'll be sending their twin boys off to school in Buffalo. And though Sylva can't help but wish they'd saved more, she doesn't waste her time worrying about possible disasters. There are too many uncertain factors to worry. *Come what may* has always been Sylva's pious attitude.

The dough tears slightly as she presses it flat. One more half turn, and she pats it into a neat ball, divides it into quarters, and shapes each piece into a loaf. Nora has been spooning gruel into Gracie's mouth, and just as Sylva finishes with the dough the child erupts with a hefty belch, and then, delighted with herself, lets it out noisily from the other end. Nora and Sylva burst out laughing, and Gracie chimes in, proud to be the center of attention.

"What's so funny?"

Sylva turns around to see her husband standing just inside the kitchen. He sets a basket of fresh eggs upon the counter; a clod of snow slides along his boot to the floor. For some reason Sylva finds her adorable man about as silly as a baby's fart, and she nearly collapses, overcome by her private amusement. She has to squeeze her thighs together to hold in her water because after three children her bladder isn't entirely dependable—and this little trick makes her laugh even harder. She can hardly stand it. *A baby's fart, that's all* . . . she can't catch her breath to explain. But her adorable man is losing patience, and he reminds her of her responsibility, warns her half seriously that the little one inside will be born with "loose screws," as he puts it, if she's not careful. So Sylva finally manages to collect herself, dabs her eyes, and tells Peter to get on out. "There's nothing for you to mind in this room," she says. She meets her husband's irritation with a smirk. He's mad because Sylva and Nora have excluded him from their laughter. He's mad because you put two females together and a man doesn't stand a chance. Sylva orders him from the kitchen, tells him, "Scat now," like he were some dirty cur scrounging for slops. And he obliges, as Sylva knows he will. In this room, her authority is total.

"Oh, you're gonna catch it later, Aunty," Nora says after he's gone, wickedness in her glance. Sylva's niece is used to a different kind of family where men beat their women for amusement, and if the same happened here she'd probably feel more at home. Seems she's learned nothing from Sylva except how to dice turnips and pluck chickens. She hasn't bothered to notice that her uncle Pete is different from his brother, Nora's daddy, that Peter wouldn't think of using Sylva as a punching dummy. It's not so much that Sylva won't allow it, but that Peter's anger doesn't slide down to his fists. He's a brainy man—in a better world he'd be a lawyer or a doctor—and his anger stays up in his head, sloshes around and usually settles into a reasonable response.

Between here and the barn, Peter will be thinking hard, and he'll tell himself until he believes it again that between meals a kitchen is no place for a man.

"Ain't gonna catch nothing," Sylva retorts in the language that Nora will understand. She sets Nora to work trying out the lard at the stove while she nurses her baby. Gracie sucks greedily, noisily, tires herself, and soon drifts into the drowsy peace that precedes sleep. The baby's eyes are still open when Sylva lays her in the bassinet, but she doesn't protest. With a finger to her lips, Sylva signals to Nora to keep hushed.

Through the next hour they work without conversation. Grease spits and sizzles in Nora's frying pan; the water comes to a boil in the huge copper pot, and the surface flattens for a few minutes when Sylva throws in the sausage. Every day Gracie falls asleep to the sounds and smells of her mother's cooking. All Sylva's children have been kitchen ratties; all have been what people call easy babies, never troubled by colic, born with fine plump cheeks and dimpled thighs. She stirs the water as it starts to boil again. Foam snakes between the bubbles and against the edge of the pot, and as Sylva stares at it she pictures a moment during Gracie's birth when she was resting between contractions, watching sleepily as the new midwife from Millworth rolled a rag into a tight cord. *Now what's she gonna do with that?* Sylva had wondered. She'd found out soon enough—the next time she tried to let out a scream, the midwife put that rag roll between her lips and yanked both ends tight, and all that came out of Sylva's mouth was a tiny scratching noise, like a lame dog coming up a gravel path.

Here's a nicer thought: Peter's fingers sliding up her thighs and cajoling her open, his member following, pushing halfway into her, drawing back, then pushing in again with all his strength so she feels his love in the center of her body. They've been married twelve years, and she's no less amazed at her good fortune than she was the day Peter first came to the Craxtons' backdoor in Rochester to deliver the week's groceries. He'd sat an hour drinking Sylva's thick-as-mud coffee—nearly lost his job for it—and kissed her on the lips when he left. She was nineteen then. Both her parents had passed on, and her older brothers and sisters were already scattered from Detroit to Syracuse. She'd stayed with the Craxtons simply because she enjoyed the work—like her own children, she'd grown up with the smell of fried onions in her hair, garlic shreds under her fingernails, her clothes spotted like a butcher's apron with the bloody juice of raw beef. She'd chewed on pork rinds when she was teething; she'd played with rolling pins, butter churns, potato mashers, strainers, whisks, and pie-crust jaggers. She took to kitchen work without any prodding from her mama, who had white-collar hopes for her boys and good-marriage hopes for her daughters. By the time Peter came around, Sylva's mother had been dead three years and couldn't disapprove.

So now Sylva lives her mama's life over again, without regrets. Baking bread, mincing boiled meat, chopping pig livers, rolling out pastry, making apple cakes and oatmeal cookies—what other job has such quick and palpable results? But the most important reward of this work is that no child of hers will ever want for nourishment. This in itself fills her with pride, since in the part of her mind that harbors all anxieties, her greatest worry is of hunger. Why this worry predominates she can't say for certain. She's never known hunger—neither had her mama. Her father died from fever when she was six, and her mother found it too difficult to conjure him in talk, so his story has been lost. Could be that he'd suffered unspeakable hardship during his early years in New York City, and Sylva had read it in his eyes when she was a little girl. Could be, on the other hand, that the worry comes from nowhere.

That's how far her thoughts have drifted by the time she removes the four loaves from the oven, overturns them onto a cooling rack, and raps the hard crusts with her knuckles. The hollow *tat-tat-tat* of each loaf assures her that the bread is perfect—a lovely sound, so resonant and simple. One loaf a day. On Christmas Eve she'll bake four dozen crescent rolls. She'll make the cranberry jelly on Wednesday. Mrs. Craxton has given up her recent penchant for plain food, and her menu for Christmas Day includes baked ham, turkey with chestnut stuffing, acorn squash and snap beans and pumpkin pie, along with an apple cake for good luck. All this for a visitor whom Mrs. Craxton despises. Sylva won't even try to guess her motive—the old woman's head is full of crannies and cobwebs and locked trunks, a moldering, forbidden place. You can't help but pity her. And yet you always have to be on guard, for her anger is vast. A slightly overcooked piece of beef or a meal served five minutes late enrages her. Sylva glances at the clock on the wall—in a quarter of an hour she'll start preparing the midday meal for Mrs. Craxton and Miss Stone, a full meal, though the old woman eats less than ever these days and seems to take more pleasure looking at a plate filled with food than putting that food in her belly.

When Sylva was a child, the Craxton mansion on East Avenue used to be so full of life—the clamor and pounding footsteps of young boys racing each other up the stairs, the music from Mrs. Craxton's piano, the bellowing voice of Henry Senior as he tried to make himself heard. This was before Sylva's time, though. First the youngest son died in infancy. The death of the Craxtons' eldest son eighteen years later silenced the household for good. The three remaining members of the family—the mister and missus and their middle son, Hal Junior—always seemed ghostly to Sylva when she was growing up, apparitions so pale and soundless as they crept around the house that Sylva used to imagine she could pass her hand right through their bodies.

A bustling in the dining room reminds her of the time. Ellen and Peg must be setting the table already. With all the preparations for the Christmas meal, Sylva has forgotten to clean the trout. But before five minutes are up she has the two fish ready to poach. She slides them from the plate into the simmering, seasoned water just as Gracie wakes up with a brief cry. With one hand Sylva stirs butter in a saucepan, with the other hand she tweaks her baby's toes, feeling secretly proud, for a cook's expertise is measured not only by her preparations but by her ability to manage the wild dance of a kitchen as the different ingredients are coaxed toward their final end.

Of course her two boys decide to enter the flux just then, when they're wanted least—they stamp snow from their boots in the pantry and burst into the kitchen demanding something to eat. That's one thing Sylva makes no rules about—a child of hers fills his belly whenever he wants. And nothing pleases her more than robust hunger.

"Mama, I want ah . . . ah . . . ah . . ." her boy Cap says, caught in his stutter.

"Piece ah sugarbread!" fills in Manny, and Sylva lightly slaps the side of his head. "You let your brother speak for himself," she says and turns back to the stove, waiting as Cap tries again.

"Mama, please may I have a pee . . . pee . . ."

"Peepee!" shouts Manny, overjoyed by his brother's slip. "Cap wanna peepee!" Sylva threatens him with her whisk, and a few drops fly through the air and land on Manny's coat.

"Mama!" He is solemn, though obviously glad to have reason to reproach her.

"A piece ah sugabread!" yells Cap.

"Ma-ma-ma-ma-ma," chatters Gracie, smacking her lips.

"Sylva!" Peg peeks her head around the swinging door and retreats when Sylva tells her, "Another minute."

Nora scoops up Gracie, who has begun to fuss. Sylva arranges the trout and potato salad on a platter, and the two boys stand aside and watch with mild interest. Amazingly, the meal is ready to be served as soon as Mrs. Craxton has spread her napkin across her lap, and for the next few minutes Peg and Ellen take turns transferring the food and drink to Mrs. Craxton, who for the third time this week dines alone while her guest enjoys another tryst out in the woods.

Sylva gives Cap and Manny their pieces of fresh-baked buttered bread sprinkled with sugar to tide them over until she can feed them properly. The dining room remains silent behind the door, and for a minute the kitchen is still, until Gracie suddenly looks toward Sylva with surprise, as though she'd solved some great riddle, and says with calculated precision, "Mama."

"That's right, chicken." Sylva collects her daughter into her arms. "Mama."

"Mama," repeats Gracie.

How complete Sylva's happiness is right then. So she doesn't expect to feel so sickly when Mrs. Craxton's trout comes back hardly touched. Nausea rises in her throat as she stares at the plate: a yellow skin has formed over the sauce and is broken in only one place by prong marks of a fork scraped slowly across the middle of the trout, from its spine to its belly.

The week passes uneventfully, the weather bitter with frequent snow squalls but little accumulation. At breakfast on Christmas Eve, Mrs. Craxton offers to have Red Vic drive Lilian back to Rochester in the truck so she can spend the holiday with her family. Lilian declines. Mrs. Craxton points out that the roads are navigable, but Lilian insists that she'd rather stay put. So they leave it at that—as it was. Mrs. Craxton's guest will remain until the first of April, to Mrs. Craxton's obvious vexation.

Lilian hasn't ordered Ellen Griswood to do anything for her since the day she arrived at the Manikin, and except for the necessary courtesies, Ellen has little contact with the girl. But she knows what kind of contact she would like to have, the bruises she would like to leave with the back of a hairbrush along those slim, silvery legs. It's an unfamiliar desire—with her own daughter, discipline has meant appeasement. Ellen has known for years that she's no match for Peg, who waits with obvious impatience for some justification to bolt. So Ellen still hasn't confronted her about Lilian Stone.

But up in their bedroom, where they've come to change into their holiday dresses for the party, Ellen almost brings herself to ask Peg whether she has ever gone hunting with Lore Bennett. Not that she doubts Lore's word. She simply wants to hear the truth from Peg, along with an explanation. *Where is the attraction in slaughter, Peg?* But she can't even bring herself to ask this question.

Peg slips off her house dress—a hand-me-down from Ellen—and steps toward the closet so the door blocks her from her mother's view. She's grown modest of late, hides herself as though Ellen were a stranger. While Peg examines the clothes in the closet, Ellen pictures what she can't see: her daughter's breasts, full though still without womanly bounce, the flat plane of her abdomen beneath her cotton chemise, the corkscrew ripples of muscles in her long legs. How much does Peg know about men? She's beyond the reach of her mother's advice now, incautious because of Ellen's neglect.

"Such dreadful scraps!" Peg's voice seems to come from the other side of the room. She stomps away from the closet, picks up the house dress from the floor, and pulls it back over her head.

"Peg, we're Mrs. Craxton's guests tonight."

"Generous bitch!"

"Peg Griswood!"

"I thought this uniform drab at first, I must admit. But you persuaded me that it is quite fashionable, Mother."

When had her daughter become so glib? And where would it lead? Ellen will have to wait to find out, for Peg decides upon another tack, no less offensive than her insolence, though more calculated. "I'm sorry"—a disingenuous apology. "I'm needed downstairs, aren't I?"

"It's Christmas Eve, Peg. Let's not argue." Ellen's present for Peg is an Indian bead necklace, which she bought last June from Red Vic's sister and has kept hidden beneath her bed all this time. Now she feels ashamed of the gift.

"I'll find something to wear," Peg says. "You go on ahead." She sits on her bed and watches her mother twist the thick braid of her hair into a bun. As Ellen checks her appearance in the small mirror on top of the bureau—fatigue smeared under her eyes but a healthy color in her face—Peg murmurs, "You look lovely."

"Are you coming?"

"I'll be down in a minute."

Ellen carries away one of their two lamps and steps soundlessly along the backstairs, listening as she descends for some noise from the bedroom. She hears nothing. Instead, she imagines the conversation they didn't have:

You'll leave me soon, won't you? You'll go away for good.

Yes.

Where? Don't leave without telling me where you're going.

You mustn't worry, Mother. I can take care of myself.

I don't want you to go.

But I must.

Why?

It disturbs Ellen to realize that she has imagined herself and her daughter almost as lovers breaking off their affair. But her discomposure passes when she approaches Mrs. Craxton's bedroom door. She gives her own identifying knock, four short taps that mean, *It is the housekeeper. May I enter?*

"You may," calls Mrs. Craxton from within.

The candelabra in the living room have been burning for over an hour and the waxy, cathedral smell mingles with the scent of the stubby Scotch pine in the corner. Ellen tucks the velvet partiere in its bracket and pushes Mrs. Craxton through the doorway. The other servants have already gathered, and they greet their mistress as nurses in a hospital ward might greet a new patient, with quick assessing glances and nods, and then they turn back to each other, sipping eggnog from crystal glasses, snatching a piece of sausage from Nora's tray as she glides past.

Every year, for a few hours on Christmas Eve, Mrs. Craxton suspends the household law. From Billie to Red Vic to Ellen Griswood, the hierarchy of rank is dissolved, and Mrs. Craxton treats the staff as family, giving each of them, including the children, the same gift: a box of dinner mints imported from France. They sing carols and eat chowder made with canned oysters. Sometimes, if the mood is right, they dance.

Yet the party is as contrived as a pageant, a splendid display in Mrs. Craxton's eyes, a specious farce to the servants. It might as well be Halloween, with everyone in costume celebrating death. Cufflinks, suspenders, striped ties, lace, and silk ribbons belie the truth: that the combined savings of all eight servants would not equal a decent fraction of Mrs. Craxton's income and securities. Questionable securities, to be sure. The Manikin itself certainly isn't worth half of what it cost to build. And Mrs. Craxton's capital is being depleted faster than ever by the expenses of staff and upkeep. But the employees are dependent upon the Craxton fortune for their livelihood, and they never resent Mrs. Craxton more than on Christmas Eve, when she insists on pretending that she has no power over them.

Only Sylva declines to play along, by necessity, since she's busy preparing the food. The others fold into pairs or trios, occasionally glancing up from conversations to gaze with mild appreciation at the collection of trophies—the snarling martin, the twig-legged dik-dik, the brown bats clinging to a cherry-wood stalactite, jaunty, bright-feathered birds. Sylva's boys run in circles until Peter catches them each by the waistband of their trousers and growls a warning in their ear, and from then on they post themselves at either side of Junket, whom they idolize for his reputation as the world's best marksman. The sausages and smoked fish help to redeem the festivities, and Nora can't fill her tray fast enough. Boggio saunters into the room, tightens his string tie, and claps his hands to summon service. Red Vic stokes the fire, building it into a powerful blaze. Ellen winds the gramophone and with a rattling hiss the needle slides into its groove and an orchestral version of "Silent Night" fills the room. And from her wheelchair Mrs. Craxton looks on with the awkward smile of an old matriarch trying to appear proud of her brood but fooling no one.

Then Lilian breezes in. The group falls silent, the candle flames tremble as she passes, and Mrs. Craxton's smile shrinks into a grimace. But it isn't Lilian in her scarlet, ankle-length tulle gown who alters the mood of the room. It is Peg Griswood. Ellen's Peg. She trails Lilian across the room with her eyes lowered, her cheeks tinged pink with rouge, the fish-scale brocade of her knee-length dress—Lilian's dress on Peg—shining like the tinsel on the Christmas tree, her legs in net stockings, her bare arms draped with a lace shawl. She might as well have walked into the room totally naked, so overwhelming is her effect. She's a reluctant spectacle and hesitates as they approach Mrs. Craxton. But Lilian takes her by the arm and says, "Isn't she beautiful?"

She gestures to both of them, so the pronoun of her question could refer to Peg, or with obsequious malice, to Mary Craxton herself. Neither replies. If Mrs. Craxton is shocked by Peg Griswood's transformation she doesn't let on—rather, she seizes Peg by the wrist and directs her to sit on the sofa to her right. Lilian takes her place on the sofa beside Peg, effectively sealing off their trio. And with the center of attention withdrawn, the servants return to their own circle, from time to time casting glances in Peg's direction and rolling their eyes as though to say, *Shame on her.*

Only Ellen continues to stare, compelled more by curiosity than by outrage. *You don't know your daughter . . .* The vividness of the memory startles her. Lore's voice. His hand resting on hers. She lifts her eyes from her daughter, searches the room and finds Lore standing by the fire, a distracted expression on his face as he listens to Sid's monologue.

In fact, Lore makes no effort to listen; whatever he is thinking, Ellen can see that it has nothing to do with Sid's loud joke. Lore is gazing toward the kitchen, where Junket has just gone, along with Sylva's boys. Junket and Peg. How natural that match would be. But one glance at Peg, Lilian Stone's devoted handmaiden, and anyone can see that such a perfect match will never occur.

"So the old feller picks himself up and shouts, 'Thanks for nothing, God.' " Sid throws his head back and gives such a shrill "Haw" that for a moment all conversation in the room stops. Then Peter raises his voice to reply to Red Vic. They're on to politics, arguing about Coolidge—"Nothing but an empty barrel, and he fooled the country," Peter insists. Red Vic reminds him of the choices in '24. "Which Santa Claus would you have put in office, McAdoo or Smith?" he taunts.

And right then Sylva bangs a spoon against the silver tureen and calls, "Come and get it."

The servants fill their bowls. Lilian carries two bowls to Mrs. Craxton and Peg and then serves herself. Mrs. Craxton languidly stirs the chowder and then spoons a slippery oyster into her mouth. "I taste the tin," she says in annoyance. "Oysters should be eaten fresh or not at all." She sets her bowl aside.

"Delicious," Lilian chirps, her pleasure clearly a touch vengeful, but Mrs. Craxton pays no attention. She forgets the pretense of equality and orders Peg to bring her two decks of cards. Peg obliges so quickly that Ellen wonders whether the girl is grateful for the chance to leave the room. Peg probably hadn't anticipated the bated hostility her "dressing up" would arouse among the others. But she knows them well enough to read their reaction in their faces.

"When I was a girl, cards were forbidden," Mrs. Craxton says to no one in particular after Peg has returned with the decks. "But my father taught me to play whist and piquet on the sly. We used to gamble with real pennies, and if he won, which he usually did, he would sweep the coins right into the pocket of his waistcoat. That was that. I lost a fortune to him over the years."

"What shall we play?" Lilian slouches back in her armchair in an explicit display of boredom.

"I'll teach you a game of patience, if you're interested."

"Certainly."

"We'll play casket patience. One of my favorites. If you ever find yourself in a hospital or sanitorium, my dears—oh, banish the thought, you're so full of life yet! But someday you'll want to know how to amuse yourself alone and to forget your troubles for half an hour. Here, then, is a pleasant little pastime." She shuffles the two decks together, and though a few cards fly away when she bends them into an arch, an echo of her earlier nimbleness is visible in the brisk way she knocks the pile against the table.

"The casket is formed," she explains, "by placing two cards at either end, like so. Four along the bottom. And five—one, two, three, four, five—rounded to form the lid. Now we count out thirteen cards—these are the jewels. Be sure to take out any aces from the casket. The ace of spades. We fill the vacancy with a card in hand. Voilà. And place the ace below for the foundation. Now we begin packing down the sides and bottom of the casket. The lid cards are off limits, except when they're needed to build up the foundation. If you take a lid card, you may replace it with a jewel. The two of spades, for instance. We're off to a good start. You'll see that the success of casket patience depends upon the frequent opening of the lid. And remember—a second turn is not allowed."

"Ace of diamonds," Lilian announces as Mrs. Craxton overturns it. "Very good."

Although like most forms of patience, casket patience involves only one player, by the time Mrs. Craxton has laid a foundation of three aces, everyone in the room has gravitated over and gathered around her, hanging on the suspense that at any other time would annoy them in its simplicity. What will the next card be? And the next and the next, all the way through two decks until the cards have been used up. "The object is to dismantle the casket," Mrs. Craxton says as she lays down a five of diamonds. It is like watching a woman darn a sock—no, worse than that, since nothing will be gained or improved by the effort. But still the servants feel compelled to witness the game in its entirety.

Sid finds a comfortable place behind Peg's chair where he can steal an occasional glimpse down her dress. Red Vic stands beside Lore and in a whisper bets him a nickel that the old lady will end in a muddle. Billie and Eva watch with the rapt interest inspired by bootleg gin, which Sid snuck into the eggnog, as he does every year, because he has his own ideas about how to throw a party.

Ellen watches from her usual position slightly behind and to the side of Mrs. Craxton's chair. As the game progresses, she senses something more at stake than the prospect of winning or losing. Mrs. Craxton has played casket patience a hundred times before, but she has never performed it in front of an audience, as she does now. It is like a pantomime, the story enacted without words. The casket remains intact, and her rubbish piles grow. If she keeps turning up useless cards she'll forfeit the game, a humiliating loss in front of onlookers, and it will be Ellen's job to console her. She could save face by cutting the demonstration short. But she keeps on with an eagerness that seems more and more inexplicable to Ellen; it's as though Mrs. Craxton doesn't care whether she wins or loses, as though her defeat will be meaningless, perhaps even deliberate.

Ellen seeks her daughter's face. Despite the makeup, she finds the remnants of Peg's childhood in the rounded chin, the delicate flare of her nostrils as she exhales, the expressive, wondering eyes. There are two ways for a woman to age, Ellen thinks: as with herself, the body may become haggard, the skin tough, with the hard elasticity of gutta-percha. Or as in the case of Mrs. Craxton, the body may grow softer, plumper, the skeleton buried beneath fluffy, whipped-cream fat. The backs of her hands are spotted pillows of flesh, without bone or sinew; the sphere of her face looks as malleable as soft butter. Mrs. Craxton has become strangely indifferent to the contest of patience. In the time it takes to overturn the remaining cards, indifference will spread until no part of her remains unaffected. She doesn't care whether she succeeds or fails. She doesn't care at all.

The queen of clubs.

The seven of diamonds.

The casket remains intact. A second turn is not allowed. She turns over the final three cards, ending with the ace of clubs. Then she looks up, a vague smile crosses her face, and she murmurs, "Henry."

At this instant Ellen understands the implications of the game and the high stakes. Mrs. Craxton is greeting her dead husband—the name signals her confusion. Yes, Ellen has been watching a woman go mad—this must account for the game's overwhelming suspense. Mrs. Craxton began the round with her reason intact and has ended it insane. The wheels of her chair creak as she shifts her weight forward. "How good of you to come," she says, her eyes vacant yet with a sureness of direction, like a blind woman gazing toward a sound, facing her object so insistently that all the servants finally follow her gaze. Their gasps of surprise are nearly synchronized as they recognize Hal Craxton Junior, Mrs. Craxton's son, who is leaning casually against the mantel, looking completely at home.

"Merry Christmas, Mother."

"We weren't expecting you."

"Didn't you receive my letter?"

"The post is so unreliable."

"But please, carry on. I'm going to have my supper and I'd just as soon you left me alone for ten minutes."

"Of course, Hal, of course. Ellen, fetch a bottle of champagne from the cellar. We'll be wet tonight, Hal—we must toast your return. But you're hungry. Go ahead, I won't disturb you while you eat. I'll play another game. Come then, girls, don't stare. He's just my son, my own flesh and blood. Hal, you remember Lilian Stone, don't you? Audrey's youngest child? But go ahead, I won't bother you anymore. Never mind that you've been away for eighteen long months and didn't bother to send your mother a single letter, not even a card on my seventy-fifth birthday, only an occasional telegram to let me know that you were staying away. Oh, never mind about all that. You need your supper. Nora, tell Sylva that my son has come home. I'll demonstrate another form of patience while Hal dines. What shall we play? Why don't I teach you demon patience, a game even more aggravating than the last, and we only need one deck. He's a clever one, this demon, so beware. When you think success is within your grasp, he'll bring you to a standstill. But we won't let our demon get the better of us, will we, girls? We'll snatch the game back. There you are, Sylva. Please see to it that my son has enough to eat. Later, Hal, you can tell me all about your travels, and we'll attend to financial matters—I'd prefer to get this out of the way tonight, if you don't mind. Now, after shuffling the pack thoroughly, you count out thirteen cards."

8

For every preserved skin and manikin, there are a thousand attitudes. And how much the finished attitude tells us about the time and place of its construction! Early in this century, taxidermists strove for mastery of detail, and the result was regiments of animals as tight-lipped and uncompromising as their Edwardian creators. But under the influence of cinema, *motion* became the mark of quality. For the directors of museums around the world, the desire to make the dioramas more lifelike took on a new urgency as the popularity of the picture show grew—the decision to depict natural history as an intricate evolutionary adventure was motivated as much by competition as by a refined appreciation of the subject. Techniques of realism became so involved that the American Museum of Natural History in New York City hired "motion specialists" to design the action and determine the most authentic attitudes for their habitat groups.

"The choice of an attitude depends wholly upon our artistic instincts," wrote one of the most famous taxidermists of the time, William Hornaday. He advised his students to choose the attitude that is the most graceful and at the same time the most representative. "To my mind," he concluded, "the attitude taken by an animal when startled by visible or suspected danger, is the one par excellence in which it appears at its best when mounted." This aspect of danger, of suspense, fits perfectly with the desire to simulate action, and taxidermists heeded Hornaday's advice, modeling their animals to portray "every sense keenly on the alert," even as they refined muscular detail to such extraordinary precision that they could show a lion's tail twitching nervously or, with two or three cunning wrinkles, they could depict the mouth of a fox about to snap closed upon a rabbit's haunch.

Combine motion and danger, and you have a cruel realism, with one story told over and over: the story of the hunt. "For a single specimen, the most striking attitude possible is that of a beast at bay"— these are Hornaday's words, and they should be engraved on the walls of New York's Museum of Natural History, in place of Theodore Roosevelt's arid scoutmaster ethics.

"My best wench," says Lily with a giggle, flopping across her bed. "My mopsy, my favorite chippy, diggity-piggity beautiful Peg. Kiss me." Over the past week their charged secret has transformed back into giddy friendship, or so the girls pretend to each other, both of them reluctant to speak of their short-lived intimacy. But their silly romps keep threatening to turn serious, especially when the hand of one girl makes contact with the body of the other, as Lily's hand does now, reaching for Peg to recline her, and with her inhibitions made coquettish by Christmas punch, Lily lets her hand rest on Peg's shoulder, lets the fingers gently knead the pocket of flesh above Peg's collarbone. And though for Peg this touch is more inviting than anything she's ever felt, though she knows she does love Lilian, though she's filled her diary with intimate declarations of love and for the last seven days has despised herself for pretending otherwise, she refuses to give in. She merely sets her jaw a little more tightly than usual, and Lily instantly perceives her disapproval. The only thing left is to fill in the cause.

"Peg? What's wrong? Why are you looking at me like that?"

"Why? Why, she says! Why!"

"What's the matter?"

"The matter is Hal Craxton," Peg retorts, and the girls gaze at each other in wonder, so mutually appalled that if someone had nudged them they would have broken up laughing. Instead, Lily sits up and replies in a hushed voice that reinforces the severity of the accusation, "What are you talking about?"

"I'm talking about the way you hung on Mr. Craxton this evening. Like you were already his whore." Peg's own encounter with Hal Craxton is one of the few secrets she's kept from Lily, and she's glad of it now.

"You're joking!" Lily can only toss her head in irritation, tinged with a shade of scorn to indicate that she finds the idea absurd. "Hal Craxton is ancient. He has gray hairs as long as my pinky growing out of his nostrils. You jealous creature, I was just being polite." Lily nuzzles Peg's neck in an attempt to close the conversation and get on with the business of friendship.

"Were you being polite when you put your arm around his waist?" Peg demands. "Were you being polite when you put your hand in his coat pocket? The next thing was to squeeze the little toad in his trousers—or maybe you did that, too."

"Crazy, crazy girl! My daddy and Hal Craxton are old friends— they were schoolboys together. Hal—Mr. Craxton—used to visit us when I was little, and he'd always hide presents in his pockets, crayons or beads or tiny harvest dolls. I was just reminding him of that old game. But I shouldn't have to defend myself against such a ridiculous accusation." As she speaks she tries to pluck loose the ribbon binding Peg's braid, and when Peg pulls away, Lily says, "You're my dearest friend. That's all that matters," her voice full of forced conviction. It hardly matters whether the false note is intentional or not—Peg feels herself sliding along with Lily into a melodrama, script in hand, the conclusion already written out.

"Prove it." Peg lowers her own voice to a whisper, as though merely to utter the challenge put them both at risk, and she says what she's been wanting to say for weeks: "Take me home with you when you go."

"What?"

"Take me home with you. Save me from this place."

"Why, that's cracked!"

"I'll be perfectly decent."

"Peg, I can't . . . my family . . ."

"Let me come live with you—just for a few weeks, until I can find a job. Then I'll rent a room nearby. We're best friends, remember."

Lily is on her feet now, pacing across the diameter of the oval rug, back and forth, her refusal lost to hesitation.

Peg folds her arms. Her bitterness is so pronounced she appears smug when she says, "I'm not good enough?"

"You don't understand."

"Your goddamn reputation."

"Do you really believe that I can introduce you to my family—like, like some stray cat I'd picked up on the street?" Her whisper is strained now, and she jumps rashly to a higher register as she completes her question.

"Oh, but I did believe it, Lily. I hoped that we could stay together forever. But we're just little girls playing naughty little games." How quickly the argument, begun as a dare, has intensified. Peg hadn't meant it to come to this, yet she can't keep her anger from finding its expression in chilling indifference. "You know, I think I'm bored. Yes, I think it's time to start another game. There's always a new game of patience to learn." As she hears herself speak, she realizes she means this to be final.

"Wait, Peg!"

Like so many of her kind, Lilian Stone has been cultivated by her parents, nurses, and teachers to uphold the standard of autocratic formality. But she's no match for Peg, who has learned her dignity from haphazard sources and will protect it at the expense of all other emotions. Perhaps there's a touch of old Mary Craxton in her irony. Even Mrs. Craxton, however, couldn't affect such vicious mildness. In the moment's passion, Peg believes she can leave behind this relationship completely, without regret, without memory. When she moves past Lily on her way to the door, she brushes her lips against Lily's cheek and whispers a haughty "Good-bye, darling."

But while Peg has a stronger, more dangerous dignity, Lily has greater powers of seduction. She catches Peg by the wrists and says in a voice that is both pleading and commanding, "Don't go, not yet."

Irony has a lure of its own, and Peg isn't ready to give it up. "Should I send Eva down, ma'am?" she inquires pertly. "Or Billie? I'm certain you'd enjoy a turn with one of the other girls. But I'm a bit weary on my feet. So if you'll excuse me—"

"Peg, sit down."

"At your service, ma'am."

"Please. I want to tell you a story about my family. When I was a little girl, five or six—please, Peg, listen to me. I want to tell you about my family. When I was a little girl, I found my daddy out."

"I'm not interested, Lily."

"Let me explain!"

"And then what?"

"I want you to understand my family. My father's money book—this will give you an idea of what it's like at home. My father kept a hollow book full of money in his study, and every few days he'd add to it. I spied on him one day. I saw him, the old miser. Counting his hoard. After that I'd sneak down to his study every morning and see how much he'd added. Altogether he put over one thousand dollars into that book. And then one day the money disappeared."

"Why should this matter to me?"

"Not long after, he began filling up his book again. I still don't know what Daddy used that money for. He caught me, you see. Early one morning he came down to his study and found me counting his money. He slapped me across the mouth, warned me never to tell anyone what I had found. Then he dragged me down to the basement and locked me in the coal bin. I spent the day staring out the little window at an anthill in the grass. It was dark when my father came to get me. He led me past my brothers and my mother, who were seated at the dining-room table waiting for supper. I was covered head to toe with coal dust. No one said a word. This is my family, Peg. I wouldn't trust them with you."

"A lowly servant girl. A housekeeper's daughter."

"Do you forgive me?"

"No."

"But you won't leave me. You can't. Not yet."

"Lily—"

"Not yet."

In the silence that follows, before she gives in, Peg's eyes search the room with almost frantic attention, as though she were looking to steal a sterner composure from some inanimate object. There is a single candle burning on the bedside table, and it lights half the room in chiaroscuro. A painting of a brace of pheasants hangs over the bed.

Velvet roses tumble down the wallpaper. Plush maroon drapes cover all but an inch-wide bar of glass; the window is dark, except for the teardrop reflection of the flame.

Peg closes her eyes. She desperately wants to resist, and if Lily's voice weren't so soothing and her hands weren't so persuasive, she would have left Lilian Stone to her wealth and self-pity. But Lily has slipped the strap of the dress down Peg's arm and is kissing her freckled shoulder, her neck, the top of her breasts, giggling over two delicious chocolates and the neat scoops of Bavarian cream—Peg Griswood, such a tasty confection—and Peg can't help but adore Lily, or at least she adores the sensation as her lover's mouth moves lightly over her body, naked now, her dress somehow cast aside, and down the curve from her waist to her hip to her thigh, devouring all lingering resistance. With a sigh, Lily pushes Peg backward onto the bed and kisses her belly. It occurs to Peg that Lily must have had plenty of relevant experience, for her hands and tongue trace Peg's willing body with an extraordinary evanescence that could only have been learned through practice. But the thought disappears like the white of an eye behind a closed lid, and Peg's own eyes shut as she sinks completely into this dream of love. She prefers blindness, where she can imagine herself lifted out of time, so she does not notice that the door is slightly ajar and that a man, a stranger, an intruder in the Manikin, is watching from the hallway. She does not see the pinched expression of jealous rage on his face. Peg does not see him at all and so does not scream in terror as he melts away into the darkness.

Night winds in this region tend to blow steadily in one direction. Or perhaps this is just the illusion created by steady darkness under the usual cloud cover. And perhaps the transformation into morning does not in itself encourage a change in the wind, and the difference is merely one of gradual light. The weather vane doesn't necessarily shift direction as the day approaches. But for anyone out walking in the fields early on a winter's morning an hour or two before dawn, the wind itself seems to change. It is not warmer, not immediately. And the wind doesn't usually alter in velocity. But it seems more playful—or more wicked. The constant night wind begins to blow in opposing currents, drenches the face with a blast of cold, subsides for a second and then slams against the back of the head. At this time of day the air seems crowded and fractious, as though all the diverse day currents had just been born and were jostling each other in an attempt to secure a pre-eminent place.

The freshness of the morning wind makes it preferable to the solid, stale, purposeful night wind. But perhaps this, too, is only a lie. An illusion of freedom—as though the wind had not traveled an infinite number of times around the globe but had sprung up just then from the earth. For that brief span of time before morning has completely settled, the wind seems like an unruly spirit released from the bondage of the land, half crazy with its freedom.

Say this spirit is a dream: the earth's dream, an unreal remembering. Red-winged blackbirds screeching. Rabbits. Chipmunks. A red fox. Long-stalked Solomon's seal umbels sagging in the heat, pairs of blackberries like a sow's teats. Wood sorrel and chickweed. Above, tired buckeye leaves, the green half washed to yellow. Everything crackling dry.

The last dream before daylight. Heat begets heat. A single flame splitting into two. The dance of fire against the white backdrop of sky. Generation. Spitting, laughing, drunken flames. The ground cowers, leaves shrivel, animals collapse into ashes. A rush and whir. Oak trees fifty feet in circumference explode. The sleeper shouts, gropes, and seizes a handful of fire.

Lore hears the panic in the knocking before he is fully awake, and he thinks automatically of Junket. Something has happened. Something has happened to his son. This is how such news comes—first with a pounding, pounding, pounding, knuckles against wood, rousing a man to a life that has changed utterly during the night. He springs from his bed, opens the door to Peter, whom he pushes away so he can get to Junket's room. He flings the door open just as Junk pulls it from the inside, so the door snaps back and the boy tumbles over Machine to the floor.

"Jesus," Lore says, catching his breath. "Jesus. Oh Jesus."

"What is it, Papa?" Junk rubs the wrist he'd landed on, then pushes himself to his feet. The dog barks until Junket shushes him.

"You all right? I'm sorry. What time is it?"

"Lore—" Peter raises his lamp to illuminate their faces. "You'd better get dressed."

"What is it?" Junk is already pulling on a sweater. Peter contemplates the boy for a moment and says, "Come on to the barn. The both of you." Then he leaves, hurrying down the stairs and out into the darkness.

Junk tucks his long underwear into his trousers and pulls his boots over his bare feet, while Lore in the same amount of time dresses fully, with socks and a flannel shirt beneath his sweater. Lore even remembers to grab their hats on the way out, and on impulse he sends Machine back into the house and shuts the dog inside. They make their way along the slippery drive through the morning darkness, planting their heels with each step to break the night's crust on the snow. The predawn sky is an eerie cobalt blue that promises a storm. The barn door is open, and inside, at the far end of the aisle, they see Peter and Sylva standing outside Emily's stall, the soft yellow glow of Peter's kerosene lamp giving the figures an antique look, as though they were daguerreotype images and hadn't moved for fifty years.

As Lore approaches the stall, he hears a soft squeal from within. *Colic,* he thinks, his worry firm and manageable now, even tinged with relief, since the bad news doesn't involve Junket. Inside the stall, Red Vic is sitting in the straw with Emily's head in his lap. He's such a large block of a man, over six feet tall with a heavy build, that the horse seems dwarfed by him. As Lore approaches, the mare suddenly reaches around and tries to nuzzle and bite her hindquarters, and Lore sees a stain of dark blood on the straw beneath her tail. *She's foaling!* But that's impossible. Lore stomps his feet to shake off the chill of this Christmas miracle. Then he notices the bloody fetlocks. Emily drops her head in Red Vic's lap again, exhausted, nostrils fluttering with her light panting.

"Papa?" Junk has his high-pitched boy's voice back again. Lore squeezes his hand and then pushes past him into the stall, takes in the familiar scents of straw and horse sweat and urine along with the sour smell of blood. He lifts the tail, its hair caked with blood and as hard as feather shafts. Emily curls her lip and tries to nip Lore, but Red Vic manages to calm her.

A long slash made with surgical precision, probably with a razor, reaches from the mare's rectum and disappears between her hind legs. The wound doesn't bleed as heavily as the more ragged lacerations on the legs. Lore probes a hamstrung foreleg and glimpses the rubbery white tip of a tendon. Emily makes a strange sound, half squeal, half whisper, and kicks out weakly at Lore when he touches her.

"Hush, honey." Red Vic strokes the broad chestnut cheek and speaks quietly into her ear.

Lore has seen plenty of wounded animals and has killed more than he can count. He doesn't mind the sight of blood when it's spilled legitimately. But this blood—unnecessary blood, useless blood—doesn't fit into his notion of things. For a moment his brain feels as though it has clenched into a fist, and he can't see anything through his pain but the blurry form of the horse. He shakes the spasm from his head, takes a deep breath, and the ghost image sharpens back into their dear old nag. Emily. Poor Emily.

"Worth bringing in Martin to have a look?" Sylva asks. Dr. Martin is the county's only vet and lives on Main Street in Millworth. "Peter could fetch him."

"I don't . . ." Lore pauses, stuck at the brink of the decision he doesn't want to make. "I don't think so, Sylva. Naw." As he stands he grabs a fistful of straw and rubs the wet blood from his palms. "Who did this?" he asks, only because the question must be asked, though he doesn't expect an answer.

"On Christmas morning . . ." Sylva says, clucking her tongue, and that sound, which usually precedes a command, causes Emily to prick her ears forward and try to roll onto her belly. Red Vic pulls her gently back; she doesn't resist. They watch her without a word, the silence broken only by the mooing of an impatient cow. Lore's initial relief has long faded—there's no place in his understanding of nature for something like this. Such an act couldn't even be conceived of by any animal other than man. And that Lore can't reach out and catch the fiends who did this and return the injury, justly, tit-for-tat—this seems the most unnatural thing of all.

"Junket, go get my rifle." Father and son exchange a quick glance—they've never been reconciled over the lost Maynard—but Junket rushes off. Lore listens to the clomp of his boots as he runs down the aisle and out the door.

For whatever reason, the boy's absence frees the adults from their solemnity, and after a minute or so Peter says, "The devil who did this—I'll kill him, if I ever catch him."

"You leave it to God or to the judge, depending . . ." Sylva says, kneeling to pick straw from Emily's muzzle.

"Who did this? Who?" Red Vic slowly shakes his head. Of anyone present, he's the one most sentimentally attached to the horse. Economically as well, since he has only three responsibilities at the Manikin: the horse, the touring car, and the truck. How this will affect Red Vic's position no one present can be sure.

"Would have taken two strong men, I think. One to hold her, one to hurt her." Lore's voice drifts off so the last words are inaudible.

"Only one pair of boots walked out of the barn before us," Peter says. "He cross-tied her, see." He motions to the lengths of rope hanging from wall hooks.

"Let's go after him," Lore suggests.

"He has half an hour on us, at least."

"Tend to the horse," Sylva insists. "And what about Mr. Craxton? Remember, he's back home." She probably means to remind them that the master of the house needs to be informed of the crime, but by calling up his name she manages to cast him as a suspect.

"Why would he—?" Red Vic loses the question to choking emotion.

"I didn't mean that."

"Strange, you gotta admit. Craxton comes home and that same night someone takes a knife to our horse," Peter says. "Maybe he's trailing a history."

"What are you saying, man? Better you keep your crazy hunches to yourself than try them out on the rest of us," Sylva scolds.

"We'll have to report it," Lore says vaguely, uncertain of the procedure. Perhaps he should bring Craxton to the barn before he puts the horse out of her misery. What should he do? No one helps him with advice. They stand around pondering the mare's suffering, unable to take their eyes off her and all of them wanting her dead, until Junket returns with the rifle—loaded, ready to be cocked.

"All right." With the weight of the gun in his hands, Lore feels more helpless than ever. After a few minutes Red Vic plants a rough kiss on Emily's nose and eases out from beneath her. She's too weary to raise her head again—she stares at Lore's weapon with mild interest, perhaps sensing that it is the instrument of her relief.

"All right," Lore repeats, infected by the horse's contagious exhaustion. The others move away from the stall. Sylva says needlessly, "Just do it, Lore. Get it over with." Almost in one motion, Lore cocks the gun, lifts it to his shoulder, aims for the small hollow beneath Emily's right ear, and fires. The whole body jerks at the impact and flops back, twitching, blessedly lifeless within a matter of seconds. Brain and blood have exploded into the straw, and from above the killing looks clean. Lore backs away so the others can see.

"Maybe we should have brought in Mr. Craxton first," Junket says. His son's voice still sounds so boyish to Lore. Stupidly, pathetically boyish.

"Maybe . . ." echoes Lore, managing with his tone to convey his irritation, and Junket glances up in surprise and shame.

"Oh, he wouldn't care if his house burned down," Sylva says.

Peter adds, "Hal Craxton will burn it down himself one day. For the insurance money."

Red Vic squats and runs his hand around Emily's belly, as though feeling the tightness of a girth. Then he covers his face with his hands.

Maybe, Lore is still thinking, watching Red Vic mourn. *Maybe.*

There were some who heard the horse's agony. Mrs. Craxton had woken early and was lying in bed waiting until the decent hour of 7:00 A.M., when she would ring for Ellen. She thought the scream was a raccoon's, though she took it as an omen for the day. "There will be trouble before sunset, Ellen," she muttered later, when she had her arms around the housekeeper's neck and was lifting herself onto the bedpan. "Mark my words."

The maid Eva was awake in her attic room and heard it too—mistaking the weird cries for a human voice, she assumed that someone in the house was having a nightmare.

And Boggio, who never slept better than fitfully, had been up for hours and was making coffee over his paraffin stove when the screams began. He misjudged the distance of the voice, thought it was coming from a deep, nearby interior.

He reached out from his chair and touched the satiny feathers of his snowy owl, probed under the extended wing until he felt the stretched leathern skin. And beneath that, he felt the outline of the wadded excelsior bound with wire, and the wooden skeleton. The cry, he believed, had originated from somewhere inside the body of the owl and was muffled by the padding and skin and winter feathers. The bird was calling out to him, over and over, barely audibly. Not that Boggio was surprised. He'd heard the owl's voice dozens of times, on nights when the wind gusted and shook the windowpanes. But he could discern a difference in these cries, even in their weakness. His lovely owl was begging to come alive, just for one day—Christmas Day—hoping beyond hope that nature would celebrate the holiday and grant a dead creature temporary life. Boggio felt a guilty pride. Thanks to him, the spirit of the owl lived on inside the trap of its false body, the stuffed bird too powerful a monument to leave behind. Boggio's little mammoth, this white muff of a bird trapped in ice, was teased day after day by its own verisimilitude.

After the screams ceased Boggio watched the owl carefully for some slight motion. He even wagged a forefinger inside the open beak, but nothing happened. Dour nature couldn't be persuaded to bend the rules. Not even on Christmas. Not even in fun.

9

The earth must be there under the snow. Dirt and gravel and marl, root-bound soil, tubers and bulbs frozen in loam, and farther down, below the frost, damp clay, water, chalk, granite, molten lava, fire. It's probably easier to imagine the fire at the earth's center from this wintery landscape than from a more temperate location, a Tuscany vineyard, say, where the caressing sun soothes curiosity to sleep and the earth seems no more than a richly decorated surface, reliably abundant. In contrast, the winter landscape of western New York hides its abundance beneath the endlessly accumulating snow and draws attention downward to the secrets of the land. Snow is like the white sheet pulled over a recently expired body. Just like the corpse, the land's contours are always visible in winter. The center of the earth is implied in a landscape transformed by snow, just as the secrets of a life are implied by the shrouded body.

As Lore clambers across a pasture on Christmas Day, he thinks about the earth hidden beneath the snow and all the burrowing animals hibernating there, a few feet below his boots. It's a small comfort to him—the thought of their comfort—what with the snow falling more heavily now and the trail disappearing before his eyes. He's not

even sure he's following a man's footprints anymore; the vague de-
pressions and scuffs in the snow might have been sculpted by wind.

A frozen stalk cracks as Lore presses it with his boot, and the sound
is so similar to the snap of a whip that his mind fills with the image of
Emily bleeding to death in the straw. After Lore destroyed her, Peter
and Sylva returned to their cabin, Lore sent Junket back to the gatehouse, and he himself left the barn and wandered off across the pasture, unsure of his purpose, feeling only that he wanted to be alone for
a time. But as soon as he spotted the tracks in the snow, he knew he had
to follow them.

By the time he reaches Hadley Road, however, the tracks have been
buried by new snow, and Lore can't tell which direction to take. To the
left lies Millworth; twelve miles to the east is the town of Kettling. Lore
decides to head toward Millworth, figuring that the closer destination
would be the more likely refuge.

The weather sides with the criminal today—there will be no justice.
The snow completely obscures Lore's own print as soon as he lifts his
boot. And the brooding black sky in the north is sure to bring more
severe snow within the hour.

Lore stops to catch his breath, squinting into the smoky storm while
he considers the situation. Unlike Peter, he doesn't believe the attack
had anything to do with Hal Craxton. Rather, he's convinced that the
message was directed at himself: Lore Bennett, groundskeeper. Lore
has plenty of enemies in these parts, since he's the one who gives and
denies permission to hunt on Craxton land. More often than not he
denies, and in the past he's been quick to fire over a poacher's head in
warning. Here's the warning turned against him: some poacher's revenge. Now the stakes have escalated. He might have to shoot the man
if he catches him. But he won't catch him, not in this weather. Of
course he won't catch him. He's been wasting his time. If he turns back
now, his breakfast might still be warm. Yes, he'll let the man go—
sooner or later, the brute will have to face up to what he did. Not
insanity, not even God, can save him from the retribution of his own
conscience.

Impulsively, Lore scoops up a gloveful of snow and holds it to his
lips. The ice crystals burn his tongue before they melt. He drinks with
a rising thirst, fills his glove a second time, holds himself perfectly still
so he may hear, behind the wind, the hiss of falling snow. The hem-

locks stand like his impatient friends on either side of the blank stretch of road, waiting for Lore to join them before they hurry home. He leans back on his heels, and the snow crunches beneath his boots. He remembers how the cold of the lake nearly killed him when he went in after Junket's Maynard. The liquid cold of a blizzard can kill too, with more finesse. Slowly, almost imperceptibly, the body gives in, the blood thickens, the pulse grows faint. He wouldn't wish such an easy fate upon the man who slashed Emily. Lore hopes that the brute, whoever he is, suffers a far worse punishment, and the hope itself gives him meager satisfaction.

But then he remembers the next duty in front of him: hauling the horse's remains to the pit where they dump and burn their garbage, a dry ravine about a quarter of a mile from the house. Lore heads back toward the Manikin, stepping gently so as not to wake the hibernating animals. The pine branches scrape and squeak overhead, the sound uncannily like muffled laughter, though he hardly notices the similarity and doesn't pause again in his journey home. He's too familiar with the antics of trees to be fooled.

The problem with Hal, Mrs. Craxton thinks, gazing somewhat blankly at her husband's collection of dead animals, is not that he neglects his mother. Rather, neglect is engendered by a perpetual boredom. He can't stand to remain in one place for longer than a month, so he keeps circling the globe, oblivious to scenery or art or the exotic tribes and animals that populate a region, interested only in his own mood. He travels simply because it is something to do.

Her only son. Throughout Hal's childhood, Mary Craxton thought of him as a mild, manageable child, and she spent the little energy left over from her parties and luncheons on her elder son, George, a more excitable and sensitive boy. And after George died at the age of twenty-two, she hardly remembered that she still had a son. Two lost boys— the injustice of this made her bitter, and bitterness settled into a constant irritation. She was grateful when Hal went off to college and she could bask in the attention of her solicitous friends. But the mildness that characterized him in his youth has transformed into ennui in his middle age. He reminds his mother of the Irish wolfhound her husband kept, a purebred so satiated by the simple business of living that it yawned as often as other dogs would bark. Henry Senior loved the dog better than any other pet and upon its death sent it to his taxidermy department. He kept the stuffed dog in his library for years, reason enough for Mary Craxton to avoid that room altogether, and soon after her husband was killed she donated the animal to a small midwestern college.

Now there are more donations to make, a lifetime's worth of donations, and in the process she'll teach her son the importance of money! He's spent his adult years indulging himself and wasting the family fortune. Well, he's going to lose what's left of that fortune, and sooner than he might expect! Hal won't be able to laugh and yawn his way free of this fate. He can't be droll about poverty. *Just wait, Hal.* She'll teach her lazy son the importance of an industrious life. She doesn't mean to punish him for his neglect—she knows she could have been a better mother—but to force him to spend his remaining decades engaged in some constructive activity. In short, by denying him the inheritance that he expects upon her death, she will force her son to find a job.

Partly influenced by her son's inconstancy, partly motivated by her own compunction, Mrs. Craxton decided shortly after Thanksgiving to revise her will and force Hal to earn his keep. She raised a parasite—he lives off the wealth that his father accumulated, without increasing or even renewing the capital. If he were a woman, unmarried and unattractive, it would be one thing, and Mary Craxton would have taken pity. But he has all the advantages of the male sex and uses none of them.

Just wait, Hal. She wishes she could stick around to watch her son's face change shades as Mr. Watts reads the document—Mary Craxton's last will and testament. She is sorry to have to disappoint her son but is convinced that over time he'll be improved by this harsh lesson. He assumes that all the assets, diminished as they are, will go to him. He doesn't have any reason to suspect otherwise.

No one knows about her plan except her lawyer, his assistant, and the gardener, Sid, who witnessed the signing of the will. At one point Mrs. Craxton had had a vague inclination to consult with Lilian Stone, but she'd quickly come to recognize the girl for what she is and stopped gushing with hospitality. Lily would have tried to benefit from Mrs. Craxton's brief affection. Now no one will benefit. Upon her death,

Mary Craxton's entire savings and securities will be given to charity, and the bank will foreclose swiftly. Henry Craxton Junior, the only surviving heir of the great natural history entrepreneur, will have to start from scratch.

An old lady's final act of grace, she mouths, solely for the benefit of the stuffed animals this time. She's felt since she entered the room— almost imperceptibly at first, and now with powerful insistence—that the animals are poised in some kind of awful expectation, waiting for her to perform. The dik-dik, the bats, the monkeys, the peacock, the snarling cougar—their dimension seems almost magical, as though they had emerged from the wallpaper or from the pages of her husband's books in order to keep her company today. They make her feel prepared for her last feat.

What time is it? She can't see the hands on the mantel clock across the room, and the little brass monkeys haven't clapped their cymbals for what seems like hours. No matter. She's had enough time in her life, more time than she ever knew what to do with, and only a routine packed full of distractions has kept her sane. It's time, whatever the hour, to put her routine behind her—as good a time as any. Time to stop wasting time, she tells herself, turning her face toward the window. Better to throw off the weight of life than to be crushed by it. Her revised will is in her lawyer's vault, her son is home, it's Christmas Day . . .

Why not now?

The question arises almost accidentally from the muck of wonder and folds itself around her consciousness. *Why not now, Mrs. Craxton?* She sits with a straight back, her expression as impatiently expectant as if she were waiting for a hairdresser to set her hair in rollers.

From the outside looking in, Ellen sees a short-tempered old woman collecting her thoughts into a mass of fury. Her immediate interpretation of Mrs. Craxton's meditative scowl is this: She will wait until her son is sitting across from her; she will watch his eyes idly skim the pages of a magazine; she will give him one more chance and invite him to stay for her birthday in February—or maybe she will simply ask him what his plans are for the coming months. She will wait for him to disappoint her. And then, without warning, she will explode into a tirade. It will be as simple as lighting a match. One moment she will be as quiet as Ellen herself, the next moment she will be screeching like a lunatic.

How annoying, Ellen thinks, that in this house so removed from time, her mind keeps wandering into the future, while the past, even the past as recent as last night, hovers over her like some great carnivorous beast. Where was her daughter last night? She didn't come back to her room until long after midnight. What does this mean? But Ellen would prefer not to ponder the question. *Attend to the present!* she tells herself. The here-and-now: wrinkles fanning out from an old woman's eyes; a split nail on Mrs. Craxton's ring finger; fat pearls clipped to her ears and draped across her bosom; the click as the pendulum in the grandfather clock in the hall reaches its summit and falls back; the fainter tick of the mantel clock.

There is so much Ellen does not want to know. To others she seems a firm, practical-minded woman, but in truth she would be too timid to leave her bed in the morning if she indulged her fears. Fortunately, she learned long ago that self-sacrifice is more profitable, at least for a woman of her station, than self-indulgence. Responsibility gets her up each morning, greets her like a blast of fresh winter air, and keeps her concentrating all day long on the task at hand.

She didn't wake with such diligent energy this morning, though, since she hadn't let herself fall asleep until long after midnight. She'd tried to wait up for her daughter, and as the hour grew late and her annoyance turned to fury, she'd started to plan a strategy of discipline. At the risk of estranging Peg, Ellen decided to assert her powers as a parent and forbid her daughter from associating with Mrs. Craxton's guest. Like should mix with like; trouble arises when different classes mingle, and Ellen intended to make Peg understand this. But the confrontation never took place—Ellen inadvertently succumbed to sleep, and when she woke an hour later than usual, her daughter was deeply, irreproachably asleep in her own bed. Where had she gone off to last night in her bangled dress and heels? Ellen would bet that Lilian Stone could tell her where.

Ellen dressed quickly and hurried downstairs. She entered Mrs. Craxton's room within minutes after she rang, so her late rising went unnoticed. Ellen and Sylva are the only ones expected to work today—by eight o'clock, though, Sylva hadn't come up to the kitchen yet, and Ellen had to prepare Mrs. Craxton's cocoa herself.

The Christmas holiday will be Sylva's excuse, Ellen thinks as she stands beside Mrs. Craxton's chair in the living room, her arms folded across her apron, her chin raised to imply a steady, dignified attention. Holidays confuse schedules, make reliable servants lazy, disrupt an orderly household. If it were up to Ellen she would do away with holidays entirely. Think of Henry Junior—that's what fun will do to you, turn you into a good-for-nothing scamp who treats every day as a vacation. Fine for a man who has the means, but for a woman as poor as Ellen, fun would land her in the gutter. Here's a future she isn't even tempted to imagine, since she dreads the misery of homelessness more than her own death.

And here's the present finally making itself felt with selfish insistence. A woman's body has its needs. Ellen's flow always comes as a surprise, often at the most inconvenient times—now, for instance, so she has no choice but to leave Mrs. Craxton alone for a few minutes. Strange, the old woman appears pleased when Ellen asks to be excused. She nods her permission, and Ellen notices that her brown irises have nearly been eclipsed by her pupils, though the light in the room is adequate. It could be she's still feeling the effects of last night's champagne. No doubt she'll be as keen as ever when her son comes down for breakfast.

A trip to the toilet, and upstairs to the bedroom, where Peg is still asleep, to secure a pad with safety pins. At first, Ellen feels comforted by the reminder of life's repetitions, its cyclical patterns: the snow collecting on the ground and in the crooks of branches will melt; a clean room gets dirty over time and must be cleaned again; a woman bleeds; a girl sleeps; a mother and daughter will be reconciled.

Or will they?

Where does Peg go when she disappears for hours? There is one place Ellen would be sure to find the answer. She has considered it before, but never so impulsively—the temptation to have a look at her daughter's diary is stronger than ever this morning. Peg is her only daughter, after all, her own flesh and blood, and has fallen under a witch's spell. Where was Peg last night? What is she dreaming of now?

Peg keeps the diary in her top bureau drawer, a worthless hiding place, since she puts it there so casually, in her mother's full view. By opening the diary, Ellen will break the pact that exists between them. But Peg need never know about her mother's intrusion. Ellen checks her watch—only five minutes have passed since she left Mrs. Craxton alone. Surely she can delay her return for another five minutes. She can't be blamed for wanting reassurance. But her daughter assumes that her mother will respect her privacy. Then why, Ellen asks herself as she reaches into the drawer, why is she going to take advantage of her daughter's trust while she's asleep and read her secrets?

Peg's diary, like most of her possessions, is secondhand—she has taken one of her mother's leather-bound planning books and replaced the calendar with blank paper punched at either end. See how clever the girl is to have bettered this old book, how smoothly the cover opens and how readily the pages turn. How innocent Peg is in sleep. And oh, how quickly her secrets reveal themselves to her mother's prying eyes.

Even as she reads, flipping backward from yesterday's entry, Ellen regrets opening the diary. Yes, she could have learned everything simply by observing her daughter, by examining her sleeping face. She could have confirmed what she'd suspected without reading the diary at all. Perhaps if she'd waited up for Peg last night she would have guessed the truth. Yes, this is the way it should have happened, the way she wishes it had happened: Ellen would be sitting on Peg's bed gazing out into the night. The door would open slowly, as though of its own accord, and Peg would be standing on the threshold, disheveled, pale with fatigue, her hair hanging like an oriole's deep nest from the back of her head, one ribbon still tied at the bottom of the bundle, Lilian's evening dress looking as spent as the body that it clothed. But it wouldn't be Peg's appearance that would give her away—it would be the guilty slide of her gaze away from Ellen.

So that's what you've been doing, Ellen thinks, finding the truth in Peg's diary as surely as if she had witnessed it herself, and yet still disbelieving. No, *tell me it's not true, tell me that you don't love her, not in that way, you don't go to her room at night, instead you go out hunting in the snow, foolish girl, or you sneak around with Junket, you saucy thing, but that's all right, young people make mistakes. But I forgive you. I forgive you. No. Where have you been, Peg?*

I'm sorry, Mother. I fell asleep in Lilian's room. She invited me up after the party for a game of rummy. It was a wonderful party, wasn't it? The best ever. Too bad Mr. Craxton had to come home and spoil the fun.

Tell me the truth, Peg.

Ellen does know her daughter. She's always known her. She can read her mind. And she would have been able to smell Peg's last encounter on her breath, if she'd been standing in the room: whiskey and love. No, not love—you can't call *that* love.

The truth?

What have you been doing, Peg?

Sleeping, Mother.

In her bed. In her arms.

How can Ellen be so sure? Her certainty keeps faltering. Maybe this diary is full of dirty lies written down to trap Ellen. Maybe she has jumped too hastily to unkind conclusions. She tries to draw back into a less violent doubt—she'd rather blame herself for her wicked imagination. Peg and Lilian? Never! Yes, indignation feels better. That Ellen could have presumed such a thing . . . indeed! Indeed. There can be no doubt. Ellen knows what her daughter would reluctantly admit if Ellen woke her and shoved the diary before her face. Unnatural love.

So this is what modern girls do for fun.

Suddenly Ellen sees through another deception: Peg is only feigning sleep. The girl is lying on her side, her face to the wall, a position in itself revealing since Peg usually sleeps sprawled on her back, arms and legs tangled in the blankets. This, along with the tension of her breathing, reveals the truth. Peg is awake and in all likelihood aware of her mother's decision to plunder her secrets. For a long minute Ellen cannot move. Then she hears a distant chime, checks her watch, and realizes with a start that she has been gone from Mrs. Craxton for over twenty minutes. The lapse fills her with a shame close to horror, and she jumps up and rushes from the room. She won't remember until hours later that she'd left the diary open on her bed, and by then it will be too late. But perhaps she meant to leave it out. Perhaps, without realizing it, she believed that her brazen curiosity must have consequences.

A house that should have been a museum from the start. An eccentric house. An extravagant house, massive and obstinate. Too many corridors and closets. Empty bedrooms. A conservatory with frosted windows, abandoned to the cold. An oak-and-leather library. A dining room with painted wallpaper. An étagère cluttered with fossils, snake skulls, shark's teeth, and butterflies. A dining table seventeen feet in length. A brass candelabrum. A living room carpeted with Persian rugs. Satin drapes. Moose-hoof ashtrays. Mossy antlers sprouting from the walls. Wild animals wearing their own flayed skins. Beetles and bones, seashells and coral. A cup of hot cocoa, cold now. A wheelchair. An old woman in a wheelchair. Mary Alicia Weber Craxton. Mrs. Henry Craxton, widow. Mother. Invalid. Lapsed Episcopalian. A mind shutting down. A slow, voluntary abatement. A magical diminishment. All the clutter that the mind contains. Its history and personality and useless skills. A house. A chair. An old woman with a bad hip. Old Mary Craxton, expert at patience. The mind at work. An ancient machine applying itself to the hardest task, grinding, coughing, sputtering. Everything else put aside, to be sold or given to charity. Only the mind working toward its own dissolution. Driving itself into the darkness. Nothing worth saving. No fear. Secondhand beliefs, useless now. The mind forcing itself beyond life. Old Mary Craxton, expert in confinement. A mind locked inside a body. A body locked inside a house. Snow outside. A gradual slowing. The pit. The barrow. Winter. Three quarters of a century. An old woman with one magnificent trick up her sleeve.

Her head still full of her daughter's terrible secret, Ellen enters the living room with uncharacteristic haste and stops abruptly, as though blocked from Mrs. Craxton by an invisible barrier. It doesn't take more than a fraction of a second to realize what the slumped body signifies. And though she wants to reach out and touch Mrs. Craxton's shoulder, she remains frozen, feeling in some primordial way that the scene is sacred and mustn't be disturbed by bumbling human hands or the sound of her voice. So she doesn't immediately call for help. As soon as Ellen sets life in motion again, the furnishings in the room will fall into place around her, her mundane sensibility will dominate. She hangs back, preferring to extend this moment for as long as possible, to let shy death settle cozily on the body of Mrs. Craxton. It is like sneaking up on some rare animal in the wild and watching as the unsuspecting creature grooms itself. For this brief yet strangely endless moment, Ellen feels privileged, like the only living thing in a museum, the sole witness.

Perhaps the privilege isn't in observing this scene but in watching without any sense of loss. Years ago, when Ellen read the telegram informing her of her husband's death in an unnamed skirmish outside Bruges, emotion had overwhelmed her. She'd already closed the door to the messenger, so there was no one to catch her when she collapsed. Four-year-old Peg had done nothing but stare wide-eyed from the farthest corner of the room while her mother howled, and when Ellen finally regained some control over herself and saw her little girl watching her, she felt embarrassed by her demonstration, as though her bereavement was just a show put on for her audience of one. The child's amazement seemed a more authentic response to the news.

Ellen observes Mrs. Craxton's unmoving body with a similar amazement, wondering how such a quiet thing as death could be so powerful. But her reverence passes swiftly—the clocks start ticking again, wind gusts against the windows, and Ellen is reminded that she must resume her role. She is the Manikin's housekeeper, and her mistress is dead. Is she? Ellen squeezes the puffy, shawled shoulder and becomes aware of the smell of soiled underclothes. She bends over to look into Mrs. Craxton's face and sees the stain of gray already spreading across her lips. She looks into her eyes, the heavy lids half closed, the whites showing like bone beneath split skin. As though she were moving backward in time, she feels a rising panic, the same panic she's been expecting to feel for months, and she responds as convention dictates: she is the Manikin's housekeeper, her mistress is dead, and the world must be informed.

Dead! Dead! Dead! chimes Mrs. Craxton's copper bell. Ellen shakes it fiercely right next to the old woman's ear in a desperate attempt to wake her.

10

Do you hear it, Peg? The bell—do you know what it means? Listen. It means your mother knows about you and Lily. There's the diary to prove it. So that's what she was doing while you lay there wishing her away. She knows, goddamn her! How dare she read the diary. Now she knows everything. Listen to the bell ringing your shame. You're a criminal, according to the law. What are you going to do, Peg? Ask for your mother's pardon? Explain yourself? Defend yourself? What you really want to tell her is that you've made a mistake. You never loved Lilian Stone—you loved the idea of her. The thrill. The danger. Lily was right, you can admit it now. Foolish of you to think that you could follow her home and share her life. Forget her. Leave this place, spare your mother the trouble of sending you away. Here's a thought: escape. Get dressed and run, Peg, run out into the blizzard, run through it, you can do it, you know how to survive. Make it to the train station over at Kettling, and you'll be free forever. Pack the small canvas suitcase, take the money from your mother's purse, and run.

Wait, Peg, listen: Don't you hear it? The tolling of the bell. *Beware, beware!* Stay inside, Peg, pull the covers over your head, go to sleep—the best refuge possible short of death. There have been too many deaths today already. A doomed day. A Christmas full of catastrophes.

Remember, as soon as you enter the hunter's line of vision, you belong to him.

Run, Peg! No, don't run. What should you do? Your mother is ashamed of you. She knows. That's the thing about mothers. Sooner or later they always know. Run, then. Spare her the humiliation. Leave her your gift—an illustrated book about home decoration, which you ordered from the *Ladies' Home Journal,* from an advertisement in the same issue with a feature story titled "Everyone Should Be Rich!" Ah, that caught your eye—in these prosperous times, everyone should and can be rich. Give yourself a few years, Peg, and you'll claim your share of the nation's great wealth. But your mother loves you as you are, Peg, you don't doubt this. Even though you've succeeded in disgusting her. If you lived in our time, a mother like Ellen would tolerate a girl like you. Unfortunately, you're seventy years behind us, Peg, and your mother doesn't want to understand. You couldn't bear to face her. What would you say? If you loved Lilian Stone it would be one thing. But it's not that one thing. You don't know what it is. Or was. An experiment? A trial run? Will there be others? What a muddle. It would be easier if you'd forgotten your own name. Peg Griswood, daughter of a housekeeper. Each time someone says your name you're hammered farther into the ground. Now's the time to go, Peg, or it will be too late. Run. You'll be in Kettling by evening. You can spend the night in the station waiting room and take the first train to Syracuse. And then go on from there, far away from the Manikin and this confusion. Lose yourself, Peg.

What is your name? Your age? Your occupation? You should be able to make up the answers to these questions on the spot, Peg. You're a lady of a sort, "finished" by a provincial academy for girls, good for nothing but marriage to a man slightly your social superior. Oh, you can take care of yourself, Peg, yes, you believe this, you believe this with such confidence that you fancy yourself immortal. Most children do. In this respect you're still a baby, even though you have a woman's body. How much is your body worth? You could ask Mr. Craxton, he'd be able to tell you. Pervert. No, you're the pervert, Peg. Hal Craxton is just an ordinary man with an ordinary taste for young girls. You could have let him fuck you, Peg, he would have paid for the pleasure, over time you could have put away a tidy sum—just like Lilian Stone's daddy. Secrets are expensive. How much will Lily cost you? More than you have, certainly, more than you could borrow. You barely have enough for a one-way ticket to New York City. What will you do when you get there? Rely upon a lot of guile and a little bit of luck. Steal, if you have to. See—your mother has three dollars and thirty cents in her purse. You have twenty-two dollars of your own. Can you start a new life with twenty-five lousy dollars? You'll have to lie about your experience, Peg. And why don't you change your name while you're at it?

Listen: Someone is shouting. A door slams. Mrs. Craxton and her son have probably had another row. Parents and children. Must it always end this way? A diary left out. A severing. Flight. Escape. See how one idea so quickly replaces another. The intoxicating danger of escape. Someday you'll tell the story of your life to someone you trust, you'll describe how you ran away from home when you were sixteen years old. On Christmas Day. In a blizzard. And all the picaresque adventures that followed. The thrill of it. Yes, you'll go, there's never been any question about that. You'll go *now*. A double layer of underclothes—layering's the key to staying warm, you know from Lore. A shirt. A hooded wool sweater. Two pairs of socks. A pleated gingham skirt. Laced boots. You wear whatever you can't fit into your suitcase. Leave the hand-me-down maid's uniform behind, of course—you won't need that where you're going.

Where are you going, Peg? To the station over at Kettling. And from there? Far away. Prove your courage. Go out into the world and make your fortune. Someday you'll return to the Manikin dressed in fox fur and kid leather gloves, a handsome husband at your side, a child in your arms. Is this what you want? Yes. No. Chop off the heel of your foot and maybe the silver slipper will fit. Who would want you? You must make them want you. You must make yourself desirable. Instead, you've hidden yourself in a heap of old clothes. Layer upon layer. A beggar woman wearing her life on her back. Hurry, Peg, or your underclothes will be soaked with sweat and chill you in the open air. Write a farewell letter to your mother. All right, then—don't. The diary will suffice. And when you've settled in some distant place you'll write to her about your travels.

Softly, softly down the stairs. The commotion below has passed, and the house is quiet again, tense with expectation. You hear a jumble of whispers. What is going to happen? What will you miss? Oh, there are adventures to be had inside as well as outside. Lock just one person in a whitewashed, unfurnished room, and there will be adventures. There's a storm raging inside the Manikin even now, Peg, and you're going to miss the worst of it. You're going to miss so much. You'll miss your mother, won't you? Even as you descend, you remember being carried down a dimly lit staircase when you were small, floating in your mother's strong arms, buoyant and trusting. And you remember watching your mother polish a silver tureen, her busy, spidery fingers a chalky pink at the tips. The same thing day after day. Or so you think. You'll show her what a modern girl can do with herself in the modern world. You'll make your mother proud.

Luck is with you today, Peg—the kitchen is momentarily deserted, the activity located in some distant room, the living room or the library. Well, it's no business of yours. You're running away, so take what you can. A loaf of bread. A bag of raisins. A piece of Sylva's applesauce cake. A can of biscuits. Wrap your scarf around your face, pull your hat down, and don't let the wind slam the door behind you. *Good-bye, Mother. Good-bye, Lily. Good-bye, Junket, little brother.* The wind drags away your whisper. Snowflakes like shattered glass. Now it's you against nature, an old story—you know it well, thanks to Lore. Snow already a foot deep, drifts up to your thighs. You don't mind. The more difficult the journey, the more heroic you'll seem at the end. *Good-bye, Sylva.* Keep to the road, Lore would remind you. Go slowly, but don't sit down to rest. Always travel with two boxes of matches—one in your pocket, one in your sack. A gun. You'd be better off with Lore's shotgun. Forget it. Forget everyone. Peg Griswood, daughter of a housekeeper. Forget her, too. Snow against your face. Christmas Day. The blizzard of '27. You will leave the Manikin without a trace. A ghost of a girl. Spirit of the wood. But you never belonged to the woods, Peg. You were born to be a city girl, and now you're merely fulfilling your destiny. A poignant scene. You imagine the silent movie of your life: a bundled girl making her way up the drive, disappearing into the storm. The audience weeps. As soon as you have a nickel to spare you're going to a picture show. You can hardly wait. What else will you do, Peg? Buy yourself a White Castle hamburger. You're not hungry now, but you're anticipating hunger. The effort. Twelve miles to Kettling. Millworth is five miles in the opposite direction. Why don't you go there, Peg? Because Kettling is on a rail line. Because the train will take you into your new life. You should have filched something from the Manikin. Something valuable. The preserved Madagascar moth with its tongue twenty inches long. The sheaf of fossil ferns. Five semiprecious stones would pay for your freedom, Peg. Change comes at a price, like secrets. Some changes cost dearly. Some are cheap. You'll have to manage on twenty-five dollars and thirty cents. Maybe if you had waited and asked your mother she would have given you more. Maybe she would have turned over her meager savings just to be rid of you. But she loves you, Peg, more than you will ever love her. Such is the nature of a mother's love. She wants the best for you. So why did you have to go and disappoint her? Now she can't bear the sight of you. It doesn't mean she loves you any less. Leave her—that's the way you can return her love. She's been expecting you to go. That you would run away like this, without warning, even in the midst of the season's first blizzard, has always seemed inevitable. It is your destiny. You both have known this for years, though you've never spoken of it. Your destiny. Her fear of losing you. As though you were a foundling, born to and abandoned by the gods, and your mother has been nothing but a temporary caretaker. It could be—have you ever thought of this, Peg?—that from the beginning your mother didn't trust you, not because of who you are but because of what she has suffered. She has lost almost everything—you are all she has left. You, and her position. She can't afford to lose her position. But all along she has expected to lose you, and you have taken it upon yourself to fulfill her expectations. It could be—have you thought of this, Peg?—that in her distracted way she loves you too much and has made you feel entitled? But maybe you don't deserve a better life. Maybe ahead of you is a lifetime of service in one form or another, and it doesn't make much difference whether you push on or turn back.

Don't worry, Peg—your doubt is as old as the story that you're living. You against nature. Go forward or turn back? Already your cheeks feel numb from the battering of snow, and you've come less than a mile. Hadley Road, dirt beneath the snow, an unbroken white strip at your feet, smooth as paint spilled from the back of a truck. Crooked, shrubby sumac half buried in snow, and shag-barked hickories on either side. Everything around you will survive the storm. You will, too, Peg. Smell the snow and pine and drenched bark. The fragrance will nourish you. The beautiful smell of life sustaining itself.

Up ahead the road curves around the huge Hadley oak. Rest, lean against the trunk, fold into the bark, disappear. How long has the tree been here? Red Vic once told you that if you feed a handful of acorns mixed with oats to a black horse, you will alter its color to dapple gray. You were a little girl then. You believed him. Remember, Peg? And you believed your mother's stories about the wood-witches. Remember? And Lore's superstitions about the souls of animals. Each beast a necessary sacrifice. When you were older you started telling the same stories to Sylva's boys—to tease them, not to teach. Those boys will be the first to notice the food you took. The applesauce cake. You reach into your coat pocket and break off a piece. Sylva's applesauce cake. Sylva's face glistening with sweat as she kneads a round of dough. Her baby is due in June. You wouldn't want to miss that, would you, Peg? Maybe you'll be back home by then, your pockets full of hundred-dollar bills instead of cake crumbs. Maybe you'll be back even sooner. Maybe, Peg, you'll spend the night at Kettling and return to the Manikin tomorrow. You shouldn't stay away too long—you'll kill your mother with worry. She loves you. So what if you've gamboled and frolicked with a modern vamp? Your mother will forgive you, eventually, just as you'll forgive her. How long is eventually? Is twenty-four hours long enough?

You're not as brave as you thought. Not as eager for experience. But you've come this far. How far? You've passed the Racket Farm—empty for fifteen years, ever since Henry Craxton bought the land. A hollow shell of a house. Roofless barn. Fallow fields. You've come more than a mile and now turn onto Gulf Road. Eleven miles to Kettling. In a blizzard. It's a story you can't wait to tell. The time you walked all the way from the Manikin to the Kettling train station. In a blizzard. On Christmas Day. You were only sixteen years old. Crazy girl. You've always been the mercurial type, always as changeable as the weather in this region. A boisterous toddler, a high-mettled child. Nothing dainty in your behavior—ever. Though you can't hold yourself steady against the kick of a shotgun like Junket can. Poor Junket. It isn't fair to leave him without any explanation. Turn back, Peg. Silly of you to have thought you could make a go of it. Alone. Twenty-five dollars and change in your wallet. You're like Alice in a winter wonderland. A child surrounded by festoons of snow. Garlands and chaplets and bangles of snow. The land bedecked for Christmas Day. Hard to believe that you aren't the only person in all the world. Even stranger, imagining yourself on a crowded city street. You don't want to go—you'll admit it. If you turn back now, your mother might never realize that you've been missing. But you must allow her enough time to forgive you, force her to forgive you. Let her suffer your absence. Let her think that she's lost you forever. You'll make it to Kettling by midafternoon, at this rate. You will keep going, won't you? How snug your body feels inside its burrow of old clothes. You'll go to Kettling, rest there, and tomorrow you'll walk back to the Manikin. Twenty-four miles in twenty-four hours. Junket will be so impressed. *All the way to Kettling in a blizzard!* Your mother will clutch you to her bosom. Lily will stand grinning in the corner of the room. A marvelous homecoming—the audience will weep. Go on, then, and come home tomorrow. But you have no home, remember? You share a room with your mother in someone else's home. A lifetime spent in service. Maids, gardeners, groundskeepers, cooks. Modern slaves working for such low wages that they'll never be able to improve their situation. Yet they insist on treating the Manikin as though it were their own property. Someone needs to remind them that it would take only a few sharp words and Mrs. Craxton could have any one of them put out the door. Or all of them, and they would share your predicament, Peg, you could lead the way to Kettling, and they'd thank you for it at the end. Another fine ending. Strange, how in the midst of the most extreme adventure of your life, you still imagine other versions, always living a double life, one actual, one theatrical. Rather a childish game, don't you think? But here's a little secret: when she was your age, Peg, your mother wanted to be an actress. She didn't want to be a star, no, in her usual pragmatic fashion she dreamed of playing numerous small parts—that way, she figured, she'd always be able to find work. She never told you this, did she? Not surprising, since she hasn't thought of it for years, and she wouldn't want to encourage you in that direction. Or in this direction, either—toward Kettling and the train station.

But you're not paying attention to anything but the effort. Freeing each foot from the grip of snow. The rough work of going forward through the storm. Your pace neither as spry as it was a half mile back, nor sluggish, just steady and careful, your torso tipped forward, as though you were tied to a log, straining to pull it along. Exertion as rhythmic as your breathing. The flutter of your pulse is like a voice urging, *Double march! Look alive! Get a move on!* But you know better than to move too quickly. Remember, you're the prey and cold the predator. *Don't yawn,* Lore has warned you, *or the cold will rush into your throat.* Don't let yourself get drowsy, don't pant or droop or flag, for the cold will trick you into a fatal sleep. Go forward slowly, at your own pace, and don't lose the road.

Stop—a sudden thickening of snow, as though a pillowcase were being shaken overhead, the feathers falling in clumps. You stand in your tracks, marveling at the bulk of snow in the air. So much snow. The wind has relented a bit, and the snow makes a wet, prickling sound as it alights, reminding you of summer, of hot, still days, of cows ambling through tall grass. During summer you could have begged a ride from a passing driver and made this trip in an hour. No motorcars now. Nothing. A prehistoric landscape. Yet even in its severity there is something peaceful about the scene. The weather no longer menaces. You've proved yourself, you've been initiated, the storm has given up trying to bury you, and now it wants to show you its magic. Each thick flake an ornament adorning the woods, the road, and you, Peg. Queen of winter with your ivory robes and silver crown. If Lily could only see you she couldn't help but commit herself to you forever. But she doesn't love you, remember? And you, being the type of girl who can withdraw love on a whim, or so you think, don't love her. Definitely not. You'll avoid Lily for the remaining months of her stay. That's if you go back, of course, and you will, yes, a comforting thought, you'll go back, so you can walk forward with abandon. It's not such a crucial journey after all—it's just one more example of Peg Griswood's impunity. *A wild girl,* people will say when it's all over. *Walked all the way to Kettling in a blizzard. Shackle her to the cellar wall, that's the only way to manage her, lock her in the coal bin.* There's a lesson to be learned from a day in a coal bin, Lily knows better than anyone, and she'll never provoke her father again, not if she can help it. When she acts up she'll do it behind his back, collect her escapades in her own secret book, which she'll hide on the shelf of her richly furnished Victorian mansion once she is married. Everything in its proper place, and if Peg Griswood wants to make trouble, she should go elsewhere. Here. Even if you move on, you can go no farther than this isolated place, this snowy abyss midway between the Manikin and Kettling.

Your own father—you wonder what he'd say about your situation.

You hardly ever think of him, and when you do it's always the same fragment of a picture: a stocky, bearded man stretched on a sofa, sleeping, a newspaper open on his chest. Not today, though—this magical place invigorates memory, takes it to the boggling point just short of hallucination. At any moment a shadowy figure will emerge from between the trees. Your father. You stare into the snow, not expecting to see your father's ghost, merely hoping that if you strain your eyes long enough you might be able to conjure the mirage of him. Your father. How would your life be different if he had survived the war? Your mother wouldn't have been so eager to put you to work, that's for sure. Maybe you would be heading to college right now instead of to the station at Kettling. A different kind of modern life. Work chosen according to your abilities—that's Plato's idea of justice. You read *The Republic* in school. You also learned how to add simple fractions. And to embroider. In the depths of winter you'd stay overnight at the Academy—your mother somehow scraped together the money for temporary room and board. She wanted to get you out from underfoot. Education as distraction. No, it was more than that. She wanted to give you chances that she never had—another old story, one that usually fails. A better life for the children. A life among the feuding, loving, gossiping gods of Olympus. That's what you deserve, in your mother's opinion. It feels like you're almost there, doesn't it, Peg? On the slopes of Mount Olympus. Half educated. Half dead from fatigue. Yes, it's true, you're tired, your body feels as though some potent sedative were working its way through your veins back to your heart, but you're not afraid anymore—you know you'll return to the Manikin tomorrow.

At the end of this stretch of road the next county begins. Already the trees have given way to sky and open fields; the tips of last summer's leveled cornstalks are visible above the snow. In the distance you can see the yellow eyes of a house, a room lit with electric lamps, the two front windows aglow. An Acme Feed Center beyond. A garage yard cluttered with rusting farm machinery. And now, only a gentle drizzle of snow. These signs of the populated twentieth century should comfort you, Peg, yet they have the opposite effect. The forest looked so magnificent in its winter garb, and the fields seem so miserly in comparison. Dirty, spattered snow along the edge of the road. A plough must have come this far some hours ago and turned back again.

Walking is much easier now, the layer of new snow only ankle-deep. And soon you see more evidence of active life: a snowman wearing a stocking cap, and the wheel ruts of a car still visible in the road. As you pass one farmhouse the front door opens, a coatless child scampers out, its mother follows, grabs the child before it plunges down the porch steps, and carries it inside. Ahead, you see a man walking with two dogs—you slow your pace to avoid overtaking them. They disappear at each low rise and reappear when you reach the summit. Occasionally, the man throws a stick for the dogs and stops to watch them leap through the snow.

The appearance of another human being out walking, just for the fun of it, apparently, adds to the bleakness of the scene. Such a paltry drama, this twelve-mile journey. A meager blizzard. You've hardly risked your life. But you've come this far, so you trudge on, irritated by the cold that has begun to penetrate now that you're not overheated by the great effort of motion. Irritated by the distance still to go, as well. How many miles to Kettling and the train station? At least four. The sole remaining purpose to your journey is a spiteful one—you'll give your mother a fright, Peg, and she'll be sorry for intruding into your private affairs. She's probably standing at the backdoor now, calling for you, wringing her hands, though she won't lose much sleep over it, you can count on that, and she won't send out a search party! Ah, you're feeling as mean-spirited as the countryside—bored, too—and there's the growing pressure of your bladder. What are you supposed to do, undress here in the middle of the road and squat? Maybe those two Newfoundlands would like to sniff the little puddle in the snow when you're through. Oh, annoyance, you'll have to hold it until Kettling. All the discomforts of travel, though you're not the first person to complain, Peg, and anyway, you've sought out trouble, you've led yourself into this predicament. On Christmas Day, no less. At least you're alone and can give yourself over to your bad mood with all of your spirited sixteen-year-old temper. Just look at you. It's your own fault, goddammit!

You're so occupied with your anger that you don't even realize you've entered the town of Kettling until the road butts into desolate Main Street, with its streetlights burning uselessly behind the fog of light snow. The train station, a small brick box of a building, looks as deserted as the rest of the town, and the front curb has yet to be shoveled. No trains running today, obviously. Fine with you, since you've long since given up the idea of boarding one.

Small Town, America, 1927, and they haven't started locking the door against transients and vandals. Footprints on the walk winding back to the platform give you pause—who else would seek refuge in such a lonely place today? But a glance through a window assures you that the room is empty. The stationmaster probably paid his daily visit already—a good thing that's out of the way. You won't have to worry about explaining yourself to him. Peg Griswood alone at the Kettling station. What would he say about that? You know him by name—Mr. Felspar—since you've had to tolerate his banter on trips to Syracuse. An elderly man with whiskers so overgrown that he used to frighten you when you were younger. But he's a harmless wolf who wants nothing more than to lift schoolgirls onto and off the trains.

No sign of him or anyone else in the waiting room. You stamp your boots on the planks, imagine for a moment the floor swaying beneath you, like the deck of a three-master abandoned by its crew, a ghost ship, and you have to navigate alone. How lonely you feel—not sweetly alone as you did in the woods, but abandoned. A homeless orphan, for all practical purposes. You peel off your wet gloves and shake the snow from your hat. A soft, metallic *ping* gives you hope that the heat has been left on, but the radiator is ice-cold to your touch. Still, you drape your wet coat over it, and with this simple gesture you begin to feel like a child inside a playhouse. *Ping.* You hear it again. An old echo of heat lost in the pipes.

You use the ladies' toilet, brush out your hair, and tidy yourself just in case Mr. Felspar does make an unexpected visit. Back in the waiting room, you arrange a modest supper for yourself: raisins, bread, cherry soda pop from a vending machine. How pleasant, really. A suitable Christmas feast. *Ping.* If only it weren't so cold in here, you'd be content. But at least you're not the weakly nineteenth-century type of heroine who, under emotional stress, succumbs to a tragic fever. You're as hearty as they come, Peg—a strong-willed, strong-limbed girl with modern aspirations. And sense enough to know that when you finally set out to seek your fortune, you'd better do it with your mother's blessing. She'll be ready to help every step of the way, once she has forgiven you. And that is only a matter of time.

Time plods along obligingly, day folds into night without passing through twilight, and outside the storm picks up again, filling the station with strange wheezing and moaning. The lamps have been left lit on the platform, and they give a gloss to the darkness inside the station. You've been leaning against your small suitcase, but you're tired enough to sleep, so you pull off your boots and stretch out on the bench. The thought of Mr. Felspar coming in now, switching on the light, and finding you here almost makes you laugh aloud.

What did the dog drag in, eh?

It's only me, Mr. Felspar. Peg Griswood!

Fancy that, Peg. The shock you'd give the old man. Pink-nosed, feet up, hair hanging loose. A modern girl. And like most modern girls you've grown unbearably bored with your latest adventure. Or so you tell yourself—so bored you could die. Instead, you'll rest. The distance of the night—from this side it seems as formidable as the distance you've traveled already today. The trick will be to reach morning without waking. Or, if you do wake, to soothe yourself back to sleep as quickly as possible. A long day. You try to subdue your mind by recalling the effort. You weren't scared at the beginning of your journey, and you're not scared now, are you, Peg? Alone in the station waiting room. Not a single train has passed since you've been here. You have the station to yourself. Your little playhouse. Remember the games you used to play with Junket—pretending to hunt, pretending to run away? Make-believe more exciting than the lived event. Even today—hardly worth telling. Twelve miles on foot. In a blizzard. So what? Just another false start. Peg Griswood, daughter of a housekeeper. Your life has yet to begin—this is your last thought before sleep overtakes you and settles like snow upon your mind, burying you.

Wake up, Peg! In your dream, Mrs. Craxton's bell rings with crazed fury, but you ignore it. *Wake up, wake up!* You sleep so stubbornly on your wooden slab of a bed, ignorant of the danger threatening you. Open your eyes, Peg! Don't you see him? A face in the window: snow crystals frozen on his eyebrows, a mustache clipped and pasted into a smiling crescent above the straight, cruel line of his lips. He is looking at you, Peg. Spying on you while you sleep. This in itself is a form of theft—stealing a glimpse of a sleeping body. What you don't realize, Peg, is that this stranger has been hovering about the station all day, peeking in this window behind your bench. More important, he has seen you before. He knows you, Peg, even though you don't know him. He knows all about you. Not an angel and not the devil, Peg. Just one man who has stepped out of the crowded world in order to do you harm.

Who is he? We'll never know. In one guise he is a gentleman—an untrustworthy one to be sure. In another guise he is a butcher. He has no permanent home, no family, no job. He trades one pseudonym for another every few months. He has been living at the Millworth Inn since December, posing as a landscape painter. He, like you, is running away from the Manikin. And it is only a coincidence—a miracle, we might call it, if it had a happier conclusion—that you and he have ended up here, alone together in the Kettling station.

Wake—

But you are awake, startled from sleep by the weight of a man's body. His hand across your mouth so you cannot scream. His other hand holding your wrists. Glint of metal like a fish's eye in water. A flash of comprehension—for a moment you understand what is happening, what he means to do, what he is doing. His knees digging into your thighs, through them, nailing you to the bench. His knuckles, and the flat edge of a jackknife cold against your cheek. Yes, for one brilliant moment you understand perfectly well what it means, and though you try to free yourself from his annihilating weight, your strength has fled, and you cannot even lift your head.

The hand that had been smothering you is groping now, digging in your groin. His mouth against your ear, whispering obscenities. But you can't hear him, Peg, nor do you care what goes on between your legs. Your only fear is that he's going to rip your ear off with his teeth. You're so disoriented that you think the pain you feel is at the side of your head, and you mistake his hot breath for your own blood. There, he's done it, the monster has begun to sever your ear from your scalp, to devour the fleshy lobe while he pounds against you, still cursing, though his words do nothing for you, Peg, since you're unable to make sense of them. You're thinking only of your left ear, unsure whether you have lost it all or only part of it and fearful that you'll lose all memory of the velvety sounds as well—crickets, rain, Sylva's chatter, motors, fire, snow, music, birds, your mother's steady breathing while she sleeps.

Another old story, Peg, what he's done to you, though it's not often told in your day. His final groan brings you to your senses, and you know clearly what has happened. You hate this stranger. You hate him enough to kill him. This is more certain than any measurable fact. Hatred. A splendid hatred. If only it were matched by physical strength, then this man—whose hatred toward you, Peg, is not nearly as pure, as powerful, as yours—would suffer a violent death.

As he plays with you, taunts you, pressing the sharp edge of the knife against your lip, your nostril, your throat, again you imagine his head blown to pieces by a shotgun blast. Imagination is a weak, inadequate defense, but it will have to do. The dream of his brutal death. And it does have some value, subdues you sufficiently so that his words glance off you. Cunts, tits, the broken puzzle of your body—you hardly care what he says because in your mind he is dying or is about to die in an explosion of blood, blown apart by a shotgun like a rabbit, or something smaller, a squirrel or a rat. He will die, and you will survive him. You're not dead yet, are you? And your ear, your ear is still in place, unscarred—you'd be grateful to him for sparing it if you didn't despise him. You've yet to realize that he has spilled your blood, though when you do see it—the thin drainage from your crotch—you won't weep for your rent hymen like some other girls would. To the end of your life you'll deny that this stranger succeeded in stealing your innocence or freshness—he took your body, used it, and returned it to you, injured, perhaps, but not less than what it had been.

And now, at last, he has tired of this sport. While you wait with your eyes squeezed shut he stands up, meticulously rearranges his suspenders, folds his knife. You open your eyes just in time to see a paper bill flutter through the darkness. "For your services," he mutters with a smirk, and you let the bill rest somewhere in the folds of your skirt, imagining his death with such intensity now that you begin to expect it. The door will open, young Junket will appear with his father's rifle, and while the monster is straightening his bow tie, Junket will fire into the back of his head.

This is the way it should happen. And when it doesn't, when the stranger mockingly tips his hat to you, opens the door himself, and sinks back into the night, you let out a howl, not in anguish or fury, but in disbelief. He should not be allowed to go unpunished. He should be killed. Instead, he has slipped away, disappeared forever from the story of your life, and you're just a small, torn body burning inside a heap of clothes, shrieking into the darkness while your mind returns to the beginning and replays the violence over and over, until gradually, one name that he'd repeated rises to the surface of the sickening memory, and you hear him repeating it in a low murmur, as though he'd meant to threaten you with it—"Lil"—the name surrounded by obscenities and hitched, you finally recall with a start, to a revealing possessive: "My," he'd said. "My Lil." It is enough to keep you on the run.

III

SEASON
OF
MUD

11

Beneath the furious skies of March, the land shudders, turns over, and goes back to sleep. *Lazy bitch,* the sky grumbles, and after considering the dormant body for a minute gives it a sound kick, sinking a boot into the brittle soil. The sky kicks again, then again, sets to beating and pummeling the earth, tearing at it in a wild effort to dispel a winter's worth of resentment. And since violence waged against an unresisting body has an intoxicating thrill all its own, the frenzy can only escalate. *Lazy good-for-nothing bitch!* screams the sky. Snow turns to sleet, the lakes and streams turn to slush, the soil thaws into mud. *Take this you loaf, you worthless vagabond!* Spasms and throes will exhaust the sky eventually, but until then it will do its utmost to destroy the thing it ought to nurture. No gentle rains ease the land out of its deep hibernation this year—spring comes in the form of torrents, eruptions, explosions, detonations, and by the middle of the month the frozen earth has been turned into a paludal hell.

But it's not the first time that the land has been abused, and despite the madcap weather and the absence of the sun, a few new plants succeed in reaching the surface of the drenched soil. Tiny shoots grow into clublike spikes and sprout stems, buds the color of frog skin unfurl, and in the cup of the leaves timid flowers emerge. Wild calla, jack-in-the-pulpit, skunk cabbage, green dragons—these are the hardy plants of early spring, and though this year they keep their petals clenched against the storms, they fill the air with the intense fragrance of new life, scents that recall cinnamon and spoiled milk, stirring the animal world to life. Whiskers tremble, hides ripple, snouts root through the wet mulch to find the young shoots, and all the while the rain lashes wildly, enraged more by this early evidence of life than by the land's indolence. For a few days it even seems possible that every living thing will be washed away by the flooded streams and rivers.

Yet behind the clamor of the rain, you can hear a few of the saucier animals laughing at the inclemency. These are the ones who defend themselves against the weather not with shelter but with sex—their courtships are more boisterous than ever, and their pleasure is infectious. On a soggy carpet of myrtle the rabbits flatten their ears against the rain and clamber onto one another's backs, not just indifferent to the weather but virtually unaware. The foxes that prey upon them are made giddy by the taste of their lusty flesh and as soon as they have finished with their dinner they rush back with their mates to their soaked bowers, where they tumble and romp with a vigor they haven't felt for months. Flashes of color in the trees indicate that the songbirds have begun to return from the south, and the flocks of geese heading north are like victory flags of troops returning home. *Shriek and spit to your heart's content,* says the land to the sky, and slowly, almost imperceptibly, the rain relents. There is not enough strength in heaven to keep up the assault, especially in the face of such blithe spirit. Once again, life proves itself indomitable, and for a few balmy days the proverbial lamb gets ready to lead the world into April.

But then, almost as an afterthought, on the last day of March the sky cracks open and lets loose its fiercest blizzard of the year—over the course of two days, snow buries the land in huge windblown drifts, erasing all signs of spring. By the third morning, it looks as though the calendar has played a wicked trick and spun the world back into the darkest midst of the fiercest winter in memory. For the first few hours after dawn the forest and meadows are absolutely silent, as though paralyzed by shock. Toward noon, a single cardinal alights upon the top of a hemlock and begins to sing. As the day warms, the snow starts to drop in wet clumps from the branches, and here and there a rodent digs its way out of a burrow. Slowly, warily, spring returns. The sky watches from the distance, laughing up its sleeve.

Stuffed! Her flayed skin wrapped around an artificial form, her hair wound into a topknot, her mouth extravagantly furnished with ivory teeth. Stuffed! Mary Craxton stuffed! What a sensation that would be! Hal could advertise, send out flyers announcing Craxton's Scientific Establishment's latest acquisition: The Missus Herself. Stuffed! An animal among animals. Hal could take the show on the road and make a million dollars in no time.

Of course, he means no disrespect. His mother remains snugly in her grave, her reputation uninjured by Hal's flight of fancy, and Hal remains on the sofa, half listening to the drip-drop of melting snow. Even with a tartan blanket covering his legs, a fire blazing, the furnace raging below, his kneecaps feel like disks of ice. Not long ago he had thought he would purchase a flat in London's Mayfair and set up home there. But thanks to his mother, Hal Craxton is only one step away from poverty, soon to be cast into the pit of the working class. He might as well throw himself into the belly of the furnace, for his grievance against his mother is too much to bear.

But Mary Craxton stuffed! Now that's a thought to tickle a man out of a sour mood. Stuffed! A seventy-five-year-old female aristocrat, a unique specimen of a precious breed, more authentic than a waxwork copy. Hal had never much liked his mother, truth be told, never enjoyed her company, not even as a small boy. She ignored him through his childhood, and once he was grown and free to travel, she blamed him for ignoring her. Her letters became increasingly cantankerous and more often than not deteriorated into a nonsensical harangue. In recent years, he had begun to wonder whether the old lady was certifiably mad. Unfortunately, he hadn't bothered to arrange a proper psychiatric evaluation. Hal had chosen to stay as far away from her as possible, making infrequent visits simply to remind his mother that he was her only son and sole heir. All for naught, as it turns out.

For an excruciating two days after his mother's fatal stroke, her body had lain in her bed, tended only by the housekeeper, while the men shoveled out the snowbound Manikin. Two long days! With her pale lips pressed tight, her skin the spongy color of buttermilk, her eyes closed in determined indifference, she seemed more powerful in her death than she had ever been in life. For two restless days and two sleepless nights Hal had to endure her company. The men worked slowly, distracted from their main task by unrelated incidents—the housekeeper's daughter, apparently, had run off on a lark to New York City. And then there was the business with the horse. Slashed, according to Lore Bennett, by some vengeful poacher. None of it meant much to Hal, who couldn't think a clear thought until his mother's body had been removed from the house and carted off to the under-taker's in Millworth.

If Hal had known what Mr. Watts, Esquire, was going to reveal to him the day after his mother's funeral, he would have wished his mother had been immortal. Or he would have refused the lawyer en-try. But Hal had no suspicions about his mother's plans—when his father died, it had been implicit, if never legally confirmed, that the entire estate would eventually pass to the surviving son. So when Mr. Watts arrived uninvited at the Manikin, Hal had opened a bottle of his finest scotch, poured two glasses, and solemnly toasted his mother's long and worthy life.

Mr. Watts was a wiry man whose egg-shaped head was topped with white stubble, and while he read the will Hal had studied the deep creases in his forehead. The wrinkles kept bobbing up at the ends so that they seemed to be smiling, though the lawyer maintained his se-rious poise from start to finish.

"I, Mary Alicia Weber Craxton . . . being of sound mind and in full possession of my senses . . ."

Get on with it, Hal had thought to himself, waiting for his name to emerge from the jargon. Mr. Watts must have noticed his impatience, for he cleared his throat and told Hal to pay close attention. Before the lawyer had finished the paragraph, Hal grabbed the page in order to read it for himself:

". . . and for no thought of remuneration but purely out of the large-ness of my heart and a keen desire to help, if possible, the cause of Mankind, do hereby divide evenly said residuary estate among the following charitable organizations. . . ."

"Absurd!" Hal had roared in protest, causing Mr. Watts such a start that his spectacles had fallen off his nose onto the table. "She was out of her mind. You, Mr. Watts! Charity! Everything to charity? That's madness!"

"Calm down, Mr. Craxton."

"Calm! I'll calm you!"

"Then you want to challenge the will?"

"Of course I do! Charity! My mother didn't have a charitable bone in her body!"

"In a codicil, Mr. Craxton, your mother does bequeath the zoological collection to you—valued, she thought, at approximately five thousand dollars. But there is more—an *in terrorem* clause at the bottom of the page. Read it for yourself, if you like. It states simply that if you, Henry Craxton Junior, sole surviving son, wish to challenge your mother's directions, your inheritance will be reduced to nothing, and the said zoological items will be distributed among museums and universities—institutions to be selected by the estate's executor, namely, myself."

"What are you saying?"

"Your mother wished to be remembered as a saint."

"She was a witch!"

"Have you ever heard of Jeremy Bentham, sir?"

"My mother was not of sound mind when she made these decisions, Mr. Watts—you should never have allowed this. You've acted unlawfully, and I will see to it that you are disbarred!"

"Jeremy Bentham was one of the great legal scholars of the nineteenth century, and of all time, I should add. To this day, his skeleton, topped by a wax replica of his head, is displayed within a glass case in the halls of University College, London. The bones are clad in Bentham's own robes, and one hand is curled around the knob of his walking stick, which he called fondly Dapple. It is a remarkable display, Mr. Craxton. And beside the case is a typewritten extract from his will, stating that the testator desired to preside, on certain occasions, at gatherings of his friends and disciples. The direction is still observed, I'm told, at banquets in his honor. Imagine!"

"You put my mother up to this!"

"No, sir. It was her own idea entirely. The hand of the dead presides. This is what Bentham sought to prove. The testator, by the terms of his will, may control the distribution of his property. But there are differences of opinion on this matter, you may be sure. As Thomas Jefferson once wrote, 'The earth belongs always to the living generation.' The rule against perpetuities is designed to protect beneficiaries like you, Mr. Craxton, who have a vested interest in your mother's property, and this may be the policy that enables your lawyer, whoever that may be (should you want to take this matter to court), to invalidate your mother's directions regarding the disposition of her property. But I repeat: Any challenge to the will results automatically in the enforcement of the *in terrorem* clause."

"Leaving me destitute."

"Exactly. Your mother will rest peacefully in her grave, and you will learn to work for a living. In the final codicil of the will, by the way, she provides for your basic expenses for six months."

"Ah, a generous Yankee."

"Truly."

"So I will have to go looking for work."

"That was her intention."

"Good day, Mr. Watts. The housekeeper will show you out."

"My card, sir, should you want to contact me."

"Good day, Mr. Watts."

And that was that, though no sooner had the lawyer left the Manikin than Hal Craxton was shouting for Red Vic to get the truck ready, and they drove at breakneck speed toward Buffalo, where Hal knew an attorney, until, twenty miles south of the city, Red Vic lost control of the truck and swerved across the icy road into a tree. Neither of the men was injured beyond a few bruises, but the collision smashed in the truck's front end and damaged the radiator beyond repair.

The cost of hiring a man to drive them back to the Manikin would have seemed trivial to Hal in his past life. But in his new life the expense enraged him, and the day after the accident he fired Red Vic. The gardener was the next to go—Sid Cheney, who had witnessed the signing of the will. Traitor! Saucebox! Then Hal told the laundress and the chambermaid to pack their bags and get off his property, relishing for a brief moment the exhilaration of tyranny. He had no qualms about sending his mother's servants away—he planned to get rid of them all as soon as the case was resolved, which, according to his lawyer, could take months, even years.

Hal's strategy was a conventional one: he was contesting his mother's claim to sanity. So far, he hadn't had much luck gathering proof. He had his own observations and a handful of her strongly worded letters. The remaining servants at the Manikin refused to provide any concurring testimony, and his mother's physician, who hadn't seen his patient for over a year, proclaimed her thoroughly and honorably sane in his short deposition. So two weeks turned into months, the will remained stalled in probate, and Hal remained inside the house, never setting foot outside, relying on the housekeeper to keep the interior cozy and the cook to keep him fed. Young Lily Stone stayed on through January, and he appreciated her cheerful, babbling company at meals, even felt himself stirred by the glimpse of a bangled arm as she reached for the saltcellar, the shallow dip of her cleavage, the triangles of dark hair in front of her ears. But she was useless to him ultimately, since she had nothing to say about his mother's sanity, and after she left in some haste during a short-lived February thaw, he didn't miss her.

By the beginning of April, Hal Craxton, who'd been traveling around the world for the last decade like a man fleeing prosecution, has grown to enjoy this torpid routine. What is outside but snow and ice, and then rain and mud, and now snow again, drifts up to the windowsills, and branches with pale, furry buds scattered across the yard? In such a godforsaken place, home to a solitary man is like a mother's lap to a young child. Not *his* mother's lap, though—he never found any refuge there. Thanks to her, he's a broken man. His life is over, for all practical purposes, and it's just a matter of waiting for the end.

Or is it?

For weeks, his mind has been veering back and forth between resignation and hope, between the past and the present. While he waits, he experiences the house as though it would be his forever. Oddly enough, he's come to wish that his mother had left him just the Manikin. Nothing else, no stock holdings or treasury bonds—only this great monstrosity of a house. Instead, she left him a collection of stuffed animals and denied him the thing he has come to need most. Cruel woman.

But he has one of the best lawyers in the state working for him, so all is not lost, not yet. There's still a chance he'll win his petition. He, for one, is more convinced of his mother's madness than ever. Who wouldn't go mad out here in the boondocks of the north, nothing but

dead animals for company? *The hand of the dead presides.* The recollection of these words, quoted by Mr. Watts in defense of Mary Craxton's will, returns to Hal as he sits on the sofa. *The hand of the dead
presides.* This is how the absurd notion comes to him—gazing at the
Craxton Collection, he summons up the image of his dead mother
raised from her grave and mounted on the platform among the animals. The hand of the dead, stuffed! Mary Craxton, stuffed!

A few minutes later, he's startled out of his daydream by the April
sun, which suddenly emerges from behind the cloud cover. The reflection off the snow blinds Hal so he can't see what he hears: the sound of
boots stomping through the deep slush. He shields his eyes and
squints—not that it matters much who is out there. But still he stares
until he can make out the stooped figure trudging toward the back
terrace. He recognizes the old taxidermist, what's his name, still hanging on here—Hal had meant to give him notice weeks ago. In his self-
pitying mood, though, he feels a vague kinship with the man. Boggio,
yes, that's the name, Boggio. There's no need to oust him. Spare the old
fellow. He can stay on at the Manikin as long as Hal has any say about
this property.

"We'll be one of a kind soon, you old beggar," Hal murmurs. Poor
old Boggio. Silly old Boggio. Necessary old Boggio. In a tremendous
moment of insight, it occurs to Hal that the Manikin's resident taxidermist must have plenty of strange and relevant stories to tell.

Sun at last, the final thaw, and somewhere Ellen's Peg sits on a bench
eating a sandwich and absently scattering crusts to the pigeons. That's
how Ellen likes to think of her: a city girl on her lunch break. Peg
has proved that she can hold her own among the millions who would
rather see such a girl lying in an alley and bleeding from her throat
than to have to compete with her for a job. It is spring in the far-off
city, and Peg could very well be sitting on a park bench enjoying the
weather.

Listen to the finches chirping—they've built a nest in the yew outside the living-room window. Listen to the drip, drip, drip of melting
snow. Sunlight on snow has a purifying effect. And with Peg's latest
letter in her hand, Ellen feels that no matter what happens next, she'll
manage. Look at her daughter's success—Peg struck out on her own,

quickly found a job in a Manhattan hotel, and now, after three months, she's the second assistant to the managing steward. It's a small hotel with only five maids employed full time. Still, a promotion through the ranks is no small accomplishment, Ellen knows, and perhaps in a few months, if not sooner, Peg will have enough influence to make space on the staff for her mother. At the very least, Ellen can share her daughter's room for a short while. Forget about the mistakes of judgment the girl has made. Peg is independent now, and she's offered (generous, grown-up girl!) to help her mother during the difficult days ahead. So Ellen doesn't need the Manikin anymore. On the contrary, she's eager to join her daughter in the city and would have done so already if she had been a different sort of housekeeper, without any sense of loyalty or obligation. Not that she owes Hal Craxton anything. But she does owe his mother, who employed Ellen for nearly ten years and came to depend upon her so completely that Ellen was expected to be present when she bathed or ate or moved her bowels. Or died. But Ellen wasn't there for those final minutes, and Mrs. Craxton had to suffer alone. For that, and for their many years together, Ellen feels obliged to keep the Manikin in order as long as it remains in the family.

The only immediate family left is Hal. Ellen tends to him with the same cold but diligent attention she gives the furniture. He still has some hope, however unfounded, that he'll be able to retain ownership of the estate. He's wasting his time here, obviously, and Ellen's time as well. She wouldn't have been sorry if he'd fired her along with Red Vic and the others. Billie was the last to go, and since her departure back in February, Ellen has given up trying to keep the house impeccable. Instead, she works to slow the quickening deterioration.

While she sweeps she occupies herself with more pleasant memories so she won't have to think back to the beginning of Hal Craxton's reign, when Mrs. Craxton was newly dead and Ellen's Peg newly missing. That time is over and done with, thank you! And since Ellen can't erase it from the past, she simply, and successfully, keeps her mind directed elsewhere.

So she doesn't disturb herself by thinking about Peg's diary, or Mrs. Craxton's stroke, or the inexplicable violence done to Emily the mare. She doesn't recall how on that terrible Christmas, darkness snatched the light away early in the day, and all night long the blizzard taunted those who were still living, clawing at the windowpanes, ripping tiles from the barn roof, whipping down chimneys, dousing candles with drafts, and forcing snow beneath the door so that by morning there were drifts in the front hall. She doesn't bother to remember how, after she'd discovered that Peg's winter coat, some clothes, and a suitcase were missing, she had gone straight to Lilian's room and demanded information. The girl had insisted that she knew nothing and then had burst into tears. The weeping girl—this is just a vague image in Ellen's mind, like the impression left by a wet leaf upon slate. And the worry that escalated into panic as the night wore on—no, Ellen has no reason to dwell upon that! The hours of not knowing. A captive in the Manikin, restrained by Sylva from rushing outside in her stocking feet while the men searched the surrounding woods. Was her daughter lying wounded, bleeding, sinking into the quicksand of snow? Was she frozen in ice, her skin a blue-gray like the color of Mrs. Craxton's fingernails? Was she dead? Dying? Through that horrible night, Ellen had subjected her daughter to every cruelty she could think of in order to prepare herself for the worst, then retracted each thought because she couldn't bear it, and then forced her mind to continue. Peg was a reasonable girl, but reason doesn't help much when there are maniacs at large. Her daughter was made of flesh and blood, flesh and blood, flesh and blood. In Ellen's panicked imagination, Peg had shrunk to the size of a toddler again, a vulnerable, downy child who couldn't even turn a somersault, much less survive in a blizzard.

The next day, Lore and Peter had combed the countryside for some sign of Peg, and though they didn't bring her back, they did return with reassuring news. Peg had made her way to Kettling, and, according to the stationmaster, she'd boarded the milk train to Syracuse early that morning. From Syracuse to where? That's what Ellen didn't know for six more days, and while she tended Mrs. Craxton's body and paid her last respects, the only scene she could picture was that of Peg on a train traveling west across a snowblown prairie, her forehead resting against the icy windowpane.

But Peg had fled in the opposite direction. A week later, a telegram finally arrived confirming that she was in New York City and already gainfully employed. From then on, as the letters began to follow, Ellen's conception moved closer and closer to the reality of Peg's experience. Though Ellen hadn't set foot in New York since she'd disembarked from the steamer in 1902, she found she could picture vividly the slush packed along the curb; she watched with her mind's eye as Peg hurtled from sidewalk to street and followed her daughter as she weaved through the lunchtime crowds.

And this is what fills her mind now, while she keeps the house in order: thoughts of Peg, her own flesh and blood. Peg feeding pigeons during her lunch break. Peg alive, her existence first felt as kicks and hiccoughs in Ellen's womb. Yes, this is a pleasant thought—Peg frolicking and flailing, a tireless thing. She looked like a stump of beetroot topped with mouse-colored hair when she was born, and Ellen couldn't help but laugh at her as she kicked her tiny padded feet in the air. Tempestuous sprite. Little steamy head, Peg's father used to call her in his letters home. *And how is my little steamy head?* From the moment of Peg's birth, until Ellen was widowed, the world had seemed as noisy, as humorous, as significant a place as it was in her own childhood.

Herself as a child—*remember?* She is like a woman recovering from a high fever, and in her weakened state her oldest memories return to her with false yet convincing clarity. Now Ellen sees her own seven-year-old self squatting on a pebble beach, the muscles of her legs invisible beneath the smooth flesh. And she includes her daughter in the scene, as though Peg were her sister. Two young girls prying up a rock at the edge of a tidal pool, their hair damp and stringy, their faces patched with white from the chalky sand. Next she adds to it the lilt of a woman's voice: "Ellen, Peg!" Two children absorbed by the minute population inside a shallow tidal pool and pretending not to hear the woman's voice calling them to supper. It is the voice of Ellen's mother, who died when Ellen was eight. Peg's grandmother. While Ellen pushes the carpet sweeper around the living room she is so deep in this unreal memory of childhood that she forgets what she's doing. Two girls squatting by the sea, watching the mouth of a barnacle open and close upon brown algae. Two girls at a tidal pool. Mother and daughter. Ellen leans against the sweeper's handle, too immersed in the past now to continue with her work.

And what about her husband? There is little reason anymore to resist the memory of loving him. His boyish seriousness when he proposed to her. How awkward, their early embraces, until they'd learned to trust each other. He'd chosen her, a penniless and plain girl, to be his wife, and her primary emotion before he'd gone marching off to war had been gratitude. And during the war, fear. And after she'd lost him, determination. Her adult life had been spent keeping up with work that needed to be done. There had hardly been time to mourn him once the first burst of sorrow was behind her.

There is time now. Mr. Craxton has practically forgotten her existence, her daughter is a grown woman with a decent job, and the Manikin will have a new owner soon. Ellen tends to the housework by rote, halfheartedly; her main interest is in herself these days. She is like a statue that has been brought to life—no, brought *back* to life—by the shock of almost losing her daughter.

Herself as a child. As a young bride. She was only seventeen when she married, and though her husband hadn't had much money of his own, he'd had the kind of tireless ambition that guaranteed her own future security, she'd felt certain. But war has a way of changing one's plans. Because of that war—the Great War, the first and last war of its kind, surely—Ellen is living the life she'd originally expected for herself.

Memories of that other life fill her with tender melancholy: her husband's whorl of black hair on his chest, his buttocks slippery from sweat, his warm breath. She'll never love another man. Whatever she thinks about Lore Bennett, she'd never want to marry him—or anyone else who might want her for a wife. Ellen Griswood, thirty-six-year-old widow. A man would marry her simply to procure a housekeeper for himself, free of charge. But if she's going to work she expects to be paid. Already her daughter is earning ten dollars a week, nearly twice as much as Ellen earns here at the Manikin, evidence enough that there are jobs to be had out there. With her years of experience, Ellen is sure to find other employment. Good riddance to the Manikin!

But she'll miss this unruly manor, she'll miss its quirks and mysteries. Most of all she'll miss the sovereignty she'd inherited with this position. Keys to twenty-seven rooms. Everything inside the Manikin, valuable or not, living or inanimate, has been her responsibility for nearly a decade. Not for much longer, though. Even now, as she bends down to straighten the fringe of the living-room rug, she wonders whether it is for the last time. All the dust and dead beetles that have found their way beneath the rugs—will they be swept away by someone else? Once all the furnishings have been auctioned off, the Manikin will stand empty, a pariah inhabited by ghosts. No, of course there won't be ghosts. Ghosts are tricks of weary minds.

Take Mr. Craxton—a conjurer if ever there was one. Ellen hears him entering the living room, identifies him by his white oxfords, since that's all she can see behind the sofa from her crouching position. It doesn't occur to her that she will startle him when she stands up, but that's just what happens—he gives a little shout, as though he were walking through shallow water and had been pinched by a crab.

"God's sake!" he says, and Ellen prepares for a torrent of angry words. *God's sake, woman, do you have to sneak around here like a criminal? Who do you think you are making me jump out of my skin like that!* Instead, in a voice so timorous and wounded that Ellen almost feels sorry for him, Hal Craxton says, "Dear Mrs. Griswood. I thought you were my mother."

Ellen tries to force out a nervous laugh, but the only sound she succeeds in making is a soft click. She can't think of anything to say, and in the silence that follows she perceives a change in the nature of his gaze. One minute he is looking at her with relief, the next minute he is full of almost manic glee.

"Were you hiding from me?" he teases, moving around the sofa to position himself closer to her. "Were you trying to scare me? You moved my mother's chair to give me a fright, didn't you, eh?"

"I didn't touch it."

"Perhaps you jostled it without realizing."

"I know I didn't touch it."

"Then we've just had a visit from a ghost!"

"Ridiculous!"

"You are a formidable housekeeper, Mrs. Griswood, if you don't mind my saying so. Yes, indeed, you're not even scared of the dead!"

"There's enough to fear from the living."

"Not in my mother's case. Tell me, Mrs. Griswood, did you like her? I mean, did you consider her a friend?"

"She was my employer."

"She was insane."

"That's no way to talk."

"She was mad."

"She was devoted to you."

"She might have fooled you and the rest of the staff. But I have proof that my mother wasn't of sound mind when she executed her revised will. The old taxidermist, Boggio—he's come forward. Old Boggio will save the day!"

"Boggio?"

"I will keep the Manikin, despite my mother's wishes. And you, I hope, will remain as my housekeeper."

Now it's Ellen's turn to start—her breath catches in her throat as she tries to take in this proposal. If she will remain. . . . Of course she'll remain, if she's invited! Of course she'd like to go on doing what she's been doing for ten years, even if Mrs. Craxton had intended otherwise. If she's not forced out, she won't leave.

"I never thought to ask Mr. Boggio his opinion before today. As it turns out, he's the one who knew my mother best." He slides into his mother's wheelchair, which he himself insisted on leaving in place beside the sofa. "Boggio has told me a story. A very strange story about my mother. A story concerning the disposal of her remains. He told me that two months before her death, my mother commissioned him— God forgive her—to preserve her body for public display. In other words, Mrs. Griswood, to stuff her!"

"You're the one who's mad!"

"My mother wanted to be stuffed! Stuffed! What better evidence than this that she had lost her mind."

"That's a lie, Mr. Craxton!" Ellen does feel like his mother's ghost now; she feels that the right to admonish him is hers alone.

"Boggio has agreed to testify."

"You've bribed him, haven't you? You're paying him to perjure himself."

"Have you ever heard of Jeremy Bentham, Mrs. Griswood?" He pushes the wheels to rock forward slightly against the resisting brakes.

"I didn't know the details of your mother's will during her lifetime. But I can say with complete confidence that she did not want to be, to be . . ."

"Stuffed!"

"You'll be punished for your disrespect."

"So you do believe in ghosts."

"She bequeathed her estate to charity."

"The estate belongs to the Craxton family. I am all that's left of the immediate family now, and I'm going to retain what is rightfully mine. Old Boggio has a story to tell, a story worthy of Poe! What better proof of insanity than this?"

"You will send Boggio to jail?"

"You don't understand. We're going to keep the Manikin, thanks to Boggio. 'We' includes you, Mrs. Griswood."

"What about your mother's reputation?"

"What's a reputation to a corpse? Come on, Mrs. Griswood, my mother was crazy, you know that as well as I do."

"I will not testify."

"I'm not asking you to testify. In fact, I'd rather you kept quiet. Boggio and I will do all the talking."

"Your mother's intentions, Mr. Craxton, are perfectly clear."

"As clear as chocolate cake."

"Excuse me?"

"The chocolate birthday cake she had the cook bake for me every year. I've always hated chocolate. I'll tell you about my mother's intentions."

"She bequeathed her estate to charity."

"You will stay on, I hope. I mean, after the legal questions have been resolved. But I won't ask you to make such a decision now, in the heat of the moment. It will take time for me to sort things out—you should use that time to consider your options. You are a talented housekeeper. I can see why my mother valued you. You are also an excellent woman."

With no more warning than this last compliment, drawled with such significance that the sound of each word hangs like a clarinet's whole note in the air, Hal Craxton pushes himself out of the wheelchair and smiles. It is a smile that diminishes even as it arouses, a smile that mocks any pretension of dignity. From a distance measurable by inches, Hal Craxton smiles at Ellen Griswood with the brazen, insulting, and yet seductive power of a man who has learned to manipulate women. For a few irresistible seconds, Ellen endures his grin, her own expression oddly childish now, gently afraid, as she admits what his eyes are telling her: that she, despite her class and prudish resolve, could be persuaded to desire him.

"Excuse me, sir." She slips past him and flees upstairs to the safety of her attic room.

If Hal Craxton is what people used to call a libertine, he is not without a modicum of self-insight, which makes possible, in turn, a small degree of transformation in his character. When his dialogue with Mrs. Griswood took that unexpected turn into romantic innuendo and then into a charged silence, he felt himself changing into the sort of man who would find a woman like Ellen Griswood "excellent." First he called her a talented housekeeper. How he moved from there to the more consuming praise he'll never know. But rather than recoil in afterthought, he is pleased with himself. That he should even consider this widowed housekeeper a desirable woman surprises him. If he can't seduce a young girl then he generally goes for the spike-heeled, debauched type. So the fact that he can even entertain this new fancy intrigues him. And when she runs off like a scared animal, he must restrain himself from pursuing her. But he does let her go, telling himself that there will be time enough to bring the old girl around. Around to what? A single romp, or something more serious?

The thought of Ellen Griswood's teenage daughter lies at the murky edges of his memory. He'd stolen a few kisses from the child . . . when was it? Last summer? A year earlier? There had been nothing unusual about the encounter. But the memory adds momentum to his burgeoning interest. Not that he longs to make the teenage girl his own. No, he wants the mother. And he wants her more because she is the mother of that beautiful girl. So what if Mrs. Griswood herself is far from beautiful? Her harshness, a worn yet brisk quality to her manner, and a certain cloistered aura all make her a unique example of available women. What will he do with her? He's not sure yet, but he already knows that he must take her more seriously than all his other lovers. And isn't this realization itself an accomplishment?

But right now there is work to do, testimonies to rehearse, letters to write. He'll turn his fate around and reclaim his rightful inheritance, thanks to Boggio. That old beggar will say anything for a dime. And as soon as Hal has his leisure back, he'll invite Mrs. Griswood to celebrate.

12

Legend has it that back in 1911, when Henry Craxton Senior offered to buy the neighboring Gill farm for a premium price, Wincott Gill chased him away with a shotgun. Whether or not the gun was ever really brandished remains uncertain, but the Gills did keep their land. For years afterward they were decent neighbors—they would send bushels of corn and greens over to the Manikin, and in return, Lore and Red Vic would drive the Gills' apples, along with the Craxton harvest, up to wholesalers in Rochester. But ever since the summer of '24, when the older Gill boy knocked his younger brother down the stairs during an argument, the Gills have kept to themselves. Apparently the older son couldn't stand the shame and left home for good. The younger boy, an invalid, hasn't been seen outside his house for three years. And the parents have neglected their land and orchards—last year they even sold their team of horses, harness and all.

Their request for help came as a surprise to Lore. "Seems it costs just as much to rot as it does to prosper," he'd observed to Junket when he'd read their letter through. After two years, the Gills were looking to scrape an income from their farm again. They'd collected twenty gallons of maple syrup to sell at the city market, and they were hoping Lore would make the delivery.

So now Lore and Junket are slopping along the muddy road in the Craxton truck, which had been sitting at a mechanic's through most of the winter. The truck was returned at the beginning of March with a new radiator and a copper-colored hood that couldn't be latched properly to the chassis. The mechanic had tied down the hood with wire to keep it from popping open, but along this uneven road leading to the Gill place the hood rattles so loudly that any conversation between Lore and Junket is impossible.

Lore takes his eyes off the road just long enough to give the boy a glance. *What next?* he wonders. Like Ellen, he's trying to prepare himself for the notice that's sure to come within the month. He'd rather it came sooner than later, so he can know where he stands. The trouble is, he doesn't know where he'll go. He's been a groundskeeper for a decade. Who needs a groundskeeper anymore? Seems the most promising direction for him would be back in time, back to the age when landowners like Hal Craxton still had money to spare. These days, bull market and all, even the richest folks aren't hiring—at least that's the news coming from Red Vic and Sid Cheney, who after two months are still looking for work. How long does it take before a man in search of a job becomes a drifter? How long before the drifter becomes a drunkard, and the drunkard becomes the body buried without a name in the nearest potter's field?

Whatever the chances for Lore, Junket has even fewer. He'll go out into the world with little more than a sixth-grade education and the clothes on his back. That's Lore's fault. He had convinced himself that the huge spread of land in his charge was education enough. So Junket can neatly tuck a bullet beneath the hide of a buck. So what? The best Lore can do is get his son through the remaining years until he's old enough to join the military.

Getting through is the order of the day. The slimy muck of the road clutches at the truck tires, the hood clatters, wet dollops of snow fall from overhanging branches and splatter across the windshield. Used to be Lore wasn't daunted by the weather. But he's grown skittish over the last few months, more easily shaken, ever since the day old Mary Craxton died. Christmas Day. A vexed holiday, to be sure. It had begun with a slashed horse and ended with the disappearance of Peg

Griswood. Well, Peg has done all right for herself down there in the city—Lore should have known she would. The mare is nothing but soggy cinders in a pit, and Mrs. Craxton is dead and buried. The disruptions behind, Lore has folded quietly back into his routines. Yet he still feels exhausted by the events of Christmas Day. Or maybe the exhaustion set in before that, maybe he has never fully recovered from his plunge into the frigid lake, in pursuit of Junket's Maynard. Or maybe it began long ago, and maybe he's been sliding and spinning like the wheels of the truck ever since he lost his wife.

Oh, he doesn't mind being a widower. Ten years, and a man can't help but become used to his solitude. There have been other women, of course: one of the summer migrants, a Danish woman named Ida, herself a young widow. And Jessie, a half-breed girl who worked at the Manikin as a laundress for six months. No serious involvement, though. No one he wanted for better or for worse, including Ellen Griswood. That Ellen would make a good wife and a watchful mother to his son—yes, this has crossed his mind. Crossed and crisscrossed. But he can't entertain thoughts of their intimacy. He has to be able to imagine it. Her. Ellen Griswood in his arms. Impossible! Even the words embarrass him, and he glances at Junket to make sure the boy hasn't read his mind. But Junket apparently has no interest other than in the precarious road—he stares ahead, his worry just short of terror. Now Lore can't hold back a grin. What Junk's expression means is that he wants more than ever to remain in the world. He wants to live, no matter how peripheral he is to the girl of his dreams. And now that she's been relegated entirely to his dreams, now that Peg Griswood isn't around to remind Junket of his hopeless infatuation, he's his chipper self again, not quite a man but trying to act like one. And failing at every nerve-racking bump in the road.

He will be stoical soon enough. He'll have to be, once his father is unemployed. There are hungry days ahead, soup kitchen days, if Red Vic and Sid are accurate indicators of the times. And over there are other indicators—the Gills, Wincott and Nancy, standing on their porch, both wearing high rubber boots and denim overalls. Sure, they'll tell you which way the wind is blowing, just as soon as Lore can put on the brake and say hello.

"Thank heavens it's the both of you and not some shark threatening foreclosure, always a different man, who knows how many bandits they got working for them at that bank, and we're just poor folks tending to our sickly boy. I'll tell you, Lore, things get worse and worse, seems the good Lord doesn't think we've suffered enough." Nancy's complaints sail past too quickly for Lore to figure out the right thing to say in response. So he steps down from the cab with a nod, frowning as he takes Win's extended hand. In two years the rough, plump, farmer's hand has withered to a shrunken replica of itself, bones covered with onionskin. He's wearing a motor-oil cap and a buttonless jacket that seems to be nothing more than pieces of flannel and felt sewn together, with pale, insectlike shapes sprayed across his shoulders— winter buds from a horse chestnut tree, Lore sees on closer inspection.

Win picks up from Nancy, voices the anger that is too spiteful to be honorable. As they lead the way toward the barn, neither mentions their older son, only their younger child, the invalid Derrick, beloved Derrick, who must be brooding in the dark interior of the house. There's no sign of him—all the shades have been pulled and the farmhouse stands in the center of the haggard yard looking as mean and unforgiving as its owners.

The smoky sweetness of boiling sap fills the air around the huge stone fireplace behind the barn. Lore stops listening to the account of financial troubles and concentrates on the pleasures of this crop. Steal the blood from a sugar maple, boil it down, and this is what you get. He squats beside a full pail left out to cool, flattens his hand above the surface, then swirls a finger into the thick, gold syrup and brings it to his mouth. The syrup is still warm and runs from his finger in a thin stream, which he catches on his tongue. The sweetness makes him shudder. The season's first syrup: It tastes of spring and of the pinewood fire that has been burning below the huge pans of sap from dawn to dusk. It tastes of the rain that feeds the trees. It tastes of the candy that the Seneca tribe made not far from here three hundred years ago.

But even more magnificent than the syrup is the sweet water that Nancy offers to Junket—a tin cup filled to the brim with clear, unboiled sap. Lore watches his son drink, smiles at his smile, and laughs aloud as Junk tips the cup again and guzzles it. They are all laughing now, and Nancy puts her lanky arm around the boy, and Win offers another cup to Lore. Water drawn from the trees—this is the wine of the forest, potent, invigorating. It is enough to wash the rage from fury, leaving only laughter. Hearty, three-hundred-year-old laughter.

Their good mood lasts almost as long as it takes to load the boxes of syrup onto the back of the truck. Almost. Junket is carrying the last pint bottle by its neck when something causes him to trip up, and he stumbles, manages to catch himself before he falls, but sends the bottle crashing upon the flat surface of a rock. The Gills and Lore have been talking with happy urgency about the going price of maple syrup— they are interrupted by the sound of shattering glass, and they watch wordlessly for a minute while Junket tries to gather up shards.

"Leave it," shouts Wincott Gill, and since Junket doesn't hear him he has to repeat it. "Leave it, I said!" The anger is back in his voice again. Anger—and contempt as well, which Lore counters with his own powerful, protective shout.

"Junk, come on!" The boy finally looks up, abandons his effort, and trudges toward the adults, his eyes downcast until Lore grabs his elbow and gives him a reassuring tug. Then Junket's eyes rise and flash back Win's anger, and with a disdainful shrug he climbs into the truck.

Win hands Lore two dollars for gas, and after a stiff good-bye he heads back to the broken bottle. Nancy disappears into the house. Lore cranks the starter and puts the car in gear. Unfortunate that the hour had to end so badly. Lore takes away with him not the taste of the syrup but this last scene in his side-view mirror: the farmhouse with its warped, peeling shingles and its blinds hiding the sadness inside, and Mr. Wincott Gill bending down to collect broken glass in his hands.

"Didn't mean to," Junk mumbles.

"Course you didn't." And that is all they say for the next two and a half hours, their meditative silence filled with the clatter of the truck. On the way to the city and back again in the late afternoon, Lore thinks about the Gills and their misfortunes. He should pity them; instead, he resents them and all that they stand for. But even more than that he fears them. Their bitterness is like a dog scratching at the crate where a convict hides—inside Lore is a dangerous, explosive emotion, his own secret rage, which he doesn't dare let out.

Junket has his own secrets, one of which is contained inside his clenched fist. Course he hadn't meant to drop the bottle of syrup, no more than he'd meant to slash his hand. It's a half-inch, shallow cut but ragged enough so the blood keeps oozing. He sneaks the handkerchief from his pocket and wads it in his palm.

And he hadn't meant to stumble. But he wouldn't have stumbled if he hadn't looked toward the house, and he wouldn't have felt compelled to look toward the house if he hadn't been wondering about the two Gill boys: Derrick, a year younger than Junket but with such a round, cherubic face that he looked far younger than that, and John, three years older and nobody's fool, the toughest boy in Millworth's two-room cobblestone school, and if you didn't believe it he'd rub your face in the dirt to prove it. No, Junket wouldn't have been trying to catch a glimpse of Derrick if he hadn't known the Gill boys. Knowing the little bit he did he wanted to know what was left of Derrick after his brother had finished with him. A broken back, people said. As Junket transported the bottles between the barn and the truck, he'd tried to see inside the windows, and it wasn't until the final trip that his gaze slid to the right of the house and then beyond, to the huge horse chestnut tree, and he saw the ladder propped against the trunk and there, tucked into the branches, an elaborate two-story playhouse. The boards looked freshly cut. Lace curtains hung in the windows, a split-rail fence enclosed a little porch, and two-foot-high pine-log colonnades stood on either side of the miniature front door. No, Junket wouldn't have stumbled if he hadn't been staring at this marvelous playhouse, and he wouldn't have dropped the syrup if he hadn't suddenly imagined the father carrying his son up the ladder.

For the rest of the long drive Junket can think of nothing else but this: Derrick clinging like a bear cub to his father, Mr. Gill carefully climbing rung by rung up the ladder. How many months did the father spend building that treehouse, and for what? For play. Merely for play.

Only much later, long after the wound in Junket's hand has crusted shut and he is back at the Craxton estate lying in his own bed, will it occur to him that for the first time since she left home, Peg Griswood hadn't entered his mind all day. Not once.

Each day warmer than the last. The tide of snow recedes, leaving behind scattered papier-mâché mounds filthy with the mud splattered by wind and rain. Mud everywhere. Mud in the crevices of rotting logs, mud coating the shrubs and weeds, mud clinging to the tiny cones of the evergreen twenty feet above the ground.

Look at the muddy ground. Look carefully, with a crow's sharp black eyes. Spring is the season of mud, and mud provides a velvety carpet for trinkets. In spring the earth gives up its hoard—broken bits of china, ginger-ale caps, pieces of ribbon, painted blocks of wood. *Swoop down, bounce with rubbery feet upon the soft earth. Circle the trinket, calculate its value and weight, and then snatch it up and fly back to the roost.* But what if one crow steals what another has found? Then a crow tribunal is called to settle the dispute. That's when the air is filled with their weird cries, hundreds of angry, opinionated voices pitched in varied keys.

The little treasures can have no real value to a tribe without a system of exchange. Crows build their nests with duller stuff: twigs, ragged canvas, clumps of fur, strips of hide, shredded bark. Oftentimes a trinket doesn't even make it back to the nest but is dropped in flight, forsaken in favor of some brighter object.

Still, until the May beetles and grubs appear in the newly plowed fields, the crows search for the glittering treasures as though their lives were at stake. Day in, day out, they hunt for the inedible refuse that the mud spits out. And if in their court of law they decide that one crow is guilty of stealing from another, they will close in on the guilty fellow and strike at his neck and head, *peck-peck-peck-peck,* until he falls from his perch, bounds heavily from branch to branch, and plummets like a stone to the ground.

All week long Hal Craxton is occupied with lengthy telegrams and letters to and from his lawyer, Mr. John George, and on the following Wednesday Mr. George arrives at the Manikin with his assistant to interview Boggio. Amazingly, Boggio sticks to the story Hal concocted for him, and afterward Mr. George declares that the testimony does indeed give strength to his client's petition. Another factor in Hal's favor is that the original will remains extant. The trick, then, is to persuade the court to declare the revised will invalid.

After lunch, while the assistant is going over the testimony again with Boggio, Mr. George and Hal retire to the library to discuss in a more casual fashion the intricacies of this unusual will and the state of mind of the testatrix. Craxton spent the morning arranging family photographs across the mantel and desk, along the windowsills and walls, so the function of the room has come to seem solely memorial. He offers Mr. George a cigar and light. The lawyer puffs to spread the spark of the flame, settles his wide-waisted body into the depths of the chair, and says, "Quite a story you've coerced from that Boggio."

Hal wonders whether Mr. Watts and Mr. George are in cahoots, then decides against it and tells himself that his lawyer's suspicion is deserved. He waits a long minute before replying. "There was no coercion," he says quietly, occupying himself with the family photographs, turning the frames this way and that. "My mother was mentally unstable."

"You do realize that your petition could take months, Mr. Craxton. Even years."

"I understand, Mr. George."

"And the costs?"

"I understand, Mr. George."

"It is unfortunate," sighs the lawyer elusively, taking out his handkerchief to wipe the perspiration from the beefy folds of his neck. Hal adjusts two framed pictures on the mantel—one a daguerreotype of his young mother, the other a photograph of his father near the end of his life—so they are facing each other. To make small talk, he says, "Boggio was the preeminent taxidermist at Craxton's Scientific for over forty years. My father trusted him with the most important projects. Maybe it's hard to see it, but that man is a genius."

"It's true, his intelligence isn't immediately apparent," says Mr. George.

"My mother never had her portrait painted. You can't blame her for commissioning a likeness late in her life. A peculiar sort of likeness, to be sure."

"Your mother was not of sound mind, was she, Mr. Craxton?"

"That's the point, isn't it?"

"It would be a shame to lose this lovely house. And the collection. The animals."

"You don't think we'll lose, do you?"

"I think we have a strong case, but by no means certain. Nothing in law is certain, Mr. Craxton."

"As it should be, Mr. George."

And so they murmur on, dancing around the subject of Mrs. Craxton's madness without ever directly discussing it. Finally, Mr. George belches quietly into his fist and announces that he must return to the office. After fortifying the lawyer with a quick scotch, Hal sends him and the assistant on their way. As he stands on the porch and watches the two men slop across the muddy drive to their automobile, he breaks out laughing—at what, he's not sure himself, but he laughs so loudly, with such a strangled, rough guffaw, that both men look up at the same time, not at Hal Craxton but at the sky, as though they expected to find some huge carrion bird circling overhead.

"We live in a matriarchy, my dear Mrs. Griswood. Whether we like it or not, the American woman rules. As well she should. Think of the American man as a driver and civilization as his motor. The man who drinks too much of this illegal beverage will drive civilization over a cliff. So it's up to women to prohibit excess. Women like you, Mrs. Griswood. Women of great moral courage and wisdom. But beware, because men like me will tempt you. They'll offer you a glass of whiskey just like this glass of whiskey. They'll invite you to sit beside them and enjoy a lavish dinner. But no matter how clever their seductions, you must refuse them. We depend upon women to refuse us. If you stop refusing, I'll drive my motor straight over a cliff. So what do you say to an aperitif, Mrs. Griswood?"

"Thank you, Mr. Craxton."

"The woman drinks! Corruption, sin! She drinks! We shall be turned out of paradise, waving fig leaves and weeping. All the same, it is exquisite liquor, isn't it? You don't have to be a connoisseur to appreciate it. Considering the concoctions that are sold these days—isopropyl laced with embalming fluid, water colored with iodine—considering these so-called whiskeys manufactured by the bootleggers, this scotch is pure gold."

"I wouldn't know."

What does she know anymore? Certainly not herself! Ellen Griswood, housekeeper. Ellen Griswood standing in the dining room and sipping scotch whiskey the color of a cat's eye in the dark. Other than the liquor that Sid sneaks into the eggnog every Christmas, Ellen hasn't had an intoxicating beverage for years. She still associates whiskey with the only man she has known intimately, and long before that, with the bitter fragrance on her father's breath in the evenings. So why she has let Hal Craxton provoke her into joining him, she can't say. At most, she'll admit a curiosity, not about him but about the possibilities. If she doesn't refuse him, what will happen? How daring can she be? There is something about Hal Craxton that gives him a mesmeric power. His tired handsomeness? His interest in her? His sophistication? Or perhaps just his would-be claim to the Manikin—yes, that is a definite attraction. And here Ellen is in a woolen dress, plaid, with a high collar and sleeves that end in lace ruffles, not an elegant dress by most standards and not even her best dress, but her favorite—and she has put it on for him. To what end? This morning when she came out to pour his coffee, he invited her to dine with him at supper so they could talk at length about domestic matters. Now she is hardly surprised when their conversation wanders toward more charged subjects.

"You have much to learn, then." Glasses clink together, lips part, liquid spills into mouths. The scotch peels the coating from Ellen's tongue; another sip cools the burn. She sets down her glass on a teak coaster and inhales the dinner smells—yellow pike spitting in the griddle, wild rice bubbling down to porridge. Though in her years at the Manikin she has cleaned, polished, set, and cleared the dining-room table, she has never sat and had a meal here, as she will tonight. And tomorrow? Forget tomorrow. She's curious about the immediate consequences of Hal Craxton's advances. Yes, she'll join him for dinner. Yes, she'll have a drink. Thank you. Thank you, Mr. Craxton. Sir.

They take their seats. When Nora brings in the first course, a creamed potato and turnip soup, Ellen stares at the table to keep from meeting the girl's eyes. But she can't escape the force of Sylva's disgust—she feels the cook glaring from the kitchen through the closed door. Sylva will never forgive her for breaking bread with the enemy. The pretense of business does not alleviate the impact of Ellen's treachery.

After Nora has left the room they eat their soup in silence. Hal finishes before Ellen. He folds his arms, leans back in his chair, and beams at her until she puts down her spoon.

"You didn't believe I could do it, did you?" he says, teasing her with an enigma to draw out her confusion. But she knows what he's referring to, even though more than a week has passed since they discussed it.

"The Manikin."

"It's mine. Easy as a bowknot. We've got old Boggio's testimony. Oh, there will be lengthy litigation, but for now we can stay put and call this house our home."

"This isn't what your mother wanted."

"Do you really believe my mother knew what she was doing when she revised her will? She was confused. And in her confusion she forgot she had a son."

"Your mother was angry with you for neglecting her."

"You don't have to take her side anymore. You'll benefit from my efforts, I assure you, Mrs. Griswood. And now you must celebrate with me, whether you like it or not."

He's right—she's come too far to reverse the direction. She can't return to the indignant beginning, when she blamed him for his greed. No, dignity won't permit her to go back. And if Hal Craxton really believes his mother was mad, Ellen won't try to prove otherwise. It could be that Boggio is telling the truth. In such a place as the Manikin, surrounded by dead things dressed up to look alive, an old woman might very well desire the same for herself, an afterlife in a museum, Mary Craxton as a natural history display, weird queen of the menagerie.

And how lively her son seems in contrast. Ellen appreciates him for this if for nothing else and listens with real interest as he discusses the changes he intends to make at the Manikin: electricity and proper plumbing, a new stove, a telephone.

After they've sipped their black coffee and finished their port and candied figs, her host falls silent. The corners of his lips twitch and then spread into that demeaning grin. If he lifted her hand and kissed the top knuckles of her fingers one by one, she wouldn't pull away—this is the effect of his smile. Instead, he lifts a cigar from his pocket, clips off the end, and inserts it in his mouth without bothering to light it. He's right, she admits to herself. She'll benefit from his maneuvering. All along she'd thought his efforts useless. Now his success seems inevitable. Maybe Mary Craxton secretly intended her son to inherit the estate, after a temporary scare. Charities were never more than necessary annoyances to the old woman, and though she'd set aside a small amount of her income each year for donations, she'd inevitably find excuses to spend that money on herself, or on her son. Whenever he needed money for his travels, she'd wire him the amount he'd requested. And though she'd scold him in her letters or in person, she never deprived him of anything.

"The other day, when I thought you were my mother—"

My mother. Ellen Griswood is queen now. She has taken Mary Craxton's place at the head of the table.

"—I saw you, Mrs. Griswood. I saw you for the first time. You are still a young and vital woman."

His eyes—like silky hands gliding along the sharp curve of her jaw, tracing the outline of her ear, cupping her chin. They fix on her lips, as though trying to force them apart. Master's insolence. Droit du seigneur. Ellen should feel insulted by his stare, but on the other side of the kitchen door, Sylva is feeling the burning shame for her, so Ellen is free to feel nothing but a lascivious curiosity.

It is not the same as love. She wants to find out where this will lead, even though she will refuse him, should he try to take advantage. Or so she tells herself. Yet here she is sitting with him as his guest and enduring his gaze without a word of protest. More than a week has passed since he called her "excellent," but still the thought of his praise makes her cheeks warm. Master and housekeeper, prince and concubine, man and woman. Maybe she'll even enjoy the debasement. Certainly she enjoys imagining his lips brushing against her work-worn hands. And his compliments please her—no denying that they please her. The evening feels as unreal as a dream, as though no permanent damage can be done. But this is not her familiar lighter-than-air dream of love, herself as a young woman floating in her husband's arms. Make no mistake—Hal Craxton is not a body with a blank face, which she can fill in with the image of a better man. He is the wicked son of the woman Ellen served for a decade, and it is his wickedness that makes possible her interest.

"May I show you something?" he asks. Yes, he is wicked, but she is obedient, and though she knows the appropriate response would be to thank him for the meal and excuse herself, she nods and rises with some awkwardness from her chair.

"The library." He gestures for her to lead, and for the twenty or so steps it takes to pass between the sliding doors into the library, she assumes he is watching her, measuring her from behind, comparing her to other women. For the first time in the evening she does feel a twinge of shame—not over what she's doing but because of what she'll never be. And then she hears the clatter of pots in the kitchen, reminding her of Sylva's disapproval and the adventure ahead of her. Oh, how her pulse flutters when Hal Craxton pulls the heavy oak doors together! How her cheeks burn as he approaches her and without touching her glides past. He opens the top drawer of the desk—his father's desk, a wide block of varnished mahogany resting on ball-and-claw feet—and pulls out a single picture.

"My mother, when she was in her thirties. See, I haven't imagined a resemblance between the two of you. You could be her daughter."

Ellen pinches the edge of the frame. She can't be sure whether she's seen this particular daguerreotype before, but she has seen others. Here, Mary Craxton poses alone on a porch swing, one arm hooked around the supporting chain, the other hand hidden in the lap of her dress, her head partly blurred by the sepia tint. Hal Craxton did indeed imagine a resemblance. With her round face and blond curls pasted in place, the woman in the picture looks nothing like Ellen. So why does he insist not only on making the comparison but proving it?

"Sad, isn't it?" he murmurs. "The mind's deterioration . . ."

Let's not fool each other, she'd like to say. He didn't invite her to dinner to mourn his mother's sanity. They both know what they are here for. Filth. Ellen wants to perfect this unfamiliar part, to impress Hal Craxton with her sophisticated interpretation of the role. But it wouldn't impress him, she knows. So she stands with a demure rigidity, still holding the photograph, her elbows pressed against her sides. After a minute or two he walks farther away, turns his back to face the cabinets below a bookcase, and says, "Brandy?"

"No."

A meaningful no. A tantalizing no. Surely he understands its paradoxical implications.

"No." He repeats it, rolls the word around in his mouth as he takes out a bottle and tumbler. "No." He pours himself a drink but leaves it, along with his unlit cigar, sitting on the shelf as he approaches her. "No," he repeats with a chuckle, positioning himself behind her. *No.*

Yes. Go ahead. He will lift her hair and nuzzle the back of her neck. He will kiss her from her shoulder's soft swoop up to her hairline. Kiss her with his long, sandy tongue, and then gently seize her earlobe in his teeth.

He is talking about liquor again, its pleasures and ill effects, but in Ellen's mind his hands slide under her elbows from behind and follow the curves of her body to her breasts. His hands on her breasts, cupping and massaging. She imagines how it will feel, at the same time insisting to herself that she must never let it happen.

Now he stands slightly behind her and to the side, peering over her arms to study the picture, murmuring something—she can't make out the words and doesn't bother to ask him to repeat himself. One half step would bring him close enough so that she could feel his breath against her cheek. His hands, his tongue and teeth. Silky palms against her breasts. The hard bulge in his trousers. Even if she tried to resist he could overpower her with a quick twist of her arm.

She has no knowledge of the encounter involving her daughter that occurred in this same room a year ago, and of course she doesn't know what was done to Peg by another man in the Kettling station. But she lets herself imagine her daughter in her place. Call it prescience, or just a coincidence—for a moment, she imagines herself as her daughter and understands why Peg would prefer to find her comfort in women. But it is too bitter an understanding to tolerate, so she turns away from it in disgust, turns, and in doing so finds herself face to face with Hal Craxton.

What is he thinking? She can't bring herself to ask. Nor will she confess her own thoughts. But they stare at each other suspiciously, and when the mystery of their gaze becomes unbearable they close their eyes and press their mouths together. She parts her lips slightly, rests her hand in the arch of his back. How compliant his body feels. She could unbutton his shirt while they kiss, open him like an envelope and drop her hands inside to feel the downy mound of his chest.

Later, she will rehearse it over and over in her mind in an effort to experience it from his side. But for now, she is lost in the excitement and kisses him as if she really did love him. A perilous *as if*—she'll come to believe it if she's not careful. How can she be careful at such a moment? She'll be bold and pay later. Pay with her own blood, if need be, the agony of labor, a bastard child. The danger should temper her passion—instead, it makes her dissolute. In her momentary wildness, she tells herself that she'll do anything for this man, even bear his child, even die, yes, she wouldn't mind if he stopped caressing and instead gripped her neck and strangled her because this is what she deserves, isn't it? An *S* branded on her cheek for shame, and then death, death to the women who love beyond their station.

He leans back, lifts his hands with the abruptness of a man suddenly repulsed, and their tongues separate with a slight sucking sound. "I . . ." He gropes for the words. "I . . . Forgive me."

"Yes." She hears a distant cough—Sylva or Nora in the kitchen. Their disapproval seems just as distant. Ellen Griswood, housekeeper. Such a naughty old girl, kissed by the master, soon to be the Manikin's laughingstock. She wants to laugh too, laugh at herself for her suicidal guilt. She's a grown woman, middle-aged, Presbyterian by birth and prudish by habit—well, it's a habit that has grown tattered from overuse, so she'll strip and start from scratch, and if Mr. Henry Craxton Junior wants to strip too, she won't stop him, no, just the opposite, she'll help him along by opening the fly of his trousers button by button.

The pale cast of his face, inherited from his mother, takes on the sheen of honey in the lamplight. The two standing lamps must have been left burning during dinner, Ellen realizes, which means that Hal Craxton lit the lamps himself. The lamps, then, are part of his design, along with the dinner, the drinks, his mother's picture. Everything has fallen in place for him, including Ellen Griswood, and now he's going to play with her, lure and repel her until she makes herself sick with desire. Her widow's body feels like soft clay. She moves sideways a few steps, leans against the arm of the wingback chair, and watches as Hal stoops to pick up the daguerrotype that she had unwittingly dropped. He studies it again, oblivious to Ellen now, and she squeezes her eyes shut to block the image of his indifference. Darkness floods her mind, and from within it emerges the silhouette of a face—her daughter's face, still childishly plump and snub-nosed. Her child sitting in darkness, staring at something that Ellen can't see.

"Mrs. Griswood, are you all right?" Hal asks with some amusement and answers himself, "But of course you're fine. Mrs. Griswood is always fine."

Of course.

She rises with a reassuring smile, thanks him for the evening, curtly bids him good night. She does not even offer him her hand.

13

James McCreery, in his book on the subject, suggests that the end result of the natural history museum is the satisfaction of human wonder. How are life-forms related? Why did differences arise? The museum promises to put such questions to rest by replicating the cyclical events of nature in all their theatrical splendor. With its lifelike specimens posed in action and mounted in muraled alcoves, the diorama—or "habitat group," as it has come to be called, since it represents different species of plants and animals coexisting within the same setting—is designed to give visitors the feeling that they have been transported to a distant part of the world, a feeling that has intensified with the advances in taxidermy. In museums across the country, the lights are kept dimmed, skeletons of dinosaurs reach to the ceiling, whale carcasses hang overhead, and the elaborate displays tell the story of nature, an exciting story that doesn't want for violence.

Today, a typical natural history museum offers hands-on computer games, creepy-crawly houses, exploding volcanoes, big-bang shows, orbiting planets, simulated rain forests, drops of pond water magnified one thousand times. The museum thrills even as it explains, illuminating nature in all its vicious and still logical particularity. For nature is logical, according to the story told by a natural history museum. Follow the story from mineral to stone to fossil to fish to reptile to mammal to man, and there you are, the net result, the reward for all the suffering that life entails, as well as the culprit: you, the reason for your questions, and the answer.

Yet there are smaller out-of-the-way museums, underfunded and poorly maintained, that display their animals like articles of used clothing, like stoles and hats and coats that have long since fallen out of fashion and are interesting only as memorabilia. In such places, you're apt to find the plate glass scratched and grimy, the light so glaring you have to strain to see the animals within the cases. These museums tell a different story, one truer to Darwin: of rough-and-tumble congregations where there was never enough food on the banquet table to go around, so they'd erupt in bloody free-for-alls. Afterward, a few survivors would creep back into the forest and carry on the species, sustaining themselves, if not thriving. It is a melancholy story, occasionally punctuated with surprises—two-headed sheep, albino starlings, mountain goats with three eyes, Cro-Magnon skulls with holes drilled neatly through the cranium. Visitors will leave more puzzled than ever, wondering whether there were any purpose to this madness, wondering whether the whole concept of evolution is some great paradigmatic joke, at their expense.

Musculus: pectoralis major and minor, easy enough to imitate, though the nearby detroideus could be trouble, and the sartorius, oh, the sartorius, now that will be fun, running as it does right beneath the plump inner thigh and heading up to the adductor longus, the seductive adductor longus, so much like the base of a braid twisted into a regal topknot, the tissue wrapping in neat strands around the bone, according to the diagrams in Henry Craxton Senior's copy of *Gray's Anatomy,* which Boggio has pilfered from the Manikin's library. The trick is to construct a perfect illusion from clay, wood, and papier-mâché, so that the stillness of a finished trophy will evoke motion, the glass eyes will evoke rage, and, most important, the mouth will evoke sound. A mediocre taxidermist cares only about surfaces. But peer into the orifices of Boggio's animals—the throats continue into the darkness of the neck, the nostrils snake back into throat, and his anuses are always longer than the longest forefinger. So much unappreciated effort, but still, Boggio worships quality, and with any one project will take painstaking care to make the form accurate so that the rippling muscles correspond exactly to the original body and the hide fits as tightly as the skin around the flesh of an apple.

And then came the supreme challenge. Not that Boggio ever believed in the opportunity. He may be a fool, but he's not so foolish that he mistakes a fiction for truth. He was responsible for delivering the testimony, that's all, just a testimony contrived by Craxton, recorded word for word, and signed by Boggio, with his characteristic flourish at the end of his name, a curlicue rising above the final o.

But Boggio has been letting himself imagine it. Strange that he never let himself imagine this ultimate trophy before. Certainly he'd noticed the uncanny similarities between, say, a woman's hand and the long-fingered paw of the lemur he mounted years ago, when Craxton's Scientific was in its early heyday. Or the human expression of the silverback gorilla Akeley brought back from Africa. But to represent the human species itself, to turn actual human flesh into a museum display—the ambition had never even occurred to Boggio. Or if it occurred to him in some shadowy corner of his mind, he didn't let himself indulge the thought. It was Craxton's idea, a lie worth one hundred smackers to Boggio, along with the guarantee that he could live out the rest of his days at the Manikin. Mrs. Craxton stuffed and mounted, frozen forever in the midst of some quotidian act. Since he agreed to take part in the plot, Boggio has spent long hours imagining the splendid detail possible, the orifices leading into the dark interior of the false form, the artificial tongue sinking into the trachea, the trachea disappearing into oblivion. And that other oblivion between the cavernous hips—the dark soul of woman. He could make a perfect imitation if he were given free reign. He'd buy the most expensive glass eyeballs from a prosthetic supply company. He'd mix up a concoction of sawdust and clay to stuff into the duodenum to plump the abdomen. He'd collect a cupful of chicken shit and pack it into the rectum. He'd commission the renowned waxwork company in Portsmouth, New Hampshire, to make a wax meal—turkey with all the trimmings, a glass of wax cider—then he'd sit Mrs. Mary Craxton at her table in all her fleshy splendor, and if anyone tried to lift her and move her to another setting, out would drop a healthy turd or two.

Boggio, you old devil, you! It is noontime on Saturday after a tumultuous week full of bribes and lawyers and questions and lies. There's no going back now, no undoing the story he's been paid to tell. *Old fool.* Maybe he's a fool, but he's a mischievous fool who answers to nobody. Old Boggio, nobody's fool. What fun he's had imagining the challenge of an old woman's body. He'd smooth away air bubbles so the skin would fit everywhere, even over the two lumps of loosely bound excelsior—the sagging breasts—even over the wrinkled clay wattle beneath her chin. He would work the skin, coax it to shrink wherever it appeared superfluous and stretch it into wrinkles and folds in the appropriate places. Boggio knows no more powerful pleasure than this: crowning a well-made manikin with a skin and seeing a specimen take on perfect shape, as if by magic. There is no art closer to magic than Boggio's art. The art of exact representation. The only thing he can't give back to Mrs. Craxton is her life.

Her life. And so the humbling thought intrudes at last: life, with all of its heartbreaks and adventures. Life. No, he can't bring Mary Craxton back to life. The admission, however obvious, is enough to darken Boggio's mood. He is sitting in front of his work table, his hands palms down on the wooden surface. It occurs to him that he has to piss. He always has to piss, there is hardly a minute when he doesn't have to piss. And his muscles ache, his entire body aroused by his flight of necrophilic fancy. He feels as though he's been old for seventy years, as though he'd been born wizened and feeble, the world too much for him before he'd even learned to walk. Poor old Boggio. Mad old Boggio. He's the butt of every joke that's ever been told, brought into existence for the sole purpose of supplying all the mudslingers with a target. He wipes the mud from his eyes with his thumb. Craxton's mud. Boggio gave him what he wanted—a false testimony about Mary Craxton's desire concerning her remains. Boggio is one hundred dollars richer for it, as well as a resident of the Manikin for life—providing, of course, that Craxton wins his petition. He will win, thanks to Boggio. But what a huge, debilitating effort of the imagination, and Boggio's god is laughing, yes, Boggio's god is thoroughly amused—and thoroughly appalled. To think that foolish old Boggio could aspire to such a grand act of profanity! There will be no forgiveness.

Damn fool Boggio. All that's left is to return the insult. *Come on, you old clown, just do what I say, don't think twice.* In Boggio's confused mind, he has agreed to a sinful act. He'll never see the angels now. He has deprived himself of salvation. It was Craxton who corrupted him. So Craxton must be punished, too. But what can Boggio do to ruffle such a powerful man? A teaspoon of gunpowder in his cigar? A dead mouse in his soup? But these are old tricks, and knowing Craxton he'd just spoon the mouse out and continue eating. What Boggio would really like to do is to put his mouth flat against the sleeping man's ear and scream loud enough to burst his eardrum. Even the most sophisticated gentleman will lose his poise if he's woken from a deep sleep with a bloodcurdling scream. But Boggio doesn't have the voice for it, nor the courage.

His head pivots, his attention drawn by the magnetic summons of his most perfect creature, his beloved snowy owl. Now here's a thought. "Yes," Boggio murmurs, continuing the conversation aloud. The owl sits on the windowsill, shrieking silently, its evil eye fixed on some spot on the wall beyond Boggio. *Ah, yes, of course.* Boggio will use his snowy owl to get back at Hal Craxton—he'll return abuse with abuse and scare the master silly. That's what Craxton deserves for corrupting Boggio's imagination, along with his name. "Yes," Boggio repeats with immense satisfaction, settling back to wait for the night. He will see to it that the man gets his just deserts. "Yes, indeed!"

What a day, what a blustery, invigorating spring day, the perfect day for a fancy gentleman to tour the countryside. And since Hal Craxton no longer has a full-time chauffeur on the premises, he has no choice but to solicit the help of his groundskeeper.

The touring car, a fancy La Salle, was purchased last summer by Mrs. Craxton to replace her Stanley Steamer, and it has been sitting in the garage for four long months. It takes all morning for Lore to bring the automobile off its block, put the wheels back on, and get the motor running. Craxton's original idea had been a morning drive with lunch at the Millworth Inn. Although he had to change his plans and idled away his morning waiting for Lore to coax the La Salle awake, he's in a cheerful, backslapping mood when he finally crosses the muddy drive—on tiptoe, to keep his oxfords clean—with his crocheted auto blanket slung over his shoulder and his cap cocked back on his head.

"Ready to go, old Sally?" he pipes, addressing the automobile directly; Lore, who is sitting on the front bumper smoking a cigarette, doesn't bother to reply. "Yes, sir, I'm ready and raring!" Craxton answers himself. "Oh, but wait, wait! We'll have company, Lore, a regular saint she is, not the kind of gal you'd call pretty, but acceptable nonetheless. More than acceptable. Don't you agree?" Lore flounders for a moment, confused by the ambiguous pronoun, but just as he's about to ask, "Who's that, sir?" he sees the object of Craxton's praise stalking in her galoshes toward the garage. It is an image so familiar that he forgets, temporarily, the suggestive description that preceded her and assumes that an old routine is being resumed: a shopping trip to Millworth or Kettling, with Hal Craxton sitting in for his mother and Lore taking Red Vic's place, different players, the same unexceptional situation. But it takes only one more glance for Lore to see that something has changed. Mrs. Griswood doesn't meet his eyes. She looks beyond him at the automobile, surveys it with what Lore detects as a vaguely covetous expression, though he quickly dismisses the judgment, for it doesn't fit his notion of Ellen Griswood, who stands before him in her drab, rust-colored raincoat and brown felt hat, as plain and irreproachable a woman as you'll ever find.

"Coming with us, Mrs. Griswood?" Lore asks, realizing too late that with this question he has cast himself as Craxton's companion, when in fact Ellen is the chosen guest for the day and won't sit in front as she usually does on excursions but instead will join Craxton in the backseat. In back, the two of them, like husband and wife! Lore cannot hide his astonishment when Hal extends his hand and with a gentle leer helps Ellen up into her place.

"Hello, Lore Bennett. Lore, are you there?" Craxton teases, and Lore snaps his hanging jaw closed. "Well then, old Sally," Craxton purrs as he climbs up beside Ellen. Lore waits only a second for him to swivel onto the seat before he slams the backdoor shut, just missing Craxton's foot.

"Damn you, Lore!"

"Sorry, sir," Lore mutters as he slips into the driver's seat, though secretly he wishes he'd been faster with the door and had crushed Craxton's dainty, aristocratic ankle. He stares at the dashboard for a moment, unable to make sense of this machine, his memory overwhelmed by the illogical situation. Ellen Griswood is Craxton's housekeeper, not his wife. And Lore Bennett is a groundskeeper, not a chauffeur. The world has been thrown into a flux again, and Lore gropes in confusion, trying to find the button that would set things right. And then his hand remembers what his mind doesn't—that the key must be inserted into the ignition, the choke extended, the clutch released, and the engine boosted with a surge from the accelerator. Off they go, like three fish in a bottle, Lore thinks, three freshwater fish caught in a bottle that is being dragged downriver out to sea.

He glances at the rearview mirror, sees Craxton's head turn toward Ellen and his cheek plump when he smiles. The words are dispersed by the wind, but Lore can tell that Craxton is doing all the talking while Ellen Griswood listens politely. Although Lore can see only the top of her hat in his mirror, somehow he senses that she's embarrassed. Or maybe he just assumes that this is her main emotion because that's what he wants her to feel—embarrassed by Hal Craxton's attention and by Lore's disapproval.

"To the right, Lore." Craxton spits out the order and then leans back to converse with Ellen. As Lore pulls out onto Hadley Road, he steals another glance at the mirror. If Ellen hadn't been so obviously gracious when Craxton helped her into the auto, Lore might still think her blameless. But no, she's to be blamed for accepting Craxton's hand, for sharing a seat and a blanket with him, for listening to his aimless chitchat.

As they drive past the Gill farm, Craxton leans forward again and tells Lore to take Gulf Road east and to pick up Marfield Road at the intersection and head south. Lore obeys the directions, though it is a route he has rarely taken before. Buffalo lies to the northwest, Rochester directly north of Millworth. There is nothing of interest to the south, nothing but potato farms and untillable slopes inhabited by indolent groundhogs and deer and an occasional black bear. But Hal Craxton pretends that he has a destination in mind. So Lore keeps south, skirting along Tonawanda Creek for ten miles or so and then continuing on through the postal-route towns of Arcade and Freedom. The scattered farms look poorer the farther south they drive, and eventually the road narrows, hemmed in by vegetation that will all but block the way by summer.

As he drives, squinting against the wind and sun, Lore finds himself imagining a bridge, a narrow stone bridge that would carry them across time into deep summer, when this road will be overgrown with sumac and creeping ivy. Lore would drive so far into the underbrush that they'd lose their way, and they'd have to abandon the La Salle, leave it trapped in the net of weeds, and make their way across the countryside to safety. That would be a humbling lesson for Hal Craxton. For Ellen, too, yes, she could stand a grueling stint in the wilderness, nothing between her and starvation but Lore Bennett, as clever a woodsman as you'll ever find. Maybe she'd come to appreciate him.

Lore is so far lost in this dream of heroism that at first he doesn't notice when mud replaces the macadam, but when he does notice, he is pleased, and not surprised. Most minor roads in this vast backwater eventually peter out in dirt lanes and then end in the middle of unmarked land—their own Hadley Road is still unpaved. Rather than slowing to better negotiate the difficult surface, he picks up speed, so they bump and plunge through the mud like a skiff on a roiling sea, hitting each mound with a smack and careening through and across the deep ruts. A glimpse in the mirror assures Lore that Hal Craxton has ceased his monologue and is concentrating only on remaining in his seat, while Ellen keeps leaning toward the front, as though to make sure that there is someone driving and they haven't been abandoned to the frothy waves. *Oh, don't worry, sweet lady, Lore will bring you safely to shore, he'll keep you from capsizing, and if you remember to, you can thank him at the end, thank him extra kindly by giving up whatever ambitions you have concerning Mr. Hal Craxton.*

And then they stop, not abruptly but with a slide sideways and a whir. Lore's thoughts spin with the wheels until he hears Hal Craxton shouting and he understands what has happened. The La Salle is stuck in the mud, the back wheels sunk deep into twin ruts. They are stuck. Stuck! And it's up to Lore to save them!

Now what is Craxton jabbering about? He's perturbed, that's for sure, and he's addressing the issue of Lore's ineptitude. Stuck here in the middle of nowhere, stuck in the mud, and all because Lore had to drive like a maniac, you'd have thought he was being pursued by the Four Horsemen when in fact the intention had been a leisurely drive through the countryside, and then lunch. Hal Craxton wants his lunch, so what is Lore going to do about it?

"We'll have to push." Ellen, not Lore, makes the suggestion, provoking from Hal an impatient titter.

"Push?"

"Push. We'll have to get out and push."

But Hal isn't prepared to sully his spring seersucker with mud, not even for the sake of a lady. And the idea that the lady herself should muck about . . . if he weren't mildly amused by the suggestion, he'd be appalled. "Lore will get us out of this fix, won't you, Lore? I can manage at the wheel, I suppose. And you, Mrs. Griswood, you will take care of yourself. No, stay there, ma'am. Let the men handle this one."

Far from minding the mud, Lore enjoys the way it slurps and sucks around his boots as he trudges to the rear of the La Salle, his feet sinking ankle deep. Hal manages to swing from the backseat into the driver's seat without touching ground. It takes him a few minutes to locate the brake and accelerator, and in the meantime Lore wedges himself firmly against the bumper, throws his weight forward, and sets the vehicle rocking. When it slides back he pushes it forward again, catches it on the backswing, and with a grunt heaves it free of the rut. In that split second he catches sight of Ellen, who is twisting in her seat to watch him, and he thinks of a skiff again, imagines that he has just pushed her out to sea against her will. He searches her unreadable face for some sign of terror, but just then Craxton compresses the accelerator, the wheels spin, and the surge splatters Lore head to toe with mud.

Shit-colored mud. Cold, pasty, stinking mud. Lore is used to mud and spends the damp months of spring and fall coated with it. But this mud, crapped by a luxury automobile, is an insult. Tarred and feathered by Mr. Craxton, with Ellen Griswood as witness. Ellen Griswood, housekeeper. Lore might as well be covered with shit. In Mrs. Griswood's eyes, it's all the same—blood, shit, clay, dirt, mud. It's all filth, and now Lore stands in front of her, a filthy brute, *a beast,* no, more disgusting than an animal because he could at least take out his handkerchief and wipe his face, but he doesn't bother.

Is someone laughing? Hal Craxton is supposed to laugh; instead, he's twisting around to get a better look at Lore, his lips raised and tucked behind the fold of his right cheek in an expression that indicates both amusement and irritation. But someone is laughing. Someone is laughing quietly, like a girl reading a novel, so absorbed that she doesn't realize she is laughing out loud. Ellen Griswood. Ellen! Ellen is laughing and at the same time pressing her fist against her mouth to contain the sound.

The insult of it. The hilarity. Lore impulsively plays along, not by laughing but by acting in such an outrageous manner that the memory will startle him for years afterward. He reaches one hand under his armpit and scratches, then leaps with an ape's hunched agility onto the rear bumper, yelling "Woo, woo, woo!" at Ellen Griswood—and jumps back down again with an obscene slurp into the mud. "Hah, hah, hah!" He cavorts alongside the auto until he reaches the driver's door, which he leans over with a violent, lunging motion. And oh how satisfying that brief sensation of power, when Hal Craxton cringes and Lore brings his filthy face perilously close.

"Lore, what are you doing?"

"Excuse me, Mr. Craxton. I'm sorry."

"Let me get back to my seat, please."

"Yes, sir."

"Now take us home, and no more of your antics, eh?"

"Yes, sir."

So back he takes them, circling when the lane widens in a dead end and driving slowly and decisively through the mud, back to the Manikin, back to that fortress in the wild.

The journey Hal Craxton makes later that night, tucked comfortably between flannel sheets—the same sheets he'd slept on as a boy—repeats the day's drive. With the lights off and the shade raised so he can see the new crescent of the moon, he follows in his mind's eye the scenery they'd passed in daylight: ramshackle cabins, roofless barns, and behind the desolate fields, forest stretching as far as he could see. He recalls the subject of his conversation with Mrs. Griswood—a comparison of the North American wilderness with the cultivated European countryside, where every tree has a surname and every square foot of land a legend attached to it. In America, the land outside the towns and cities has little historical interest for a man of Hal Craxton's temperament. Still, he enjoys an excursion now and then, and perhaps he'll come to like the region better as time goes on.

That image of her windblown face begins as an ice sculpture in Hal's memory and melts into his bold advance. *Mrs. Griswood. Ellen. May I call you Ellen?* His hand, his sly hand. Her lap covered with the auto blanket. His hand on top of the blanket, resting feather-lightly on her leg. His hand beneath the blanket. As Hal drifts toward sleep, he feels that peculiar pocket of heat that a woman keeps trapped between her thighs. With each bump and lurch of the car, his hand had gripped her leg more firmly, and yet she hadn't protested or shifted away from him, hadn't uttered a single word for that matter, and Hal wonders whether she would have stopped him if he'd tried to slip his hand beneath her skirt. How willing is she? He must find out. Ellen Griswood is a mother and a widow, a combination Hal has never known before—the complex mystery of this plain, uncanny woman makes her irresistible.

Hal sleeps and his memory drifts on to the moment when the La Salle slid into that wretched mud. And here the dreaming mind takes over, scattering the remembered images, and Hal is running through a soupy marsh, or trying to run, but his imagination plays one of its common tricks and turns his blood to lead—he can hardly lift his legs, and then a loop of tangled bog grass catches his toe, and he falls forward to his knees. He catches sight of a woman's gray-coated back between the tree trunks. *Hello!* he calls, but she disappears. Is he running toward her, or are they both fleeing from a common predator? Hal can't be sure. All he knows is that he must try to run, so he clambers to his feet again and slogs off. And just when the fear becomes unbearable, he finds himself in a clearing dappled with sunlight, and there in front of him is Mrs. Griswood on her hands and knees, scrubbing the moss with a brush. She turns to look at him, bending her neck like a horse snapping at a fly on its hindquarters. *Mrs. Griswood! Ellen, what are you doing?* Without a word she lifts her skirt and apron above her waist, lifts her bare arse higher, and waits for Hal to have his fun. So he falls upon her, ravenous, his earlier panic forgotten. He enters her roughly, gripping her around the waist. But instead of peaking, his excitement diminishes, and he plunges deeper, pumps so hard it feels to him as though he is sawing poor Mrs. Griswood in half.

But he's not clutching his housekeeper now—he is sitting at the dining-room table and carefully cutting a piece from his seersucker suit with a steak knife. He spears the cloth with his fork and places it in his mouth, chews slowly, with more interest than distaste.

So the night goes, his pent-up imagination exhausting itself in its typical fashion after the dormancy of his waking hours. And when dawn throws its arc of light over the trees, Hal is dreaming that he's trapped on an outcropping of rock high above a raging river. And there's his mother—a young, athletic version of her—leaning over the edge of the cliff. She extends her hand but can't reach him; she disappears, presumably to fetch a rope. Hal tries to keep his heavy eyelids open, since he's afraid that if he lets himself sleep he'll roll off the rock. But his eyes insist on closing, so he gives up and rests them for what he intends to be only a minute. Then he realizes that he has been asleep, for how long he doesn't know—he blinks, reaches out instinctively to grab the rope he hopes his mother has lowered for him, and instead his fingertips brush against the feathers of a huge winged monster, half tiger, half bird, that is diving toward him, screaming, her beak open wide enough to swallow him whole. Before he realizes that the ungodly voice he hears is his own and the monster just a trophy, a stuffed bird, some kind of predator bird, an owl, yes, just an owl mounted on a piece of wood, he loses his hold, slips sideways, and falls. He is falling, falling, falling backward into the rapids. Above him, the monster settles on his bedside table, tucks in her wings, and watches.

14

My dearest Peg,

Having received your latest correspondence, I shall postpone the washing and write an immediate reply. First, here is the sum you requested. More will follow if you need it. I am sorry to hear about your troubles at the hotel. Doubtless you were designated the scapegoat by some wicked fellow worker. Do you have any suspicions as to the identity of the true culprit? We had a similar incident here long ago, when Mrs. Webster was still alive. The item missing was a silver wedding goblet with the Craxtons' names and the date of their marriage engraved on the base. I was wrongly accused and given notice. I expect you were too young to remember much about this scandal. Suffice it to say that before nightfall, justice was achieved. The second maid, a seventeen-year-old girl named Jesse, confessed and returned the goblet. Mrs. Craxton apologized to me. I wonder whether the incident had something to do with my speedy promotion following Mrs. Webster's departure three months later. You see, oftentimes there is an opportunity for reparation. Perhaps you will be rewarded for your difficulties should the truth be revealed. For now, I hope this money will help. If you cannot find another position soon, please, Peg, return home. It seems that Mr. Craxton expects to retain possession of the estate after all, and I have decided to stay on, though in what capacity I am not certain. You will be interested to learn that Mr. Craxton has asked me to marry him. I am thinking it over. My beloved daughter, you are always welcome here no matter what, and if you have an opinion regarding Mr. Craxton's proposal, please let me know. As always, Mother

This is the letter Ellen will never write:

My dearest poppet,

So they've accused you of stealing, have they? No surprise. Every woman who works as a maid will be accused sooner or later. It is one of the hazards of the job. Virtually the same happened to me right here at the Manikin, way back when I was new on the staff and working under Mrs. Webster. Luckily, the true thief came forward, and I was exonerated. But I learned my lesson, you may be sure. A domestic servant is easy game. The trick, then, is to make your employers dependent upon you. Make them incapable of doing anything for themselves. Make them love you. But you could tell me a few things about the nature of such love, couldn't you, Peg? You know what it is to win the heart of your superior. Let me just say that I am sorry for reading your diary without permission and I want you to come home. We'll leave it at that.

Home, yes, it is my home, more mine than Henry Craxton Junior's, you may be sure. Remember Mr. Craxton? Well, he woke up early this morning shouting and blubbering, making all sorts of commotion (you recall that his bedroom is directly below ours). Being the only other resident in this cavernous house, I rushed down to help, thinking he'd fallen asleep with a cigarette in his hand and set himself on fire. I found him lying on the floor in a heap of blankets, his eyes open but his mind still asleep. I've seen it before, Peg. When you were a wee child, you had the night terrors most every night. So I did to Mr. Craxton just what I'd do to you. I wrapped my arms around him and whispered, "Hush, hush now."

But Mr. Henry Craxton Junior wasn't still asleep as I'd thought. He was wide awake, scared by nothing but a stuffed owl left on his table by some prankster. And he wasn't so confused that he couldn't tell it was Ellen Griswood holding him. Ellen Griswood in her nightgown, nothing on underneath, for you know I like to air myself out at night. So he huddled in my arms, his teary face pressed against my bosom, his whole body trembling, and he sobbed, Ellen (understand, there was no presumption here, since yesterday I gave him permission to address me thus), Ellen, he cried, Ellen, I love you. Imagine that! Henry Craxton Junior in love with his housekeeper! If that's not unreasonable, I don't know what is.

If you were still here at the Manikin, Peg, I would have had a different response to Mr. Craxton's overtures, you may be sure. I would have picked myself up off the floor and marched straight back to my room. Our room. Your bed is there for you, should you want it. But without you I find myself less concerned with manners. In your absence I have let myself go. I am no longer respectable. I am dissolute, without purpose. I am only interested in pleasure, and for this I deserve a good whipping! And what do I get instead but an avowal of love. It's not that I'm unworthy. Hah, quite the opposite! I am too good for such a man! And still I held him and let him cover me with kisses. And I have no regrets.

For here's the thing, Peg: he loves me, no denying. What do you think accounts for it? I'm no beauty. Never was. I've got no special talents. I have no more education than what my aunt Lila took the time to give me. I wager he is more affected by his mother's death than he'd like to admit and is looking for comfort. She was quite mad toward the end, I've come to realize. Mr. Craxton feels confident that he can invalidate her will on grounds of insanity. I predict that he will come to regret his maneuvers. This house is more of a burden than he realizes.

I don't think he will regret what he said to me this morn-

ing, though it is my fault for taking him in my arms there on the floor, the morning light filling the room like murky water, just the two of us, Mr. Craxton and Mrs. Griswood, as opposite as night and day, melting together into the dawn. Now I'm inclined to tell it to you in a roundabout way, to hint and hope you guess it on your own because the truth is like a pin piercing my modesty, what with it being so sudden, so unexpected. But you're my daughter, so I'm going to come straight out and tell you what Mr. Hal Craxton has proposed, astonishing as it will seem, and it is astonishing, unbelievable, really, so I'm not going to try to convince you that it's true. You decide whether I'm pulling the wool over your eyes. Or maybe I'm the one who has been duped, which is the far more probable scenario, I should point out, and maybe Hal Craxton is merely buying time by falsely offering me a future when in fact he'll have forgotten his proposal by noon today when we meet for lunch; rather, meet at lunch, for he has not invited me to share his table with him again, so I will simply carry the plates and refill his wineglass and watch his face for some sign of affection, some indication that he meant what he said to me this morning and that I should take seriously his proposal.

Simply put (though it's not simple at all, is it, Peg? It's not just a matter of a poor woman saying yes to a kindly benefactor, what with Mr. Hal Craxton's questionable history regarding women . . .), Mr. Craxton has offered his hand in marriage. Of course, there's a chance it could be just hokum and nothing has changed. I will continue in my position as housekeeper and Mr. Craxton will continue in his position as employer, I will scrub the floors and he will pay the bills, and we will pretend that what happened never happened. Or else—and this possibility will seem the more unlikely because it is the more difficult to imagine—by the time you return home your mum will be Mrs. Henry Craxton Junior. And then the question becomes, Do we want this? We including the both of us, Peg, you and me, for though you're a working girl now you still have some growing to do and I wish you'd do it at home, our home, where I will be the mistress of the manor and you without a care in the world. You'll come home if I marry Hal Craxton, won't you? You'll come home to money, or you won't come home at all. Your taste for luxury was acquired on the sly, Peg, I had my back turned, but now it's too late to do anything about it, so if with a single word I could lure you back to me, then I will say that word, I will shout it from my attic room. Our room. There will be no doubt about my meaning. I will scream "Yes!" at the top of my voice, and Henry Craxton Junior will look up from the magazine he is reading in the library and know that he has a wife.

How could I refuse him, given what is at stake? And whatever complaints I might have about Hal Craxton, they pale when I consider his love for me. That's if he truly loves me, of course, and though it's hard to believe, I think he does love me, Peg, he can't help it, though it's come over him as fast as a fever. This morning he confessed his love not to deceive me but to persuade me. And he did not try to take advantage of me in a moment of weakness. That he feels compelled to make his love legitimate convinces me that he is a changed man, less vain, more responsible. And I have changed, too. I have had feelings I wouldn't have dreamed of allowing myself six months ago. I can't say honestly that I love Mr. Craxton, but when I consider the benefits for you, my poppet, I am convinced that they far outweigh the losses. I hope you agree and will come home to share in my good fortune. As ever, Mother

Lore is not a trophy hunter. Never has been. Doesn't give a damn about antler points or unperforated hides. Come spring, he even starts to wonder why he doesn't just leave the pesky creatures alone. With the grouse underfoot, the fawns like speckled shades following the does, the otters teaching water dances to their young, Lore feels like an intruder, a trespasser in this bountiful world. By fall he'll be carrying his rifle again, to be sure—somehow the sharp smell of cold in the air makes killing seem as sensible, as necessary, as harvesting. But as daylight stretches out and the world revives, Lore has little appetite for blood.

Now his only business is to groom the land and make it presentable. He spent the morning cropping the box hedges below the Manikin's front porch—Sid's old job. When he's being honest with himself, Lore knows that there aren't many chores Sid Cheney did that he can't cover on his own. Still, he misses the gardener's company. With Junket's help, he's devoting the afternoon to clearing the main trails of branches and trees toppled by winter storms. Usually he enjoys this work, but today he's got a bothersome tooth that sends a shiver of pain through his head with every pull of his handsaw. Not that the pain is anything to complain about. There's no reason to lose a tooth if the pain isn't unbearable, so he'll wait months before he drags himself to the Millworth dentist. And in his present mood, the pain in his jaw even seems fitting—not deserved, exactly, but appropriate.

He is cutting a thick maple branch into stove wood, his face squinched from the effort. Back his arm plunges, and the saw sinks deeper into the bark; forward, and dust wafts up and coats the edges of his nostrils. It feels as though he is scraping his own teeth through the wood, and he saws faster to be done with it. Sweat drips down his cheek and into the corner of his mouth. When he tastes the salty moisture he stops sawing, thinking for a moment that he has been weeping without realizing it and has swallowed a tear. But no, the wad of straight hair hanging like a loose sock over his forehead is drenched in sweat, his eyes are as dry as chalk, and if he felt a momentary sadness over lost possibilities, he feels just fine now, a little breathless from the effort of work but certainly not undone by a woman who will never love him.

Here, she's in his mind, Mrs. Griswood herself vying for space in his consciousness while the pain from his tooth tries to push the thought of her away. As though to settle the dispute, Lore heaves his boot down on the branch, breaking through the last wedge of wood and sending it crashing to the ground. With it the pain from his molar bursts and spreads like a thick, warm liquid behind the surface of his skin. He is surprised to hear a moan escape from his throat, and when the pain has subsided to a dull throbbing, he glances around, half expecting to see his son hurrying toward him. But Lore would prefer a woman's solace if he had a choice, Mrs. Griswood's steady, sympathetic hand. . . . And here she is again, a nuisance of a woman buzzing inside his head.

He would never have guessed that Ellen Griswood was so interested in material fortune that she would encourage the advances of Hal Craxton. Apparently, she's been harboring a secret, greedier self all along, sustaining this side of her until an opportunity arose. That's the way it is with women—they can't be trusted. Better to leave them alone. Now Lore is alone and Mrs. Griswood is yielding to the ministrations of the laziest son of a bitch Lore has ever known.

In the distance he hears the tear of underbrush—Junket must be hard at work while Lore wastes time pondering a woman's deceit. But she never swore she'd turn away other men, and though that's what Lore expected, he can't accuse her of breaking a promise she hadn't made. And if after so many years he finds himself able to imagine Ellen Griswood as his own, it's not because he's been inspired by jealousy. Rather, her new romance has made Lore dissatisfied with old routines. For ten years Mrs. Griswood went about her work with quiet efficiency, and Lore depended upon her to stick to her routine, just as he depended upon his reflection to meet him in his mirror every morning. Suddenly he's lost his reflection, whether to the devil or to Hal Craxton it hardly matters. What matters is that he's lonely.

The sound of his son at work serves to emphasize that they are intruders here—the only way they can exist on the land is to destroy it, rip it apart like an obsolete map and scatter the pieces. Lore kicks away a stone, feels a jab from his rotting molar, kicks again. He was taught early in his life to give up nothing but shit and piss to the earth, to hoard even his breath and always sleep with his head under the blankets, for the warmth from breathing equals the warmth of a buffalo hide, according to his father, a man whose temper calmed only when he was sleeping out in the open air on a mountaintop, lying with his head to the wind, blankets folded under his feet. Then his temper would fade with the embers, and he'd tell Lore about places neither of them had ever seen—tamarack swamps, canyons, salt deserts where the surface was as thick and soft as pudding. And though Lore has always treated nature more generously than his father would have liked, in his present mood he regrets every breath that he let dissipate into the air. He should have taken his father's advice to heart. The natural world is a lovely adversary whose beauty may never be trusted.

His father finally decided that he couldn't live without his beloved rival, so he packed up his camping gear and left home for good. Lore was Junket's age at the time, old enough to understand his father's reasons. His mother didn't understand, though—for months she kept setting a place for her husband at the dinner table, and he didn't show.

Sometimes it seems to Lore that he sees his father's wildness in his son's eyes, a wildness that is ultimately self-destructive. What Junket needs is a mother, preferably a hardworking mother like his own, or like Ellen Griswood, yes, Mrs. Griswood would do just fine, that's been the truth all along, even if Lore hadn't been able to admit it. But he's desperate enough to convince himself of it now, and for Junket's sake he will fall down on his knees before the woman he never bothered to love and plead with her to forget Hal Craxton and consider him, Lore Bennett, instead. Yes, Junk needs a mother, and his need will serve neatly as Lore's excuse.

How faint, almost impalpable, the pain in his jaw. How distant, the sound of his son's labors. How ridiculous Lore Bennett will seem to Ellen Griswood when he courts her, as ridiculous as a grown man imitating an ape. But he's willing to put dignity aside, to debase himself in order to save his son from the wildness. And in the process he'll save Mrs. Griswood from Hal Craxton. That bastard couldn't really care for her, not in the way she deserves. Craxton's out to win a competition with himself, to add another *X* in his list of seductions, and despite what Ellen Griswood may think she wants, Lore is her only honorable hope.

While he hesitates, he observes the life of the woods. A yellow finch spills like a drop of brightly colored paint from the heights of an oak and flits away, a bluejay clings to a knob of a crab apple, the young leaves of a sugar maple glisten in the sunlight, and the creamy white flowers of an ash tree dapple the background. Junk must be resting—Lore hears only the light drumming of a woodpecker hidden inside the foliage. The boy will come looking for his father any minute, but Lore would prefer to go back to the Manikin alone, so he calls out his son's name, calls twice more before he hears an answer.

"I'm going down to the house for a bit," Lore shouts, and though Junk remains out of sight, he calls back, "See you later, then!" and Lore answers, "See you." He stomps away, trying to make his footsteps sound confident, even cheerful, when in truth the task ahead fills him with a peculiar dread. What if Ellen refuses him? But Lore won't spin out answers to what if. Instead, he repeats the lie that inspired him in the first place: he is acting on behalf of others. His son and Ellen Griswood both need his assistance, they need to be saved from accidents of passion, and by the end Lore will be the celebrated hero of this story. *Hey ho,* away he goes to rescue the woman from a terrible fate.

No buckskin fringe flutters in the wind as he strides along, no musket graces his shoulder, but still he feels like an anxious pioneer, each step carrying him ten years forward in time until he reaches the collar of lawn surrounding the Manikin. Only then does he falter. The long grass reaches inside his trouser cuffs and tickles his ankles, and he reminds himself that he should mow the lawn. Wild crocuses dot the green, and he stoops to pluck one, plucks another, collects a handful of flowers as he approaches the house.

The windows are like dark pools of water, undisturbed by any motion. The odd stillness gives the impression that the occupants have fled in panic, taking nothing with them but the clothes on their backs. Lore enters through the backdoor, emerging from the pantry into the kitchen, where steam rises from the stove's hot-water reservoir and a pot of soup simmers unattended. Everyone has gone away, Lore assumes, his logic distorted by fear. They have fled, leaving Junket and Lore behind. What made them go? Lore is the only sentient presence in the house, and everything—the crocuses in his hand, the braid of garlic hanging beside the window, the statue of a woman bent over the table, her face hidden in her hands—everything has turned to stone.

"Sylva!"

"Dear God, you startled me!"

"I didn't see you."

"I'm sitting right here in front of your eyes, Lore."

"You were so quiet."

"I was thinking."

"Thinking?" Lore is still baffled by the sudden emergence of life in this tomb, and it takes him a minute to orient himself. He sinks back into a chair and lets the flowers fall in a little heap on the table.

"You doing all right, Lore?"

"Fine, fine, just out of breath." He forces himself to pant a bit.

"Well, here's something that's gonna take your breath away alto-gether, Lore Bennett."

She's right—Lore finds it hard to catch his breath, for though he's not sure what Sylva is preparing to reveal to him, he perceives from her tone of voice that his disappointment will be great. Only then does he notice Sylva's two boys hunched together with crayons and paper at the far end of the room, away from the hot stove, and the little one, Gracie, too big for a cradle now, sleeping on a quilt in the corner. As though the baby can feel the force of Lore's stare, she opens her eyes with a start and begins to cry. One of the boys calls, "Mama!" without looking up from his picture, and Sylva says tiredly, vaguely, "I know it," and goes to the baby, scoops her up, rubs her hand in a spiral on the child's back. Lore watches her hand as Sylva murmurs comfort. "You're awake now, honey, you must have been dreaming, dreaming about monsters for sure, but your mama's here, your bad dream is over, and you know I wish I could say the same about another bad dream, but this one's just beginning, a dream about monsters. Can you guess what I'm after, Lore? Lore?"

He looks up when she repeats his name—he's hardly been listening and doesn't understand the question.

"Course you can't guess it, the way it came out of the blue like that. There's sickness in this house, Lore. Mr. Craxton brought it with him. Took his mother's life. Now Ellen . . ."

It must be grief choking her. Lore leaps from his chair, finishing in his mind what Sylva hasn't finished saying out loud. "Ellen . . ." He can't say it either, but he understands that she's out of reach forever, that she's dead, Ellen Griswood is dead!

"No, no," Sylva bursts out, "it's not . . . oh, she's fine, Lore, there's nothing wrong with Ellen, nothing wrong with her body at least, but her soul . . ."

"What are you saying, Sylva?"

"I'm saying that Mr. Craxton asked our Ellen to marry him. And she's up and accepted."

Now the baby is crying again, and the boys erupt in a tussle over a picture that's been ripped in half. Lore helps out Sylva by grabbing each boy by an arm, and somehow he manages to hold them while Sylva gives them a dressing-down. Still the baby is crying, and Lore wishes that just for a second or two they'd all turn back to stone so he can think about what Sylva has just told him and try to understand.

It is up to a woman to know the affliction in her own heart, but only God knows the hearts of all his children, so Sylva tells herself that she mustn't interfere in Ellen Griswood's affairs, except to say a prayer for her and ask the Lord to open Ellen's eyes and help her to recognize the sickness and mend her ways by withdrawing her promise to Mr. Craxton. But maybe Ellen prefers ruin to widowhood and has accepted Hal Craxton out of desperation. She looked desperate enough as she announced her plans to Sylva and Nora while they were preparing lunch: desperately pleased with herself, and with desperate coyness she wrote out her consent on a piece of paper, which she folded and tucked into Mr. Craxton's wineglass. He was losing patience, Ellen claimed, though he'd proposed to her only hours earlier. She feared that if she kept him waiting, he'd find himself another bride.

Though it shouldn't be her business, Sylva couldn't help speaking her mind to Peter far into the night, until he grunted his last agreement, turned his face into the pillow, and fell asleep. Now Sylva has pretty much finished her talk with God and there's just the little one inside her to listen, and if it doesn't understand, so much the better. A woman can't help sharing thoughts with an unborn child. It's listening now and wants to hear more, judging from the impatient prods. Sylva slips her hand under the blankets, lifts her nightgown, and molds her palm around the right quadrant of her swollen belly, feels a rolling motion and then three determined kicks: *knock, knock, knock.*

Are you there, Mama?

I'm here, child. Thinking. Just thinking about a poor woman who's been blinded by the dazzle of money. We've got to pity her, child.

What is pity, Mama?

Pity is forgiveness without knowing.

Her little one blinking, stretching, quickening, kneading her belly from the inside. *Are you there, Mama?*

I'm here. Thinking about a white woman who's beset with a sickness only God can cure. Foolish Ellen. Won't even take the time to think twice about it. Must be she loves the house because no woman in her right mind would love Hal Craxton. But she's not in her right

mind, and if there were roots to cure her, I'd find them. But there's
nothing I can do now but pray, and when I'm done praying I'd better
mind my own business and let Ellen Griswood mind hers, and if she
truly wants to get married before the end of the month like she says, I'll
prepare such a wedding feast she'll think it's all a dream.

What is dream, Mama?

You are, little one.

On through the night the child tumbles, punches, kicks against its
confinement, and Sylva keeps her hands on her belly to catch the im-
print of its motion on her palms. And though she hardly sleeps even an
hour, when she finally leaves her bed early in the morning she feels
refreshed, or more precisely, unburdened, having decided at some
point during the night that there is still one person who can save Ellen.
So while Peter and the children sleep, Sylva kindles the stove and settles
at the kitchen table. She has to steady the rickety pinewood table with
her elbows while she writes, and she uses only those words she is sure
she can spell. As she finishes she hears Gracie beginning to whimper
down the hall, so she folds the paper, slides it into an envelope, and
copies the address from the back of a postcard she received last month
and ever since has kept tacked to the kitchen wall. The card shows an
aerial view of Manhattan. Peg's joke on the back of the postcard was
for the benefit of the boys. She'd written: *I live at the top of a sky-*
scraper and on a clear day can see across the ocean to France! Come
visit me sometime. And though Sylva knows better, that's where she
has pictured Peg: in a fancy penthouse apartment, smoking and laughing and presiding over the world. Such a willful, fun-loving girl, not
too old for a spanking, Sylva thinks with more than a little indignation,
but whether Peg is mature enough to recognize her mother's foolishness and hightail it home remains to be seen.

15

At 7:00 A.M., the first of May, a train leaves Grand Central, chugs somewhat hesitantly through the crowded suburbs, slowing for crossings every fifteen minutes or so before it passes through the Shawangunk foothills and descends into the lowlands of Dutchess County. In a more determined fashion it moves north along the Hudson, slipping in and out of the shadows of the Catskills and eventually veering west at Albany. As it wends its way through the deep valleys and along upland pastures, cows lift their heads just long enough to watch it pass, ruffed grouse and pheasant and jacksnipe cower in the hedgerows, and once in a while some carefree cottontail hops across the tracks, catches its paw beneath the rail, and is turned to blood and gristle in an instant. Onward the train goes, over the high plateau that extends across the state, the landscape defined aeons ago by the continental glacier, which formed moraines and gouged out waterfalls, turned aside streams and scraped mountains into rounded hills as the ice receded. To the north of the tracks, the orchards of the Ontario plain are covered with the snow of white blossoms; to the south, beyond the Mohawk River, the overlapping greens of hickory and chestnut and pine color the hillsides, and the pastures are dappled with buttercups and violets. Farmhouses built on nearby hillocks seem to watch the train, and occasionally a child stands on a front porch and waves, but the train passes without so much as a toot, intent upon its mission, fancying itself indomitable, as oblivious to the world as it is to the diverse lives inside its cars.

Gusts from the wheels tip the cattails toward the swollen river, reminding Peg of hundreds of slender-legged birds positioning themselves to drink. Hard to believe that she is going home, though, truth be told, in her four months away she never really understood why she'd left home at all. Nonetheless, in good Griswood fashion, she tried to make the best of the situation. Somehow she managed to find a job at the Dome Hotel on East Fifty-sixth Street, a job that kept her occupied twelve hours a day, seven days a week. When she wasn't working she was either asleep or at a picture show, often both, since she found it hard to stay awake in a dark theater, even when the audience was howling at Harold Lloyd steering the city's last horsecar into the side of a truck.

The other maids at the Dome figured her a snob because she insisted that she had no stories to tell about herself or her family. She went about her chores without complaining, changed stained sheets, scrubbed toilets, wiped up pubic hairs from bathtubs, and whenever an unwanted image tried to push into her consciousness, she'd dull it with the effort of mindless work, a skill inherited from her mother. Of course, she knew that she'd been raped, just as she knew that she'd grown up at a place called the Manikin, where her mother was the housekeeper. But she recalled these things as distant and unimpressive facts. She convinced herself that she didn't much care one way or another about her past experiences, including what she'd felt for Lilian Stone. So at one time in her life she'd been enamored of a stylish young woman. So what? What mattered, all that mattered, was that she collect her weekly check and save for the future.

She reassured her mother in her letters that she was fine, even better than fine with her ample salary, room and board included, the picture shows and window displays and parks. Even when she lost her job without warning and had to ask her mother for money, she'd made her troubles seem as uneventful as if she'd rolled over in her sleep. It didn't occur to her that Ellen herself might be revealing even less, and when the last letter arrived with a ten-dollar bill stitched to the paper, Peg read it so carelessly that she didn't realize what her mother was telling her until Sylva's note arrived the next day.

Peg stares out at the land, the flat terrain bending up to the foothills above the Mohawk Valley. She sees a goshawk perched on a fence post and immediately thinks of Lore Bennett. Thanks to him, this country-side is the subject Peg knows best, or at least knows effortlessly. Look what happened when she tried to leave it behind. She will be in Kettling, twelve miles from home, before five. This proximity makes her feel strangely aware of her body. The dry air of the train's interior scrapes against her skin, making her shudder, and she listens to the crank of wheel shafts and the sound of metal against metal silencing the rest of the world. Peg Griswood, daughter of a housekeeper and, formerly, second assistant maid at the Dome Hotel on Fifty-sixth Street. Funny how fate can match up coincidences—Peg lost her job, wrote to her mother for money, and within a fortnight she was summoned by Sylva to the Manikin. Whether or not she'll succeed in dissuading her mother from marriage remains uncertain. Sylva believes that Peg is the only one who can influence Ellen. Perhaps. But Peg has never known her mother to retract a commitment.

They know so little about each other, really. Less than ever, since Peg has been away. Ellen would never guess what happened to her daughter after she left the Manikin, and Peg has no intention of telling her. And from her side, Peg can only presume that Ellen has been bewitched. In Peg's judgment, widowhood entailed as much responsibility as housekeeping. So how could Ellen, the most responsible of women, throw it all away for the likes of Hal Craxton? The trap must have been ingenious, the seduction so casual and quick that Ellen forgot to be cautious. And Peg is supposed to save the day by turning her mother against the man she has come to love—if such corruption can be called love. At least Peg's mother can make her love legitimate, unlike Peg, who, on the basis of her one romance so far, tends toward the same sex, in particular, toward modish and sly young ladies. But that's all over, and if Peg ever falls in love again—something she's determined to avoid—she'll keep the relationship safe and respectable. No more hanky-panky with beautiful heiresses for this girl, no ma'am,

Peg is on the right track, she's going home, traveling back into her childhood, to a time before she'd met Lily, a time when her body felt whole and independent and it hadn't yet occurred to her that love could be so perilous.

That Peg can fool herself into such a state of nostalgia has more to do with the motion of the train than her own personality. This journey home seems an immense yet simple accomplishment—immense because she had to pass through Kettling and spend four months in the city before she could return, and simple because she'll be home by dark, without much effort. But why did she leave home at all? She has tried to blame her mother for reading her diary—without this intrusion, Peg and Lily might be meeting covertly to this day. Peg wouldn't have been at Kettling on Christmas night if it hadn't been for her mother, and in all likelihood she still wouldn't know that Lily had another lover.

But even before Peg had fallen asleep in the Kettling station, she'd already decided to return home, a decision lost in the terror of that terrible night and remembered now, as the train slows past warehouses and grinds into the city of Rochester. She lifts her suitcase from the compartment beneath the seat and steadies herself against the jolts of the train. She'd like to blame her mother for everything awful that has happened to her—after all, she is a teenage girl, with the usual mix of petulance and pride, and anger is one of the most refreshing of emotions. But she feels more helpless than angry and wishes she could tell her mother the truth about what happened in Kettling and let Ellen heal her with comforting words.

On the train to Kettling she listens to the wheels pounding, the cars dragging as the engineer eases the train forward, then slows again for a junction. Beneath every car—passenger and head-end cars alike—the double metal shoes press against the wheel treads and fill the air with slaughterhouse squeals, and Peg discovers that she's been clenching her fists as though to squeeze the brakes even tighter. She releases her hands as the train picks up speed. Soon, too soon, they arrive in Kettling, where there are no demons, only local residents waiting for visitors, grocery boys sent to collect provisions, two postal workers, and the manager from the movie theater here to pick up this week's three-reel entertainment. Peg avoids walking through the station. Instead, she hurries along the platform and into the parking lot, where a single taxi idles. She'd intended to take a taxi home, to arrive at the Manikin in style, but at the last minute she changes her mind and sets off on foot. It is four-thirty on a pleasant May afternoon. If she keeps up a good pace she'll be home before dark.

Home. This is what Ellen has wanted for herself and Peg, just a home where they can live regardless of the whims of an employer. Hal Craxton must have seduced her with the Manikin, given her the opportunity to experience it as a mistress rather than a housekeeper. A magnificent home somehow being wrested back from charity into the Craxton family. Peg understands the lure and could forgive Hal Craxton almost everything if he would write her mother's name on the deed to the Manikin. But she can't forgive him for choosing Ellen Griswood as his wife, since he can have no honest reason. He is taking advantage of her poverty and plainness in order to gain a woman to tyrannize. A simple purpose, so obvious that Peg wonders why her mother doesn't suspect it, though she doubts that at this point such an accusation would alter Ellen's plans.

Still unsure what she will say to influence her mother, Peg leaves Kettling behind and starts the long trek to the Manikin. Ankle-high stalks of corn carpet the fields, red-winged blackbirds chatter in drainage ditches, and the crows swoop from treetop to treetop. Peg swings her canvas suitcase to clear the thick clouds of gnats. How crowded and busy the fields seem on this late spring afternoon. So the contrast is all the more disturbing when the open land gives way to forest. Immediately, Peg is struck by a disturbing lifelessness. The trees look freshly painted, their young leaves like pieces of wax, moss upholstered to their exposed roots, the forest floor synthetic, the whole scene beautiful, perhaps, but too colorful, too silent. How strange and dreamlike in its proportions, with the massive trees shrinking Peg to a miniature. Perhaps it is the effect of the late afternoon sunlight or the newness of the leaves, or maybe it is the result of four months in the city, but the forest seems a man-made replica of itself, as useless as an old stage set.

When a passing driver stops to offer her a lift, Peg declines, preferring to continue on foot despite her fatigue, hoping to see some sign of life, to catch a glimpse of a deer, a fox, even one of the fat groundhog pups so common along the roadside. On the train she'd felt as though she were returning to a simpler, more authentic place, but now she feels as though she's left reality behind.

Three hours later she is standing in the dust on Hadley Road and wearily contemplating the Craxton gatehouse in twilight. She slips inside the gate, closing it quietly behind her. If Junket and Lore are inside the house, they don't notice her pass, and Machine is nowhere to be seen, so Peg continues up the drive alone. It is right that she has arrived at this hour of transformation, with the cooling breeze perfumed with wild honeysuckle and the Manikin itself looking so picturesque and yet so secretive. And it is right as well that for the first time on the Craxton estate she hears the whine of a small plane flying overhead. She watches as it passes out of sight over Firethorn. The fading sound of the engines signals to Peg a mournful finality, warning her that since she's chosen to come back, she will never be allowed to leave.

"Tell me, Peg."

"You were asleep, Mother. Everyone was asleep. I'd gone down to the library. It was so quiet in the library at that late hour. But he found me there. I thought he'd gone to bed. Mother, are you sure you want to hear this?"

"Tell me."

"He kissed me. That was all right. But then he was leaning against me, pinning me in the chair. I don't know why I didn't scream. Maybe it was because I thought I deserved it. I'd given him ideas, what with the dress and all. Lily's dress. I was still wearing Lily's dress. Mother?"

"Go on."

"Sylva?"

"Tell us, honey."

"He pulled me to the floor. I couldn't stop him. It felt like, like he was holding me under water, I couldn't breathe, I couldn't save myself. When he was through he took twenty dollars from his wallet and left it on the table."

"Lord Jesus."

"Dear little poppet."

"I bought my ticket to New York with that money."

"You shouldn't have run away. Your mama was sick with worry."

"I was ashamed, Sylva."

"My poor girl."

"You won't marry him, Mother?"

"Never."

"I'm sorry."

Many years later, Peg will tell the truth to her mother. She will look up from her cup of five-cent diner coffee and without warning she'll say, "Hal Craxton didn't rape me." And while Ellen stares in speechless wonder, Peg will tell her what really happened—not on Christmas Eve but on Christmas night, not at the Manikin but in the Kettling train station. And though Peg will try to explain why she felt compelled to lie to her mother and blame Hal Craxton for a stranger's crime, Ellen will just shake her head, momentarily overwhelmed by the thought of the different life she might have led if Peg hadn't deceived her. Mrs. Henry Craxton Junior. That she could ever have been tempted by such a man will astound her into speechlessness, so when Peg asks, "Do you forgive me?" Ellen will just stare in wonder. And then she will see the dismay in her daughter's eyes, and she'll grab her hand and begin kissing it with all the fervor of a starved dog gobbling a shred of meat.

But for now, the lie is intact, and the amazing relief that Ellen felt when she saw Peg coming in through the pantry has been replaced by a horror nearly equal to what she would have felt had she witnessed the assault herself. She hugs Peg's head, strokes the hair thick with dusty tangles from a day's journey, pets Peg with the flat of her hand to calm her sobs, murmuring as gently as she can, "My poor little poppet, my poor little poppet," even while she tries to calm herself.

The pressure of Sylva's hand on her shoulder reminds her where she is: in the kitchen of the Manikin, and out there in the dimly lit depths of the library, Hal Craxton sits waiting for his evening coffee, surely impatient by now, since Ellen left to make a fresh pot over half an hour ago. But he won't ring for her now that she's his fiancée—he'll have to wait for Ellen to bring the coffee in her own good time. Two cups, of course. He doesn't know that Peg has come back, though he'll know soon enough, Ellen tells herself, strengthened by Sylva's touch. At last she understands why he wanted her for his wife—still wants her, since he doesn't yet know what she knows. Marriage was his foolish penance, a way to make up for his crime by sharing his property—property that doesn't yet rightfully belong to him. But jail is another way of doing penance. The idea of justice is a small but invigorating comfort. Yes, Hal Craxton will pay for what he did to Peg.

"We'll go to the sheriff," Ellen mutters.

"Promise me—no, Mother, promise me . . ." Peg is suddenly scrambling out of her sorrow, and both Sylva and Ellen try to hush her. But Peg is desperate. "Don't you . . . don't you understand? I let him do it to me. I didn't try to stop him. I could have screamed. I didn't scream."

Although Peg has been saying this from the start, only now does Ellen comprehend. She remembers Lily's sequined dress, pictures it in a little heap on the floor of the bedroom. The memory of the dress somehow conveys better than Peg's words the meaning of her protest: Hal Craxton will go free.

But he'll go alone, thanks to Ellen. She yanks Peg up by the arm, no less sympathetic to her daughter than before but so eager to be rid of Hal Craxton that she needs to confront him this minute. So without a word she drags Peg out of the kitchen, hitting the door with such force as she goes that it continues to swing for a long, creaking minute.

Left behind, Sylva catches glimpses of the mother and daughter as they cross the dining room, Ellen lunging forward, Peg stumbling to keep up. Then the door settles in its place, and Sylva doesn't bother to open it to take a peek. Instead, she stares at Ellen's empty chair and thinks to herself that if Henry Junior were a colored man, he'd be dead by now.

He might as well be dead. The woman he loves—yes, he has come to love her, to need her—despises him. "You disgust me!" are the words that accompany the unkind expression on her face, and she thrusts her daughter in front of him as evidence.

Such a sweet, young, firm-breasted thing. He kissed her once, didn't he? Tasted her with his wicked tongue. Mrs. Griswood won't forgive him. Just like his mother. His mother never forgave him, though he's not sure what he did in her lifetime that offended her so. His own mother. Sad, how she lost her mind in the end. Oh, he's had to stretch the truth a bit with Boggio's help. But it's all for the best, his mother would agree. All he ever wanted was her forgiveness. Once, long ago, he'd made her furious. What had he done? Now Mrs. Griswood is furious. He loves her like a mother—no, instead of his mother. His mother is dead, he knows that, he can tell the difference between truth and hallucination. He had been confused the other morning, but that wasn't his fault. Blame it on the owl. The owl came out of nowhere. Scared him silly—now he knows what it feels like to wake up into madness. But he's grown rather fond of the creature and yesterday he took it upon himself to nail the trophy to the wall above his bedroom door. The owl will protect him against evil. What he really needs is protection against himself. Here he had the opportunity to make things right and live out the rest of his days in peaceful domestic splendor married to a tidy, reliable, docile woman, and he's managed to make a mess of things. He gambled with the daughter and lost. Mrs. Griswood will never marry him now. No one will marry him. In his dream his mother was supposed to fetch a rope and save him. Where is that rope? Where is his mother? She was buried on the last day of last year, lowered into a hole torn out of the frozen ground. Hal himself wants to be cremated at death, his ashes scattered. Wants to stay dispersed on Judgment Day. Wants to play hooky. That's an odd thought, and it brings an inappropriate smile to his lips. Only seconds have passed since Mrs. Griswood and her daughter entered the library. He realizes too late that he shouldn't have smiled. They have disappeared in a huff, leaving him alone.

His mother was alone when she died. He wonders if she suffered much pain when she slipped from this side to the other. His father, according to the pathologist who did the autopsy, was killed instantly, his head crushed by the truck's rear tire. We should be born with knowledge of our death so that we can spend our lifetime preparing ourselves. He wonders whether he would have died in his sleep last week if he hadn't woken just before he hit the river. That's what they say: if you die in your dream, you'll never wake up. Then Mrs. Griswood had appeared, hushing him, not because he'd been naughty but because he'd felt so frightened. He fell from his dream into her arms. This wasn't love based upon attraction. This love was as spontaneous and necessary as the first breath a newborn takes. Gone now because of an innocent kiss. If Mrs. Griswood had more experience of the world, she wouldn't take a single kiss so seriously. Just a kiss planted on the irresistible lips of a young girl. Not even love involved.

He can tell the difference between love and not-love, thanks to Mrs. Griswood. Thanks for nothing. Who would have thought that such a woman—a mere housekeeper, a widowed housekeeper—would refuse him because of a single harmless episode involving her teenage daughter? The wedding had been set for the following Wednesday, and Hal had already picked out a diamond wedding ring from his mother's jewelry box. Now Mrs. Griswood will never wear his mother's ring, nor will she have any further claim to his estate. This latter thought gives him some satisfaction. Good riddance. Better to be alone than to be compromised by an uneducated, penniless widow, a domestic servant no less. That she would give up so much because of one little transgression suggests to Hal that she didn't understand the extent of his sacrifice. Didn't understand the consequence. The loss of stature. His punishment: the peculiar mocking ire of the leisure class. A house-keeper for a wife? That would have been reason enough for his wealthy acquaintances to exile Mr. and Mrs. Henry Craxton Junior into the netherworld of the unpopular. No more invitations to country houses in Sussex, to Tuscany villas, to Greek islands. By marrying Ellen Griswood, Hal Craxton would have made them both pariahs.

He has been saved from such an awful fate by the future Mrs. Craxton herself. He is free to pick up where he left off. He has never been more free. His mother is dead, and he will remain a bachelor. That he should have desired otherwise perplexes him.

Yet even more perplexing is that he still desires it. To be forgiven. He will do what he should have done when his mother was still alive—he will fall down on his knees and beg for her forgiveness. Prodigal son. He shouldn't have kissed the daughter. He is sorry for it. He will tell her he is sorry. His mother. No, his mother is dead. Mrs. Griswood is the one he wants. Mrs. Ellen Griswood: He thinks of little else these days. He offered her his name. How could she refuse it? He will persuade her of the advantages. He will promise never to kiss her daughter again. There is still hope—the living can always change their minds. He wishes he could change his mother's stubborn, unreasonable mind and persuade her that he is deserving. Short of that, he will work on Mrs. Griswood and try to convince her of his noble intentions. He is sorry for kissing her daughter. He will never do it again.

He fortifies himself with another sip of port. Over the course of the long winter he has drunk up half of his father's wine cellar. By the end of summer the Manikin will be dry. They'll have good reason to move to the Continent then. Together. Mr. and Mrs. Henry Griswood Junior.

Craxton! His name is Craxton! It's been a long, confusing week, and a resolution seems only a distant possibility. Mr. and Mrs. Henry Craxton Junior. He will offer her money. The title to the house, pending the resolution of *Craxton v. Craxton*. His life. Ah, here's something no woman could ignore—he will threaten to take his own life unless she marries him. If she refuses, his blood will be on her hands. Murderess! This ivory-handled paper cutter will do the trick, he will hold it to his throat and make Ellen Griswood understand the depths of his need. There is no refusing a man so violently, irrevocably in love.

And so he wiles away the evening pondering the potent idea—suicide, or at least the threat of suicide. He broods instead of sleeps and sips his port. Hal continues to sit in his library, contemplating his next move but unwilling to disturb this temporary peace, time sliding by, his beard sprouting, his fingernails growing. He could go on like this and bother no one. He doesn't even feel hungry. Days will turn into weeks, weeks into seasons, in the blink of an eye it will be winter again.

But first the night has to peak. His mother's clocks announce midnight in a tumble of clashes and chimes and cuckoos, and out of the clamor arises another ruckus, a hammering at the library door. *Who's here at this ungodly hour? A thaumaturge come to make things right? If it's anyone else, tell him to go away.*

Hal rises from his chair to greet his visitor, discovers that he is more than a little unsteady on his feet, and holds an armrest to regain his balance. Before he can manage to take a step forward, the door opens and the room is full of people, dark-clothed bodies, their faces shadowed by the single lamp he has kept burning. Is this a celebration in his honor? Why, everyone's here, he sees on closer inspection: the groundskeeper, the Negro cook and her husband, even Mrs. Griswood. And at the front of the group stands the ringleader himself: crazy old Boggio, preening, straightening his collar, and laughing silently between clenched, crooked, saffron teeth.

Hal can't guess what they want with him, so he just stands dumbly and waits for someone to explain. Finally a voice arises from the pack of servants, a woman's voice, Mrs. Griswood's voice. Hal recognizes it and feels more at ease. Then he realizes what she is telling him.

"Leave us."

What?

"Go."

The word is followed by a ripple of murmurs as the servants close in, surrounding Hal. For a second he thinks they are going to start beating him with their fists. Instead, the library fills with hissed commands. "Go away," they are telling him, "you don't belong here, leave us, go on, get out." He feels the hard grip of an old man's fingers around his wrist. Boggio's fingers. Hal Craxton knows of no one uglier than Boggio, no one more bestial. Now he understands. Boggio is the devil, undisguised, and Hal stupidly made a pact with him. Boggio is here to lead him to hell. The servants have come to see them off. "Go away, leave this house, get out, get out, get out!" Out of his own house? Well, it's not quite *his* house, not entirely, not yet. Pending resolution. What will be resolved? Craxton versus Craxton, servants versus master, the devil versus man. Hal doesn't stand a chance. He'll be lucky if he escapes with his life, his wits intact. "Get out! Get out!" All right, then, he'll go, yes, he'll leave willingly, no time wasted. "Go on!" He'll go tonight, right away, if that's what they want.

He rushes past the servants and out of the library. His first impulse is to run out the front door and down the drive, to keep running through the darkness until he drops in exhaustion. But he has just enough sense left to know better, so he stumbles upstairs to pack his bags.

Appropriate that the stroke of midnight brought justice, for this is Astraea's hour, the end of a day, the end of a golden age. The goddess was the last of the divinities to leave the earth, and since her departure, any act of justice has been at best a courageous hunch and at worst a conviction inspired by hatred. The servants of the Manikin acted courageously and gambled with their livelihood in order to treat Hal Craxton to their kind of justice—a fair punishment for what they all believe he'd done to Ellen's Peg, who slept soundly up in her garret bedroom while her mother and Sylva assembled a troop five strong, a troop as powerful as a band of dead soldiers, fleshless, full of vengeance. Hal Craxton won't bother their children anymore. The confrontation will probably cost them their jobs, an even exchange, given the stakes. Hal Craxton had to be punished, and they were the only ones who could do it.

Afterward, they gather in the kitchen, huddling around the table while Sylva boils water for tea. No one is sorry for what can only be called a mutiny, but they need time to think about the consequences, since it had been arranged in such haste. They hadn't even rehearsed. The report of Craxton's offense was passed by Sylva to Peter to Lore and finally, on impulse, to Boggio. Without quite knowing what they would do, they buttoned their coats around their nightshirts and went up to the kitchen, where they heard in full from Ellen the story that Peg had told earlier that evening. Then they took their curses into the library.

Five against one. Hal Craxton didn't stand a chance. Where he will go from here they can't predict. They know only that he will leave and until he returns they will stay here and maintain the house and grounds just as they've been doing for years. This is as it should be, even though they hadn't any strategy when they entered the library. It was Ellen who said the first words, inevitable words, they believe now: *Leave us.* Yes, they agreed at once, Hal Craxton must leave the Manikin—they would have expelled him by force if necessary, but luckily he has chosen to leave of his own accord and right this minute is carrying his suitcase down the stairs with a *thump-thump-thump,* across the hall, and out the front door into the frosty spring night.

The servants gaze at one another over their cups and listen to the clatter of gravel as the garage doors swing open. But no one speaks, not even when the engine of the La Salle coughs awake and the automobile slides out, swerves in reverse across the drive, skids to a halt, stalls. The engine turns over and over, catches, and the La Salle moves down the drive. Hal Craxton, a dangerously inexperienced driver, is driving off into the night. Only a guilty man would be that desperate, and if there was ever a question in anyone's mind that Ellen's Peg might not have been telling the truth, the sound of the La Salle as it chugs off dispels all doubt.

Hal Craxton is gone—the length of his absence depends upon the depths of his guilt. Until they are sent away the servants will remain here and continue with their work as though nothing has changed. This consensus is implicit somehow, and they finish the soothing tea in meditative silence, then one by one they head back to their beds—first Boggio goes, then Sylva with Peter immediately following, reaching for his wife's free hand as she opens the kitchen door, leaving Ellen and Lore facing each other, their features like the hollow apertures of masks in the light of a kerosene lamp set at the near end of the table.

Now that they are alone, the silence that had been acceptable grows awkward, the space between them vast, and Lore has to squint to see Ellen's eyes, which narrow in return as though to deflect Lore's gaze, to stare him down. A long minute passes while they engage in this subtle battle of wills, neither of them uttering a word, until the competition becomes so tense that Ellen, exhausted by the events of the night, finally cuts the game short with a question obviously meant to embarrass Lore.

"What are you staring at?"

With surprising ease, Lore replies, "You."

IV

ETERNITY

16

Come with me and discover up close the wonders that await you in the wild. Look carefully, check under logs, below the ice, at the tops of trees. Can you find one bullfrog? Two turtles? Ten dragonflies? Now press the button on your left and listen. No, you're not hearing a thumb rubbing against the side of an inflated balloon—that's the leopard frog croaking, and if you press the next button you'll hear the northern cricket frog, which sounds quite like two steel marbles clacking together. Scratch the red paper tab and smell primroses. Scratch the purple and smell lavender. Scratch the brown and inhale the sour wetland fragrance of a cypress swamp. Now come this way, I'll take you through the seasons, and you'll see for yourself the ingenious plan of a deciduous forest, where the end of every story leads back to a familiar beginning and everyone plays a part. Four habitat groups, four typical scenes of life in motion: autumn, winter, spring, and summer depicted in rich and exact detail, nothing left out in the name of economy, nothing distorted or misplaced. Here is nature in all its infinite and yet predictable variation, with time suspended by the able hand of man.

Begin with autumn: Seventeen thousand wax leaves pressed from seventeen thousand molds and painted with bright colors, the molds made one by one from seventeen thousand fresh leaves. Seventeen thousand leaves scattered across the forest floor, each leaf wrinkled, worm-eaten, and still unique. Now look up—a blue jay perches on a branch, and over there in the corner a striped skunk slinks back to its den, while nearby a marbled salamander basks in the sun. Painted on the rear mural, a peregrine falcon flies off with a rabbit in its talons. At the front of the scene, a buck tucks its head and charges, its immense rack positioned just inches from the glass.

Next, winter: Here you'll see the hungry crows scavenging an abandoned campsite for food. The slight but ancient yellow birches. The cotton snow imprinted with hoofmarks. And the deer themselves, two females, their white tails raised in alarm, their entire bodies taut, haunches shrunken into hollows, their ears perked forward.

Spring: Green emerges in the background mural, jack-in-the-pulpit blooms in the marshy turf, a young peeper clutches a tree trunk and extends its tongue to catch an inchworm hanging on an invisible thread from a branch, a robin chomps a bloodworm in half, and a doe leads her fawn along a path, stopping to nibble a tender green leaf that glistens from the recent rainfall.

And summer at last. Gentle, abundant summer. Do you see the scarlet tanagers, both male and female? The yellow finches and ruby-throated hummingbird? The blacksnake and the unsuspecting wood rat? The ichneumon fly and orange moth? The mud daubers and cicadas and red ants and centipedes? The beetles, the gnats, the water striders and mosquitoes? Notice how sleek the hides of the deer are at this time of year. How lithe and capable the young bobcat. How happy this summery scene, this paradise on earth. And yet who doesn't feel a melancholy twinge at the sight of the green leaves edged with brown, the dry, cracked creekbed, the hungry snake poised to strike? Even in this timeless scene, change is visible. And evidence of change reminds us of death, and death, no matter how necessary to the cyclical scheme of life, reminds us that everything we love will be lost.

Had enough? Come with me then, leave nature behind and visit the transplanted tomb of a great Egyptian prince, the stone "house of eternity," where nothing purports to be real, where everything stands for something else, and the door separating the living from the dead is a false door, as permeable as fog.

Are you willing? Follow me.

. . .

They are ten altogether, living in a big house on a hillside in the fruit belt of western New York, and they love their home in its every aspect. Sylva's child, due any day now, will make eleven. They drew straws for the bedrooms, all except Ellen, who prefers to remain in her cozy garret. Peg moved down to the grand guest room in the east wing, the room that had belonged to Lilian Stone through most of last winter. Sylva and Peter and their children have adjacent rooms in the west wing, and Lore and Junket share Mrs. Craxton's first-floor suite. Boggio, lucky at last, drew the long straw for the master bedroom, where his beloved snowy owl stands guard over him while he sleeps on the feather tick, the satin sheet tucked snugly beneath his chin.

No one remembers who first suggested that the Manikin's bedrooms be assigned by lottery or who decided that the servants should move into the house at all. Nearly two months have passed, and they've stopped waiting for Hal Craxton to return and throw them out. Money will be a problem eventually—the adults are using up their small savings to pay for various supplies and materials needed to make general repairs. But thanks to the three dairy cows, they have more than enough milk. And though they're reluctant to slaughter even a single chicken without the permission of Hal Craxton, they do eat the eggs. Add to that the fish that Lore and Junket catch daily, and the residents of the Manikin are nearly self-sufficient.

The fruit has suffered this season—a month of drought has stunted the peaches, and the apple blossoms dropped early. By the end of June roads are dusty, the ground hard, the lawn already patched with brown. But the flowers are thriving, thanks to Lore's watchful care— the borders of all three terraces are brilliant with geraniums and daisies, and along the southeastern corner of the house the trumpet vine has reached the eaves. In the lower garden, the air is saturated with the scent of roses, on either end of the arbor moonvine and bittersweet have woven themselves through the trellis, yellow alyssum carpets the slope, and the hydrangea planted at the two corners of the front porch are in full pink bloom.

"Thank the Lord," Sylva says at every meal's grace, "for gardens, for orchards, for pure springs, for evergreen hedges and sunsets, for the night breeze that pushes the curtains up against the ceiling, for our food, and for our loved ones."

"Amen," Peter chimes. And Lore adds, "I never guessed that life could be so good." They speak softly not just at meals but at all times, as though they were afraid of waking one another from a beautiful dream. The dry summer heat helps to mute the sharper sounds and to slow motion, and though the adults go on weeding the garden, shelling peas, milking the cows, they take their time with the chores. In the evening they wonder idly why they haven't made more efficient use of the day.

Sylva's boys and Junket have settled into the job of building a tree fort for themselves and are gone from the house from breakfast to supper. Peg can usually be found on the greensward at the edge of the east terrace reading a book—to herself or to little Gracie, who is old enough now to get in Sylva's way in the kitchen. And Boggio wanders about with an air of aimless propriety, sampling Sylva's breads and pies and pronouncing judgment or directing Lore toward a stray locust sapling in the garden or once in a while complimenting Ellen on a gleaming, freshly waxed table. That Boggio has taken it upon himself to fill in for the deposed master bothers no one, not even Lore. Somehow, foolish as he is, Boggio seems the appropriate choice for the role. Master Boggio. He serves as the perfect symbol for the new order, a clown in place of the king, a walking joke, his pretension so incongruous that all he has to do is clear his throat and his audience will burst into laughter.

Which is just what the boys do when they meet Boggio on Paradise Path at the top of the orchards, where the dirt is covered with the brown crackle of old apple blossoms and the air still lightly fragrant. After supper, the boys wandered off from the house without any purpose in mind, and having looked for fun and come up empty, they are glad for the entertainment provided by the Distinguished Person himself. Boggio clears his throat to prepare for his solemn oration, and the boys start giggling, anticipating all sorts of foolishness. But Boggio simply reports, "No need," and with a little salute disappears up the path, repeating the phrase as he goes—"No need, no need, no need"—as though practicing a birdsong. *No need, no need, no need.* Manny and Cap look to Junket for an explanation, but all Junket can think to do is shrug, and with that the two younger boys burst out in laughing echo—"No need, no need, no need."

Down Paradise Path the three boys run, slipping, leaping, skipping to the lower garden, and from there *patter-pat-pat* in their bare feet up the slate steps to the east terrace, where Peg is reading, catching the last of the day's sunlight on her open page. Cap snatches the book from her hands, tosses it to Manny, who hands it to Junket, and they run away again, *patter-pat-pat* down the steps and up the slope, Peg shouting as she slides her feet into her sandals and then on second thought kicks them off again, the boys racing out of sight, chanting, "No need, no need, no need" between fits of laughter, Peg in pursuit now, gaining on them, catching up at the spring and facing off across the black, gurgling pool. When the boys run clockwise, Peg runs after them; when they reverse direction, she veers around. And so the chase continues, back and forth, forth and back until Manny and Cap collide and Peg just misses slamming into them and instead bends to the inside, crosses one foot over the other, and tumbles right into the spring.

But there's no terror in this dunking—the boys have all had their turn this summer, and when Peg scrambles out of the icy water with a roar, there's nothing to do but make fun of her and try to snatch a good look as she pulls herself up, her sleeveless summer dress melting against her body, creasing between her breasts and thighs, her nipples poking against the thin membrane of wet cotton. Listen to her shout. She's mad now, boys, you'd better run before Diana turns the hounds loose, but here she's caught Cap by a thin wrist and will tear him limb from limb if she can manage to hold this slippery eel, but she can't, and he's gone, racing after Manny and Junket, Peg in pursuit again, as good as naked, her wet hair sticking to her neck and chest as she screams threats of murder, the boys heckling her from the distance—"No need, no need, no need"—until Peg collapses in exhaustion. She lies on her back staring up at the dusky expanse of sky, arms folded in a hug, and the boys return and gather silently around her, edging close so they can watch her chest heave but keeping far enough away so she can't grab one of them by an ankle.

"I'm freezing," she says at last, startling them out of their reverie. Junket sets down the book he's been clutching, takes off his shirt, and tosses it to Peg, who catches the wadded cloth on her face. She sits up, and as she slips her arms into the short sleeves mumbles, "Ya little pig shit."

A pause. A silence, while they all assess the implications. And then through the air that has turned grainy with the descent of darkness comes Manny's timid reply, "Asslicka."

"Horsepiss!" Peg retorts.

"Slugbutt!" Junket says without missing a beat.

"Snoteater!"

"Twatface!"

"Cocksucker!"

"Titties!"

"Balls!"

"Bitch!"

"Oh," moans Peg, clutching her belly and then rolling right over in a somersault, laughing with great sucking gulps. "Oh, no more, please, no more."

"Goddamn chickenshit slut!" wicked little Manny howls, and they all dissolve into giggles, unable to speak now or even stand up, pressing their heads into the dry grass or into their hands, groaning from the excess of hilarity. And suddenly Machine romps from nowhere into their midst, barking and straddling Junket, licking his face with such urgency that her tongue pokes far up a nostril, and Junket makes a sound so obscene that even Machine seems pleased, and she sits back on her haunches, swishing her tail crazily and curling her lips in an expression that must be a smile.

And so the children of the Manikin pass a typical evening, Peg stripped of her latest reading matter and lured from her diffidence into the randy fun that only children can fully enjoy. Whether Junket feels privately burdened by his disappointed love, he can't say—he lives on the surface these days, as they all do, even the adults, experiencing their freedom like so many discharged Ariels, servants only to the elements.

On another part of the estate, the elements of love are being tested. In Lore's formulation, defined over the course of the past few days, the full moon does for the emotions what the sun does for plants, washing the body in transforming light and enabling lovers to reach across the great divide separating individuals. For a man it inspires a momentous courage, as Lore had so delicately phrased it, a quickening of the pulse. . . .

"That so, Lore?"

"I'll prove it to you, missy."

"You will, eh?"

"I will!"

And so here they are, adrift in a birch-bark canoe on Craxton's Pond, waiting for the fat globe of the moon to rise. Already they can see the crown of light at the top of Firethorn. But the moon needs to be high in the sky to work its magic, according to Lore, who sits in the stern smoking, his tongue working the raw gum where the dentist pulled a molar just last week, the continuous line of his eyebrows pinched into a thoughtful V, suggesting not that he is worried about the truth of his thesis but that he is uncertain of the strategy best suited to the immediate situation. Should he approach his lady with romantic words, or should he simply take her in his arms, without warning? You'd think they'd never kissed before from the way Lore sits there so solemnly, so politely. But for the past two months, ever since Lore neatly replaced Hal Craxton as the object of Ellen's affection, they've been snatching kisses whenever they can—in the pantry, in the garden, in the broom closet or the library—earnestly secretive, though their secret is common knowledge just waiting to be sanctified.

So what are Lore and Ellen waiting for? Ostensibly, Lore waits for the moon to rise, while Ellen waits, with puritanical resolve, for Lore to make the first move. In the distance they hear the tinkling sounds of the children laughing. The breeze hits the water like a dozen skimming stones, glancing off the surface and leaving behind patches of ripples. From time to time the crunch of dry leaves signifies some wild animal's stealthy journey through the woods, and on the south shore they can see Boggio's silver hair, so bright over the short mass of his body that it seems to emanate light. After a while he wanders back into the darkness of the forest. Lore tosses his cigarette overboard, then catches water in his hand and splashes his face. The moon is partly visible now, but still Lore makes no motion toward Ellen, and she gives no sign that she is impatient. They drift across the center of the pond with complete acquiescence.

"Did I ever tell you, Ellen?" Lore murmurs at last and then stops, as though he's forgotten what he meant to say.

"Tell me what, darling?" She's never called him that before. Darling. The word hangs in the emptiness beside the moon.

"About the white owl. Junket's owl."

"The snowy owl?"

"I did tell you, then."

"Boggio's owl?"

"Junket's owl."

"The owl in Boggio's room, Lore?"

"What owl?"

And so they work through the confusion, Lore explaining to Ellen that here on the pond, from this very canoe, Junket took aim and put a bullet through the head of the arctic bird. And Ellen explains what Lore never knew—that Junket saved the carcass by passing it on to Boggio, who then gave the stuffed owl to Craxton (to *him*, Ellen says with emphasis, refusing to utter the name), who mounted the trophy over his bedroom door. Lore's quiet "That so?" suggests that he doesn't much care about the fate of the owl anymore—the betrayal that would have infuriated him earlier only bemuses him now. And Lore's bit of information—that Ellen's Peg had been with them that night last fall, the night Junket shot the owl—draws from Ellen merely a whispered "Right here?"

"Right here."

Hands entwined. The moon bright enough to make shadows, the canoe splashing from side to side as Lore moves up to sit beside Ellen. Their lips meet, tentatively at first, bobbing apart, touching, mashing together. He slides one hand around her midriff and with the other unbuttons the collar of her blouse and reaches his fingers in, sliding them under the top rim of her brassiere. He kisses her chin and neck, tugs at her sleeve to expose a shoulder and drags the tip of his tongue across her skin. She lifts his head and kisses the sunburned skin above his beard, kisses his forehead, inhales the smoky scent of his hair. And then, as she tips up her face to catch the full blaze of moonlight, she accidentally shifts her balance, tilting the canoe far enough so that water sloshes over the side.

Ellen braces herself, clutches the bench while Lore clutches her, and the canoe rocks gently back to an even keel. The breeze raises goosebumps on Ellen's arms. Water swills around her bare toes. In the heavy silence, a frog chirps and is answered on the opposite shore by the throaty grunt of a bullfrog. Ellen smiles, without thinking leans back her head again and manages to pull Lore off balance—he slips sideways across her lap and his weight knocks Ellen off the bench. She drops seat first into the bilgewater as her feet kick up, and Lore gropes for the rim, catches the stem of the paddle instead and sends it tumbling into the water while he collapses onto his knees, his face sandwiched between Ellen's upraised legs.

"Oh, excuse me," he says, as he would to a stranger he's just bumped in a crowd.

"Goodness," Ellen responds, her lower torso stuck rather absurdly in the narrow prow. But she doesn't make a move to lift herself to a more civilized position, and neither does Lore. Instead, since it is a night to laugh, what with the awed, bulbous-nosed moon watching their antics, that is what they do. Laughing, Ellen wiggles her bare feet in the air, and Lore wraps his arms around her knees. They laugh with giddy helplessness, with sighs of *oh, no,* sandwiched in between gasps, *oh,* because they are well aware that they are being ridiculous, and *no,* even though they mean the opposite.

At last they feel satiated, even dizzy from the extra oxygen they've been taking in with their gasps. Lore reaches with both hands beneath Ellen's rump, lifting her back onto the bench, and he carefully folds up the hem of her tousled skirt to keep her bony knees bathed in moonlight. Magic light. There can be no doubt about its effect. He glances at her, Ellen smiles again, and he nudges her skirt up and nibbles the wedge of muscle on the inside of her thigh. She gives a little start, then settles into her pleasure and begins running her fingers through his hair, absently unbending the tight curls. The canoe spins in a slow circle, erasing its shadow as it turns, while the forgotten oar drifts out of reach.

Who's there? Sparks of fire or drops of light falling from the moon? Nothing to be afraid of. Just a handful of fireflies cast off into the air like dandelion puffs. Boggio would like to catch one. And do what with it? Why, swallow it, of course. Boggio would like to swallow a firefly and light up his dark soul. There is laughter everywhere tonight—in the orchard, by the spring, on the lake. Boggio is alone. But being alone he can do such things as scratch the private place where the sweat tickles him. Being alone he can fart to his heart's content. If only his mood would rise to the occasion. Here he stands on a clear, balmy summer night, in fair health, give or take occasional incontinence, the palsy in his hands, and a temporary light-headedness, and he can't make himself feel happy. Proud, yes. He is proud to reign over the Manikin. And content with his accomplishments. A life well spent. No remorse. But he is not happy. Or is he? To be honest, he doesn't have a clue about what it means to be happy and might well have experienced the feeling without realizing it. "I am happy." He experiments with the phrase, whispers it, then says it loudly. "I am happy!" But it doesn't convince him.

He wanders on in the direction of the marsh and his hut. He hasn't been back there since he found the pair of panties—mostly because he was afraid of stumbling upon the lovers in the midst of the act. The mysterious act. All he knows of it is what he's gleaned from hearsay and the occasional pornographic pamphlets he has purchased from a little stand set up every year in one corner of the state fairground. He has remained a celibate man not out of conviction but because that is what came naturally to him. He never even felt the urge to be embraced. He is instinctually self-sufficient. Alone with his trophies. They will live on without him, and once in a great while an observant viewer will admire not just the animal itself but the artistry of the object, the way a person might admire the mother of a well-behaved child. The trophies are his children. He is happy when he is working on an animal, isn't he? But work involves too much disappointed ambition to allow for pure happiness. Which means that Boggio has never felt purely happy.

Who's there? Just a mosquito, its sting embedded in the soft flesh of his arm above the elbow. The engorged thorax smears beneath his palm. He is on Marsh Path now. The locusts buzz loudly all around him, erupting at once in their metallic chorus and then fading in unison. And the frogs keep chirping behind and in front of Boggio, falling silent only as he walks past. A sudden, violent flapping of wings and tearing of underbrush suggests that a predator, a fox perhaps, has seized a nesting bird. Boggio walks on, the mud squishing water into the hole in his right shoe. He doesn't need a lantern tonight, not with the moon lighting up the landscape. He slaps another mosquito on the back of his neck. Twenty or so yards ahead stands his old hut, looking forlorn, sagging from neglect.

Poor old hut. Rotting, infested hut. His footsteps across the boards sound intrusive to his own ears, and he almost turns around and leaves. But he is drawn to the window by the sight of another visitor, a red bat hanging in the glassless frame, its delicate fur the color of rust in the moonlight. Boggio reaches out, touches a wing, and the bat drops and flies off swiftly, darts as fast as a swallow toward the nearest line of trees, and suddenly turns and doubles back toward the hut, heading straight for the window again with the speed of a bullet. But the nimble bat bends upward at the last minute, wings outstretched across the span of sky, its verminous squeak so obviously mocking that Boggio is stunned, humiliated.

But a quick jerk of his shoulders, a cough to clear his throat, and he is dignified again, undaunted by man or bat, nobody's fool, as proud a fellow as you'll ever find.

Not happy, though. Boggio has no reason to feel happy because he has no need for happiness. So he's been telling himself. But his self-sufficiency has been shaken by the moon, by the smell of honeysuckle, by the laughter of children. No need, no need, no need. What a strange, bright darkness. The melting blue of twilight has been replaced by a weird fluorescence. Boggio feels as though he is floating on a boat in the middle of a silvery ocean. He sees no sign of his red bat. The sky separates the silent heavens from the noisy, chirping earth as the empty space of the window separates Boggio from the natural world. He has spent his life celebrating nature and helped to make it available to everyone. But nature shows no gratitude. That would make Boggio happy: some recognition of his sacrifice. Nature remains indifferent, even hostile, and will seize any chance to make a fool of old Boggio. King Boggio, puppet monarch of an anarchic kingdom. The thing he loves most cares nothing for him. No need. No need. No need. Down he spins, down the bottomless well of despair—

—when suddenly, plummeting from the center of the moon, comes a miracle to rescue him. His bird. Not just any bird. His owl, alive again. *Hannah*, he thinks, watching the long, nearly vertical dive of the bird. He never named his trophy, but the name comes to him now, inexplicably. Hannah. He is not imagining her. He couldn't imagine this—the sudden braking, fingered wings flapping against the shallow pocket of swamp water, then the slow, mothlike rise, some hapless amphibian caught in the talons. Once level, the owl flies off to the north, wings springy on the upstroke and beating heavily down against the pull of gravity. Hannah. Boggio watches the silent flight until she is swallowed by the distance. Then he scans the marsh for some evidence of the visit. *Hannah?* he whispers. Hannah. A fragment of memory. A woman named Hannah. Who was she? Where did the bird come from? Nature's gift.

Hannah?

From a mile away he hears the low-voiced shriek of her reply.

Come back. He wants to see her again. His Hannah. His angel. He has finally seen an angel. He wishes she would come back and glide close enough to the open window so he could reach out and touch her. Is an angel insubstantial, like fog or smoke, or would her feathers feel like the finest silk? Dear Hannah.

It occurs to him that he'd better sit down or his weak legs will collapse beneath him. With some difficulty he lowers himself to the floor. Demons have sewn stones into his hands, poked pins and needles into his legs, drenched him with a bucketful of fever. He is shivering, his sweating skin ice-cold on the inside, hot on the surface. He recognizes the malady as one of those sudden summer fevers he's prone to, fevers as short-lived as they are powerful. He needs to rest, that's all. A midnight snooze. Nothing else to do but stretch out on the floor and pull the blanket of moonlight up to his chin.

It is a night fit for profound mysteries, and Sylva is stumbling along a woodland path, trying to make sense of the mystery of her pain. *Child of light, come out, come out!* She is God's humble servant so why won't He make it easy for her, why won't He let the pain wash upon her body not like a cold ocean wave, drowning her, but like the moonlight, soft, warm waves of moonlight, magic in the air, and by tomorrow . . . ? She cannot imagine it, cannot imagine her child outside, her body singular again, can only imagine over the next swell of pain to the other side. *Now this I affirm.* There will be another side, subsidence, and though the next pain hasn't even crested, she is already envisioning relief. Moonlight. Molten light radiating heat. This is no lie she's telling herself. Tonight the moonlight warms the earth. Warms Sylva's skin. Protects and reassures her. The Lord is her shepherd so she doesn't need any midwife around to gag her, no, Sylva will manage just fine on her own, and only at the last minute will she go find Ellen and ask her to please catch the baby.

It hasn't yet occurred to her that she might run into trouble out here in the woods, a laboring woman alone, midnight already behind her. All intention is focused on the next pain, and the next and next. Sylva must ready herself so the pain doesn't take her body by surprise. The tightening should be willed, not simply reactive, Sylva must concentrate and meet the pain as she imagines she would meet a curling wave, muscles clenched to steady herself against the shock. Yet no matter what she does, the pain destroys resolve. The great squeeze of pain. Insides churning, tightening, forcing a grunt from her throat. And then the subsidence. Blessed peace between spasms. The child may rest. Sylva may rest. Back at the Manikin, her family sleeps and dreams, unaware that Sylva has snuck off like a mama cat to endure her pain in privacy, all because last time round the Millworth doctor, who had no special fondness for Negro folks, sent a young midwife in his place, and the woman treated Sylva roughly. Well, no white woman's gonna stick a hanky in her mouth ever again, not if Sylva can help it. Could be, though, that she's making a mistake, trying it alone, feeling it alone. As the next swell crests and her gut tightens, peace turns to panic, she is scared by her body's ferocious strength, the clenching, "Good Jesus, please see me through," scared not of what might happen next but of what is happening now. Her body twisting, squeezing. Death would be a relief. Instead there is pain. Pain severe enough now to knock her to her hands and knees. Salt beads stinging her eyes. The heaving and tightening inside. She strains to vomit, retches mucus—*Don't worry, girl, your heart ain't burst yet, oh dear sweet Jesus, I can't take it no more, no more*, and then, at last, the peace. Makes her want to laugh, this interval between the pains. She wipes her lips with the back of her wrist, chides herself silently for falling to such a state—out here in the dark like an animal all because she doesn't want some white witch attending to her needs. Now has she ever done anything as foolish as this? Wandered from her bed in the middle of the night, left her doting man behind, nobody within calling distance, no help to be had if she needs it, and she does need it, "Merciful Jesus, please, oh Jesus, oh," grunting, whining, retching, mucus thick as pine sap dribbling down her chin. And then the peace again. The necessary calm. World as still as the child inside her. Deadly calm. That the child might not survive its birth—the thought that she's managed to ignore suddenly enters her mind, and her muscles tense against the awful fear. Stillness inside and out. Silence. That the infant might not live through the pain, that it might strangle itself in an effort to be free. . . . It would be her fault. Murderous dignity. No help within calling distance, thanks to Sylva. No sound. Fool woman, she'd spend the rest of her days gagged and bound if it meant saving her baby. But the good Lord will save the child—her baby will be born and live and go to school and grow old. Beyond this temporary labor, a lifetime. And then Sylva is back in the midst of her pain, back arching, eyelids squeezed closed, her body retching again, grunting, spilling clots of blood and water and mucus and shit. In the midst of the pain she is compelled to look at the sky, sees the blaze of light in her mind first, blinks, then sees the star crossing the sky. A falling star—proof that she will see this ordeal through. Ah, she didn't mean to get this far along all by herself. Where is she? Somewhere on a forest path. She should go back. Or ahead. The closest refuge. "Ellen, where are you?" Anyone will do, man or woman, white or black. All Sylva needs is a soft hand tracing the outline of her spine, stroking her, caressing her through the pain. Stupid girl. She's so ashamed she won't permit herself to call for help. Instead she's determined to make her way back to the Manikin, ever so quietly lie down beside Peter, and wake him gently. *It's time.* Isn't that what she's supposed to say? *It's time,* meek but still poised. Fearless. All that's expected of a woman. And once Sylva is settled in her bed and Ellen is in attendance, she'll thrash and scream to her heart's content. Until then, "Oh God," the long spiral of pain, and so soon after the last. She drops to her hands and knees again, arches into the pain, gropes inside herself for some relief, and without thinking finds the muscle in her belly to push against the pain. Immense and irresistible pain. *Not yet!* She's not ready to push, she's not home, she's not lying in her own bed, her Peter fidgeting, hopping from one foot to the other, Ellen there to boil the water and snip the cord and put the baby on Sylva's breast. Magnificent push. She's not ready. She's not—and now the peace again, but not for long. Taking her by surprise, force of birth, can't fight it, can't endure it, can't even run home. *It's time, dear Lord in heaven, someone help me, oh Jesus!* Soft summer moonlight. Last year's leaves now dusty mulch. She's not ready! Water and blood dampen the dry earth, dust to mud, mud to life. *Push!* But the effort of expulsion fills her body with a different kind of pain. Pain not shocking like cold water, more like a blast of heat. Fire, its center somewhere between her hips, and now the slide toward relief is followed without pause by another explosion of pain. Here's the urge to push again, a mistake but she can't help it, can't help herself, can't help her baby. Her body isn't ready but the urge to push and expel the pain is irresistible. Pushing her baby into the fire . . . what is she doing? She needs help but can't stay on her feet long enough to get anywhere. Never occurred to her that she wouldn't be able to walk. Can hardly breathe with this fire in her middle. The child will pay for its mama's pride. No midwife's gag across her mouth, sure enough, but neither does she have the guidance that every woman needs to see her through. Another pair of eyes when hers are squeezed shut against the pain. Another woman. Confidence of reason. The agony is almost constant now, the intervals of rest only seconds long, and Sylva is still alone, can't get home, can't find the way out of the woods, so she might as well stop looking forward to relief, yes, better to shrink within the crush of pain and let the animal sounds escape. Pleas to heaven lost in deep, ugly groans, her voice unfamiliar to her own ears, the sound so distant and strange that she mistakes it for the sound of rescue. Jesus has sent help—"Over here, I'm over here!"—but no one comes, no Samaritan lifts her upon his back and carries her home to the comfort of her fancy, borrowed bedroom. Sylva remains hidden in the woods, invisible, her groans so bestial that no one would recognize a woman's distress in the sound, but still she pushes up and out with all her might to make the sound as loud as possible, foghorn groan for the whole world to hear until the sound turns to retching, her body divided, half the muscles pushing up toward her mouth, the other half pushing her insides out through the birth canal, tearing her heart from its place, forcing it downward. She'll die if help doesn't get here soon, but still she feels grateful that Peter can't see her now because he'd die just from watching her suffer, these throes too much to witness, better off alone, sure, better off alone— this is her last thought before her mind devotes itself entirely to the pain, the physical struggle so consuming that if someone held a mirror before Sylva and persuaded her to open her eyes, she wouldn't recognize herself, wouldn't know her face, not because of the contortions but because her personality has disappeared. She is all body, all pain, endless pain, gravity working within to force out the separate self, crushing, consuming—and then, a strange, popping sensation deep inside her. She finds some relief by shifting to a squatting position, balancing herself with her hands. Now she can push not against the pain but in tandem with it, the effort sensible again. She understands what is happening and why. Her baby. She is pushing her baby into the world. As she should. As God wills. His righteousness. Labor is not in vain, labor is never in vain. Nor life. Heaven at the end. A long, splendid respite. So the child will be born in the wild, delivered by the hand of God. She feels her body gathering, gathering, preparing for another immense push, and exclamations of "Oh, oh, oh" escape in puffs from her lips. The wind pants through the leaves in rhythm, the trees point their gnarled fingers, and the moon stares with the slack-jawed patience of an expert fisherman.

Remember me. Now the moon is sinking from the sky, and Boggio lies in darkness in his hut. Never mind. The fever warms him, burns away the chill. He shivers in the heat. Such a night, a night to dream away illness. Sweat puddles in the pouches beneath his eyes, and the boards feel cold against his skin. He remembers everything that has ever happened to him, one experience connected to and reviving all the others. Nothing separate, nothing irrelevant. A meaningful life.

Remember me. The command just beyond the reach of thought. Echo of a voice—whose voice? Hannah's. A woman named Hannah once told him to remember her. Boggio senses that he is indebted to her, though he doesn't know why and doesn't much care. And yet he cares enough to keep pondering the mystery. Such is the attitude induced by fever. A Cheshire-cat sort of attitude. This way or that. You'll go somewhere, as long as you keep walking. So Boggio wanders in his mind in the direction of the voice. Fearless. He doesn't care what he finds. It's a way to pass the time, after all. Going from here to somewhere else. Boundaries made permeable by the fever and the summer night. He moves easily to the other side of consciousness, into darkness, takes another step forward, and suddenly he remembers what he has never remembered before: sliding, sliding, sliding headfirst down the fun-house chute straight into a carnival. Or else he is dreaming the memory, yes, this must be a dream: the carnival, the noise, the lights, and the grinning clown who greeted him, the face speckled with the dark craters of his pores, the clown's teeth soot-colored, his breath so foul that Boggio had to turn his head—and found himself staring at the blank white apron of a nurse. She reached for him, but he managed to squirm from her embrace, fell to the ground, and dashed off. He remembers running this way and that—in his panic he almost tumbled straight into a lion's gaping mouth but managed to backpedal, bumped against the clown, careened past him and slipped through the crowd, shouting for his mama, oh how he wanted his mama, he never wanted anything as much as he wanted his beloved mama right then. He couldn't bear not having her, and in the middle of the crowd he collapsed, folded his knees up, tucked in his head, and cried.

A tiny, sobbing child. Someone handed him a damp washcloth and he sucked on the corner. Otherwise he was ignored. Hours passed. Days. He cried himself to sleep. When he woke he was in his mama's arms, his soft bottom resting in the crook of her elbow, his hands clenched into puffy, dimpled fists. The tip of her nose was cold against his neck. But such bliss couldn't last—sure enough, the nurse returned, her fingernails scratching his skin as she reached for him. *Not yet,* Boggio pleaded. *Wait,* his mama said, and she held Boggio's face close to hers, whispered, *My name is Hannah. Remember me,* without tenderness, more like a military commander giving directions to a spy. Memory as espionage. The assignment: to keep alive the memory of his mother, merely another careless young woman loved and abandoned. But just as she would always hate the man who used her, Boggio would hate her for giving him away, vowed to spend his life proving that he didn't need her. Didn't need anyone, thank you, though before he could stop her the nurse lifted him up and lumbered off into the crowd.

He passes in an instant through the many years of his life and returns to the floor of his hut at the edge of Craxton's marsh. Passes beyond the peak of the fever, as well. Now he remembers only vaguely, fondly, his mother's face—not beautiful by the usual standards, though exquisite to Boggio. They share the same bent nose and tufted eyebrows. He is sorry for his years of resentment. He'll make it up to her, he tells himself. A new beginning at the age of sixty-seven. Mad old Boggio, stretched out on a pinewood floor. In his present mood, he blames no one, not himself, not his mother, and not even the cad who took advantage of her.

It must be close to morning, judging from the rising volume of the birds. Boggio still feels too weak to move. The fever has settled in his bones, melting the marrow, but his head is clear again, and after a few solid hours of sleep he'll be able to walk back to the Manikin. He concentrates his mind's eye on Hannah's face so he will dream of her again. *Silly old Boggio.* All his life he's been pretending that he's not a sentimental fool, and the only person he's succeeded in deceiving is himself. Now it's time to stop pretending. He's a child at heart, everyone knows the truth, and he might as well indulge his childish whims, such as: imagining that his mother is nuzzling him with the cold tip of her nose. Hannah. *Are you there?* Hannah. And something else . . . a last sound floats down to him like a single feather. A familiar name. Craxton. What does the name of Craxton have to do with Boggio? He isn't supposed to understand—he knows this much, at least. His mother chose to keep it from him: the meaning of a name.

For the first time in years, Boggio begins to cry. It is a pleasant sort of sadness, rich with meaning. He turns on his side, as indifferent to the discomfort of the pinewood floor as a man in love.

Ellen thought she knew about love. The responsibilities. She has always been a responsible woman. Even her short-lived engagement to Hal Craxton was the consequence of a highly attuned sense of responsibility—she'd wanted to become mistress of the Manikin for her daughter's sake. That she allowed herself to feel thrilled by the improbability of it all seems irresponsible to her, in hindsight. But this, this! She hardly recalls how they managed to reach the shore, paddling with their hands, so overcome with hilarity they nearly capsized a dozen times. And here they are, Ellen lying naked beneath Lore on the mossy, sloping bank, Lore's shirt beneath Ellen to protect her from the damp ground, Lore's lips on Ellen's breast, her knees raised, the soles of her feet sliding along the backs of his calves as he eases into her.

So this is love. Wherever they are touching Ellen feels the warmth from his body spreading out across the surface of her own skin. But the sensation inside her is something else. Lore pushing into her, lifting, gently pulsing. The feeling has no center, instead travels through her in twisting, spiraling currents. She raises her hips to draw him deeper and watches the compression of love on his face, his mouth silently shaping a single word. "Ellen," he is saying. "Ellen, Ellen." Even her own husband hadn't loved her enough to love her plain, familiar name as Lore does. Astonishing devotion. He is everywhere inside her. Pleasure without consequence. This is love for its own sake, no responsibilities, love as natural as breathing. Swirling, careening love. She feels her muscles gathering, tightening into a tight knot of pleasure, and she closes her eyes to sink into the feeling, grinds against Lore until the pleasure bursts and fills her completely. Ellen loses herself in this happy mood, for a moment feels Lore's body from a distance as he loves her more fiercely, then floats back to him and shares the ecstasy of his release.

Shared warmth. Separate bodies sharing heat. The warm pad of his belly pressing against hers. The outline of his ribs. His heart beating next to her ear. They lie together without speaking, drowsy and content. Maybe they even sleep for a short while—Ellen can't tell whether she rises from the depths of bliss or sleep. But gradually she becomes more aware of the world—the bristly sphagnum moss beneath her legs, the morning star glimmering through the web of birch and poplars. And in the distance, the roar of a ferocious beast, some carnivore stalking the woods, a bear or cougar or some other sharp-fanged, hungry man-eater. The animal will catch the scent of their lovemaking on the breeze—perhaps it has already done so and is racing toward them, greedy for its pound of flesh.

"Lore! Lore, listen!"

"What?"

"Listen to that!"

"I don't hear anything."

"Listen!"

The beast roars again, the sound closer than before, and Lore jerks upright, tugs at the shirt still partly beneath Ellen, and hastily plunges his arms into the sleeves and his legs into his trousers.

"Come on, Ellen."

He holds the neck of her dress wide so she can fit her head through. As soon as she is clothed again he grabs her hand, pulling her straight toward the source of the roar, straight toward danger.

"Lore, what are you doing?"

Another roar, and Lore tugs at Ellen as though she were a kite that hasn't yet caught the upsurge of wind. She has to concentrate on the ground now, for they've left the mossy bank behind and are running up the path, over sharp-edged rocks and pine cones and sticks.

When she hears the next roar Ellen recognizes the sound, at least detects the human cadence of the voice and concludes amid the confusion that some poacher has caught his ankle in his own steel-jaw trap. Later, Lore will tell her that this was exactly his thought, and when they break onto the wider path and the next moment stumble upon Sylva, who half squats, leaning forward over her hands, both Lore and Ellen stop in midstride, frozen by surprise. Sylva is naked now, her nightgown cast aside a few minutes earlier, and she looks up at them with a sheepish smile, reminding Ellen of a woman caught on the toilet.

The realization that they are about to witness the birth of Sylva's child is clouded by the mystery of the location, the *why* of it all. But the *why* will have to wait because the baby, apparently, won't wait much longer. As though she's just been slapped, Sylva's grin twists with pain and she begins to scream.

"Not here, Sylva," Ellen pleads, but Sylva shouts, "It's coming, it's coming," and rocks back on her haunches, her heavy breasts flattening against her chest. Lore catches her just in time, supporting her beneath her shoulders while Ellen, by force of necessity, moves to the position between Sylva's knees.

"Merciful God," Sylva moans, her body limp from exhaustion, though before Ellen can think of any comforting words Sylva has squeezed her eyes shut again and emits a sound unbearable in its implication. Her bulging labia open around the bloody crown of the child, and as she gives a huge push the head pops out and hangs there like a bubble, its eyes squeezed shut, its tiny lips pursed in a pout of such amusing indignation that Ellen breaks into a shaky laugh as she supports the infant's head in her palms.

"Look, Sylva, look what you have!"

"Oh Jesus, thank you, thank you."

And then Sylva tenses for one final push. Ellen helps to free the infant's shoulders and feels the weight of the small body fill her hands. Without quite knowing her own intentions, she spreads her skirt into a hammock, and lowers the slippery, squirming, outraged little girl into her lap.

"You've got a little girl, Sylva."

"A girl," Lore practically sings from behind Sylva.

"A little girl," Sylva cries, or laughs, Ellen can't tell which but hears herself echoing Sylva with small, shuddering gulps of relief. She doesn't notice that the sky has brightened slightly, but later, when she recalls the birth, she'll remember the scene being lit by a strange, electric sort of light. And she'll remember feeling slightly puzzled by the situation, uncertain of what to do next, how to separate the child from the umbilical cord, what to use as a wrap. She'll remember how time seemed to flow around her while she floated in a halcyon place between the present and the future, until Sylva brought her back with another cry. At first Ellen thought the placenta was a second child, a monster twin, but when the raw, blue-veined tissue dropped to the ground, Ellen understood what it was and identified it for Lore, who, she noticed, stared over Sylva's shoulder with more than a little fear.

She won't remember how Lore's jackknife came to be in her hand, but she will recall vividly sawing through the cord while the furious creature in her lap screamed, its tiny mouth open in a perfect oval, so Ellen could see its pink tongue flattened beneath the surge of its wail. And for the rest of her life, whenever her hand happens to brush against fine silk or vellum, she'll recall, abruptly and completely, the newborn child's soft, soft skin.

17

What Maling Mortimer, the butcher and second tuba player of the Millworth Citizen Band, told Lewis Gutekunst, drummer and pawnbroker, had to be retold by Maling himself to Sherm Case, owner of Millworth Hardware and lead tuba, who'd heard it from the grocer and solo fiddler Cecil Farr, who'd heard it from Lewis Gutekunst. Sherm listened politely as Maling told the story through again, then he ran his fingers through a boxful of halfpenny nails and shook his head, not in disbelief anymore but in amazement, subdued amazement to be sure, but any response beyond a reticent skepticism was unusual for Sherm, and the men gathered in the store—Lewis, Cecil, and Maling Mortimer himself, still wearing his bloodied apron because he'd been summoned in the middle of a rib job by Lewis to come next door so Sherm could hear it straight from the horse's mouth—agreed that Sheriff Thompkins should be the next to hear about the goings-on.

The story, first told to Maling Mortimer by his sister-in-law, Edith Pockett Mortimer, a receptionist for Dr. Spalding, took various and somewhat contradictory shapes as it was passed among the members of the Citizens' Band, but in Maling Mortimer's hands the story was returned to its original version—if not exactly word for word the same as Edith had told Maling, then damn close. And it went something like this:

"Now you all know that Mister Hal Craxton left on one of his extended vacations last May, but what you didn't know is that he was turned out of his own home, chased out by the live-in help—that's right, the live-ins, none other. That Bennett fellow, the one who calls us trespassers when we track a deer onto Craxton land, why, he brandished a club and threatened to bash in Craxton's skull. Then the housekeeper pitched in with a carving knife, and the rest of the folks let fly with pots and pans, making such a god-awful din that Hal Craxton had to hightail it off his property right in the middle of the night. And what do you think has happened in his absence? Why, the live-ins have taken over the Big House. 'All this time' is right, Cecil, we've been thinking nothing was new up at Craxton's when as it turns out even the coloreds have settled themselves in the Big House as though they're family, sleeping in those feather beds and wearing old lady Craxton's hats and silks, playing like they're wealthy as sin when the truth is they haven't seen a week's pay since the missus died back last Christmas.

"Which is why the live-ins went after Craxton in the first place: for four months he refused to pay them a dime for their work. They must have scared the devil out of him with their midnight posse because he hasn't been heard from since that night. Left no instructions, no forwarding address, no nothing. Except, of course, the estate and all its furnishings, and the live-ins, being common folk, have claimed it as their own. I'd say they've all gone senseless, coloreds and whites boarding side by side, but that's hardly the beginning. What philanderings have taken place at the Big House we may never know for certain, but there are intimations of godlessness, according to Edith, who got it from Dr. Spalding, who says the proof of it is what they did to the colored woman on the last full moon. Why, they dragged the laboring woman into the woods, and in a moonlit glade they danced in a circle around her and chanted witch chants while she birthed her baby. Well, witches or not, Sherm, it's clear that things have gotten out of hand up there. Bennett's boy came for Dr. Spalding yesterday morning because the colored woman split herself in the birthing and needed to be stitched up. Dr. Spalding went himself, since the midwife was tending to another patient, and after he was done with the colored gal he turned around to find that crazy old taxidermist half dead of fever, so he gave him some pills and told the old man to get straight into bed. Dr. Spalding had seen enough by then to want an explanation. He took Lore Bennett aside and asked him what the hell was going on, and Bennett told him the story I've just told you, never indicating for a moment that the goings-on were a source of shame. Just the opposite! He was busting with pride and even invited Dr. Spalding to a wedding party to celebrate his marriage to Ellen Griswood. That's right, a wedding party at the Craxton estate, hosted by Mrs. Griswood and Mr. Bennett."

"Mrs. and Mr. Bennett, you mean," interjected Meade Ewell, the town clerk, who had entered the store unnoticed. Without another word he went straight to the back to fetch a rubber stamp from the stationery shelf and left a quarter on the counter before hurrying out, accidentally paying an extra five cents for the stamp, which he needed, the men learned later, to mark the date on Lore and Ellen Bennett's marriage document, having lost the town's official stamp after months of idleness. But Sherm never bothered to return the money, a small enough profit compared to the two dollars that Cecil Farr made later that morning, thanks to the newly betrothed Mr. and Mrs. Bennett, who came to his grocery store with their two youngsters, filled a basket with delicacies, and paid him in cash that had only minutes before been counted out by Lewis Gutekunst, in exchange for a pawned gold locket. And Maling himself made out like a bandit, charging Mrs. and Mr. Bennett seventy-five cents for what was supposed to be five pounds of choice sirloin but was in fact four point two pounds, the error attributable to the stealthy activity of Maling's thumb on the scale.

By high noon, when the members of the Citizens' Band gathered again for lunch, they agreed with Maling that the business up at Craxton's place needn't concern Sheriff Thompkins. The live-ins should be allowed to have some fun. "Hear, hear," said Lewis softly, raising his glass of orangeade. "Hear, hear," the others whispered, and tapped their glasses together in a quiet toast to anarchy.

The harp seal is not only the handsomest of all seals, it is also the species most valuable to man, literally worth its weight in gold, especially the babies, which are covered from nose to flipper tips with a soft, woolly, snow-white fur. The Craxton specimen, however, is an adult female, five or six years old at the time of her death and colored with yellowish patches—not exactly what an aristocratic lady would want to wear on her back as she wanders along Fifth Avenue. So this harp seal lives on into eternity with her hide intact. Boggio rubs her dusty glass eyes with his hanky before he drags the animal down from the platform, where it has sat and watched the world for the last thirteen years. The animal, so bulky in form, is surprisingly light—Boggio has no trouble carrying it across the hall and into the dining room. Lifting the seal is another matter, though, given the width of the body, so he has no choice but to leave the animal on the floor.

Next, he carries in the colorful macaw to preside at the head of the table. He positions the horn-beaked bird in its throne and slides over a moose-hoof nut bowl, giving the impression that the macaw is in the midst of a meal. To keep the macaw company, he carries out the peacock and the quetzal and sets them each in a chair.

Then Boggio lifts the cougar from the upper platform and after some thought drags the beauty into the front hall, where the tawny cat from now on will crouch, announcing with its snarl, *Ye who enter here beware,* for this is the Badlands, home of the prowling mountain lion, star of hundreds of thrilling adventure stories though in reality the cougar is a cowardly animal, easily found by dogs, chased into low trees, and shot.

But not here, not in the Badlands of the Manikin. Here, thanks to Boggio's impulsive and uncontested decision to redecorate the house, the wild animals will reign. Lore and Ellen, along with their children, are still off in town getting hitched, Sylva and her family are upstairs, so Boggio may arrange the animals just as he pleases. The point is not to situate them in a natural setting. No, Boggio will turn the human habitat over to the beasts. A carnival of the dead. With the help of the pills Dr. Spalding gave him yesterday, Boggio feels as though he's passed through a long, restful month of recuperation. He woke up this morning full of energy and purpose. He knows what it's like to be a child lost in a strange, wonderful, terrifying world. Boggio's carnival will be just as strange and wonderful and terrifying, with the fancy macaw presiding at meals and the cougar greeting visitors and the gibbons . . . where shall he put the pair of gibbons? Those delicate, shy primate-lovers, with faces so like tiny old men that Boggio feels a special kinship and wants to give them a privileged position. Why, they belong in bed, of course. Which bed? The only downstairs bedroom is the large one formerly occupied by the invalid Mrs. Craxton and now home to Lore Bennett, soon to be graced by the newlyweds. The nuptial bed will have a trial run, Boggio decides, and lifts the slender female from the embrace of her mate. He remembers with affection the difficulty he had in building the wiry, muscular manikin. The result of his efforts is a stunning specimen, not nearly as fierce as his later work yet lovely in her own way, with hands an astonishing six and a half inches long and arms stretching nearly five feet, equal in length to her supple legs. A beautiful, powerful creature, so perfect that she brings tears to Boggio's eyes. He considers how much he's missed in his life, specifically, the sight of a gibbon leaping, galloping down an open hillside in Borneo, catching herself with her hands, swinging her legs under and leaping again. Nor has he seen a cougar in the wild or watched seals cavorting in the surf. He has missed so much and now he has so little time left.

Nothing to do, old man, but to lose yourself in the carnival.

He carries in the male to join the female in bed, tucks them in, and returns to the living room. He transports the bats, the crocodile, the skunks and raccoons, the giant turtle to various corners of the house. Next he disperses the beetle collection along the windowsills, and while engaged in this work he notices that his fingers are twitching, his breath coming more rapidly than usual—attributable, he assumes, to the excitement rather than to the effort. He's a naughty old fellow, isn't he? King of the Badlands, and if the Founder were alive to see what Boggio has done to his little museum, he'd go after him with a whip.

At the orphanage school Boggio had worked his way through the long, tedious study of the System, as his teachers had called it. The System. Without it, the doors of Animate Nature would have remained locked to his curious mind. *Beware of all chaotic jumbles of unrelated facts*, he was warned. But here's the fun of nature—in chaos rather than in classification. Forget the perfect System of Nature. Instead, wander through the carnival, give a personal how-do-you-do today, meet the individuals—curiosities indeed, when you take them one by one! Oh, Boggio is punch-drunk, feeling as deliciously mischievous as a little boy spreading glue on doorknobs. Crazy old Boggio. No scientist he! Boggio is a true artist, rebellious in spirit yet fearful that the carnival, his own creation, will prove too much for him.

But still he persists, distributing wild animals throughout the house. And by the time Mr. and Mrs. Bennett return, their baskets filled with such delicacies as pickled pigs' feet and canned hearts of palm, the Manikin has been transformed.

What makes a successful party? Some experienced hosts and hostesses might make a list of necessary food items, such as:

> *18 turkeys*
> *18 fattened pullets*
> *the* noix *of 20 pheasants*
> *45 partridges*
> *72 stuffed larks*
> *a garniture of cockscombs, truffles, mushrooms, olives,*
> *asparagus, croustades, sweetbreads, and mangoes*
> *1,000 colorful petit fours*

Others might suggest an abundance of drink, or, in the language of the day, coffin varnish, craw rot, horse liniment, tarantula juice, sheep-dip, nitric acid, hypo, belch.

Some would insist that no party is worth attending if champagne doesn't flow from the faucets. Others would swear by a few prodigious strawberries dipped in chocolate. Still others would say that dress is all that matters. Or location. Or the guest list. Or the number of willing and available gentlemen. Or ladies.

In other words, there is little agreement on the essentials of a celebration. So when Mrs. Ellen Bennett, formerly Griswood, and her new husband set out to throw a party, they are, as Ellen puts it, at loose ends. Neither has had much experience with parties. Ellen doesn't know where to begin, and when she finally does manage to open a jar of herring roe, the formidable task of preparation absorbs her so completely that she forgets what the party is all about.

Not until she stumbles in her ankle-length pleated skirt over the harp seal, nearly dropping the plate of canapés onto the floor, does the thought of fun occur to her. But the near accident is proof that she is inept at contriving fun for others. She is too diligent, too responsible. What are all these animals doing out, anyway? Only now does Ellen notice the invasion, and her mood, temporarily foul, brightens at the sight of the macaw poised to snatch a nut from the center of the moose hoof. She notices the bats clinging to the mantel, and in the hall, the giant turtle is planted in the middle of the floor like a huge stone mushroom, while by the door the cougar waits to leap upon the first visitor. For a moment Ellen imagines that she sees the tail twitch ever so slightly, then she shakes her head clear and exclaims aloud, "We've been taken over by animals!"

And by children. Watch out, here come Sylva's boys, howling, sliding one after the other down the banister. Ellen tries to jump out of their way but little Manny bumps smack into her legs, looks up anxiously, sees her smile, and scampers after his brother.

The next thing Ellen knows, the front door flies open without a warning knock, and Red Vic stands before her, a bushel's worth of roses in his arms.

"Congratulations, Mrs. Bennett!"

And behind Red Vic stands Sid Cheney, looking a bit more ragged than when he left last winter.

"What a wonderful surprise!" Ellen says, gathering the roses.

"Lore invited us," Sid explains, hesitating on the threshold.

"I sent a wire from town yesterday," explains Lore, appearing beside Ellen, sliding his arm around her waist. And now that Sid has his verification he slips past the newlyweds, announcing to anyone who cares that he, Sid Cheney, is starving and can anything be done about it?

So the celebration begins with backslapping, kisses, boisterous conversation. Sid scoops up a handful of nuts as he passes the macaw, casts a feckless "Howdy" at the bird, then moves into the kitchen, where Sylva's boys, along with Junket and Peg, are plundering a box of chocolate-covered cherries. The adults join them, and soon they are all eating out of boxes and jars and drinking whiskey supplied by Lore. Peter enters the kitchen holding the bundle of his new daughter—named June after the month of her birth—and Sylva appears behind him, still walking slowly, as though the soles of her feet had been burned, but looking fresh and rested, eager to take over the preparations.

The next hour is full of rapturous sighs over the infant and not a small amount of ridicule directed at Lore—*Ten years, ten long years it took him to get up the nerve to ask for Mrs. Griswood's hand in marriage, eh, Lore, were you scared she woulda turned you down?* Lore merely chuckles at their taunts, accepting as truth what is so obviously false—that he actually loved Ellen Griswood for ten years. Everyone knows he hardly noticed her for a decade, nor she him, but the lie generated by this celebration will persist: Lore Bennett and Ellen Griswood were destined to marry and must have loved each other at first sight.

Gradually the gathering moves outside and spreads across the lawn. It is a hot, still afternoon. Wherever the warm air hits a baked, solid surface—the terrace, for instance, or the Manikin's shingled roof—a strip of air undulates in a liquid mirage. Everyone's thirsty, and no sooner does the whiskey run out than a jug of pear wine is discovered in the garden. How it got there no one will ever know—or admit—but after Peter takes a swig and declares it potable, the wine becomes the beverage of choice. The group breaks up into twos and threes, and the conversation follows. As stories replace banter, those who aren't telling settle down to listen.

On the terrace, Sylva nurses June and tells Peg the story of the birth.

By the spring, Red Vic tells Lore and Peter about a job that took him up north to Canada to pick up a shipment of skins for a Buffalo furrier.

On the front lawn, Sid tells Ellen about the sensational trial of Ruth Snyder, who was sentenced to the electric chair along with her lover, Judd Gray, for murdering her husband.

From the shore of Craxton's Pond, Junket, Manny, and Cap skip pebbles across the surface. Junket describes how he threw his brand-new Maynard rifle into the water last fall, and when Manny says he doesn't believe him, Junket tells the story again, in finer detail.

Red Vic describes how as he drove through the Algonquin Forest, a plane flying overhead spilled a huge cloud of pesticide into the trees. The dust turned the truck's gray chassis yellow and made Lore cough something horrible. He's had a sore throat ever since—and it happened nearly four weeks ago.

Sid explains what twenty-five thousand volts will do to a body.

Sylva says, "Make no mistake, Peg. Never try to manage on your own." Peg lifts Gracie onto her lap and announces that she has other plans for herself, plans that don't include children.

Junket doesn't go on to tell how his father dove for the Maynard and nearly drowned.

"Melt you like a wax doll," Sid explains, while Ellen scans the yard for Lore.

"Least you found work," Peter says to Red Vic. "It's good to know there are still jobs to be had out there."

"Far and few," Red Vic replies, kneeling to dip his cupped hands into the spring.

"Eyeballs slide down your face," Sid says, trying to goad from the new bride an exclamation of disgust, but Ellen remains silent.

"What plans, Peg? What plans can a young woman have besides children?" Sylva asks in that weary tone of voice she assumes when she doesn't care about the answer.

Peg waits for an ambition to define itself spontaneously, but when nothing comes to mind she says with a shrug, "Don't know yet."

Junket throws a pebble in a high arc and watches it drop into the water. He imagines that the Maynard lies directly below the concentric middle. He starts to take off his clothes. Manny and Cap back away a few steps, and Machine whines for something to fetch.

"You think that furrier needs other drivers?" Lore asks, examining a cluster of pea-sized grapes.

"He doesn't need me anymore, that's all I know. I haven't had much luck finding work. My age doesn't help. But Sid hasn't done any better."

"Unemployment's down," Peter points out.

"Down and going up," Red Vic replies.

Junket squishes through the muskeg and mud until the water is up to his thighs, then he glides onto his belly, splashes crazily to bring the warmth back into his limbs. Once he's become accustomed to the chill, he dives beneath the surface and begins combing through the water weeds for his lost treasure. Machine swims in circles above him.

Boggio, alone as usual and still inside the Manikin, flips through the Craxton family Bible in search of a long-forgotten verse.

To the west, the sky has darkened to a bruised turquoise.

Junket rises for a breath and dives again, trails a hand along the bottom in hopes of finding with his fingers what he cannot see. On shore Cap points to a grayish object about the size and shape of a pie plate floating on the surface. "Snapper!" he screams, and Manny joins in. "Snapper! Snapper! Snapper!"

The Book of Isaiah, Boggio recalls. The verse he's looking for is in Isaiah.

Red Vic, Peter, and Lore all agree that Smith is preferable to Hoover and Roosevelt is the state's only hope. Lore, who considers himself a man determinedly without prejudices, privately reassures himself that he'll be luckier at finding work than either Peter or Vic, since he is white.

When Junket rises again, he hears the boys shouting. He waves to them and dives. Machine barks in delight.

Ellen notices a brush of lightning in the western sky. Sid has given up trying to disgust her. He's singing rather aimlessly now—"You have a smile like an umbrella . . ."—trailing Ellen as she walks toward the terrace.

Boggio sinks back into the velvet wingback chair. " 'They shall name it No Kingdom there,' " he reads aloud, " 'and all its princes shall be nothing.' "

The men wander back up the steps and arrive on the terrace just as Ellen and Sid round the corner of the house. The infant has fallen asleep in Sylva's lap. Gracie is following the journey of a ladybug along Peg's forefingers, across her hand, over the joint of her wrist, and up her arm. *Fly away, fly away, fly away home!* Peg sends the ladybug into the air with a gentle puff. The wind carries it off. A distant rumbling of thunder to the west warns them of the approaching storm.

"Where are the boys?" Sylva asks.

"Down at the pond," Lore says and offers to go for them. Peter hurries off in the opposite direction to bring in the cows.

Thorns shall grow over its strongholds, nettles and thistles in its fortresses. It shall be the haunt of jackals, an abode for ostriches. . . .

Cap and Manny aim rocks at the snapping turtle but keep missing their target. Junket rises with a forked branch, tosses it for the dog, and dives again.

The storm eclipses the sun, casting the earth in twilight. Behind Firethorn's summit, lightning pulses rapidly. The thunder sounds like rumblings of pain escaping through clenched lips.

Lore follows the sounds of children's voices and finds Sylva's boys on shore. "Look there," Cap says. "Snapper!" Manny announces. Junket kicks to the surface, and Lore calls him in. "Snapper!" Manny shouts importantly, though it's only a piece of broken bark, Lore knows. He doesn't correct Manny, since the threat persuades Junket to swim back to shore. He reaches the shallows and stands, beads of water dripping down his heaving chest. Beautiful boy, Lore thinks. Back on land, Junket won't meet his father's eyes as he rubs himself dry with his shirt. It occurs to Lore that Junket was probably searching for the Maynard, and he feels sorry and oddly embarrassed for the boy.

" 'Yea, there shall the night hag alight and find herself a resting place. There shall the owl nest and lay and hatch and gather her young in her shadow. . . .' "

Lore leads the way back to the Manikin, Cap and Manny chirping about the snapping turtle—big as a goat, big enough to take off Junket's foot.

Rain hits with fierce suddenness, surprising everyone, and in the few seconds it takes to reach the backdoor they are drenched, all except little June, who is bundled in a cotton towel and clutched against Sylva's breast. Lore and the boys dash in a minute later, and soon the party peaks in laughter again as Peter arrives hugging the jug of pear wine for dear life.

"Rain on the wedding day means wealth!" Sid roars, and he starts singing his smile-like-an-umbrella song again. Ellen drinks a full glass of sweet wine as though it were lemonade, feels dizzy, and lowers herself into a chair. The men take advantage of her momentary incapacity and lift her chair above their shoulders, carrying her in the wobbly throne out of the kitchen and through the hall while the children scream and dance behind them and Sylva claps and Sid keeps singing. Round the procession winds through the dining room, past Boggio in the library, who tags along in the rear, across the hall, through the living room that looks strangely unfurnished without its assembly of animals, around the conservatory, back into the living room, Boggio holding a baby skunk on one shoulder, a weasel on the other, Sylva's boys shrieking, Ellen slightly terrified by all the ruckus, the thunder crashing against the sides of the house, the sky spitting through open windows, joy as engulfing as a flood. Of course no one hears the automobile skid along the gravel drive, no one notices the two figures dashing toward the house, though from her perch Ellen does see the front door swing open, but the sight robs her of her voice, and she can only stare in horror as the giddy revelers move out of the living room into the hall, where they find themselves facing, across the varnished green hump of the turtle, none other than Hal and Lilian—née Stone— Craxton.

The celebration is over. The master has returned with a wife. Nothing will ever be the same.

18

They say that the thunderstorms that night were the region's worst in twenty years. They say that at the top of Firethorn an old oak tree, long dead, was struck by lightning and burst into flames, and that the flames shot up so high into the galaxy that they touched a star, and the star exploded, filling the sky with a cascade of sparks.

They say that up at the Manikin, it wasn't the wind that broke three windows and a mantel clock—it was Henry Junior, who went temporarily mad on account of the storm. Or was it bad home-brewed liquor, iodine and tapwater disguised as whiskey? No one could say for sure. But the fact was, he smashed up his own house and even tried to kill a colored child but was stopped by Lore Bennett, who beat him soundly.

The servants vacated the house that night without bothering to pack their few belongings. Peter tucked little June inside his shirt and led his family through the downpour back to their cabin. Lore and Ellen fled with Junket and Peg to the gatehouse, Red Vic and Sid Cheney close on their heels. Only Boggio chose to stay behind. He went up to the master bedroom and locked himself in. When Hal pounded on the door, Boggio refused to open for him.

So Lilian and Hal spent their first night together in the Manikin in the main guest room, Lily's old room, recently inhabited by Peg and still strewn with her clothes and various books borrowed—rather, filched—from the Manikin's library.

Offended by this new disorder, Hal threw every article of clothing out the window; then he lay back on the bed, his head raised by pillows, and stared at the white forepart of his Ralston sailor-tie oxfords. Lilian sat in a wicker chair by the door. To onlookers, they would have seemed more like a prisoner and guard than husband and wife, with Lilian keeping watch—keeping her thoughts to herself as well, while Hal muttered about the goddamn servants, wondering aloud why he hadn't set the law on them long ago.

If it had been up to Lily, the celebration downstairs would have continued in all its frenzy—she'd obviously loved what she'd seen. But she hadn't seen enough. She hadn't been there the night the servants mutinied, no, she hadn't suffered the humiliation, when Hal Craxton became the unhappy victim of an insurrection. He'd been licking his wounds ever since, the episode never satisfactorily distant in his mind, and he'd gone ahead and married young Lily for the same reason that soldiers get drunk after a defeat—in an effort to distract himself.

But Lily, as it turned out, hadn't been able to sympathize with her husband in this matter. She spent most of the drive to the Manikin trying to persuade him to go easy on the staff. For the final miles she'd fallen silent, and Hal's anger had intensified with the storm. He'd expected to find the servants making themselves at home, but he hadn't been prepared to walk into the midst of a carousal. A wedding celebration, no less—Ellen betrothed to Mr. Green Thumb himself, a natural match, and why Hal had ever been inclined toward such a plain and uninspiring woman as that, he couldn't say.

He hadn't been able to say what he thought when he first opened the door, so tongue-tied was he by the image of Ellen teetering on her precarious throne. He had stared at her and she at him for what must have been a full minute. And then he'd gone wild, heaving the giant turtle onto its back, and seizing a walking stick from the hall stand, swinging it over his head. Ellen almost tumbled headfirst out of her chair. But the men managed to lower her to the floor without injury, and they moved in a tight herd out of Hal's reach. He growled at them. They backed into the living room. The room had been altered, he saw at once, though it took him a moment to identify the change. Why, his father's Cabinet of Curiosities—it had been scattered! The famous Craxton Collection, the only thing of value his mother had actually wanted him to keep. The bats were hanging like old stockings from the mantel, the windowsills were covered with bugs, rodents roamed underfoot, beasts lounged on chairs and sofas. In a rage, Hal swung his stick, spun around, smashed his mother's mantel clock instead of the bats, smashed a windowpane and another, object by object destroying the house he had come to claim.

What happened next, like most accidents, did not adhere to the normal rules of time. Or that's how everyone would remember it: the stick swinging forcefully but without constant velocity, so it seemed to move forward and then stop, move forward and stop, move straight toward Gracie's head with stop-start accuracy. There stood little Gracie, still burbling with delight, unaware that the celebration had ended and that Hal Craxton was the enemy. . . . The stick swung round, Hal swiveling on his feet rather than at the hips so he didn't see what he was about to strike. But the others saw, and Sylva managed to fill the gaps between the seconds with a scream while Lore dove through the air toward the child, covering her like the shadow of a cloud and catching the head of the stick on his buttocks.

Thwack! The master had struck his servant, an outrage that wasn't supposed to happen, not in this democratic twentieth century, not in America. Lore yelped, turned round to face his assailant, gave another yelp, not in surprise and pain this time but in fury, and barreled head-first into Craxton's belly, pushing him against the wall and pounding his face with the work-worn knuckles of his right fist until Red Vic pulled him off.

He left Hal Craxton bent over, dripping blood. They all left him, except Lilian, who without thinking used the gold-threaded armrest cover from the sofa to stop his nosebleed. Obviously impatient, she helped her husband upstairs, and after the brief standoff with Boggio, she led him to the room that had been hers for the past winter.

So they spent that first night separated by the vast expanse of Hal's anger. Lilian dozed in the chair while Hal studied his shoes and plotted revenge. He was still plotting when, hours later, Lilian woke with a shriek, clutching her throat, forgetting at once the content of the dream but still so overcome by a sense of peril that it took her a solid minute to catch her breath. And then she gave another little shriek and pointed at the floor.

"What in God's name is that?"

Why, the head of a twenty-two-foot-long reticulated python (dead, of course), peeking out from beneath the bed, that's all, Lily. Just a python left by naughty old Boggio to scare a girl witless.

Once upon a time, a giant turtle was overturned by a cruel man and left to die. "Someone help me!" Turtle cried, wagging his leathery legs in the air.

Dame Cougar, who just happened to be nearby stalking a young rabbit, came along and nudged the shell to set it rocking, but try as she might she couldn't put Turtle right side up. "Wait here," she instructed and slouched down the hall looking for an assistant. Finally she came upon Mr. and Mrs. Gibbon, who were having a romp in bed. Dame Cougar waited impatiently for the loving couple to finish with their business, then she cleared her throat to gain their attention.

"I need your assistance," she said. "Both of you." So Mr. and Mrs. Gibbon, always compliant, swung after her down the hall, hands to feet, feet to hands. Together, the three of them managed to turn over poor Turtle.

"A sordid affair," Turtle said, bending her neck to improve her circulation.

"That's people for you, pee-people, hardy-hah!" piped Macaw, who'd hopped in from the dining room to watch the rescue effort and was chewing on a cigar, scattering tobacco everywhere.

"Stinking homo sapiens," mumbled Bat.

"Such a sight," Daisy Dik-Dik said. The animals contemplated the refuse: broken glass, cracker crumbs, a pickled pig's foot here, a sardine tail there. Not that they were surprised. Having lived among people for so long, they knew that the fundamental desire in a human heart was to destroy things, and from day to day they weren't fooled by a show of propriety—even the housekeeper couldn't deceive them. Mankind had been put upon the earth to create havoc, and as long as the species flourished, nothing was safe.

But the animals had grown accustomed to domestic life, and for their own sakes they had to make the Manikin inhabitable again. So despite their indignation, they spent the rest of the night restoring order. They washed and returned dishes to cupboards, discarded half-eaten food, swept up crumbs and broken glass. Dame Cougar dusted the windowsills with her tufted tail, Mr. P. Cock took care of the tables, Turtle pushed the carpet sweeper over the rugs, and the Gibbonses polished the silverware. Meanwhile, the domestic cockroaches organized their lesser fellows into groups and ushered them back to their display boxes. Daisy Dik-Dik plumped cushions, and Macaw stationed himself on the mantel and called out orders. All through the night the animals cleaned the house—not because it was their job but because it was a matter of survival. And what a job they did! Leave it to animals to repair the damage done by man. Leave it to animals to set everything right.

At least that's what happens in a fairy tale—reparation so total it is magical, and everyone lives happily ever after.

After Hal bravely evicted the python from the bedroom, Lilian fell into one of those selfish and provocative slumbers so typical of beautiful young women, Hal knew from experience, having watched scores of them sleeping. She lay with her lips parted in an all-too-suggestive smile, her tongue flickering inside her mouth like the flame of a gas lamp. Annoyed by her self-sufficiency, Hal left her to her dreams and descended the front stairs.

Someone must have crept back into the house during the night and cleaned up—other than the broken windowpanes, Hal could find no sign of the merrymaking or of his own violent spree. Even the animals had been returned to their platform. Still, he half expected to hear the echoes of mayhem bouncing off the walls. He touched his hand to his nose—no blood flowing, but the bridge ached beneath the light pressure of his finger. The worse pain, though, was the memory of his latest humiliation. First he'd been evicted from his own home by his employees, and upon his return he'd been manhandled by his groundskeeper. Well, he'd come back to stay, to take control of the Manikin again. He was Henry Craxton Junior, worthy and legal heir to a natural history magnate, or so the court had ruled with unexpected alacrity, not because of Mary Craxton's supposed insanity but on the basis of a legal glitch in the revised will, transferring to Hal the property that his mother had tried to deny him. His first task as master of the household would be to dismiss all the servants.

He wanted nothing more to do with them after what they'd done to him. While distraught over the loss of his mother, he'd been tricked into loving Ellen Griswood. Then the others had tricked him into fleeing. It had taken him a full month of recuperation to realize that he'd committed no crime and to understand the import of his mother's death, which had affected him more than he'd thought. The Stone family had kindly nursed him back to sanity, hosting him while *Craxton v. Craxton* moved through probate. And on the very day the judge ruled in favor of the plaintiff, Lilian Stone's father offered Hal his daughter's hand in marriage.

Between the dowry and his own income, Hal could have afforded to close up the Manikin and travel with Lily. Perhaps they would someday, but not until they had purged the house of demons. "Demons" was the word on the tip of his tongue when he entered the library—it was the word he'd fled from seven weeks earlier. So when he saw a woman's knees covered by a pleated skirt poking out from the chair, he almost turned and ran again.

Instead, he inhaled deeply to regain his composure, wandered over to the mantel, and finally spoke.

"I'm giving you twenty-four hours' notice, Mrs. Griswood," he said.

"Mrs. Bennett," she corrected him.

"Your impudence," he muttered and let the phrase float without a predicate.

"Mine!" she echoed. "Mine, indeed!"

It angered him that she had occupied his wingback chair without permission, but he couldn't bring himself to order her away. Instead, after a pause he asked, "What do you want from me?"

"I want compensation," she said.

He thought he detected a surreptitious embarrassment in her tone of voice. Or maybe he was hearing what he expected to hear, given the nature of the demand. It wasn't just back wages she wanted—she expected him to pay her for the disagreeable business behind them, the business concerning that kiss he'd thoughtlessly bestowed upon her coquette of a daughter. Compensation? Why, he'd pay his housekeeper exactly what she deserved.

"Certainly, Ellen. Excuse me. Mrs. Bennett, I mean."

He glided around the front of the chair and dropped a nickel into her lap.

Oh, what a dynamo! The force of her temper, which Hal had glimpsed only briefly that night she'd turned on him, was astonishing—Ellen, thin-lipped, staid Ellen, leapt up and flung the coin at Hal's feet. It glanced off his shoe and rolled across the floor until it was stopped by the rug's fringe.

"You bastard, you!"

He expected her to come at him then, almost hoped she'd strike him so he could hit her in self-defense.

But Ellen just leaned against the chair, clutching the arm for balance as she rocked forward, bloated with hatred to the point of bursting. Hal had never known a woman to show her hatred so blankly, so honestly. For a minute he was shaken, until he recalled the absurd image of Ellen riding high above the men's shoulders on a kitchen chair, Cleopatra of the Manikin. She'd obviously been frightened by his sudden entrance last night, perceiving as she did the scope of his authority, and Hal needed only to coax the fear to the surface.

"You won't get any reference from me," he grumbled, "so don't ask."

"I'll take what I'm owed."

"You're a sharp beggar, Ellen Griswood. Bennett, I mean. Mrs. Bennett. Now if you sent your pretty child to collect, I might find it in my heart to be generous."

"I curse you. I curse this house."

"Good God, a curse! The sorceress has put a curse upon me! Whatever shall I do? I'm turning into a frog, help, croak, oh! Why, Mrs. Bennett, you're not amused."

"You disgust me."

"And to think we might have been man and wife. Mrs. Ellen Craxton—no, it doesn't sound right, does it? But your daughter, now there's a catch!"

Smugness tends to dull caution. So Hal Craxton, whose smugness had flourished during this dialogue, was not prepared for the full consequences of Ellen's temper, and he caught the milky foam of her spittle on his lips and chin before he could turn away. Shock froze him in place for the few seconds it took her to escape—a good thing because if he'd been able to move he would have grabbed the woman by the neck and choked the breath from her.

They would have taken the dogwoods and honeysuckle, the grapevines and wintergreen. They would have carried away the apple trees as well. The pastures. The spring. The azaleas and dahlias, the holly, the basil and wormwort and parsley, the cows and chickens, the lop-eared barnyard tomcat, the rock bass, walleyes, and trout, the songbirds and crows, the deer, beaver, muskrats, groundhogs, skunks, raccoons, and field mice. They would have loaded the Manikin itself piece by piece onto a broad-bed truck and carted it off. But everything, or almost everything, belonged to Hal Craxton. The servants might as well have been watching a fire sweep over the estate, leveling all that they loved. The Craxton land, the Craxton manor, the Craxton Collection—all had been used and appreciated by the servants, and now they felt cheated. The Manikin and grounds had been theirs in spirit, or so it seemed. But semblance made for an insubstantial claim, and here at the end of their terms of employment, they discovered what should have been obvious all along: they were taking away only what they'd brought to the Manikin, nothing more.

Peg could have dispersed the illusion long ago. She'd never been confused about ownership. Nearly every material thing within the boundaries of the estate belonged to the Craxtons, except, of course, the servants themselves. They'd always been free to leave. But having left and returned, Peg understood what her mother feared—a worse, more constraining evil that could drive decent people to ruin.

If only Hal Craxton had abandoned the Manikin forever. If only summer would never end. If only crimes could be undone, love withheld. Peg had spent the last weeks pretending that she had no past. But the past had overtaken her in the form of Hal Craxton and his new wife, so Peg had no choice but to go forward.

First, though, she would go backward and do what she should have done long ago: confront Lily face to face. She waited a few minutes after her mother left for the Manikin to gather her belongings, then Peg went up to the house herself, ostensibly to collect her own clothes from the guest room. Entering through the pantry, she found the kitchen immaculate, as though a regimen of elves—or perhaps her tireless mother—had scrubbed and straightened during the night. She crept quietly up the rear stairs, pausing when she heard the far-off rumbling of voices, which called to mind her stealthy departure on Christmas morning, when she'd snuck down these same stairs and fled the house, intending never to return.

She was moving in the opposite direction now, her attention so fixed on the imminent meeting that she didn't care who was talking. On the second floor she went straight to the guest room and without knocking opened the door. She wasn't surprised to see Lily's creamy shoulders and head poking out from beneath the crocheted spread. What surprised Peg—though it shouldn't have, given the voices she'd heard from the stairwell—was to find Lily alone.

She entered the room as quietly as possible, hesitated at each creaking board, but Lily didn't move. Peg stood beside the bed and studied the contour of her body—she lay prone, her arms folded and tucked beneath her belly, her legs stretched out, her whole body as rigid as a plank, tense even in sleep, though her face, while not exactly relaxed, looked more thoughtful than anxious, like the face of a woman trying to recapture a lost memory.

Peg had come here for a dramatic showdown but found herself slipping back into love, dragged by the force of Lily's beauty. Who could compare? Such intelligent, exquisitely drawn features, shoulders so slender and yet so soft. *Remember how soft they are, Peg?* She let her hand hover for a moment, then dropped her fingers to the back of Lily's neck. Lily squirmed a little in sleep, just as Peg must have done while the stranger who had come to assault her in the Kettling station stood examining his prey. Lily's vicious lover. Lily couldn't necessarily be held responsible for his jealousy. It could be that she'd preferred Peg and had admitted it to him and sent him away with a few harsh words, never foreseeing the toll he would exact for a love that excluded him. It could be that Lily's only fault was to have loved recklessly.

Under Lily's spell once more, Peg forgave her almost everything, and without considering where it would lead began stroking the back of Lily's neck with her forefingers, rousing her into a docile, half-awake state, coaxing a dreamy smile of recognition from her, falling into her embrace as Lily rolled over and lifted her arms.

Peg was enchanted, yes, in love again, adoring and adored. But if given the opportunity, she would have revenged herself. And sure enough, the opportunity arrived in the form of Hal Craxton, who came up the hall and stretched his head around the open door to take a peek at his young wife. But she was murmuring the same old meaningless vows to Peg, so lost in her bliss that she didn't notice her husband. But Peg saw him—rather, she saw a man leaning out from behind the door, not Hal Craxton but the other one, the nameless one. Peg felt the stranger's presence as surely as she felt Lily's arms sliding up and down her back. It occurred to her then that the man who raped her in the Kettling station might have seen for himself what Lily had tried to keep secret, might have spied on the two girls and discovered their secret love. That was what had enraged him so, a secret inadvertently revealed, and he'd revenged himself on Peg.

Now she would give her beloved Lilith a turn with the devil. Peg held her face between her hands and kissed her, sinking her tongue deep into her mouth. On the threshold, Hal Craxton broke into a savage howl.

19

Babel. Pandemonium. Marrowbones and cleavers. The world was about to end, or so Ellen thought when Hal Craxton's voice came roiling like thick smoke through the upstairs window. How she knew that her daughter was in danger she'd never be able to explain. She had left Peg with the others in the gatehouse. But she sensed with instinctive certainty that Peg had followed her up to the Manikin and was entangled in whatever crisis had prompted Hal Craxton's yell. Ellen ran back along the drive in the direction she'd just fled, into the house, up the stairs, and came to a panting halt just inside the guest room, where Hal Craxton was methodically slapping his wife back and forth across the face.

At first Ellen thought he was trying to revive her from a drunken stupor, until she noticed that he held Lilian's wrists in one restraining hand. Only then did she become conscious of her daughter, who after moving a few steps away from the bed suddenly lunged forward and threw her fists against the man. He was insensible to the assault, too intent on hurting his wife, and he kept on beating her without pause, as persistent as a factory machine slapping labels on bottles. He hit Lilian's right cheek with his open palm, slammed her left cheek with the back of his hand, slapped her right cheek again, then left, then right, smearing blood across the pale skin while Lilian's head rocked beneath the force of the blows. And in the next moment Ellen found she was no longer a spectator—she had scrambled into the midst of the tempest, intending to stop the violence, hardly a simple feat, though she did succeed in planting herself between Hal and the bed, which enabled Lily to roll away and gave Peg a chance to claw Hal's face. Peg was eager to kill, and if she'd happened to have a knife handy, the blade would surely have ended up in Hal Craxton's heart.

But she had only fists and teeth and nails, and with these she pursued her offensive. Soon Lily was caught up by the momentum of the attack, then Ellen, too. They set upon their common enemy alongside Peg while he flailed wildly in defense. The women knocked, kicked, battered blindly, and just when they were beginning to get the better of Hal Craxton, just when they were about to devour him alive, he slipped out from the center of the melee and, true and honest craven that he was, retreated from the room.

Leaving behind three women, three weird sisters, or so they looked to themselves in their bloody, disheveled state. Three powerful sisters. When Lily covered her split lip with her hand and began to giggle, Peg joined her, as though the amusement were a song, a cackling round, and Peg laughed along so eagerly that Ellen couldn't help but add a few chuckles herself.

They laughed the way bruised survivors of an accident might laugh, relieved to the point of madness. But their relief was short-lived. It took just a connecting flash of recollection for Ellen to see in her mind what she had never witnessed—Hal Craxton taking advantage of her daughter. Nothing funny about that, or about a husband beating his wife, and these girls had no right to feel so lighthearted. No, it wasn't proper—Ellen indicated her disapproval with a scowl, and as soon as Peg became aware of her mother's change of mood she sobered, too, catching a gulp of laughter in her throat and holding it there. Only Lily's gaiety continued. With Ellen and Peg looking on in silence, her laughter grew more hysterical and gradually, steadily, transformed into a wail.

That should have marked a turning point—a turning away from the hysteria and confusion back to the events leading up to this night.

Together the three women should have explained and confessed, comforted and admonished. Some resolution, however forced, should have been reached. But the effort toward a resolution was never begun because Hal Craxton decided to return right then and take control, using words instead of force this time. He stood in the center of the room and mopped his face with a hanky. After staring at the women for a moment with a frightened, trapped-fox expression, he shook his head as though to rattle his memory, and said, "I don't know what came over me." He waited for someone to respond, but the women contemplated him in silence. He caressed his chin with his palm and after a minute murmured, "Mrs. Griswood, please accept my apologies. And you, young lady." He nodded his remorse to Peg. "And Lily, my dearest Lily. I beg your forgiveness. I didn't mean to hurt you."

A strategic apology, Ellen thought. Although she didn't doubt Hal's sincerity, she resented his tactic. By apologizing, he was reclaiming his honor and asserting himself as the directing presence in the room. And to Ellen's disappointment, Lily gave in, subordinating herself with the most melodramatic of gestures: she ran to him, collapsed to the floor, and embraced his knees, pressing her bloody lips against his trousers as though begging for her life. And it was just this—her life as Mrs. Craxton—that she clearly wanted to preserve.

A glance toward Peg confirmed to Ellen that she shared her mother's disappointment. Indeed, without waiting to see where the reconciliation would lead, Peg whirled around and rushed out of the room.

Ellen started to follow her daughter but first was compelled to take one last sweeping look around the room. She assigned it all to memory—the drapes, the wallpaper, the flagstone fireplace, the chest of drawers, the barren whatnot, and the oil painting hanging above the bed. She'd never taken the time to study the picture at any length before. There'd been no reason, since it was obviously an amateurish still life. But despite its ordinary qualities the image of the brace of pheasants sprawled across a table lingered like a light spot behind closed eyes, and it became conflated with the scene she left behind. As she descended the stairs after her daughter, the spindled banister wobbly beneath her hand, she pictured the slaughtered pheasants with human faces, husband and wife, their colorful plumage caked with blood.

. . .

On the final night, the stars in the heavens turned into sugar sprinkles, the moon was a twist of lemon, and all the servants and their children slept soundly, gathering their strength for the various journeys ahead of them. All except Junket and Peg, who, unable to sleep, had wandered separately to Craxton's Pond. Peg was dragging a stick through the shallows when Junket came upon her. Fishing for lost memories. Two childhoods spent in this unreal place. Tomorrow they would enter the Real World, or so Junket believed. He didn't much care where they went, as long as he kept Peg near him. They were brother and sister now, irrevocably connected, an inadequate intimacy but better than nothing, from Junket's point of view. The taboo made it necessary for him to love her without wanting her—or such was his self-deception. Artifice of kinship. Peg would be his sister forever.

"Whatcha thinking?" he asked gently, settling on the ground beside her.

She threw a pebble into the pond. In the darkness, it seemed to Junket that the water swelled into the shape of a hand that reached up and grabbed the pebble.

After a minute, Peg said, "I don't know what I want anymore."

Junket tried to comfort her with his own enthusiasm. "We'll be in a new place by this time tomorrow, and by the end of the week we'll have reached my uncle's house. The ocean . . . I've never seen the ocean. Maybe I'll be a fisherman!"

"I don't care what happens."

"But don't you want to leave? You ran away once. Why did you run away?" Junket had never asked Peg this question because the answer seemed too dangerous—it had something to do with Hal Craxton, who had mistreated Peg, used her rudely. The nature of the abuse was clear, though the extent of it remained hidden behind the whispers of adults.

Peg let the pause lengthen into what seemed a permanent silence, a noisy, nighttime silence filled with the cicadas competing with the frogs for attention, the crickets rubbing their wings raw.

"Stupid, stupid boy," Peg finally said, repeating the insult that had so shaken Junket that night he shot the snowy owl. But this time she did not throw the words at him. She charged him with his stupidity in a fond, slightly ironic tone of voice. And Junket, rather than feeling diminished or insulted, simply felt frustrated by his ignorance. Peg knew so much about how the world worked and what to expect from it. And she had reasons for everything. Junket had lived too narrowly to understand such complex things as a girl's motivation for running away.

"I ran away from myself," Peg said after a minute, her words obviously packed with meaning, though Junket still didn't understand.

"You're . . . you're perfect," he blurted, and immediately felt ashamed for revealing his admiration in such simple terms. But Peg put her arm around him, giving him the sort of hug that both comforted and discouraged him.

"You think so, eh? If you only knew."

"Knew what?"

"Knew about me and Lilian Stone. Now do you understand?"

He answered her with silence. What was there to understand? Peg admired that hotshot girl. So what? Such admiration wasn't a flaw in her character. It was just a temporary mistake.

"Forget it, then," Peg said, which made Junket feel that understanding was his responsibility. So he worked at it while they both contemplated the water and waved away mosquitoes and blackflies. He tried to consider Lilian Stone through Peg's eyes, tried to fathom the meaning of the conjunction: *Me and Lilian Stone.* Maybe Peg felt like she had lost her friend to an unworthy husband. But it was more than that. More, perhaps, like love.

Now a boy of such provincial experience might be disgusted by the inkling of what he perceives to be an unnatural love. Or such love might seem as natural as any other variation he'd ever observed in the wild. For Junket, the possibility that Peg actually loved Lilian Stone in the same way that he loved Peg filled him with respectful awe. So she could love, too. He had never quite believed her capable of love—or, more accurately, he'd flattered himself to think that if Peg wouldn't love him, she couldn't love anyone. But she'd loved fancy Lilian Stone. Junket thought he knew exactly how Peg felt and tried to find a way to convey his sympathy without embarrassment. That the intimacy Peg desired had been anything more than imagined never occurred to Junket. He assumed that Peg had restricted her love to a fantasy, and he was honored by her confidence. *Me and Lilian Stone.* He thought he understood the implications; he would go on believing that he and Peg had loved and suffered equally.

He squeezed her hand. This gentle pressure had a stunning effect, releasing from Peg a rush of sorrow so engulfing that Junket's first impulse was to throw Peg into the water and rid himself of the burden. But this selfish and all-too-familiar urge was as short-lived as it was contemptible, and Junket collected the sobbing girl into his arms.

"Don't despise me," she cried, clutching him, "don't ever despise me."

He stroked her hair and soothed her, assured her that he wouldn't despise her, promised to love her forever. This was what he'd always wanted, wasn't it? To hold her and speak of his love. Yet how subdued this love was—celibate and dependable. They would go to each other for comfort through the rest of their lives. The purity and strength of this affection couldn't mask the fact that it was insufficient, that Junket would always want more of Peg than she was willing to give him. But he found comfort in the knowledge that he could provide comfort. No one would ever come between them. They would live in that glass world they'd invented as children, loving others but trusting only each other.

After Peg had calmed, they sat together listening to the night sounds—frogs and insects, a hoot owl in the distance. The air itself seemed to radiate a soft, buzzing sound, the sound of energy, of conduction and flux, of tiny particles in motion, spinning in a wild, rigorous dance.

It must have been nearly midnight when they stood up and headed back to the gatehouse. They'd already packed their suitcases. Tomorrow Win Gill would drive them in the truck the twelve miles to Kettling, and from there they'd set out on the long train ride to Halifax, where an uncle of Lore's had settled years ago—and prospered, by all accounts.

When they stepped from the wooded path onto the grass, they both halted, as though struck by an identical insight. Ahead of them, the Manikin was flattened into a silhouette, and the windows, painted black by darkness, hid the empty space behind the surface. Junket suddenly wanted to shatter a window—if he'd had his Maynard he would surely have fired it. Instead, he heaved a rock toward the house, but it fell far short, landing in the middle of the lawn. He wanted to try again, wanted to keep on throwing rocks until he'd shattered every window in that useless mansion. But Peg was tugging at him, so he gave up and accompanied her toward the drive and down to the gate-house. As they walked along he hooked his arm through hers, desiring only to keep her close and to protect her, or to be protected.

Leviathan house, unwanted. Triton among the minnows. Folly clothed in warped, mossy shingles, a portico collar, false pillars, with a dirt basement for bowels, sloping floors, crumbling walls. Pity the house. Failed sanitorium. Giant kennel built to restore others and doomed to rot alone.

Don't go, the Manikin would plead if it could speak. *Don't leave me.*

Soon the house will lie empty, uninhabited. First old Boggio's heart will give out and he'll be found dead in the master bedroom after surviving behind that locked door for nearly two months, subsisting on meals carried up to him at night by the new cook—Nancy Gill, whom Hal will hire on the spot when she comes to the door one day begging for potatoes—and emptying his slops from the window into the garden below. Then Mrs. Gill will quit, choosing to endure poverty with her family than to exist in a state of tenuous dependency, vassal to Hal Craxton, as unpredictable an employer as you'll ever find. And shortly before Thanksgiving, the mistress will desert the master— flocks of honking geese heading south will undo her, and she'll drop to her knees in one more show of abject humility, entreat him to escape the coming winter, and when he refuses she'll leave for Millworth on foot and from there catch the bus to Rochester. Hal Craxton will spend one horrific night alone in the Manikin, though what, exactly, he experiences during the wee hours he won't tell; the next day he'll take off after his wife, never to return. He'll persuade her to join him on his travels, and together the two will wander the globe, miserable but determined tourists, dodging wars, both of them refusing to settle anywhere for long. Lily will die of cancer in 1949, but Hal will live on in stubborn health for another thirty years. And in all that time he won't visit his country estate, won't even arrange for the upkeep, though he'll go on paying his taxes and will refuse all bids on the property, suggesting to the residents of Millworth that someday he intends to come home.

So the Big House will be granted, at last, a tranquil quiet, its privacy vast and impenetrable. All those spacious rooms and corners, nooks and crannies, cupboards, bookcases, closets, and the animals, don't forget the stuffed animals—they will be left alone. No more children tormenting, no tireless housekeeper heartlessly scrubbing and dusting everything in sight. True, occasional intruders will be a nuisance, and the rats will claim the basement for themselves. But mostly the Manikin will remain free of the inconveniences of habitation.

There's something wonderfully beguiling about an abandoned mansion. And the stuffed animals will only add to the mystery. Stories told about the house will become legends. Local gossips will invest the Manikin with magical qualities, and over time it will be turned into a provincial shrine, a necropolis of curiosities. Preservation experts will be called in, funds will be raised. The house will have a second life as a museum. Now there's something to look forward to!

But I can practically hear the voice of despair: *Toss me a match. An ember. A lit cigarette will do. I'll give you a show for your money!*

The Manikin, being just an inanimate structure and thus completely unreasonable, doesn't realize that it has an obligation. What the thieves don't take will be sacred one day. The house will be worshiped and eventually sustained by the citizens of Millworth, so there's nothing for it to do but to wait patiently, in its untenanted misery, for time to spin out its plan.

You could say, I suppose, that time's the culprit. Seize-an-opportunity time. Whereupon, anno Domini time. The Manikin will be left behind and eventually preserved as a representative of an extinct species, directly related to our feudal ancestors in Europe but still distinctly American, reminding us that the entire country once posed as a haven. But time has a tendency to plunder existence, to steal our sense of purpose. Abandoned by its owner, the house will have to endure the natural elements for over half a century without any material help from mankind.

Amazing, really, that it will survive such lengthy neglect, for the natural world looms on all sides, eager to take possession. Brier and holly will spread into wild tangles, the overgrown lawn will fill with nettles, climbing ivy will strangle the flowering vines. All evidence of the cultivated gardens and orchards will be eradicated by the jealous wilderness, until the Manikin will resemble nothing more than an ark floating upon a sea of weeds. If it were capable, the house would console itself by recalling pleasant memories—the sound of laughter, the smell of hop-yeast and salt-rising bread, the feel of fresh springwater coursing through its pipes. According to the stories, however, the house will survive its fifty-year abandonment not because of an inherent hardiness or even luck. It will survive the vandals and brush fires, lightning, hail, floods, and blizzards because it is guarded by the spirit of its most famous trophy—the snowy owl, an animal as formidable as it is rare in these parts, fierce carrion bird and, so they say, interlocutor between hell and earth.

In all likelihood, the Big House will stand intact far into the next millennium. There it perches on its broad hill-spur in the shadow of Firethorn, surrounded by a sloping lawn that falls and then rises again to the upland orchards. Half hermit, half monarch, it will remain insensible to the remarkable advancements of civilization—penicillin, television, fluorescent lamps, Mickey Mouse, crossword puzzles, women governors, John T. Scopes, Gertrude Stein, vitamin B—and as oblivious to the great betrayals of history, the broken treaties and mass murders, as a newborn child.

20

I returned only once, in 1958. On a whim, I left my home in Connecticut early one Saturday morning and drove west along Interstate 90. Many hours later I turned south, following the Genesee River for forty miles before crossing through Millworth and over Firethorn on Gulf Road. I arrived at the Manikin shortly before dusk.

At the time, Hal Craxton was still alive, and the Manikin had been left unattended for three decades. The surge of development in the Northeast hadn't hit the region yet—Millworth was destined to remain a poor village, the railway no longer ran through Kettling, and no major highways had been built to connect the region to the upstate cities. A few small industries had sprung up, though, and Gulf Road was home to an occasional four-room ranch house. But traffic remained light, and on Hadley Road, between the old Gill farm and the Manikin, I didn't pass a single car.

The huge pocket of Craxton land, crowned by its Greek Revival mansion, appeared at the end of my journey like a hidden world behind a mirror. A soft breeze blew cottonwood puffs through the air while swallows swooped through clouds of midges. I sat on the hood of my car and contemplated the Manikin's north facade with the attention I would have given a letter I'd written as a child, not quite believing that I'd been the author, or that I'd been a resident of this Golgotha. How strange to think that I'd spent much of my childhood here, while my mother exhausted herself trying to keep the house in order and her employer distracted. I wouldn't wish such work on anyone. Yet my mother had proved herself a capable rebel. "The Craxton Uprising," we called it in the family stories retold every holiday. And the part I'd played, the lie I'd told my mother to keep her from marrying Hal Craxton—the thought of it made me laugh aloud as I sat there.

Although age had eroded my youthful audacity, my memories began to come back to me with such force that I grew curious about the Manikin, and curiosity made me bold. I'd come here to see how the house had fared through the years. I decided I couldn't leave until I'd explored the interior.

The first-floor windows had been boarded shut, but after circling the house I found an open basement window. A path indented in the weeds suggested that I was not the first trespasser to use this entrance. And evidence of others made me wary. But I persisted in my adventure, and with some difficulty I managed to squeeze through the basement window and lower myself onto a trestle that had been moved against the wall. A splinter on the window frame snagged my trousers and ripped the denim open, luckily without catching my skin. Once level on the dirt floor, I moved toward the ladder that led up to the first floor. I had to keep hunched over, since the basement was only four feet in height. The old furnace stood in the same place, the ash door open to reveal the pit where the grates had been. The boiler lay on its side. The wooden boxes used by Sylva to store apples and potatoes remained exactly where she'd left them. They were empty, of course, along with the coal bin, the furnace, the house itself. I stood still for a moment, trying to gauge the extent of the emptiness. The pulse of this great, vague place had stopped. And here I was sneaking across the basement like some wayfarer intent on plundering a tomb.

As I looked up the ladder to the open hatchway, I couldn't help but think that something awful awaited me there—a dead body, a skeleton, pieces of matted hair torn from a skull, a ghost. I am not the sort of woman who normally indulges in superstition, but the threat was both so real and abstract that I couldn't stop my imagination from drifting.

Lore had cut that hatchway into the kitchen floor back when I was seven or eight, and in the years that followed I used to marvel at my mother's fortitude as she descended the ladder into this well of darkness. Now my own courage fed upon itself as I ascended until my fears faded to nothing. I climbed to my feet in the kitchen and brushed myself off with composure that was almost contemptuous in its indifference.

Here I am! I announced silently, and sensing no objection from the Manikin I began to look around.

The kitchen—along with the other first-floor rooms—had been stripped of furniture and appliances. Even the immense cast-iron stove had been carted away, and the emptiness contrasted sharply with the recollected images that cluttered my mind. At first the memories were those improved by time. What a simple country childhood I had enjoyed—fresh-baked cobbler cooling on the table, Sylva shucking corn, little Junket poking me in the ribs. And what a simple, easily dismantled lie that was! I had spent my early years trying to understand the complicated rules of servitude that my mother knew by rote. And now my freedom to wander the house at my own discretion only intensified my memories of the endless restrictions. Except for the kitchen and one corner of the attic—and the library eventually, at Hal Craxton's dispensation—the territory had been forbidden.

Irresistible, forbidden rooms. For years I had risked my life—or so it had seemed then—in an attempt to penetrate the mysteries of this oversized house. My mother still attributes my early restlessness to her easy hand. She let me grow wild, she insists, and blames herself for the consequences of that. I have given up trying to persuade her otherwise. But I don't blame my mother—I blame her occupation. I never could figure out why the freedom my mother allowed me was compromised by an invalid woman named Mrs. Craxton. A person I wasn't allowed to speak to governed my life, determining where I could and couldn't go, what I would eat for supper, even which school I would attend, since the salary she paid my mother was just enough to send me to the Millworth Academy. Given the inscrutable logic behind the household law, of course I entertained myself with an endless variety of transgressions.

Mrs. Craxton was an oddball not only in her habits but in her choice of servants. Most employers of the day refused to hire live-in help with children, for obvious reasons. But Mrs. Craxton preferred servants who came with a young child or two—a shrewd preference, I see in hindsight, since it made employees like my mother and Lore more obliged to their employers and therefore more dependable workers. If she could have surrounded herself with slaves, she would have done so. Short of that, she made it nearly impossible for her servants to quit.

Or that's my explanation for my mother's excessive loyalty, though here again we disagree, my mother insisting that she was truly fond of Mary Craxton and didn't mind her petulance. Of Hal Craxton we speak only vaguely. And the Manikin itself has come to seem an independent entity, a long-lost wonder that never belonged to anyone.

As a child, I hadn't quite understood what it meant to say that the Manikin was Craxton property, but as I wandered through the dark, vacant rooms I felt the presence of the mother and son, their habits, their privileges, just as I felt the coolness of the winter months stored in corners and crevices.

Eventually I wandered upstairs. The hall carpet had been pulled up, and chunks of plaster had fallen from the walls. In the master bedroom I discovered the animals—dozens of forgotten old impostors abandoned to this dusty purgatory. It had never occurred to me that Hal Craxton would have sold all the furniture and still kept the animals. I had come upon a buried treasure. During my childhood, these crones and graybeards had turned the Manikin into a playhouse for me, a prohibited playhouse, to be sure, but all the more tantalizing because of the censure. Dressed in their own skins, with glass marbles for eyes, they had appeared unreal and yet unbearably lifelike to me—terrifying doll-animals that came to life as soon as I closed my eyes in sleep.

I'd moved to the Manikin with my mother when I was five, and for many years the Craxtons' Cabinet of Curiosities haunted my dreams. Inevitably, though, I began to take the animals for granted. Children are inclined to think that all people live identical lives—I figured that every house in America was full of mounted animals, that antlers grew from all the walls, that people flicked ashes into severed hooves and housekeepers brushed the fur of dead cougars. The only thing that continued to confuse me about the animals was the prohibition against playing with them. Outside, Lore gave us permission to kill, but inside we weren't supposed to touch a finger to the giant turtle's hard-baked shell.

After the servants chased Hal Craxton out of the house, it was old Boggio who marked the new order. He turned the Manikin into a diverse habitat, made it a true home for a wide variety of species. The fun hadn't lasted long, of course—Craxton came back and evicted us in short order. Yet, inexplicably, he kept these poor veterans locked in the Manikin, where they had been languishing for thirty years.

The turtle was gone—stolen by thieves or sold by Hal Craxton—along with some of the more colorful birds and exotic mammals. The remaining trophies eyed me not with the sparkling outrage of their early years but with tired, sour expressions: *Why did you abandon us?* They were rather disgusting, I admit, especially the furry ones—mangy, with little trees of fungus growing up legs and along leathery noses and horns. The smell in the bedroom was of fruit covered with mold. But I found myself pitying them. Beasts of the fields, fowls of the air, vertebrates, marsupials—their confinement seemed unjust, and I considered releasing them from their captivity and taking them home with me.

Then I noticed how daylight had faded to dusk, and I decided that I'd better vacate the house before night trapped me there. I resolved to take a single trophy, the only one I'd ever seen alive, if only for a moment. The snowy owl had been mounted above the threshold, its plaque nailed to the door frame so the bird loomed overhead, ready to bury its talons in the skull of an intruder. With its dusty, gold-flecked armor, it was still a lovely warrior. Without question, this was the trophy I wanted to take away. But I couldn't reach it from the floor, and there was no movable piece of furniture to stand on, nor a quadruped sturdy enough to support me. So I picked up a gnarled walking stick that had been propped in the corner and began striking at the plaque in an effort to break it apart.

Shame on me! Peg Griswood, a no-nonsense, middle-aged working woman going at that mess of feathers and clay as though my life depended upon it! With just one strike I knew I was doing something horrible, unforgivable, but I couldn't restrain myself. I was determined to get that bird, to take a piece of the past with me when I left. Another strike split the panel above the door—the crack ran up from behind the bird and disappeared into the molding. I searched the ceiling for a new crack, found none, and was preparing to strike at the bird again when I experienced a sudden and indescribable fear. Did I shiver? Isn't this what a person does in response to fear? No, nothing moved, not my body and certainly not the house. The fear had sprung out of the air, and it was my mind, my consciousness, shivering inside me.

The fear had a definite form, though I can't define it with words. It was a material thing, as real as the vast, grim hush of the Manikin. I felt myself in the presence of something unnatural and dreadful, spectral yet physical. The intensity of my cowardice could only be justified by a precise description of the fear, which I can't give. The best I can offer is the metaphor of a ghost. For though there was nothing to be seen, the fear was as momentous as the appearance of a ghost, as astonishing as a dead thing come to life.

So I ran. I ducked my head beneath the surface of the liquid air and dove through that hellish house, the density increasing with every step, the pursuit involving a steady constriction around me, a suffocation. I think I held my breath for the entire descent. When I reached the basement I threw my body upward toward the open window, drew in a cleansing gulp of air, and pulled myself free.

I know I didn't imagine this monstrous, predatory fear, though I have nothing but my own memory to prove that the experience actually occurred. I drove away from the house, heading west toward the last red streaks of sunset above Firethorn. As I drove I felt myself succumbing to an actual, physical trembling, a belated response to my temporary madness. I had trouble negotiating the road, so I slowed and pulled over to the shoulder.

The place I'd chosen to stop turned out to be directly in front of the old Gill farmhouse. A light on the second floor, along with an old Ford sedan in the drive, suggested that someone was home. I felt a sudden desire to knock on the door and tell the occupants, whomever they were, about my encounter at the Manikin. But I wasn't sure what, exactly, I'd encountered, and I knew I'd succeed only in looking foolish, so I drove on to Millworth.

I restored myself with a quiet dinner at the Millworth Inn. The owner was out of town for the weekend, and the manager, a sullen young man, obviously preferred to be left alone in his corner of the otherwise empty dining room. I slept fitfully that night—the squeaky springs of my mattress must have echoed through the empty hallways of the inn, though as far as I knew there were no other guests to be disturbed by the noise. Early the next morning, after settling the bill, I started out on my trip home.

I had no desire to repeat my visit to the Manikin—by then I was rather embarrassed by the experience. But Gulf Road kept pulling me eastward, so instead of heading up to the interstate, I continued on over Fireworth for the second time in twenty-four hours. I turned down Hadley Road, and as soon as I was in sight of the Gill farm I decided to stop again.

I'd had little contact with the Gill family as a child. All I could remember was that the older boy had pushed his brother down the stairs. I'd heard that Nancy Gill had worked as the Manikin's cook for a few months, and Win Gill served as a driver from time to time. Mostly, they'd kept to themselves. I assumed that such a family would have held on to their farm through the years, and when a plump, gray-whiskered woman answered my knock, opening the door only a few inches, I addressed her as Mrs. Gill. She wiped her hands on her apron and said sharply, "What is it you want?"

I explained that I used to live at the Manikin, thinking that this was reason enough for my appearance at her door.

"Well I ain't Nancy Gill," the woman said, pausing to consider whether or not to divulge more information. Finally she flung open the door and motioned me inside. She stood so close to me when she spoke again that I could feel her breath on my face.

"You want to see Derrick?" she asked, throwing out the question to taunt me, apparently. But I stood up to her and said, "Yes, if you don't mind."

She lifted her chin and broke into a throaty yell, booming Derrick's name through the house. "Derrick, oh Derrick, darling! You got a visitor!" Just as abruptly she fell silent again and without expression led me up the stairs. I had the distinct feeling that I was the first visitor to the house in twenty years, and that my presence alternately impressed and annoyed her. I was about to apologize for the intrusion when she opened a bedroom door.

And so I encountered Derrick Gill. We'd hardly spoken as children, and though back then I'd known him by sight, I wouldn't have recognized this shriveled, forty-three-year-old version. The only part of his body visible above the covers was his head, shaped like an apple, hairless except for the faint lines of his eyebrows, with buffed, shiny skin and perfect teeth. His two weaselish eyes narrowed even further when he burst out laughing.

I looked behind me, but the old woman had disappeared, so I just stood there, arms folded impatiently across my chest, and waited. He groaned with laughter, he roared, he flung his head back and forth, crowed and coughed, then smacked his lips together and said, "Little Peg Griswood!"

I was surprised that he knew me, of course, but more than that I was intrigued by his ability to recall a familiar face. If he'd kept a place for me in his memory, then surely he could tell me something about the house, something that would help explain yesterday's experience.

"Well, well, well," he said, sucking in his cheeks. I saw his eyes glance at the chair against the wall, so I pulled it over to the bedside and sat down.

"Little Peg Griswood. What have you been up to these last thirty years?"

I laughed then, amused by the interest of this person I hadn't thought of since I'd moved away. "I'm all grown up," I teased.

"I can see, chippy!" he replied with a lewd snort.

"I live in Connecticut now."

"Children?"

"No."

"Married?"

"No."

"Waste of womanflesh," he clucked. I knew I could do no better than ignore the comment, so that's what I did. I wanted information. But first I made the necessary inquiries about his own condition. He told me that he was happy as a lark, and though both his parents were deceased, he was attended to by benevolent Mrs. Muldoon, his nurse, who sat her pussy on his face for a dollar a taste whenever he so desired.

I waited for the fit of laughter to die down, then said quietly, "I visited the Craxton place yesterday."

"Did you go inside?" he asked, those narrow eyes growing round, the lids controlled by unusually elastic muscles. I suspected that he already knew what had happened to me in the house.

"I did go inside," I echoed.

"Through the basement window."

"Yes."

"And did you go up to the second floor?"

"Yes."

"You found the collection?"

"Yes."

"And you tried to steal the angel?" He cackled this last question, the interrogative rise nearly lost in his laughter. Obviously, there was no need to answer him.

To my surprise, he became abruptly serious, throwing out the next observation in a whisper. "You survived."

"I don't know what happened."

"You're lucky, you know. The first looter who succeeds in dislodging the angel won't live to tell it. If you'd put a bit more muscle into it, deary, the house would have collapsed, and you'd be buried beneath the rubble right now instead of chatting on a Sunday morning with Mr. Derrick Gill."

"The house is haunted. Isn't that what they say?"

"I say the house is haunted. How could I know what others say?" He chewed lightly on his tongue for a moment, then continued. "That old taxidermist Boggio. He cast a spell upon the house before he died."

"A spell?"

I should have scoffed at such fanciful talk. Instead, I lost the inclination to disbelieve anything that Derrick told me.

"While he wasted away right in that same room where you found yourself yesterday, he cast a spell upon the house. No one lasts long inside. Sometimes on a summer night I hear the screams. I heard you last night, little Peg. Ellen's Peg."

I imagined the sound of my voice traveling on the back of the evening breeze, over the land, and through his window. I hadn't realized I'd screamed, but I didn't doubt the truth of Derrick's words.

"Why did Boggio do that—cast a spell, as you say?"

"Why does the bastard kill his legitimate brother?"

"I don't understand."

"Boggio was a Craxton!"

"What?"

We were both speaking in whispers now, and I had the sense that behind me a jealous Mrs. Muldoon had returned and was eavesdropping at the door. But I couldn't bring myself to turn around.

"Boggio was the son of the Founder."

Henry Senior had been tagged the Founder by the employees of Craxton's Scientific Establishment—it took me a minute to remember that, and while I struggled through the confusion, Derrick rattled on. "Son of the Founder. Now there's a savory. A little mistake of youthful derring-do. The mother was a simpleton, they say. The Founder was a mere mite of fifteen when he planted his member in that most sacred place, heh heh heh . . ."

"Henry Senior?"

"The girl killed herself. The son was sent to an orphanage. But the Founder gave the boy a job in the company as soon as he came of age. He never told Boggio about the Craxton connection, though. Never told anyone."

"So how did Boggio learn the truth?"

"How should I know? Maybe the good Lord sent him a telegram. Maybe the Founder's ghost paid a timely visit. It doesn't matter how Boggio came to know it. What matters is that when he finally learned the truth, the power of his rage turned him into a wizard." He squeezed the last word out with a creaking breath. *Wizard*. His flawless teeth were a solid white shape, a glowworm between his parched, smiling lips. I looked away then. I closed my eyes, surrounding myself in darkness so I could take in his strange story.

Somehow it made sense, and though there might have been a thousand other explanations for what had happened to me in the Manikin, a thousand more probable causes that could have brought me to that crisis, Derrick's version was the one that I preferred.

When I opened my eyes, he was asleep, or perhaps feigning sleep. That he was a trickster and a lech, I had no doubt. But I needed to believe what he told me, so I ignored the evidence that pointed to a half-truth and took away a new and accurate history. Old Boggio was a Craxton. This would explain why Henry Senior made a place for the taxidermist on his country estate. Perhaps Henry Craxton had bought and renovated the Manikin more for Boggio's sake than for his own, as a secret sanctuary for the son he'd neglected. And Boggio had achieved a magical vengeance at the end and put the house under a dreadful curse—*Ye who enter here beware. . . .* This was the unnatural explanation I'd come looking for. This was all I needed to know.

I didn't see Mrs. Muldoon anywhere as I walked downstairs—she must have concluded I would not permanently intrude upon their special intimacy. I let myself out as quietly as possible. The bright sunlight shocked me. It should have been midnight, dead leaves swirling in the wind, creatures with neon eyes watching from the edge of darkness, bones rattling inside hollow trees. Something in the landscape should have reflected the submission of the living to the authority of the dead. But the world wouldn't cooperate. Instead, the reality of daylight and summer along with the smell of gasoline as I started my car and the oom-pah of "Seventy-Six Trombones" on the radio helped to dissipate my mood, until I felt fairly steady again, even purposeful. I had to be back at work at 8:00 A.M. the following morning, and I had a four-hundred-mile drive ahead of me.

I continued east toward Kettling. This route gave me one final opportunity to see the Manikin. I tried—and failed—to convince myself not to stop. I needed to see the house now that I knew its story, though I shouldn't have spared the time. As the car rolled and bumped along the grassy drive, I vowed to linger no more than a few minutes.

My impatience to get back on the road brought to mind the beginning of another journey. I remembered how Sylva had sat in the passenger seat of the truck, baby June in her arms, Nora had balanced Gracie on her knees in the truckbed, the boys had straddled the side, and Peter, Red Vic, and Sid had caught and stacked suitcases that Lore lifted up to them. Then Junket leapt onto a wheel rim and from there into the truck while Machine barked frantically from the ground. Lore appeased the animal by hauling her up to Junket, then he climbed in and took a seat on a tower of boxes, which seemed to be the signal for Win Gill—our driver—to start the motor. The chassis shook, the air filled with exhaust, and above the coughing of the engine I heard a voice—old Boggio was leaning out the bedroom window, waving and yelling good-bye to us while the master and mistress hid their faces inside the curtained library and pretended that we had never existed.

And there was my mother standing near the passenger door, urging me on, a gray silhouette behind the cloud of exhaust extending her hand to me. "Come on, poppet, hurry up, poppet," she was saying, rolling her tongue in the playful brogue I hadn't heard her use for years. "Hurry up, poppet, let's go and find the sea."

What became of us from then on—the effort to find and keep jobs, the illnesses and injuries, the love affairs, the education erratically gained—all of it begins beyond the Manikin, beyond that moment when I climbed into the front seat beside Sylva, and my mother squeezed in next to me. Win Gill looped the truck around to head down the drive, and over the backfires I heard Boggio calling out, "Good-bye! Remember me!" and again, "Remember me," and still again, the sound of his voice muted by distance, transforming into a more languorous command as we chugged toward Hadley Road, and though I twisted in my seat and leaned across my mother's lap so I could see the old man waving from the upstairs window, the voice I heard only faintly now belonged not to him anymore but to the Manikin itself, the house shaping the words with its wood-and-plaster tongue, begging us, the lucky ones, to remember.